THE LOST
CREATION

THE BEGINNING OF AN END

Armen Davtian

ISBN: 978-1-950576-49-4 (Paperback)

Any references to historical events, real people, or real places are used fictitiously. Names, characters, and places are products of the author's imagination.

Dedication

To both of my daughters: Evolet Saga & Emilia Sera.

Daddy Loves You Both

"If you can see it in your mind, you're going to hold it in your hand"

- Bob Proctor

Table of Contents

Prologue–When Earth Was Lost

For the creation waits in eager expectation for the children of God to be revealed. For the creation was subjected to frustration, not by its own choice, but by the will of the one who subjected it, in the hope that the creation itself will be liberated from its bondage to decay and brought into the freedom and glory of the children of God.

We know that the whole creation has been groaning as in the pains of childbirth right up to the present time. Not only so, but we ourselves, who have the first-fruits of the Spirit, groan inwardly as we wait eagerly for our adoption to son ship, the redemption of our bodies. For in this hope we were saved.

Romans 8:19-24

The loving Creator stared deeply into her eyes, vast and shining as they stared into His own. They both sparkled before him, one blue like the sky and the other a blue-green like the ocean. She was so young, he thought, and so naive. He clutched His chest, and He gently handed her to the Son. Jesus held her close to His chest with a loving smile of His own. The Creator sat down on His throne for a moment, knowing her future and feeling even now the agony that would soon be hers to bear. If only she knew the pain that Earth's children would cause her, the children of Adam in all their sin.

Visions flashed before His eyes of smoke and flame to deafening booms accompanied by screams of pain that joined together to form the orchestra of war. Gravel flew in the air, transforming before His eyes into shrapnel. Arrows flew overhead, lighting ablaze as they soared for formidable fortresses and soon turned to bullets before Him. Deafening cracks and boomed resounded throughout the Earth, shaking its most firm foundation while mushroom clouds rose from the ground throughout its surface.

Tears flowed down a million cheeks from two-million weary eyes, then more as they multiplied, both young and old from every nation. Their cries grew louder, more filled with agony and fear. They rang in His head for what felt like years. "Why?" they all asked the same questions, but He wanted to ask them the same.

"Why?" the infant, Earth, looked up at Him with hopeful but questioning eyes. He could read the question in them, but He had no answers for her. A playful coo hid the pain that was to come for her, but already He could feel, and it wouldn't be long before she did too. He then looked deeper into her eyes and gazed again upon His children and the creation He made for them. His chest felt warm, and the burden eased on His heavy heart for a time. A sense of peace overtook Him as He beheld the wonders of His creation and theirs.

He saw the beasts that crawled the Earth as a twinkle in His eye. He watched them come into being, from the smallest creature swimming in the sea to the most ferocious bear roaring as it prowled about the woods and the lion who stalked the jungle for prey. Looming over them, he turned His eyes to the massive dinosaurs that once roamed their world. Man would overcome them as nature rolled the dice in their favor, and they would rise to rule over His creation. To them, He would assign the tasks of naming every marvelous living creature the crawled upon the face of their world of wonders. To them, He would bestow His knowledge, His intelligence, and His ability to create. They would be such great Creator, He thought, but also such terrible destroyers.

Sprawling up to match the glory of His mountains, He watched as many built towers and strongholds surrounded by mighty walls and gates. He watched them forge machines to race across the skies and put His birds to shames. He watched as their great ships took to the water, bringing men and women to explore the depths of His ocean floors and the wonders to be discovered there. Massive flashes of fuel and flame launched rockets into the air to explore the vastness of space and discover the treasures of His endless universe. Yet the same rockets would also be used to destroy it all.

Many of them swam through the waters of the ocean to sink their mighty ships. Others moved to wipe out their fleets and burn their communities. Thousands, then millions soared across the Earth and through His skies to devour nations and swallow their cities, consuming the innocent in their path and erasing all life for decades. Only the winds could be heard afterwards, whistling over craters where life once thrived among the civilizations of men who boasted of many wonders. He wept, watching as they dumped the waste of their insatiable appetites into His oceans. Toxic fumes of their endless desire to create but never learn to do so in His plan and timing, poured into the air and choked the life from the firmament.

He watched as men and women wasted the potential of their hands and mind on the lust for war and the greed for endless, hoarded wealth and piles of possessions on their dying world. The wealthiest and most powerful among them knew their time was near. They watched as the powerless continued to dwell in ignorance, too miserable and too downtrodden to search for the truth. Their world was dying because they had surrendered to sin and darkness and allowed the leaders they appointed form among themselves to lead them astray.

The father cried aloud, tears shining as they streamed down His cheeks, and the Holy Ghost moaned so that all creation could hear, though they couldn't understand the source of its wailing. Then, at last, the Son joined them in their suffering, and Jesus wept. They watched helplessly as the baby grew from infant to woman, and Mother Earth began to lose her way and wander from her place in Heaven. By the time she realized her many years of folly, it was already too late. The Earth was lost, and He could never again be one with His dying creation.

Mother sobbed, falling upon her knees as if to beg for mercy as she held her stomach in wrenching pain.

"Make it stop! Make it stop!" she cried, falling further and further from Heaven and deeper into the depths of the void. So cold it grew, and so lonely she felt, as she drifted further and further into its unforgiving plains of nothingness. The silence seemed so loud, so agonizing in her ears. Worst of all, however, she thought as she lies shivering and suspended in the vacuum of space, was the separation from His love.

Where was that endless, eternal love, where was the warmth it once had brought her? What love?

She couldn't even remember anymore. Even more, she forgot His name and face. Whose name? Whose face? Her eyes went wide with terror as the truth set in. There was nothing, no one at the end waiting for her but the void. In an endless universe of unforgiving darkness, she was truly alone.

Chapter 1-Snake in the Garden

… and there was a great earthquake, and the sun became black as sackcloth, the full moon became like blood, and the stars of the sky fell to the earth as the fig tree sheds its winter fruit when shaken by a gale. The sky vanished like a scroll that is being rolled up, and every mountain and island was removed from its place. Then the kings of the earth and the great ones and the generals and the rich and the powerful, and everyone, slave and free, hid themselves in the caves and among the rocks of the mountains, calling to the mountains and rocks, "Fall on us and hide us from the face of him who is seated on the throne, and from the wrath of the Lamb

The woman shuddered lightly as she lied there on the ground. With a slight gasp, she pushed herself up, weakly to her knees, and at last ascended to her feet. Where was she? Everything was black and empty. Even the ground she stood on, though it seemed to hold her, was formless. The silence all but deafened her, and though she could hear herself cry aloud, her voice barely carried. There was nowhere for it to go and no one there to hear it. She might as well have to shout herself.

The only glow she caught was one of flame that came from a lifeless sphere of rock and lava. It floated there, all that remained of a decimated universe. She stared into it for a moment, drawn to its glow. She felt connected to it somehow. With that connection came an intense sadness. She wept, not knowing why, but mourning as a mother who lost her precious children.

The flames continued to pop and crackle as a few explosion continued to erupt around. Had she come close enough, the heat may have consumed her. Yet there it floated quietly before her, calling to her and tugging at her very soul. It was almost as if it were reaching out for help. It was too late now, she somehow knew. The ball of fire would soon be more as its flames cooled forever floating in the vacuum of the void. One last crackle sounded off, louder than the other. She gasped, startled by it and looked away. No longer could she bear the sight of it.

"Is anyone there?" she asked in vain, already knowing the answer. She fell to her knees, feeling faint and caught herself on trembling hands. A few tears forced their way through despite her attempts to remain calm and stifle them inward. She felt a sharp pain in her stomach, screaming aloud as it intensified with every moment. It couldn't have been more unbearable than if she were suffering the pains of childbirth. "What's happening to me?" she asked, sobbing with every word. Tears gushed now from her eyes as she cried aloud and buried her face within her folded hands.

Her tears stopped for a moment and she froze, her jumping as a light ring sang in the distance, growing louder and more harmonious. A bright white light shined in the distance as a place on the void began to split like sliding doors. As the gateway of light cracked open before her the ringing grew to form an angelic chorus. Blinding light bathed her in its rays and certain reassuring warmth came with them. Her pounding heart began to still and her aching gut began to find relief. Slowly her tears dried as the light fell over and then a voice startled. It was a soft and feminine voice, sweet innocence resting in its tones.

"Please don't cry!" it called, echoing throughout the black chamber she found herself in as it called to her from the light. The reassuring voice resembled that of a little girl who couldn't have been much more than nine years old. "You will be restored, and everything will be new again."

"Who are you?" the woman asked.

"You can call me Venus," she said. "I am a shining star, a messenger of God. I'm here to help you."

The woman soon transitioned to ask the even more perplexing question. "Who am *I*?"

"You don't remember?" she asked, almost giggling. "You are Mother Earth, divine creation, beloved of the highest," she explained. "I can understand why you don't remember. It must have been very painful for you."

"What must have been painful?"

"When you turned from God and everything you were was destroyed by it."

"I don't understand."

"Then we should start from the beginning." the girl said.

"What of the end?" the woman asked.

"It lies before you..." she answered. "This is all that's left of what you were, but it wasn't always like this. You should have seen it...." the girl stopped herself, another giggle. "Well, ok, I guess you kind of did you just don't remember. Let me show you." A small and shadowy figure stepped out of the light and it revealed a small girl. Her smile was kind and bright as she approached the woman and took her by hand. The woman flinched, caught off guard by the gesture. She soon stilled as she felt a tingling from the little hand that pressed against her own. Her ears rang lightly and she felt at ease and even managed a smile at the gleeful giggle she released.

The gateway of light spread before her, and a loud hum was buzzing in the void while it expanded as if to form a screen. First, the screen went black, the light vanishing. Her heart jumped, was the little girl gone, did she leave her? All remained silent but only for a moment as small figured

4

of light formed on the darkened screen. She could hardly make it, but it almost resembled a man but formed of pure and holy light. His light reflected from wavy waters as he hovered over the emptiness of the universe. A booming voice like thunder echoed, sending ripples through every drop of water. Its deafening echo reached the very ends of the universe.

"LET THERE BE LIGHT!"

Shades of yellow, blue, and white begin to glow and swirl on the face of the void. Onward they expanded as their radiance grew brighter with every moment. Rays of white began to dominate and wiped the darkness from the face of the universe. In its stead, if left only the radiance of a sparkling glimmer that rang with a chorus of soft and soothing tunes of angels. The spirit that hovered over the now shimmering waters cracked a smile. His eyes glowed with radiance in them lied a spark of infinite love, one the called heart of those beheld it. The woman felt His presence tugging at her heart. She somehow felt safe gazing upon him. A feeling of love she never knew washed over her, and she gasped aloud as she seemed to catch him paying her a smile. It warmed her heart somehow.

As the light continues to sparkle, its pure and perfect essence were dominating the universe, God saw that the light was good. He pulled apart the very fabric of the universe with mighty hands and tore apart the darkness and the light. He spoke with roaring thunder and first addressed the darkness. "You shall be 'night'" he said, then turning in a more somber tone to the light. "And you shall be 'day'"

You too are a light a voice seemed to whisper in the woman's mind.

"Who is that man?" the woman asked the girl.

"He is the Creator of all things, the master of the universe," she explained. "He's your father." she smiled and continued to tell the story of creation as it unfolded before her eyes.

The light shined in perfect radiance, bathing a sphere of water in light and warmth from its illuminating rays. God beheld the lights with a peaceful glow in His eyes. He smiled widely at His creation, and he saw that the light was good. God spoke again, this time with a mighty wind releasing from His lips. It spun about like a whirlwind with His every word.

"Let there be the heavens and the skies. Let there be an atmosphere to surround the waters of the deep. Let there ascend from the waters the breath of life!" Then the world wrapped the sphere and began to stir its bubbling water. Steam ascended and joined with the winds to form the clouds and skies. A cool mist hung in the air and cooled the sphere. The light rose forth to pour its rays on the new creation, and the sky transformed into a majestic blue.

God spoke again, His voice like a chorus of drums as they bent the very fabric of the universe to His will. "Let there be the earth and let there be soil and solid ground within the waters of the deep" he spoke, and it was so. With a mighty rumble that shook the face of the void the planets formed. Fire and clay filled the sphere of water. A low roar shook the earth as the master lifted His hands called it forth. The solid ground of clay rose to form land. The Creator named the solid ground 'earth' and the waters he called the oceans and seas. The land cracked to also form the rivers and the lakes from bubbling and cooling waters.

With a radiant smile and peace in His eyes, God hovered over the face of His new creation. There he gazed over glowing waters, shimmering green and blue as far as the eye could see. He watched with pride as the light descended over the waters he hovered above them. The earth spun in the darkness for a time along with other planets unseen in the void. In a blink, it seemed the darkness descended and the light began to peek over the horizon. The Creator smiled again, a new day of creation began. He watched with joy in His eyes as he prepared His world for His most precious creation.

"What creation is that?" the woman asked, anticipation overwhelming her.

"You'll see." the little girl smiled and continued.

The sun rose and the new day began as the light came again to bathe its Creator in glorious rays of white. God spoke again this time in soothing tunes, yet His voice resounded throughout the earth.

"Let there be life. Let there be trees and crops, and flowering plants. Let there be vines and all manner of vegetation."

A garden sprawled forth as shades of green and rainbow colors painted the face of the once plain earth. At His command, trees erupted in bursts from the earth and vines sprung up along with flowering plants and fields of grass that grew into meadows. Succulent, and vegetables came forth as well, each bearing seeds. Nuts and berries burst up as well with perfect crops forever free from rot or blemish. Night fell again as darkness claimed the world once more, but quickly yielded to the light as the day began again.

God spoke again in a commanding tone. "Let there be lights," He said. "To light up in the void in day and night. Let there be the stars, and the sun to rule my world in the day and a moon to share its rays and rule the night. And let the light and darkness be separate, forever divided." With a mighty sweep, much of the darkness returned, but only to be adorned sparkling lights that covered the heavens in bright and burning stars. Explosions resounded and shook the face of the universe massive spheres of flame and burning gases formed. Near the Earth, the sun burst forth in all its glory. The sun poured its ray upon the earth and bathed it in its soothing warmth from afar.

God watched with pride in His eyes as the sunset over the world he was creating. With a wide smile, he watched as the stars popped out and the moon came forth to share the radiance of the sun during the night. He nodded His head with satisfaction, and he saw that it was good. The night gave way to the morning and a new day began. With a calm tone, His voice rang through the waters and in the air as it boomed through the earth. "Let there be life fill the waters, living creatures to swim their depths and dwell in the seas. Let there be singing birds and creatures to fly over the land and soar through the heavens." Out of thin air, birds appeared in the air filling the world with their sweet songs and gracefully gliding over the earth. Fish began to pop out bubbles that burst throughout the seas and the lakes and the rivers. There they swam along with all the creatures of the sea from mighty sharks to crawling crabs and tiny shrimp. The seas and the air teemed with life. God folded His hands with peace in His eyes and another smirk. He saw that it was good and nodded again. The sun dipped below the horizon, yielding to the stars and the moon that popped out into the night. Soon it rose again over the mountains and the elegant gardens. It illuminated the sparkling waters, now abundant with life, and air that hummed with the tunes of various birds. The new day began, and God spoke once more commanding forth His next creation.

"Let there be the beasts of the earth to inhabit the land and feast from its bounty."

The crying of elephants and the roaring of lions joined the fraying of horses and buzzing of crawling insects joined together to form a chorus of a wondrous life. Every manner of species, great small appeared to inhabit the earth, and they lived in harmony and from the bounty their Creator provide them. Their very existence became a testimony to the Creator as he watched with laughter and joy as they moved about the earth, giving thanks to him for their existence. He spoke once more this time, every living creature of the earth, the skies, and the seas.

"May you feast upon the bounty I have provided you, on every seed-bearing plant and every precious crop I have blessed you with."

And so the animals began to eat and sow and spread His seeds upon the earth. The world provided endless sustenance, an eternal creation. The sunset once more the day became night and the darkness fell once more. In another blink, the sun rose again, and God folded His hands with a smirk under its light. He saw that all that he made was good and breathed a sigh of satisfaction. He looked over the face of the planet and all that contained.

Waters bubbled from the earth to irrigate its plants and provided sustenance for every beast upon the face of the earth that bore living a soul. The birds, the fish, and the animals of the land lived in perfect harmony and peace. They never found themselves in want and enjoyed existence in the paradise of their Creator. On the seventh day, he rested and blessed the final day of divine completion. His work was done.

The Creator grinned with glee and anticipation as he reached His hands into the dirt. He stroked the clay with slender fingers as he formed the shapes, colors, and texture that would form His newest creature. He molded the clay with an artist's care and precision. This one had to be just right, His most important, most beloved creation. From the clay, he formed the shape of a man, and there he named him Adam.

With a gentle smirk, he leaned over him and blew gently over His face, the breath of life. The air formed a lightly glow as it slowly steamed from His lips and went into nostrils. He chuckled lightly as he watched His eyes shoot open. The man drew back initially, startled. He looked up in wonder the shining face of His Creator. His pounded and His breathing was heavy as His hands shook in the presence of the divine being. He gasped, falling back upon His hands and crawling back space.

"Do not be afraid my child," he reassured him, placing a gentle hand upon His forehead. The man fell instantly asleep. "You will not be alone. A man should experience life with a companion. As I have made you for my love, I will make one for yours."

He reached His hand into Adam's chest and retrieved a rib. He placed His hand gently against His chest and closed it up again and turned His attention to the rib. "Flesh from the flesh, love from love," he said. He ran His slender fingers gently along the surface of the rib and from it, he formed a woman, and gave her too, the breath of life. Slowly the man awoke the two looked at one in other with wonder on their faces. Adam froze as Eve approached and gently took him by the hand. His face went flush with red as her fingers stroked His palm. She giggled softly, and he responded with a chuckle. Before the day, all three were roaring with the left as they roamed the world that God created.

The two watched with a smile as he bid them farewell for now and leaped into the heavens. He flew into skies, vapors passing over him as the heavens swirled with majesty. Clouds formed around him as he floated over His creation and admired it from afar. An arch like a rainbow of white formed behind the clouds and over His head shining along with the Creator radiance. His glorious rays of light pierced through the clouds and all of the creation paused to admire His wonder.

God looked over them all with nothing but love in His eyes. He wore joy all over His face as he smiled over them. The beasts the land stirred and scurried about the face of the earth, while creatures the sea spun and flipped around with excitement. The birds circled the air exclaiming their love for their Creator through soothing tunes of joy. He then turned His gaze on Adam and Eve with a shining grin. His heart swam with excitement. He couldn't wait to teach them all His secret and share with them in the wonders of His creation. He couldn't help but laugh as he wiped a tear of joy from His eyes. Never had he seen two souls so precious, and someday there would be billions of them. The wonders they'll accomplish, he thought.

Streets of gold and sparkling crystal cities rested under the blinding light of heaven. The soothing tune of a seducing golden harp sang throughout the kingdom. The tunes were beyond what any man or angel could ever hope to produce. The angels gathered around, glowing with their Creator's radiance. Yet in all their glory and all their light, they paled in comparison to the harpists, the brightest angel of them all. The haunting tunes continued to bring the angels from all over heaven, God's greatest warriors and messengers, all coming to listen to the highest angel. Lucifer, the Angel of Light, was once God's most beloved. The harp had been a gift to him and with it the most wondrous tunes of heaven and earth. Yet where was he now? Too busy with His new playthings to bother with angels anymore. Some of the other angels wondered too; he was sure of it. They were about to be replaced. The song stopped and everything fell silent.

Lucifer paced, back and forth a few times, his face stiff and tone solemn once he spoke. With roaring he words, he stirred the angels to his attention. "You are all here, my friends," he said. "Because we are God's angels. His warriors, His messengers, His most loyal servants. Yet it seems that God has forgotten us. I ask you," he pointed a finger downward. "Where is He? Down with His creation, gallivanting around with the pieces of flesh he made of mud, and calls 'Adam and Eve'."

Gabriel stood first to interrupt, boisterous as always, Lucifer would say, loyal to a fault.

"This is nothing short of blasphemy. God has not forgotten us and, he is simply tending to His new creation. We are still above humans, and we are their guardians! They are not our enemy if anything they need our guidance as well as His."

Some of the other angels chattered in agreement but only before Lucifer regained the floor. "Do you not see how he swoons over them? Do you not see how he smiles every time he looks at them? How he leaves heaven each day to be among them? He is teaching them the secrets of heaven; He is training His heirs, our replacements!"

"Without God, we would not even exist!" Michael objected sternly, but with elegant diplomacy. "He did not create us to question him. God knows what He is doing, and we should trust in His wisdom. We were made to serve and to obey, and that's what we as angels will continue to do!" he cried, other angels joined him in agreeing with shouts and cheers.

"If you want to watch him give this kingdom to those animals, those low creations that is your choice!" Lucifer declared. "But I, for one, will not stand by and let it happen! We are angels, God's most glorious beings, and we deserve better than this!"

With that, he turned away, defiantly some of the angels went with them, grumbling, muttering, and voicing their dissent. Yet most of the angels stood loyal and firm with Gabriel and Michael to obey their Creator.

"Should we go after them?" Gabriel asked Michael, the highest angel.

"It may be unwise, we may have them outnumbered, but Lucifer is strong, and His harp is powerful. Plus we don't want a conflict in the kingdom. We must consult God when he returns."

"But what does he have planned," he asked.

13

"I don't know," Michael answered firmly. "But it can't be good."

The sun rose again with the morning dew as Adam and Eve wandered the garden. Laughing, splashing in the water, and enjoying its many succulent fruits. A snake slithered into the nearby beads of grass. The snake's scales shimmered a little in the sun, but within the grass, he remained concealed. His tongue slithered from his mouth, and his narrow eyes were fixed intently on Eve. God called to them and they came forth from the soothing pool to meet him.

"Today," God said to them" We'll be doing something new."

"What is God?" Adam demanded, barely able to contain his excitement.

"I can't wait to learn more!" Eve exclaimed. "What will be doing, though?"

"You see creatures in the water?" he asked.

"Of course!" said Adam.

"And those ones flying in the air?" he asked. "And that one over there, nibbling at the grass?"

"Yes!" Eve exclaimed. "What about them?"

"We're going to give them a name, each of them."

"What are you going to name them?" Adam asked.

"Actually," God answered, resting a hand on each of their shoulders. "You're going to name them."

The serpent hissed and glared their way. Adam and Eve turned their heads to the sound, but the serpent slithered away before he could be found. God only slightly glanced his way. He knew. The serpent could hardly believe what he had seen and heard. *He's letting them name His creation?* He thought with fury. *That task belongs to the angel; this must be stopped!* Then the serpent wondered, how much God would love His precious new creation when these bags of flesh will soon enough turn on Him.

He wants to teach them our secrets. He thought. The serpent hissed again, this time screeching with agony as the spirit left its body and it regained its soul and body.

"Let's see if there's a quicker way that we can teach him." he said aloud, laughing as he returned to discuss what he had seen with his fallen angels."

"The serpent was Lucifer?" the woman asked.

"Yes!" the little girl said, sounding sad.

"Are you OK?" the woman asked, seeing the sadness in her face.

"What happened next was..." she took a deep breath and brushed the emotion away. Her voice echoed eerily throughout the void as she continued to explain the story while it flashed before their eyes.

Chapter 2-First Life, First Blood

Now the Lord God had planted a garden in the east, in Eden and there he put the man he had formed. The Lord God made all kinds of trees grow out of the ground—trees that were pleasing to the eye and good for food. In the middle of the garden where the tree of life and the tree of the knowledge of good and evil.

A river watering the garden flowed from Eden and from there it was separated into four headwaters. The name of the first is the Pishon; it winds through the entire land of Havilah, where there is gold. (The gold of that land is good; aromatic resin and onyx are also there.)The name of the second river is the Gihon; it winds through the entire land of Cush. The name of the third river is the Tigris; it runs along the east side of Ashur. And the fourth river is the Euphrates.

The Lord God took the man and put him in the Garden of Eden to work it and take care of it. And the Lord God commanded the man, "You are free to eat from any tree in the garden; but you must not eat from the tree of the knowledge of good and evil, for when you eat from it, you will certainly die.

Eve wandered the garden alone that day, or so she believed. The follow

16

the sounds of a bubbling spring. The waters sounded cool and welcoming. She cracked a smile at taking a dip, a refreshing break from the warmth of the garden canopied in life. Everywhere she looked she could see falling rays of sun passing through the canopy of the trees and vines, some of them as high as small mountains. Everywhere she stepped, there was something sweet and healthy to eat. Colors greeted her as well as she walked. Roses without thorns and undying flowers of hundreds of shades, colors, and variety sprawled up wherever she went. The small animal scurried about the garden, crossing her path. Nearby she saw a lion gently stroking the head of a lamb with its nose. She smiled.

Her heart raced, and the smile grew as she heard splashing in the distance. She ran to meet the sounds. Her speed picked up, but she did not grow weary. The cool mist soothed her skin as it hung in the air and a gentle breeze carried in her stride. A loud splash arose as Adam ascended. Streams of water fell over locks of hair as he shook His head, joining her in a laugh. He arose from the stream to greet her, snatching a crisp green snack that grew on its edge.

"There's my lovely lady!" the two managed another chuckle. "I've missed you."

"And you," she said warmly, love in her eyes as he wrapped His arms around her. "Will the Creator be joining us today?" she asked as he released her from His sweet embrace.

Rays of blinding light quickly answered her question, as did the warmth that seemed to soothe her chest. Joy bubbled within her and the feeling was familiar. She was in in the presence of God. The only feeling that even came close was when she found herself in her beloved partner's embrace, but the Creator's presence, His love, it was a different kind of love altogether. She and Adam often eagerly awaited His visits with them in the garden. He had so much to teach them and so much knowledge to share. They could hardly wait to learn it all. That's what He loved about them, so eager to learn. He smiled as he revealed himself from the light, wrapping His arms around His creations as the serpent watched in envy from afar.

"How have you been? How have you been enjoying the world I created for you?" he asked.

"We love it!" Adam eagerly spoke first.

"We really do!" Eve jumped with joy to voice her agreement.

God smiled, though more of a grimace, even so, it was a smile of love. He could hear their thoughts before they could even think them. He knew the desires of their heart, though they dared not speak them. Even so, he also saw the good in them, the great and wondrous things they would accomplish with the universe he gave them. He chose to see the good, and in His eyes, it outweighed the bad. They were worth everything, especially in a heart that only knew infinite love. It was a love that could only be found in the heart of God.

"I think I saw that love." the woman interrupted the little girl. "He looked up me, when you were showing me the beginning, I'm sure of it."

"He exists in all time" the girl explained. "He saw you now, and he saw you then, even before he finished creating you. The same love He had for them He has for you too. It was that love that sparked the beginning of all things, and continued even as they came to an end, as all things in the old world do." The girl smiled up at the woman and her inquiring eyes and squeezed her hands again to reassure as they continued.

"I found these for you, my love," Adam said, staring hauntingly into her eyes.

"They're lovely" Eve returned the gesture with a kiss.

"I made myself." God smiled.

"Like everything else you make they're beautiful." Eve wrapped her arms around him, but less tightly than before. Adam smiled went to embrace the Creator as well, but His smile wasn't as wide as it was before. God nodded as they greeted him with a heavy heart. He knew why. Even so, he waited for them to speak.

In the silence, they enjoyed an orchestra of lovely birds and massive beasts that screeched in the distance. Buzzing insects also filled the air, bustling about through the garden in games of "tag the flower" The sun bathed them in rays of white through the green canopy as it sits in a sky as clear as crystal and as bright as diamonds. All of creation was perfect. They knew this. Nothing they could ever experience would ever compare to it, and they could only imagine the joys of sharing it with their little ones someday. They wondered what that might be like, but even so...something was missing.

"You want to ask me something," God said, His tone reassuring as he smiled on them both.

They stood silent in an awkward pause, but God waited, always patient. Adam spoke first. "Why can't we know?" he asked. "Why can't we go with you when you visit heaven and see your angels and your kingdom, and why can't we know...?" he hesitated. Did he really want to know? He did. "Why can't we know the difference between good and evil?" he asked.

With a deep sigh, the Creator cast His gaze to the lush terrain beneath him. "You're not ready," he said gently.

"Just one bite!" Eve insisted. "What could hurt?"

"You will die," he said sadly. "And your children will die, and so will their children. It will be the death of you, your people, and my most precious creation."

The pair nodded, wearing solemn faces, but though they paid the matter no more words, the Creator knew it was far from settled in their hearts. The three marched in silence as they climbed a high hill to catch a view of the sunset. The view never failed to stun them both, and their reactions never failed to bring warmth to the Creator's heart. They were such curious creatures, but he feared the consequences of their insatiable lust for knowledge. Even more, he knew what they could do with the power it afforded. He released another heavy sight as the moon rose bright and full before. Over the hours the stars came out to join it in its dominion of the night and the lights took their place in the dark. Stunning as the sight had been, the pair seemed uninterested, as if the spectacle were getting old. Had they really grown bored already of His creation?

He watched with a heavy heart, and yet managed still a loving a smile.

Even more so as he watched them lie down side by side to rest. He knelt beside each one to press His lips against their forehead and plant a gentle kiss. His body went opaque and then transparent. Over moments it faded from their view, and he departed from the world as he left His beloved ones to rest another night.

"What was this fruit?" the woman asked. "Why was it so dangerous?"

"It was the fruit of the Tree of the Knowledge of Good and Evil." the girl answered. "It is the very thing that caused the fall of man and the destruction of the old world. Every ache and pain you felt when you awakened, everything you saw, every cry of despair that you could hear from the old and fallen world...that began with fruit from that tree."

"Wouldn't knowledge be a good thing?" the woman asked.

"If it's used properly, but limitless knowledge without God's wisdom is a dangerous tool capable of more destruction than any person at the time could ever have believed. It has led to great triumphs and unimaginable horrors. Knowledge, true and thorough knowledge cannot coexist with innocence, for knowledge is a bringer of great and terrible things."

"Then there is good in knowledge?"

"When the Creator came to Adam and Eve, their first task was to the name the animals. They would also name the plants, the materials God used to build their world and structure life. They would even name the very smallest elements of the universe. The Creator walked with them in the garden and shared His knowledge with them, and even allowed them to put that knowledge to good use." she said. "But knowledge apart from

God, unrestrained by His perfect will, eventually ruined everything."

"And that is why the old world is gone."

"All that is old has been and will be destroyed, and all that is old must eventually be made new."

"What happened next?" the woman asked and the girl continued.

A cool breeze passed over Eve, lightly brushing her hair. It carried with it the soothing mist that always hung over the garden and in the air around them. The plant life thrived because of it. Adam and Eve, along with the beasts of the earth, needed only enjoy it, and without lifting a finger. She found it remarkable sometimes, how the Creator could create such a wondrous and intricate world for her to enjoy. The usual song of birds joined the squeaks giggles of playing animals. A deer pranced across her path, galloping away as a wolf playfully chased the doe away. Eventually one of his fellow pack members caught up, and together they tackled her to the ground. The deer wriggled away they licked her, barking and yipping playfully in what seemed like a game of tag where they were always "it". Even the deer seemed to rather enjoy it.

Her feet rustled through grass, leaves, shrubbery covered in sweets berries and flowers. She stopped for a moment. An unfamiliar sound came from a patch reeds nearby.

"Sssssss!!!!" it hissed softly, trying to gain her attention. "Ssssss!" it hissed louder, beckoning her closer. With hesitation and a tight chest, she approached with care as the sound grew louder, fiercer. She slowed her approach as the serpent even seemed to growl slightly, growing louder still. What startled, even more, she swore she heard it speak. Were those words hissing from the reeds?

"Come here!" it seemed to whisper, but she must have heard it wrong. Only Adam and the Creator had ever said a word to her. The animals never spoke. They were fun and playful little things, enjoyable to watch for sure, but never things for conversation. She had seen a snake or two before but paid hardly any mind to them. Of all the beasts she met in the garden, she had favored them the least. But this one wasn't like the others. This serpent was something more than what met the eye.

"Clossser!!" it bid her again, more insisting. "SSSo, we may speak."

"What do you want?" she asked. With each step nearer she approached, she felt it call to her not just in hisses and honeyed words but even calling to her very heart and soul. Something in her chest got tighter and bound her closer to scaly thing. She gasped aloud as it crawled to meet her on all fours, its limbs forked and disfigured.

"Follow!" he bid her.

"Why?" she asked.

"Don't you want to sssee?" he asked in a growl this time and a raspy snicker. He crawled into a grove of nearby trees and called out from them again, "Aren't you...curious?" he asked, laughing again. Eve waited a moment. She knew the crafty serpent could be up to nothing good, but what? What did he want to show her? She tried to think of other things. Where was God, what about Adam? What would they say? Still, her mind shifted back to the serpent's beckoning, her heart racing with the thoughts he incited in her. What could it possibly be? It almost felt as if she began to lose control of her own two feet when she took after the serpent into the woods. Where was she going? Where was he leading her? The questions taunted her. The longer she followed him, though, the less she began to care what the consequences may be. She just wanted to *know* where she was being led. What could this mysterious creature want with her?

She almost stumbled over a nearby violet-sparkled vine as she allowed her thoughts to distract her from the path ahead. She would hardly let a stumble, stop her now, however. The serpent quickened his pace, snickering as if to taunt her he vanished into some nearby shrubbery.

"What do you want from me?" she asked, angry now. Was he leading her on a pointless chase, was this some silly serpent game? "Where are we going?"

"You'll see!" the serpent giggled, snorting as he vanished into an overgrown path into another patch of woods. Eve grunted and groaned, even screaming a few times in her frustration as vines and branches smacked her. They tried to block her way, but she forced, ignoring the resistance they presented as she determined to see what the serpent wanted. She spit and sputtered a few times, and wiped her hair from the dirt and leaves and blades of grass that were strewn all over it. She looked with gasps once she finally came to a clearing and wiped the debris from her eyes.

The massive oak towered over her, bigger than any tree she had ever seen. It must have stood higher than and mountain and its trunk covered held at least four mammoths easy, she reasoned. Yet even more impressive than the imposing trunk and massive branches the little spheres of red its branches bore. The fruit sparkled, its skin firm and crimson like an apple but its flesh soft like a peach or plum. The pulp held so much juice it even seeped through the skin and droplets fell like light rain from its spreading branches. The branches themselves bore flowers of every shape and color to compliment the fruit and together they released a sweet aroma into the air. The scent of carried a sweeter odor than any breeze that had ever passed her nostrils. She'd never smelled anything like it. A droplet fell lightly on her nose. She flinched at the very feel of it and wiped it with her finger.

The sticky nectar spread like melting butter as she rubbed her fingers together. It made her skin feel soft and cleaner than the clearest water. She looked at it with wonder in her eyes and saliva on her lips. It looked so good.

"You should try, sssome!" the serpent side. Her heart skipped a beat, and her chest constricted. With a gasp, she realized where she stood.

"Is this..."

"Thisssisss, the Tree of the Knowledge of Good and Evil." the serpent snickered as his twisted limbs dragged his slithering body to the tree and began to climb. Surprising they stuck well as the snaked raced to the first branch. There he smacked that hanging fruit and watched with glee as it tumbled to the ground. He descended from the tree with a grin of razor fangs as he retrieved the fruit and presented it to Eve. She caught the narrow gaze feeling ill at ease as the wide-eyed serpent presented her the

25

gift. She licked her limps and waved her hands, hesitating. She couldn't.

"Doesssn't it look ssso good?" the serpent asked her.

A gentle warmth could be seen in Adam's eyes as he tended to the little lamb.

"Baaa!" it cried pitifully as he rubbed it on its back. He chuckled, watching it lie down and rollover. The lamb looked up at him with eager eyes as if to ask him to rub his belly.

"There you go little one!" he said. "So soft too!" he exclaimed, chuckling when playfully nibbled at his hands. "I wonder where Eve is," he said. With a deep breath, he stood to his feet, looking around. The sun seemed lower than before. It seemed that he had been having so much fun with the animals that he'd lost track of time. "I'll bet she got lost again." he chuckled. "Just like Eve." He shook his head as he took off to search for her.

Eve tossed the fruit to the serpent who looked up at her questioning eyes and a wagging tongue. "Does it not look tassty?" he asked, snickering again.

"The Creator told us to stay away from this tree. You should never have led me here!" Eve said, eyes wide, and heart-pounding. She knew she wanted, but she remembered her Creator's warning.

"Everything in this garden is yours. I have given you a feast that earth has provided as a bounty," he said with His usual loving smile. She still remembered the warmth of the Creator's hand on each of their shoulders. "There's more beyond the garden too," he said that day. "Someday your

26

offspring will fill this world, and all that I have created for you. But this one thing, I ask. Stay away from this tree."

"What is this tree?" Adam had asked.

"It is the Forbidden Tree of Knowledge," he had told them. "And if you eat it you will die, and you bring death to all that I have created for you."

Eve returned to the moment, watching serpent's sly smile grew while crawled to her enticing, though unsettling eyes.

"What'sss, the matter?"

"If we eat from the tree, it will ruin everything. Anyone who eats from it will die," she told him. "I need to go!" she turned away.

"And you believed him?" he almost seemed to be cackling now. "How sssilly of you!" he said. "I know the Creator. I've been to Hisss kingdom."

"You've been to heaven?" Eve gasped.

"The only reassson He won't let you eat that fruit isss because he'sss afraid of you!"

"Afraid...of Adam and me?"

"If you eat the fruit. You'll know everything, like Him. You won't need a Creator anymore, and you'll be wissser and greater than he ever wasss!"

"How can you say that?" Eve objected.

"If you eat the fruit, you will be like God, and you will know everything!"

The serpent rattled as he moved his eyes closer to hers. She froze, staring into them lost in the sinister gaze. "Trussst me!"

"I'll die." she shuddered, her stomach turning with desire. She licked her lips, mimicking the serpent as she caught the reflection of the fruit in its eyes. Her mouth watered for just one taste. What would it be like? She wondered. What would it be like to know what God knows?

"You surely will not die!" the serpent reassured her, a cheerful tone in his sinister chuckle. "Eat!"

The scaly finger felt like claws as the serpent clasped his gnarled fingers around her wrist and gently guided her hands closer to her lips. "Jussst one bite," he whispered. Her teeth sank gently into the skin and the pulp. Juice dribbled out from her quivering lips and down her chin. She trembled with pleasure and gasped with awe. In all the time she spent in the garden her tongue had never touched something so weak. She paused for a moment to savor. She held the taste in her mouth, breathless with hesitation. She swallowed. The juices and the pulp soothed her throat and cooled her stomach. She had never experienced anything like in all her existence, even in the very presence of her Creator. But then...

"No!" She gasped. "What have I done?" The serpent snickered once more before he slithered away in the bushes nearby. Eve fell to her knees, weeping. What had she had done?

Surely God would banish her from the garden. She would die alone in misery, her sweet Adam no longer by her side. Her weeping went silent. A scowl of anger burned on her lips. The Creator would make him a new "Eve" to take her place in the garden. He would forget about her and fall in love all over again. The new "Eve" would bear the children that were rightfully hers. She couldn't let that happen. She jumped suddenly as the sound rustling blades of green startled her from behind.

"Eve?" he called to her. Her heart raced and she turned frantically to find cover.

"I can't let him see me like this!" she whimpered softly. "I'm naked."

"There you are!" he chuckled aloud. Eve ducked behind a stalk of nearby reeds, gasping, but forcing a smile.

"Oh, Adam!" she laughed nervously. Suddenly she reminded herself that unlike her, he wasn't aware of her exposed skin. She cautiously stepped out as not to arouse suspicion. The serpent hissed nearby, a slight snicker as he watched. With his narrow eyes, he caught a glimpse of the fruit she hid behind her back. He couldn't believe it had been so easy. These humans really were naive. What did God see in them anyway? He watched with a sly smile as everything went according to plan. Adam drew closer for a playful kiss, innocent as ever, for now, the serpent chuckled.

Eve blushed at the gesture, slowly backing away as his naked body drew closer to his.

"What were you doing out here?" he asked.

"Oh, nothing," Eve said coyly.

Adam's mouth fell open as he looked up gasping at the looming tree. He went silent for a moment, dumbfounded as he stood beneath its shade.

Was this tree the Creator had told them so much about? Was this the Tree of the Knowledge of Good and Evil? He backed away slowly. "Eve?" he said her name question, did he even know her anymore. Could his suspicions be true? "What are you doing at this tree?"

"There was a serpent crawling through the garden," Eve explained. "I followed it here."

Adam's eyes went wide and watered just a little. Eve had never seen them do that before. His face went pale with terror. His hands shook, trembling along with his cracking voice. "What did you do?" he knew something was different about, though he couldn't say just how. She wasn't the same Eve he'd known in the garden all this time.

"It seemed so good. It *was* so good, Adam. When the serpent presented it to me I-." she gasped. "I just couldn't resist." her eyes flooded with tears. Adam wept, his eyes flooding too, as she presented him the ruby fruit. How could she?

"You left my side for but a moment, and you did *this?*" he screamed in rage. "Don't you remember what the Creator said? If you eat it, you'll die..."

"Yet you ssstand!" the serpent snickered, coming once more. "Ssstill alive!"

"He's right!" Eve exclaimed. "I didn't die! God must have lied to us!"

"No, Eve!" Adam cried. "It can't be!"

"Just eat it and you'll see!" she said. "You'll see!" she handed him the fruit.

Adam held out his hand to retrieve, but with uncertainty. He gazed at it for a while, staring at the place where Eve had left her bite mark. His hand trembled at the very thought of disobeying His Creator. "If I am to die, Adam," she said. He looked up, tear-filled eyes growing even sadder. "Will you allow me to die alone? Will you discard for a newer Eve of God's creation?"

Don't you love her Adam?" the serpent laughed, hissing with glee.

"You are my 'Eve'" Adam said. "Flesh of my flesh, bone of my bone!" he sealed his teary eyes and bit the fruit in defiance. Less than a second, and he swallowed with pride, not a hint of hesitation. "Where you go, I go my love!"

"Sssosssweet!" The serpent laughed, slithering away again as the branches from a patch of trees shuffled and crunched. A cool breeze picked up as the sun rose to the highest point in the sky. The breeze startled them, for in its winds, they heard the voice of God. He sang softly, songs of love and life, as He often did. Their hearts pounded as they raced to find a place to hide. Adam looked down, jumping.

"I can't let God see me like this!" he exclaimed.

"We have to hide!" Eve agreed. Together they dashed for the trees. The Creator may have chuckled on other days, watching His creations at play, but He knew this was no game. His cheerful song ended, as he knew it someday would. The soft breeze picked up to be replaced by a sad an eerie wind. It almost seemed to whistle some tragic tune as God stood silent before the tries. They trembled quietly, sure he couldn't see. Eve was gasping quietly, Adam shushing her as they tried to hide.

"Come out!" the Creator called sternly. Adam and Eve tensed in their hiding places, their hearts skipping a beat. They'd never heard Him use that tone before. It sounded a far cry from His usual soft and tender speech with which he often greeted them. His eyes harbored disappointment in place of the look of pride they had come to recognize. All remained silent as the Creator patiently waited for His creation to come out. The silence couldn't have been more deafening. It broke at last with the cracking of branching and the rustling of leaves. Adam and Eve came out doing the best they could with leafy branches to cover their bodies in shame.

"Adam, come now!" God called as they came out. "I've been looking for you. Where have you been?" God knew, of course, but He wanted to hear it from him.

"I'm sorry God, it's just..." he almost stuttered now. "I heard your voice in the distance. I was sure you were looking for us. I'm sorry..." he stammered away.

"Were you hiding from me?" He asked.

"Yes, God, you see." Adam hesitated, looking down. "I didn't want you to see...well...I'm naked."

The Creator's eyes narrowed at Adam. Adam flinched. He seemed angrier than ever before. Despite it, He refrained from raising His tone, asking Adam gently, "How could you possibly know you were naked?"

"Well my God, you see, well Eve came to me and..."

"Did you eat the fruit, Adam?" God cut him short.

32

"Well, I was looking for Eve!" Adam put in frantically. "She just ran off, nowhere to be found. I had to find her, you see, and I was able to find her here." he explained. "When I found her she had...water coming out of her eyes and her voice...I've never seen her like that. She was so upset. She handed me the fruit and begged me to take a bite. How could I resist? How could I say no to the love of my life, the partner you made me?"

"And you Eve?" God looked to her in question. "What have you to say for yourself?"

"God I had no I idea...this snake came to me out of the garden. He spoke to me he showed me the fruit. He said that you were lying and he put the fruit in my hand and," tear streamed and her voice broke as she tried to come up with the words to express her regret. "The serpent deceived me! He lied to me!" she screamed, pointing to the bushes. "It was the serpent!"

The Creator looked to the bushes, scowling in anger. He extended a finger to point, and His eyes glowed with the flames of His rage.

"Come out, serpent!" He commanded in a booming voice. Thunder followed, cracking the air around them and drawing a fright form Adam and Eve. The serpent crawled out, hissing, even growling his defiance. He looked up at the Creator with hatred in the slits that formed his eyes. He tried to speak, spitting his hateful defiance against the Creator, but with a gesture of His fingers and the Creator sealed His mouth shut. "Be silent!" he spat at the serpent with a scowl. "Because of this, I will curse your kind for worming about the earth on your bellies. You will wiggle and writhe like a worm and you will eat from the dirt on the ground all the days of your life!" He scorned. "There will be hardship and rivalry between the serpent and the woman, and her children will resent you. They will unite against you. The woman will crush your very head under your feet as you lie in wait for her merciless heel, a fitting death for a *snake!*"

Adam and Eve stood solemn and silent, trembling as they watched their Creator snap His fingers. The serpent shrieked with agony and writhed away. His limbs dried and crumbled, steaming and turning to dust. In shame and in defeat the serpent sulked, slithering away and swearing vengeance yet again on man and his Creator. The Creator stood silent for some time with sadness in His eyes whilst He shook His head on them both. They found little comfort in watching His wrath unleashed on the serpent, hoping perhaps he may distract from their wrongdoing. The serpent was the craftiest of all the beasts. Surely their maker would see they were deceived. Surely he would understand. Deep down inside they knew better, however. It was a fool's dream to hope the Creator of the universe would simply ignore His own rules, the very rules that bind all that exists in the heavens and the earth. It was a dream to believe He would bend the rules He subjects even His highest angels too. Soon He would strike them dead and start with new creations as well He should. So there they stood, trembling, and naked in their shame. They turned their gaze downward, not even bothering to cover themselves anymore. Tears came as they joined hands, ready for their fate.

"Why?" His soft words broke the silence as he turned in tearful anger to Adam and Eve. He hid His grief from them, though it overwhelmed Him more than did His wrath. "Why have you done this?" he waited for an answer, but only a moment before he continued. "I gave you everything. I gave you this garden and every type of plant to enjoy, every type of animal to play with and love. I gave you fruits, nuts berries, grains, and vegetables. I gave you *life*. And you too would have known the joys of creating *life*." His head too was now hanging low, but in sadness not in shame. "Your offspring would have been the masters of this universe. They would have been the heirs to my divine secrets. It would have been a perfect creation. But now there will be only death, for your kind will wreak destruction on this world." He sighed deeply. "You had so much potential."

"We're sorry, God." Adam and Eve spoke in unison, heads hanging in shame.

"As am I my precious creations. You have brought sin into this world, and I can no longer dwell among you. I can no longer walk with you and speak with you each day. Most of all, I can no longer allow you to dwell in my garden." He looked to Eve. "You will still bear children Eve, and they will still fill the earth. But you will die, and they will die. Bringing them into this world will be long and painful for you."

Adam gulped noticeably as God turned His gaze to him. "And you Adam, you will sweat and toil. Because of you, the earth is corrupt. It will experience drought and famine and you will have to beat it with a plough for it to bear seed. You will have to bring it freshwater, and you will have to labor hard for everything. Every breath you will take, you will earn. There will be war because of what you have done." he said sternly. "Both of you will die, no longer able to take part in my once perfect creation when you are gone. I have made you from the dust of the earth, and one day you shall return to the dust when you are laid to the grave. Now you will leave my garden!" he said. "But first we will cover your shame, and you will see what you have brought into the world. Blood will be the price of your disobedience and only a sacrifice of blood will cover your shame and your nakedness."

Adam and Eve watched in stunned silence as their Creator drew what appeared to be a crude blade carved from sharpened stone. He approached the whimpering ram and wrapped His arms around with a loving smile. The ram snuggled up against its Creator, bleating softly. With a tear in His eye, the Creator drove the knife into its hide. The ram whimpered. Its blood gushed out to form a puddle and the Creator drove the knife in once more to end its suffering. Eve flinched and whimpered. She buried her face in Adam's chest to avert her teary eyes. Adam stood in solemn silence as he held his partner in his reassuring arms. He winced against the gruesome sight. He watched in disgust and horror as God finished skinning the second ram. With master craftsmanship, he cut the skin into clean and even cloths and presented them to Adam.

"Cover yourself!" he commanded them. He swallowed hard, knowing what he must do next. "Now go and never come back!" he orders sternly as he brought them to the exit to the garden. Adam and Eve stood with mouths and eyes hanging open. All their eyes caught, beyond the garden's gates, was a wasteland in comparison. There the beasts were wild and they could hear them growling and whining as the hunters among them pursued their prey. Plant life grew, but it hardly thrived like in the garden. Vegetation and fertile spots of land lied few and far between. An eerie cloud hung over the lands beyond as if signify the uncertainty they would face.

"How can we survive out there, God?" Adam asked, gasping as it he overlooked the barren lands beyond.

"I have given what you need to survive, and what knowledge I've withheld from you well..." the Creator paused sadly. "That you took by force. I have clothed you, and I have given you the tools you need. Go! You will never return to Eden!" A tear forced its way through, something the two had never seen from their Creator before. Their hearts sank as they turned away in sadness. With every step, the painful yearning grew. Tighter their stomachs turned in knots with every foot and every inch they placed between them, Eden. Darkness overwhelmed them as they realized they had surrendered paradise.

They turned back but once to look as a towering warrior shook the earth, landing on sturdy sandals that were laced about his feet and ankles. Massive wings like those of eagles folded. The figure glowed with golden rays and even kneeling before His master towered over the very trees.

"They must never return to the garden." the Creator explained to the angel, clad in heavenly armor, the likes of which they'd never seen. "Already, I can see the evil they will bring into this world in their short lifespans. Imagine what they could do if they were allowed to eat from the Tree of Life. Imagine what they could do if they lived forever." the angel nodded his understanding again.

"Nothing will get past this gates my lord, much less the sons of Adam. You have my word on that!"

"Good!" the Creator nodded, gesturing for His angel to stand. "Now draw your weapon and protect my garden with your life." He commanded.

The angel nodded one last time and beat his chest. He bent forward in a slight bow and then put his right hand by his sheathe. The blade screeched as he retrieved it and the flames roared to set the blade ablaze. Adam and Eve gasped frightfully at the very sight of it. The flames crackled and the heat of them blurred the air as the angel held high his flaming sword.

"No one will enter!" the angel swore in a booming voice that shook the ground and brought those who heard it to their knees. Then with a wave of his sword, a wall of stone flame rose around the guarding, sealing it off forever to every mortal soul. Over time the garden died as the ground's curse took effect. Weeds sprouted but soon joined the other plants in drying out. The living creatures there began to fade from hunger and over time the garden died with no one left to tend to it.

* * * *

Adam and Eve had wondered for a year or two before, at last, they took refuge in a cave. Adam scouted its small space for a few days. He watched and waited to ensure no creature had already made it home and may return. When all seemed clear, he brought his precious Eve into the shelter he provided for her. She had kissed him on the lips that day, so happy to have a home. That must have been what led to what happened next, and where they were now.

Adam jumped a ninth, Eve shrieking in utter agony. Her deafening cries carried through the cave and rang his ears like bells. He winced in pain as her sweating hand wrapped tightly around his own. He wasn't sure which seemed worse: her iron grip that threatens to crush his swollen hand or ear-splitting cries of pain. Even worse was the blood. He had hunted before and skinned his share of beasts, but nothing could prepare him for all of this.

"He's coming, Adam! He's coming!" she screamed, and indeed he saw the little one popping out. He reached his hand into her womb, emerging His hands in the placenta. He ignored its slimy touch and dug His hands in deeper to retrieve his newborn babe. Bringing the child into the world seemed to be all that mattered now. His heart pounded. His chest constricted as he held his breath and retrieved the child. With a crude tool, he cut the umbilical cord clean and tossed it aside. He tended to them both with wet rags they'd cut from goats' skins. A proud smile lit up his face.

"It *is* a boy!" He exclaimed, laughing he turned to Eve as he held the babe close. "How did you know?" he asked.

"A mother knows." Eve smiled. "And how could such a strong husband not give us a son?" she added with a playful wink.

"I can't believe it. We've brought the first person, the first little person into the world!" Adam's voice cracked, his eyes welling with tears he handed the child off to Eve. "Through the miracle of our God, we have brought a *man* into the world."

"A real human life, just like ours." Eve agreed with a smile. "What should we name him?" she asked.

"I..." Adam gasped, trembling and still unsure of himself it seemed. His hands trembled and his eyes refused to blink as he gazed upon his son with pride. "He's a strong one!" he grinned, watching as the tiny hand grasped his finger tight. "We will name him Cain!"

"Welcome to God's creation, Cain!" Eve said softly, snuggling the little one while he cooed in her arms.

The woman watched as the pair enjoyed their new son, their faces lit up with joy as she had never seen. In her eyes, she saw so much love. It was almost unfathomable. How could any living creature love so much? Was this what God's love was like?"

"It's greater," the little girl said as if reading his mind. "When you are in the presence of His love, you'll know. Nothing can compare to it."

The screen flashed with images of Cain's life. The boy grew a little and took his first steps. Adam and Eve laughed aloud, their eyes bright with joy as they listened to him speak his first words. Eve grinned widely as she held his little hands and watched him take his first steps. He grew older still and even learned the love of a brother as he watched his father help Eve bring another boy into the world. They named him Abel.

"So Eve did have children." the woman said. She turned from the screen and to the little girl. Her heart fluttered, catching a glimpse of the sadness in her eyes. She continued nonetheless, as the children's lives played out before them. "They didn't die like God said they would."

The little girl looked up at her and forced a smile. "Sometimes humanity doesn't believe God when He says He's going to do something," she explained. "That's because God does not perceive time as humanity does. All-time is in Him, and He is in all time. Because of that, He often sees what humans do not."

"What does that mean?" the woman asked, confused.

"It means that all things happen in his timing. Watch!" the girl commanded. "Cain and Abel grew up together. As children, they engaged in childish games. They fought sometimes." she explained as the boys engaged in shoving matches on the screen. Other scenes showed them in the running together over hills, and another showed Cain teaching his younger brother to climb a tree. The woman laughed at scenes that warmed her heart as they played before. She watched as the boys grew into men and began to labor with their father, Adam. She smiled at the beauty of their progression through this thing that they called "Life". Another smirk crossed her face as the young men laughed together over a meal, playfully smacking and punching one another softly. In their eyes, she saw the love of brothers.

"They loved each other as brothers do. But things changed..."

Abel cupped his hands and filled them with water from the nearby river. He splashed his face with freezing water. It offered cool relief from the afternoon sun. His flocks agreed as he led them to the riverside to graze and drink. He looked over His livestock with love in his eyes. Some of these sheep, and goats, and other cattle he had swaddled in cloths on the day they were born into this world. He knelt down to gently kiss one of his fattest lambs. The creature bleated gently as he stroked its wool and pressed his against its slimy snout. He chuckled softly as another of his flock ran snuggled him too, clearly jealous. A hint of sadness came to his eyes as he led his flock away from the waters, allowing only a moment more to finish their drinks. A heavy sigh and he turned away with a walking stick, crudely carved by blades of stone.

A lump formed in his throat when he turned again to gaze on his most precious lamb. He gives a pat on its back once more as he led it away with the others. He had wished there was some other way, but how could withhold the most precious of his flock from God Himself? He had no choice. It wasn't His fault, of course, he remembered his mother telling him. Their parents had brought death into the world when they disobeyed God, and because of this, sacrifices must be made to God to atone for their mistakes. It seemed unfair to him, but who was he to question the laws of God?

Tears welled when the lamb bleated one last time. He laid the pitiful creature upon the altar and bound it with strings crudely cut from some kind of washed sinews. The lamb whimpered as he retrieved the crude stone knife. He knelt for but a silent moment to offer his sacrifice to God before he stood again. He raised the knife above his head and squeezed his eyes shut just before he did the deed. He almost sobbed as he drove the blade in and watched his little lamb breathe his last. The lamb faded from this world, and Abel knelt once more, trying hard not to mourn it for too long. Thereupon his knees, he spread his arms offered his sacrifice to God, the most precious of his flock.

"A token of my love and reverence for you my God," he called out softly, tears choking his voice.

Cain wiped a bead of sweat from his brow as he tended to the fields. Dirt stained the rough hands that pulled at weeds to make room for his proud garden of greens and grains. Cuts covered the hands along with dirt and blisters, another sign of his hard labor. A satisfied smirk formed as he watched his masterwork sprout from the earth. With a long blade, he cut down some random samples of some of his favorite cops. When he finished cutting them down, he gathered them onto a sheet of cloth rolled them up to prepare for his journey. The stroll always exhausted him. The labor of his garden always forced him to his feet and under the heat of the sun. He should've been used to it by now, but that long walk was always what finished him. He carried the cloth over his shoulder and walked up the steep slope that led to an altar he and his brother had built with Adam when they were younger. It just looked like a pile of rocks from where he stood, but it was so much more. The three had put their sweat and toil into piling those stones, and the boys had been so proud when it was finished.

Cain approached the altar but stopped his journey short, startled by the spectacle ahead. He pressed his hand against his chest to still his pounding heart. He watched awe as rays of golden light fell like drops of rain around his brother. A beam of blinding white fell on Abel like waterfalls of light and bathed him in its warmth and purity. The feeling of sent tingles through his skin, and somehow set his heart at ease. A booming voice echoed from the skies, projecting through the beam of light.

"You have given me the first-born among your flock, the most precious of your labors and your loves!" God told him. "With you and with this sacrifice, I am well pleased."

"Thank you, my God," Abel called back, kneeling still. "I am glad it has honored you."

The light cleared and the angelic ringing dimmed, but Abel remained in silence for a few quiet moments before he stood. Cain nodded his approval. He was glad to see that God had accepted his brother's sacrifice. His stomach turned a little, butterflies finding their way in somehow. He hoped that God might do the same for his. He smiled at his brother and greeted him with a nod as he passed by. Abel grinned and clasped his brother by the shoulder.

"Best of luck, brother!" he said. "I hope the Lord is pleased with your sacrifice."

"As he was for yours," Cain remarked, sounding uneasy. "We can only hope."

"You spend all day tending to that garden, and even some of the wild plants surrounding us. I know He'll appreciate your hard work."

"Thank you, brother!" Cain said with a smile and a nod. The two joined in a quick brotherly embrace and parted. Cain approached the altar, his wrapped crops in hand. He dumped them on the altar along with old sticks and straws of dry grass. He knelt before the altar and offered a silent prayer. He rubbed the sticks together until a stream of smoke began to form. The grass and sticks lit ablaze and fire consumed his crops on the altar. He spread his arms to present his burnt offerings to God. He breathed deeply, his eyes sealed shut, waiting for his Creator to speak. The flames flicked as smoke continued to rise from the altar, but all remained in silence.

"God?" Cain broke the silence at long last. He opened his eyes and turned his head to heaven; his hands still outstretched. "Has my sacrifice not pleased you?" he asked. "Have I not won your favor today?" he asked. Minutes passed, but they must have dragged like hours as Cain waited in deafening silence. Nothing. After all the labor he performed. After all the long seasons he spent tending to his fields and suffering under the scorching sun. After all that, God said nothing? A few more moments of uneasy silence and Cain watched as the flames faded and his crops were reduced to ash. With bitterness deep within, his eyes began to well with tears. Cain stood, his legs stiff and his fists clenched before the altar. He nodded after waiting one more minute, and still, God refused to speak.

"Very well!" he sniffled bitterly and stormed away.

Adam and Eve laid together by a tree and watched with smiles as their first son returned. Abel greeted them with a wave and hardly grin.

"They are so handsome." Eve smiled at Adam as she watched Abel return to his flocks.

"Good workers too." Adam offered with a chuckle. Eve returned it with a giggle and a light peck on her partner's lips. "Just like their strong father."

"Two fine sons, and a woman more beautiful than the stars themselves." Adam smiled. "A man could not ask God for greater blessings."

"It's not fair! It's not fair!" Cain cut their conversation short. He threw down his cloth and his farmer's tools in rage. Adam and Eve stood, nodding at one another with solemn faces. Cain screamed in rage as he kicked over one of the fences that protected his crops. With fury, he continued to beat the fence and tear it limb from limb. He jumped and turned, startled by a soft and slender hand that rested upon then gently squeezed his shoulder.

"My son!" Eve exclaimed, pressing her palms against his cheeks and turning His gaze to her own. "What is wrong?" she asked. "Talk to your mother."

"God refused my sacrifice," he said, turning His head down, calmer now. "I worked for months on these crops. I plowed the soil I planted the seeds. I protected them from pests, and I have cuts," he threw out his palms in frustration. "All over my hands from pulling weeds. I drive away pests, and even those pesky livestock Abel can never control."

"Calm yourself, my son." Eve tried to reassure him. Cain pulled hard away from her gentle grasp and turned his gaze down to the earth.

"He sacrifices a few pitiful livestock, and one pitiful lamb and the love and glory are his to claim!" he spat bitterly. "God loves Abel and all his filthy little beasts! But I work all day and give my finest fruits to him, and he doesn't even speak!"

"My son!" Adam said firmly. He wrapped His arm around Cain's shoulder. "All is well. This is not your fault. Just consider this..." he beckoned him. "Abel gave his most precious lamb to God, the first-born and the fattest of his flock," he said. "And he gave God a sacrifice of blood," he explained.

"What is your meaning?" Cain asked, sounding annoyed. "That work I do for God means nothing? What would you eat but meat all day if I let my gardens rot?"

"My son," Adam told him. "If you want to please then gather up the finest of your all crops. Find the biggest and most beautiful among them. Bring them your brother Abel, and ask him for a lamb to sacrifice."

"I should be able to give to God from the works of my hands! If they were not pleasing to God then..."

"My son." Adam stopped him short. He spoke softly and squeezed him tighter to try and calm him. "Your mother and I made a terrible mistake many years ago." Cain pulled away, huffing now. Not the story of the tree of again!

"I know you disobeyed God!" he sighed, rolling his eyes.

"And because of it, we brought death into this world. So we must remind ourselves and God that we remember that death and how shameful it was. Death is an ugly thing, and we brought that among God's creation. We still suffer for it, and because of that, only blood can atone for the evil we have sown."

"So my labor, my love, and my passion are not good enough for God because there's no blood?" Cain asked. "How is that fair that he should favor my brother so?"

"My son listen," Adam said, his voice breaking as he stared into his eyes. "We do not understand the ways of God. We separated ourselves from Him before He could teach us. But now we only obey God. He is our master, our Creator, and He is our God. It is not for us to understand Him, but to obey Him, Do you understand?"

47

"But father it isn't..."

"Do you understand?" Adam asked more sternly. "If you want to live among us, you must honor God. Do not repeat your parents' mistakes. Do not bring His wrath upon yourself and on the ones you love. I have lived with the weight of doing so since the day your mother and I were caste from the garden. So I'll ask you again. Do you understand?"

"Yes, sir." Cain nodded and stormed away, fists still clenched as he returned to his garden. He beat the dirt hard with his blow, going into a rage. A bitter scowl grew when he slammed the plow one last time into hardened clay. He winced aloud as he watched the plow break. He collapsed to his knees and buried his blood-red face in his trembling hands. Once more, a firm hand on his shoulder startled him from behind.

"Are you well, brother?" Abel asked, his usual comforting smile, but Cain could hardly bear to look at him. Why was he so special? Why did he so easily earn God's favor? He could hardly bear to look at the smug grin he now seemed to wear without shame. "Our mother said you were upset."

Cain knelt in silence for a moment before he lifted his head with a bitter scowl. Too choked by tears to speak, he simply glared at his brother in silence. "I understand you're upset because God accepted my sacrifice, and not yours?"

"It wasn't just today." Cain sighed, breaking his silence at last. "I've never heard his voice as loud and as joyful as when he spoke to you. He never shed his light on me, revealed himself to me. My sacrifices have never been pleasing to him."

48

"I'm sure that's not true," Abel reassured him.

"God doesn't love as he loves you, Abel," he said bitterly. "It's the same with our mother and father. You were always attention hoarder."

"We'll figure this out, Cain." he insisted. "We'll talk to God together. See what we can do to earn you his favor. What do you say?"

Cain scowled noticeably but tried to hide. After a moment, he forced a smile and nodded his head. Abel helped him to his feet and two exchanged a light familiar chuckle. Abel felt uneasy. Normally when they laughed together, it was different. This time his brother's laugh seemed forced. Cain must have still been upset, he reasoned. When he looked away, Cain returned to his bitter scowl even as they walked together.

"Remember playing on these hills together?" Abel asked him after an hour so of walking.

"How could I forget?" Cain said, hiding the resentment from his voice. His hand shifted, moving quietly for the knife that hung at his side.

"You promised you'd always protect me no matter what. You said we'd always be brothers until the day..."

"Until the day we return to dust," Cain remembered, drawing the knife with a grin as his brother turned away. Who would God favor after that day came, he wondered, and who would He bestow all his blessings on when Abel breathed no more?

Abel smiled. "You rem-" He grunted hard as his brother set upon him. He

49

saw the knife with widened eyes and grabbed his brother by the wrist before he could drive it home. Abel was quick and agile, but his bulky brother was stronger and a far superior specimen in battle. In seconds they tumbled to the ground, rolling back and forth but a few short moments. Cain growled when he felt the blade slip from his hand, Abel on top of him, crying out for help as he tried to retrieve the blade. Cain pushed his body up, knocking Abel on his back before he could reach. Another heavy roll, he laid flat, looking up at Cain who pinned him. He struggled to roll out of the bear-hug grip, but to no avail.

Only after a heavy toss from Cain would he roll free and try to return to his feet. Before he rose, however, Cain bore down upon. A sharp pain rang through his chest as the blade came down, sinking into his heart. He gasped, trying to shriek in agony, but no air would leave his tightening lungs. Cain brought back the blade again and sank again, this time into his stomach. Abel gasped again, this time gagging blood. "Cain!" he tried to cry, choking and gurgling with a second stab into the stomach.

"Why don't you just die?" Cain screamed in rage bearing the knife three more times, then five more times in rage. Blood spattered as the knife crashed into his brother's torso, again and again. Long had he been dead, but blind with rage Cain continued his assault. Covered from head to toe in blood, he finally backed away. His heart slowed and his breathing grew easier, but only before he'd realized what he'd done. He wept profusely, his hands still trembling. Tears joined with blood as he buried his gushing eyes in his murderous hands.

"What have I done?" he cried. "What have I done?" he shrieked louder. In a panic, he jumped into a nearby river to wash the blood from his body, but his clothing still bore its stain. He threw himself, cried out to heaven for a way to undo what he had done. He looked down at his trembling hands in horror and wondered how two such small and feeble hands could end a life, especially that of his own brother.

A voice startled him from behind, but when he looked, he only saw a vague figure, a silhouette in the wind. The booming voice sounded too familiar, however, as it echoed its question to Cain.

"Cain," the figure asked. "Where is your brother?"

"God is that you?" he asked, already knowing the answer.

"Where is your brother?" the Creator asked, drawing closer. His voice carried and echoed in a heavy wind that seemed to be picking up. "Where is he?"

"How should I know, God?" he asked. "I am to watch him every hour of every day? Am I to hold his hand as he tends to his flocks? He's a grown man. How should I know where he is?" he asked, standing straight and bold in his defiance. "Am I my brother's keeper?"

Thunder seemed to crack the air and the winds picked up nearby, swirling with dust as it drew closer to Cain.

"Do you think me a fool?" God's voice grew in volume and in rage. "Do you think you could hide your deeds from the Creator of all things, form the ruler of the universe?" he asked. "I can hear your brother now. His very blood cries out to me from the earth that I spoke into existence. Do not think to deceive me, Cain!"

"Then I suppose you will strike me dead," Cain said, his head hanging down in shame. "And I will join him in the ground today."

"You will live." the Creator replied harshly to him. "But you will be destitute. You will live as a wanderer and a vagrant. You can labor in your fields and your gardens all you want, but no crop will grow. You will be cursed and in want, and will be an outcast from your family and your tribe, all the days of your life."

"Then I am dead already!" Cain cried, eyes welling in sorrow. "For I will be poor and hopeless, wandering these wild lands alone. Someone will rob me and kill me."

"I will give you this one mercy, and only this one mercy." the Creator answered. "Anyone who puts a hand on you to harm you, they will be punished with seven times the force they tried to use against you." Cain winced aloud as burning mark began to form upon his forehead. Like a rash, it burned and itched, forming the shape of a skull as a warning to those who would try to slay. None would dare to try.

Cain departed from the lands of his family, and with a bitter scowl bid his old life farewell. Only the wild lands of the earth awaited him now, and he would live on what little kindness they would provide.

* * * *

God had told them what had happened with Cain and Abel, but Eve needed to see it for herself. Adam had urged her not to come. He'd reassured that he would bury the body himself. She refused to stay behind. A strong arm wrapped around as Adam walked by her side, but it

52

was hardly reassuring. Not today. Tears welled up and her nose clogged with snot. Her nose grew puffier, and her heart heavier with every step they took. The hills loomed before them and drew closer whilst they ventured forth.

"You don't need to see this." Adam reminded her. "You shouldn't..."

"I've lost two sons Adam." she insisted, tears flooding in now. "At least let me say goodbye to one of them." Adam nodded with a heavy frown. He took her by hand and she wrapped her fingers tightly around his own. Just a few more steps now. Her stomach swirled in knots, and her tightening chest made it harder for her to breath. They approached the body. She knelt by Abel's side and closed her eyes, tears leaking from the lids. Adam grunted lightly, turning the body over. Eve screamed in her despair. She hadn't expected the face to appear so lifeless. Soulless eyes stared into her own. She swore she saw her son in there somewhere, but she knew the truth. Able was gone. She shrieked in agony and threw herself over the body. Her cries echoed in eerie winds for a mile. She beat the ground in rage, screaming, whimpering, and finally sniffling. She fell to silent sobbing, her entire slender form trembling under the weight of her sorrow. Adam wrapped an arm around her yet again, but still, it failed to give her comfort.

"Why, Adam? Why?" she cried, wrapping her arms around him and burying her face in the chest. Adam tried his best to console, but he could hardly even be pressed to console him. He choked back the tears and swallowed the bitter lump inside his throat. He sniffled a light, and a few tears came through. He stifled them back again. He had to be strong for Eve.

Eve wept louder still as images began to flash through her mind. She watched herself in helpless agony, following the serpent to the tree. She clenched her fists in rage, watching as she bit the apple. It seemed so good at the time. Then at least she gave way to endless weeping. She slipped from Adam's arms. Her body slumped onto the ground and she buried her face in the grass. She cursed the fates and herself for her foolish mistake. She should never have believed that serpent's venom lies. The voice still echoed in her mind, taunting her. The words rang and screeched like scraping kneels, torturing her with her mistakes. Now she could hear the mocking tone in the serpent's voice as he had whispered them.

"You will sssurely not die!" he snickered, hissing with endless laughter that taunted her for hours after.

"So..." the woman stood gasping and almost speechless. The little girl could feel her sadness and squeezed her hand in a vain attempt to comfort. "Her children *did* die."

"Yes." the girl answered. "And she would die too, and all her children until the end of all things."

"That's so tragic!"

"It was." the little girl agreed. "Eve was the mother of all life, but through her sin brought death into the universe."

"One mistake ruined everything." the woman mused sadly. "One mistake and all of creation were ruined, and after that, it was too late..."

"When there is death, God makes way for a new life." the girl explained.

54

"Adam and Eve would have another son, and they would name him Seth. But the world only got worse after that. People became corrupt, selfish, and began to murder one another. Sin became so great that God had no choice..."

"No choice?" the woman asked, sounding startled. "What did he have to do?"

"Just like Adam and Eve lost their child to death, God would have to destroy His creation, but just like He gave them a new son, He had a plan to make His creation, and His people new again.

Chapter 3-Heaven's Rain, Heaven's Fire

The woman stood stunned, tears welling. She averted her eyes from the tragic scene and hid her face to sob. She could see no more. The little girl wrapped an arm around her and laid her head against her shoulder to reassure her.

"Don't cry."

"I just..." the woman sniffled and stuttered. She paused for a moment to sob a moment more before she could regain her composure. "How could God's creations *kill* each other? And brothers? Brothers in God's creation, and the seed of Adam and Eve?"

"This was the curse that Adam and Eve brought into the world: death and destruction through sin and disobedience to God," she explained. "We do not always see the consequences of our actions at the moment. Sometimes they are like soft ripples, rolling out slowly before they take their full effect."

"There was so much blood." the woman trembled just recalling it.

"Blood is the price that must be paid for sin." the girl explained. "Things only became worse after that. Plants began to die, and it wasn't just man that began to slaughter one another. The stronger of the beasts began to hunt and consume the weaker ones."

"The animals...ate each other?" the woman sounded shocked.

"It became their nature. And yet inwardly the long to return how things were in Eden when God's creation was pure and as intended."

"But it was too late, and there was no hope."

"God had a plan." the girl cracked a smile. "And it started with His messengers. People of faith would bring His message back to humanity and prepare the way for His plan to restore harmony between God and man."

"What would he do?"

"There were many prophets and teachers of His Word, but perhaps it began with one righteous man by the name of Noah..."

"Noah?" the woman's eyes lit up for the first time in a few moments. "Who was he?"

"After the fall of man things became worse..." the girl said sadly. "There was only one man whose family still served God. He was loyal, he was righteous, and he was faithfully obedient to God. For that reason, God chose him to begin a new generation."

"A new generation?" the woman asked.

"Centuries passed," the girl continued. "And the man began to populate the earth. As they increased in number, so did the multitude and severity of their sins. Along with their wicked deeds, they brought death and sorrow."

The screen flashed before them and revealed images from around the ancient earth. The soothing dew still hung in the air but only for a time before it began to dry. Plants began to wither from lack of water and died in soil that hardened like clay and grew infertile. The animals that dwelt on the earth cried out with want and hunger, and in yearning to return to oneness with their Creator. By force, they felt their souls torn from His embrace, bound to Man whom God had made their trusted steward. The stronger of the beasts began to consume the weaker ones as rain forests and lush gardens were replaced by hostile wastelands. Much of the ground grew hard and covered in stones. Even the smallest of God's creatures began to rise as pestilence, consuming every good fruit that came from the earth. Rot and diseases tore through the soil and poisoned every living being with certain death.

The woman shed another tear but forced her gaze on the screen. She needed to be strong. She needed to remember. Yet she could feel the groans of the living creature after the fall, crying out for unity with God. Though man ignored it, he too could feel the yearning. God looked down at His creation with sadness in His eyes. He watched with horror as His most prized creation took up arms against each other, even over petty things. She saw a woman slipping poison in her husband's chalice as she eyed a younger, stronger man. She gasped, watching a young strike an older man and spit on him.

"How dare you?" the man snarled, drawing a blade. Before the boy could, the man slipped a knife into His heart and watched him die with laughter. She turned to the little girl in question, but little Venus shushed her and her bid her to return her gaze to the scene before them.

God watched from on high as His creation became worse and worse. His heart sank as he watched His most prized creation turn from him to follow other gods. Was there even one that even bothered to remember their Creator? Even more, he turned a tearful gaze to all the suffering brought upon them by their evil deeds. War and famine joined with tragedy and disease to infest the earth.

God leaned forward on His shining throne overlooking sparkling granite steps. Tears welled up. What had He created? How had they fallen so far from Him? He hid His eyes in His hands and the tears broke loose. He wept aloud so that all of heaven could hear him. Booming thunder seemed to follow as all of Heaven dimmed for but a moment.

"Why did I ever create this world?" He sobbed profusely now. "Why did I create man? Why did I ever think that I could make a suitable companion out of clay?" he wiped His nose and sniffled. "Everything must be destroyed. They are beyond redemption and will only sow more suffering." He paused. A gleam of hope shined in His eyes. He watched with pride as he turned His gaze to the one man left on earth who still brought honor to His name. "Noah!" he spoke the name with love and warmth in His voice.

Noah walked home from a long day of labor, but not before stopping by the market place to spend his earnings. The markets were packed today as his pagan neighbor prepared for a day of feasting and orgies. Already he could see the men ready in their makeup and extravagant costumes. Women lathered themselves with oils and perfumes, along scant coverings Market patrons pushed and shoved one another as they clamored for the first picks of swine and other unclean beasts they would roast. They fought over the strongest brews and finest wines, ready for a night of indulgence in a feast to honor the gods of their creation. Noah coughed, even gagging slightly, as the smoke and vapors of their intoxicating substances swirled in the air around him. He never did enjoy going out.

Noah shook his head and looked the other way as he watched a man shove a child to the ground for a fresh loaf of bread. The drunkard laughed aloud as he snatched the bread from the lad's hand. Noah paid for his provisions and nodded to the merchant. He held his head down to avoid his friends and neighbors, especially on this day. Noah and his family were perhaps the last to honor the "Old God". Tonight, he and his family would be having a feast of their own, though a quiet one.

Noah sat around the table to a feast of lamb and lentils with his wife and three sons. Together they joined hands and bowed their heads in reverence to their Creator and divine provider.

"Thank you, my lord, for all that we have, and may we eat in remembrance of your blessings. In this sacred feast, as we consume this lamb and remember its blood, may we remember the price of our sins. For it is by toil, we atone for the curse we brought to the ground, and by blood, we atone for the death we brought to your creation. Thank you, Lord, for providing us with sustenance and undeserved mercies. Amen!"

"Amen!" the three boys said heartily.

The sunset as they enjoyed their final meal for the day and prepared for a night of rest.

"Do we have to go to bed?" one of the boys objected. "It's the only sunset!"

"You can stay up a little longer," Noah said. "But when it's dark we sleep."

"I wanted to go out with friends!" the boy demanded.

"Not at night," Noah said softly. "Nothing good ever happens at night. Not here."

His wife nodded in agreement.

"But my friends wanted to play hide and seek in the hills. It's so much more fun in the dark!" the boy exclaimed.

"No, Ham!" Noah's wife said firmly.

"We never get to do anything fun!" the boy whined. "Why can't we be like other families?"
"Because we still serve our Creator!" Noah interjected. "We live in a wicked world, Ham, we can't be like the other families. But understand that it is more important to be as our Creator intended."

"But why?" Ham demanded.

"Because he gave us the gift of life," Noah said with a smile, placing a hand on the boy's shoulder. "Someday, you'll understand."

The sun fell that night, and despite their objections, the boys did eventually fall asleep. Noah watched with a smile as the moon rose and stars came out to announce the glory of their Creator. He wondered how amazing it must have been to live at the time of creation when all had still been pure. It had been a time, he imagined, when man and creature alike could share in God's bounty free of toil and death. He longed for a time when God himself walked among His creation. What was it like, he wondered, to know the Creator of all things? What was it like to talk to Him?

"Noah!" a whisper in the wind startled. To and fro, he turned but saw no one there. In the distance, he heard a drunken feast of laughter and debauchery. Muffled in the distance, lively music played as promiscuous women danced for the amusement of drunken and monstrous men.

"Noah!" The voice called softly, this time louder than a whisper.

Noah shielded his eyes against a blinding sphere of light that burst forth in a patch woods a few paces away. "Noah!" the voice called again.

Noah gasped, covering his gaping mouth with wonder. His knees trembled as he carefully knelt before the light.

"Is that you, Lord?" he asked, his voice shaking with awe.

"Noah!" the voice said softly, but as clear as if He spoke right into his ears. "You are the only man left on Earth who still gives honor to his Creator. The hearts of your neighbors have grown wicked and their souls are corrupt. They have turned from me and to every kind of wicked pleasure. They cannot be saved!"

"What do you mean Lord?"

"I will flood the earth and destroy everything. Everyone you know, your friends, your neighbors, and strangers in the street, will be wiped from the face of the planet. My cleansing water will fall from heaven and my cleansing waters will rise from the deep springs of the earth." God warned him. "My flood will swallow everything that dwells on once dry land, including every man and every living beast. I will destroy my creation so that I can start anew."

Noah held his hand to his chest, trying to still his troubled heart. "Bur God!" he cried out in trembling voice, falling to his shaking knees. He stretched his hands out as if in holy surrender. "Have I not served you? Have I not taught my boys to honor your name? Have I not led my family in the path of godliness despite those around me?" he asked. "Does my family deserve to die with those who have turned from you?"

"Of course not," God said gently. Noah felt warmth and the deepest of love in its laughter. The feeling of it overwhelmed and placed his mind at ease. "I have seen your heart, Noah. You and your family are the only hope left for this forsaken world. We will start again with you. Yours will be the new generation."

"How will we survive a flood that will devour all creation and all that dwells on dry land?" Noah asked.

"You will obey," God said. "Listen very carefully to my instructions."

"I will do anything you ask my Lord!" Noah exclaimed in awe. "I have served you all the days of my life. What do you ask of me?"

"You must build a great ark. It will not be an easy task, but if you follow my instructions, it will save my creation. The ark must be large enough for your family to include your sons and their families. It must also be able to hold two of every single one of my land-dwelling beasts. You will need one male and one female of each species."

"How can I possibly hope to build something so large, Lord? I'm a fair carpenter but..."

"Your sons will be old enough, and your family will lend you a hand. More importantly, I will be with you. I will empower you. All I ask is that you step out in faith, and never turn back."

"I will go to the ends of the earth for you my lord!" Noah swore.

"Then you will go by boat."

Though Noah could barely make out His form, he could almost feel God cracking a smile. He frowned, watching the light fade in the distance as God returned to His heavenly abode.

* * * *

Noah's smile stretched with pride as he watched his sons at work. Ham and Japeth hammered away at the sturdy wooden vessel, their thick beards symbols of the years the project had taken them.

"Is Shem back with that grain yet?" Noah asked his two sons.

"He should be soon enough," Japeth answered.

"Good." Noah nodded nervously. "I hope there's enough. Only God can know how long we'll be on that boat."

"I just hope it floats," Japeth remarked.

"If we followed our Creator's instructions, I have no doubt it will," Noah said.

"*If* it rains." Ham scoffed. "Do you think water is going to fall from the sky?"

"Do you doubt the word of our Creator?" Japeth asked his brother.

"I'm just saying. We're the only people in this village who believe it's possible. It's never happened before. Why would it now?" Ham sighed. "I'm just saying I'm getting tired of being the grand jest of the community. Our family is a joke for everyone! Look how they stare at us as they walk by, how they laugh and mutter their ridicule."

"Don't mind them, my son," Noah said. "What matters is how we are seen in the eyes of our Creator. He will see our obedience and reward us."

A low rumbled startled the men, and the fright extended to all those in the village who heard. The sky was eerie gray today, and a soft breeze swayed a thick banner of clouds their wave. The sky had never looked at this foreboding. The clouds drowned out even the light of the sun. Noah's wife came out with Shem and other members of the house to oversee the loading of the grain onto the ships. Some of the neighbors who happened by didn't bother to stop for their usual time of laughter and mockery. Instead, the hurried home to hide from whatever omens the sky was carrying.

Another rumble shook the earth and Noah nodded firmly as he watched the clouds bunched together. He spread his arms and turned his eyes to heaven, closed tightly, and waiting on his Creator to move. At first, only the winds would break the silence. Nothing happened. Perhaps he had not pleased God with his ark. Perhaps it had been too late. But then.

Twigs cracked at first, but then louder noises arose. The ground shook with mighty footsteps. Trees swayed as animals of every kind emerged from nearby woods and hills and plains. Pairs of them one by one, no guidance from any man, entered the ark in perfect order. Two of every kind arrived, just as the Lord commanded. With each step, they took the animals announced their presence on the ark. Together they formed a symphony of creatures great and small. The loudest was the greatest among them. The elephants sang like trumpets while the lion's roars rolled out like war drums. Cattle frayed and rodents squealed as well, two-by-two as they each entered the sturdy and massive vessel. With stunning precision, they formed a perfect line to enter the ark, much to the bewilderment of Noah's gasping family. Without guidance from any man, they entered and waited quietly in the ark.

Two-by-two they went, just as the Lord had commanded. When the last of them climbed aboard a booming roar of thunder shook the air around. Blinding lightning cracked the skies. The spectacle announced the beginning of a storm. Water drizzled first, then poured from heaven and wells of water begin to ascend from the very earth. Noah's family in only minutes were trudging mud as they clamored for the ark. They slipped and slid in their course and many times they stopped to help one another. The very dew in the air or all that had remained began to fall as well, soaking the ground in its heavy mist. Puddles formed at first, then ponds filled with desperate people.

Meanwhile, aboard the ark, Noah prayed the vessel would stand up to his Creator's standards. Only time would tell, and they'd all know soon. The boat creaked and swayed sharply to the left. The passengers cried out in terror along with whining animals who slid down the slope that formed with the tilting ark. They stopped in time for the mighty ship to return to balance with a mighty splash. The boat swayed and rocked in the mighty winds that shook with the rising waters and the waves that crashed against its base. The boat stilled for a moment but quickly started to rock. Despite the mighty storm, it seemed to stand, and they remained above the water. It worked.

"It floats!" Noah chuckled. "It floats!" he laughed aloud as he wrapped his arms around his three sons. "With the help of God, we've done it!"

In moments, his family joined in cheering and applause but most of all in praise to God. The animals too, restless as ever, also joined in the festivities. Jumping up and down, turning to and fro, they shouted praises to their Creator. Outside the ark the scenes we're very different. Children cried for drowning mothers. Men, both young and old lost the wind and sank at last, helplessly into the depths of the waters. Some of Noah's neighbors cried and begged to board the ship, but the Lord forbade him to let them enter and even, so it was too late. The water was falling heavy now. With a heavy heart and a hard swallow, he watched them drown. In only hours floating corpses infested the vast and mighty waters. Noah shed a tear and turned away from the window; he could see no more.

The ark was warm and welcoming, but anything but quiet. A chorus of frays, roars, squeals, and even the songs of bird joined to form a chaotic chorus. Over time a beastly odor infested the air. The boat was poorly lit, especially in the evening when candles were scarce and to be used sparingly. Weeks on the ark dragged on like years, and months began to feel like decades. Would they die on this boat?

Noah stared out as the wind and the rains began to clear, and the sun revealed itself once more. A glimmer of hope came to his eyes. The storm was over. He watched with a smile as he released the bird and watched it fly away. Like the other birds, it circled the ark, afraid to stray too far. The ark was the only solid ground they had for miles. Even so, Noah smiled. It brought him a joy to hear their songs ago. It had been too long since they sang like that. They were so much happier then able to fly free.

"Thank you, God," he whispered, watching rays of light fall down from the open skies. "Thank you for sparing your humble servants."

"How can you thank him?" A bitter voice asked him from behind.

"My love." Noah turned to his wife with a tender smile. "Have faith," he reassured, pressing his open palms gently on her cheeks. "God will provide for us."

"Look how He has provided so far." so she pointed out. "All of our friends are dead. We're on a huge boat in the middle of nothing but water. We have limited food and we're expected to provide for hungry mouths, both man and beast. The ship stinks and will be sure to bring us all disease. There is no land and there is no sign there will ever be land. Our God has spared us his flood, but instead, he has doomed us to die at sea on this dark and crowded boat. God has abandoned us."

"Have faith my love!" he insisted again, gazing into her eyes, then

71

looking to a nearby wind. She spoke to object, but he soon shushed her. "Listen!" he said. "How they sing for their Creator. They know that He will provide for them. Soon our little birds will find a home, and He will provide a home for us too."

"I only pray that you are right..." she answered plainly. "I'm just not so sure He hears me."

"He hears you, my love!" Noah reassured her. "And all these years we have stood together, serving Him faithfully in a world that has abandoned Him. He has carried us this far. Have faith!"

His wife forced a smile and changed her tone to one of tenderness. She planted a surprise peck on the old man's lips. He grinned. The gesture was unexpected, but always a welcome one.

"I wish that I could have faith like you, my love," she said with a smile.

The fluttering of wings and ruffled feathers startled the pair as dove burst through the nearby window to cut short their conversation. Noah's wife screamed, and Noah swore he felt his heart attempt to erupt from his very chest. His eyes went wide, and he drew a gasp as the bird released a gift from its little fingers. The tiny branch of leaves and berries fell into his palm and the bird took off. Noah held the little branch closer to his gaze, laughing. He could hardly believe what his eyes were telling him. Could it be true?

"Don't you see what this means my love?" Noah asked her.

"I think so!" she exclaimed, eyes watering and voice cracking with tears of joy.

"The waters are receding. Soon the birds will find our new home."

Days passed, but the promise remained unfulfilled. The birds returned with leaves and branches, and even flowers and the occasional blade of grass. Did it matter? The birds could not show them the way. Even if they could how would they navigate the ark, where were the winds? They had died since the rains had cleared. Only the songs of seagulls outside remained to reassure them, but even they grew dimmer. Some of the birds weren't coming back. Had they strayed too far? Had they failed in their vain attempts to find a home?

Noah and his family gathered in the heart of the ark but sat in silence. No one wanted to say what they were truly thinking. Only Noah seemed to believe that God provides them with a new home. Their supplies were running low, and they needed to make hard decisions.

"We can't feed the animals anymore!" Ham spoke first. "Our lives and our families are more important, and we're almost out of food."

"God asked me to take care of His creation," Noah said calmly, but firmly. "We are going to do that. We will preserve His beasts."

"We are going to starve!" Ham objected loudly, and others murmured in agreement.

"He's not wrong." His wife said sadly. "I don't want to watch my grandchildren die of hunger, Noah, and it's been months, and God has yet to fulfill His promise."

"Just days ago did we not pass a mountain?" Noah asked. "That once was submerged in water?" he asked.

"That doesn't mean..." Ham began to object.

"We have also seen that somewhere trees are beginning to grow, and not just trees but flowers, grass, and other smaller plants that grow closer to the ground. There is a land out there!"

"Then when is God going to fulfil His promise?" Japeth put in his thoughts as well. "How can we be expected to keep feeding this many? We're all going to starve."

"God will keep His promise!" Noah insisted. "He will not let His servants-" A loud crash shook the entire ark. The force of it stirred the animals to panic, and what birds remained flew in a frenzy to the nearest windows to escape whatever struck the vessel. All those who stood found themselves on back and faces, tumbling to the ground. Many screamed while others gasped in terror. A deafening cracking noise continued as splitting gave way to solid stone. One last heavy thud and the ark stopped, much to the relief of those on board.

"We've landed on a mountain!" Shem came running from a window nearby. "There's land! There's land!" he cried, jumping up and down. The rest of the family soon joined him, rushing for the exit to the ark. Noah and his sons released the hatch and the heavy wooden door landed with a crash. The animals, coming to sudden stunning order, departed the ark first. The family followed but in a more disordered fashion. Though slow they came in staggered lines, pausing to look around in wonder. They chattered amongst themselves, gasping in relief at last at the sight of solid ground beyond the confines of the ark.

Some danced with glee while others fell to weep with tears of joy. Some of them cheered aloud, dry land at last, while others paused in wonder to utter silent prayers of thanks to their Creator. Noah's wife wrapped her arms around him and placed her cheek firmly on his shoulder.

"I'm sorry I ever doubted you, my love."

"It is not I, you doubted my love," he said, looking to heaven. "Don't apologize to me," he added with a chuckle. His face lit up as she pressed her lips against his cheek to plant another tender kiss. Noah returned the kiss before he turned away to gather his carpenter's tools. Then there he built an altar and presented a sacrifice to his Creator in humble thanks. He ignited the altar and knelt to thank his king. The smoke rose to heaven, and God returned the gesture with a smile, a gesture of his own.

The crowd went silent, man and beast, and bird alike as an unfamiliar sight lashed out across the sky above them. An arc of many colors flashed across the sky, a gift of the sun which bestowed her rays upon the vapors of the clearing storm. Its many colors streaked across the now clear sky, as bright as the dawn of a brand new day. Every living creature stopped to admire the rainbow, God's promise of mercy and His symbol of hope for a new creation.

"All those colors! It's so beautiful!" the woman gasped.

The girl cracked a smile. "It is!"

"What does it mean?

"It served as a promise from God, a reminder to man each time it rains that God will never again destroy the world with water."

"But he would destroy it again?" the woman sounded disappointed, her awe-inspired smile turning to a frown.

"Noah and his family were a new generation, the hope for all of humanity. The world started anew with them. But it wasn't meant to last." she sighed. "Not all of Noah sons and descendants were righteous people. Man would once again turn from God," she explained.

The images of the mountain shined for but a moment more. The woman took them in while she still could. Staring intently, she absorbed the image of all of Earth's animals gathered around the mountain, along with men and women and boys and girls that had survived a global flood. She blinked once more before it faded along with the massive rain that beamed above them.

The image scattered then faded into black. Darkness remained for but a moment before the image reemerged as something else. A great city appeared and crowds gathered around a building site. Bricks and mortar stacked to form a tower, while those who built shouted curses at the name of God.

"With this great and mighty tower, we will prove we don't need God!" one of their rulers cried.

"Let Him flood the earth again!" another dared defiantly. "With this tower, we'll reach the heavens and claim them as our home!"

The woman shook her head in disbelief. "Who are they? What are they doing?" she asked, confused.

"They are the people of Babel. Once again, man fell from God and even rebelled openly again Him. There they thought they could defeat their Creator."

"It seems like their tower is coming along well..." she remarked.

"Just watch." the girl said.

The next ruler approached the building site, dressed in shining robes of silk, adorned with jewels on silver chains and golden rings. He opened his mouth to address the crowd, but their dismay pure gibberish came out. Someone in the crowd spoke out as well, but they too spoke only nonsense. As time elapsed, the whole crowd began to erupt in chaos as everyone spoke a different language.

"What...?" the woman began to speak.

"The land was called Babel because God scattered their languages. They were forced to go their separate ways, parting by language, and spread across the earth as God had originally commanded," she explained.

Brick by brick, the woman watched the tower collapsed, abandoned by its builders. The gem of a city decayed, its once impressive architecture crumbling into dust.

"So even after all of that with Noah, was there no one left who remained faithful to God?" the woman asked. "Was there really just no hope for Abraham?" she asked.

"There was one man." the girl answered, a glimmer of hope in her voice. "He would be called the father of many nations. His children would bring God's message into the world and would give Earth their Messiah as God's chosen people. His name was Abraham." the girl told her. "Abraham was a man of faith in a world that had once more lost sight of God." The girl continued.

Abraham looked over his estate with a sense of pride. As far as he could see rich and healthy livestock dotted the lands before his eyes, and they all belonged to him. He nodded with a smile to the servant girl who handed him a cup of wine.

"Thank you," he said with a smile. He sipped the cup, spilling just a few drops on his hanging beard. He looked back at a lavish home with a heavy sigh. He forced a smile as he watched his wife Sarah come out. Life in Harran had been good to him, he thought. He had livestock and servants as far as the eye could see, a nice home, friends, and even his good health. Yet there was one thing he found missing, and it left painful ache someone in his heart. He knew Sarah had suffered for it too, but they had tried for years, and she was too old now for children. Even so, Abraham had always wanted a son

Abraham watched with wonder as the sun dipped gently below the horizon. How breathtaking, he thought, it was to behold the beauty of God's creation. He wished that man could live forever, so that he may cease to take it in.

"Will you be coming in soon?" Sarah asked, wrapping her frail arms tightly around his round, but solid build.

"Soon my sweet Sarah," he said with a smile. "The stars really are beautiful when they come out though, are they not?"

"They are..." she agreed. "But not as beautiful as it is to behold the face of my sweet husband," she said with a tender kiss to her husband's lips.

"And the children we would have."

Sarah's smile quickly became a frown, her heart sinking at the mention of it. "If only..."

"I'm sorry..." Abraham said, watching his wife pull gently away.

"No..." she reassured him. "All is well. I...I should go in. I will await you inside my husband."

"I will join you shortly, my love."

As often happened, Abraham failed to keep his promise. Instead, he waited for the night skies to arrive so he could admire the stars. How many of them could there be? He wondered. He often tried to count and even wondered if they might be some curious soul across the seas who did the same. Could anyone know for sure? They seemed to so many as the skies seemed so vast, and yet God the almighty created each one. How glorious such a being must be, he thought, and how unworthy he was to even exist in his very creation. Each night he thanked his maker for the privilege. With a final nod, he finished his prayer of thanks and turned to meet his wife inside. Best not to keep her waiting any longer than he already has, he reasoned.

"Abraham!" A man in white called from a distance. Abraham could barely make him out from a distance, but the glowing robes were hard to miss. The voice startled Abraham as much as the sight of the figure itself. Despite how far he stood, he could have sworn the man stood next to him and spoke into his very ear. "Abraham!" he said.

Abraham gasped aloud. He felt a certain tingle starting on his crown and rolling through his spine. A certain warmth enveloped him. His hands trembled and his heart picked up in speed while his breathing grew heavier. A certain sense of ecstasy washed over him and he, at last, fell on his knees before the approaching glow of white.

"Abraham!" the voice called again, this time clear as day. "I have seen your faith. You honor your God."

"Is that you, Lord?" Abraham asked.

"I Am." the voice answered plainly. "You are a righteous man in a den of the unfaithful. Your friends and neighbors, and the people of your country do not know me and have no desire to know me."

"Surely Lord if you reveal yourself..."

"When the time is right, but that is not for you to know." said the Lord. "You'll ask only to obey."

"What must I do, Lord?" Abraham looked up at him in question but quickly averted his gazing from the flashing light that nearly blinded him.

"Leave all that you have built here. Go to the lands that I will show you. Serve me and follow me into the Land of Promise, and I will give you a son. Of you, I will make a great nation that will introduce my message to all of humanity."

"But my Lord, I am old as is my wife. We have tried but we cannot have children. Forgive me, Lord, but I cannot give you a great nation."

"Your descendants," God persisted. "Will be more numerous than the stars and beyond what any man can count," he said. "If you took every grain of sand on Earth and counted each one only then could you know the number of Abraham's children who will dwell on the earth."

"My Lord, I don't know what to say!" Abraham exclaimed. "I am honored. Of course, I will go as you have commanded."

"There is more." said the Lord. "I bless those who bless you and curse those who curse you. I will make you into a great nation, and all men on Earth will be blessed because of you, Abraham. Now go and I will fulfill my covenant with you if you show me your obedience and faithfulness."

Abraham lied down next to his wife Sarah, trembling slightly as he climbed into the bed. What would he tell her? What would he tell his nephew Lot, his nephew who had all these years been the closest thing he would ever have to a son? How do you tell anyone that you intend to leave behind your entire life and fortune because a voice told you so in the middle of the night? Yet Abraham knew in his heart that this was what God wanted him to do.

"So a man wearing robes of light, whose face you did not see came to you in the middle of the night after some wine and a long day's work, and told you to leave everything behind and you're not even sure where he wants us to go?" Lot seemed to sum up the sentiment of the gathering. He even provoked murmurs of agreement throughout the crowd of gathered servants, laborers, and members of Abraham's household. "You can understand why I may have a hard time convincing my wife, my two daughters, and all of my men to come along for such an uncertain journey?"

Abraham nodded and waited a moment. "I do understand," he said, placing a firm hand on lots shoulder. "But I have known you Lot since you were too young to speak or even stand on your own two feet. All these years, you have been like a son to me. Have I ever led you astray?"

"You are asking us to leave everything!" His wife objected. "But you cannot even tell us where we will settle!"

"We will settle in the land that God will show us!" Abraham spoke firmly. "My friends, my family, and my faithful servants, please listen. All these long years, my household has served the one true God, the God who was with us from the beginning. We have honored the one true Creator, despite the wicked lands that we live in. We are surrounded by pagan people who have defiled themselves with every kind of strange practice and tradition. They have mocked us and have threatened us with violence. They have harassed. What's more, we are surrounded by wicked kings who prey on the vulnerable and shun the one true God. Yet all these years He has provided." he said. "He has brought grain to our fields and has placed four walls around us and a roof to cover our heads at night. Each day we awake is His gift. Who are we not to follow if he commands us to go?" he said. "I am not asking you to leave all that you have for me. I am asking you to have faith in the one true God, that we may make for Him a great nation and a people who will honor His name and His commandments."

"Wherever you go, we will go to Abraham!" Lot agreed after some hesitation. "What say all of you?" Lot asked his men.

"We are with you, Lot!" they cried in unison.

"And what of you?" Abraham asked his men.

"We are with you, Abraham!" they cried.

The small crowd gathered spent the rest of the day preparing for the journey. Together they gathered as many supplies as they could carry along with whatever personal belongings they could afford to

84

bring with. Abraham and Lot gathered their cattle and their flocks and herds and all their belongings together with their servants and every member of their households. Together they formed the caravan that would someday create a great and Godly nation.

For years they traveled from place to place selling the goods derived from their cattle, and that they could gather and carry in their journey as a caravan. Going from city to city, they never settled in one place for long. They traveled to the lands of Bethel, and onward through Egypt until at last they came to a vast and all but empty desert. The Negev was oft unkind to them, but they found ways to survive from the land, and God in all His mercies provided for His people who walked beneath the banner of Abraham.

The desert was free and open and stretched out wide before them, but it gave little in the way of provision for man and beast alike. Over time it became clear, especially for the herdsmen and the shepherds that the land's bounty would soon run out. Lot went with his men to try and find suitable grazing grounds for his herds. For hours they marched to find a patch of green one of his scouts had discovered only days before. At last, they could finally lay their claim, good news for their thirsty and starving companions. Yet when they arrived, Lot and his men would only find more disappointment.

As far as they could see herds of cattle, and sheep could be seen grazing, feasting off of the bounty of the land. Lot's men murmured among themselves as he struggled to still their troubled hearts.

"Let me speak to their foreman." Lot reassured them.

The foreman crossed his arms with a sly smile, watching Lot's approach. He had expected a conflict. It had become all too common these days as the two groups competed over the desert's dwindling resources.

"My men scouted these lands out days before. We've already laid our claim to them!" Lot explained. "Surely you men and animals can find somewhere else to graze?"

"*My* men and I have been wandering these forsaken deserts for hours, and you want us to just walk away and continue to watch our herds starve?"

"Hasn't Abraham hoarded enough silver and gold!" someone among Lot's crowd called out. The others joined in their boisterous agreement, and Abraham's men soon barked back comments of their own. The shouting and bickering grew to deafening levels before a commanding voice called the crowds back to order.

"What is happening here?" Abraham demanded of his men before he turned to Lot. "Lot is everything alright?" he asked.

Lot shook his head sighing. "Abraham..." he took a deep breath. "This isn't working. There is simply enough room and not enough resources in this dessert for us both. My men are hungry, tired, thirsty, and they're frustrated." His men voiced their agreement. "We can't continue scraping these fields for what little they have to offer. I can't continue to stay with Abraham...I'm sorry."

Abraham shrugged his shoulders, His mouth and eyes gaping wide. "Lot, I had no idea..." he stammered. His eyes filled with sadness, his voice breaking. "Lot, we are family, one blood and one people. I don't want us to fight. I won't watch this conflict tear us apart! Whatever lands you want are yours. If you go east, I will go west, and if you go west, I will go east. Our bond is more important to me than earthly land, which God generously provides to us both. Tell me where you want to go and my men will know the lands are reserved for you."

Lot nodded solemnly. "We've been exploring the plains of The Jordan. They're well watered, there's plenty of space to graze and the lands are fertile, rich with crops." He took a deep breath, knowing well the audacity of what he was about to ask. "I want to go east then, to claim the plains of The Jordan. There are cities there too, plenty of markets to sell our goods and make a fortune. I will pitch my tent near Sodom."

"These are dangerous lands," Abraham warned Lot. "But I honor your wishes," he said, placing both hands firmly on his shoulders and wrapping him in a tight embrace. "Send word to me when your journey is ended so I may know you and your family are safe.

Know that I, your uncle, will be here if you ever need me."

"Thank you, Uncle," Lot returned the embrace. "I won't forget you!"

"Nor I forget you." Abraham returned the promise. "May God keep you safe on your journey."

The journey had been safe for Lot, along with his family and men. Over the time they dwelt in the lands of Sodom they prospered, selling their goods to the nearby cities and building a fortune for Lot and his family. They lived in peace and luxury, but the peace of Sodom, as always, proved to be short-lived. Four kings marched upon the lands as other kings warred with one another. Death struck the cities as soldiers came to slaughter and to plunder the wealth and supplies of the city. Lot camped farther outside the city these days but even was not so foolish as to believe this would keep him safe.

* * * *

Abraham wept as he knelt upon the altar he had built so long ago. Tears flowed and his voice cracked as he cried out to his God.

"You said that you would make me a great nation! You said you would give me descendants more numerous than the stars, yet here I am, unable to lead even my only family. I have no son, and the closest thing I have to one is far off in the wicked and war-torn lands of Sodom." he cried. "Oh Lord, I only pray he's safe."

"Abraham!" One of his servants cut short his prayer. "One of Lot men is here to see you. He says it's important."

Abraham wiped the tears from his eyes and stiffened his upper lip. No time for crying now. He had scarcely heard from Lot in so long if he sent one of his men, it must have been important.

"Please," Abraham nodded firmly. "Send him to me."

"Master Abraham, Master Abraham!" the servant cried, throwing himself at Abraham's feet. "Something terrible has happened!"

"What is it? Is Lot fine? What of his wife and his two daughters?" Abraham demanded frantic. "Speak!"

"There was a great battle in Sodom. The armies overtook the city. They took everything. Wealth, food, and even Lot and his family, along with what few men we had left. Only I escaped to come and inform you."

"Gather fighting man and every weapon we have!" Abraham ordered without hesitation. "These kings have made a grave mistake in taking God's chosen people. We will not rest until our family is safe again!"

"Master Abraham," one of the servants objected. "What can we do against so many?" he asked. "They outnumber us, and our weapons and armor are no match for theirs!"

"God will fight with us!" Abraham cried defiantly. "We will prevail!"

Night fell and the armies halted in their march to make camp for the night. Their new loot was stored in chests, except of course for their living prizes, those he stored in cages. Lot watched in horror as his wife and two daughters wept, bound and gagged in the cage across from him. He struggled to be free of his bonds, but the rope was too strong and too tight.

"What do you say we have some fun with the ladies?" one the soldiers suggested. With hearty laughs, they voiced their agreement approached the cage with Lot's loved ones first.

"I don't know about you, but I like the younger ones, pretty little things."

"The older might be sweet as well. Let's take turns sampling all three." a drunken soldier guffawed aloud. Lot struggled harder to break his bonds but to no avail and gagged he failed as well to cry out. Despite his bondage, he tried to scream and even kicked the cage, but it did little. A single kick and he fell silent the very moment the soldier's boot met his bloody face.

"This is going to be fun!" one of the soldiers exclaimed with glee, watching as the girls also struggled to scream. They writhed and wriggled and even kicked to be free of the soldiers, who held them laughing and even hooting as they watched their pointless struggle. The soldiers stopped suddenly, hearing something. A battle cry sounded in the distance with one man shouting, his cries so loud they could hear him all the way from here. The men who followed up him joined him in the chorus and as they drew closer their battlecry drew clearer as it grew in volume.

"God is with us! God is with us! God is with us!" they cried in frantic charge.

Abraham and his men descended like rushing waterfalls from the hills nearby, bearing spears, swords, and horses, while others supported them from behind with slings. The drunken and weary soldiers rushed for their weapons and armor, but their reactions proved too slow. The fight had already begun. Abraham drew first-blood, thrusting his sword into a screaming soldier's heart. He ripped it out with a snarl and quickly turned to do the same to a soldier who failed in his attempt to surprise him from behind.

Abraham's other men moved swiftly to make short work of the soldiers as well, and in a matter of moments, they set fire to their tents. The cages lock's and the prisoners' bonds were broken, and they too soon joined in the fight until at last the kings' armies began to retreat. Abraham and his men, along with the freed prisoners cheered wildly. Some clapped, while others jumped up and down for joy, all giving praise to the highest God, and to Father

Abraham."

"God has given us victory!" he announced to a cheering army. "So few of us, we have defeated the armies of kings. God is with us!" he wrapped his arms around his nephew, who returned his uncle's embrace, but didn't seem to share in his excitement.

After a few moments, Abraham noticed his grimace, which matched that of his wife. All of them stood in uneasy silence.

"Do you see now Lot? God has given us victory. Now you can trust in his promise, and we can claim what is ours as God's chosen. Come back and join us, Lot! This is your home, and *we* are your family."

Another moment of silence passed before Lot's wife spoke first. "Are you going to tell him?" she looked to her husband in question.

Lot nodded solemnly and drew a deep breath. "Abraham," he sighed, unable to even lift his gaze from the sand beneath their feet. "We are returning to Sodom. We're going to make lives for ourselves in the city."

"Lot..." Abraham objected. His face wore his disappointment. "Many of my finest men have died to rescue you, to bring you *home*. Come with us!"

"There's no future for us out here. Will, we simply wander the wilderness forever, claiming what few mercies the desert will offer us?" he asked. "In the city, we'll find work, refuge, and a future for our children. Come with us, Abraham!" he insisted.

Abraham shook his head sadly. "I will follow the promise of God. He has promised us a great nation, and he has shown me where I am to go. If you must go to Sodom, then I wish you well, my nephew, but I cannot come with you."

Lot nodded solemnly. "I understand. I suppose this is goodbye again."

"I suppose it is." Abraham swallowed hard. "Goodbye, Lot. Know that my love goes with you."

The woman shook her head as she watched the scene play out. She watched with a heavy heart as Abraham turned from Lot after one last embrace, the final one that would ever take place between them. The little girl could see that she was confused. She didn't understand.

"How could he just turn away from him like that? After everything, his uncle did rescue him, how he could move into that wicked city. Did he forgot the promise of God, the great nation his uncle would bring?"

"Lot and his family wanted a life of ease and pleasure," she said. "It's what every human wants, or so they think. But God does not build his people through an easy life. It is through struggle and hardship. He tests our faith and makes us great."

"Was the city attacked again? Did Lot and his family still live on after that?" she asked.

"The war ended." the girl explained. "But another great king would judge the city of Sodom, and would pronounce it worthy of destruction."

"What great king was that?"

"The greatest king there ever was. He is the master and Creator of all things, the king of Heaven and Earth," she answered plainly. "The King would send two messengers to pronounce judgment on the city, but first they would pay a visit to Abraham." she continued.

Two men approached, their silken robes shining like gold and civil. Their faces bore strange features, and their forms were tall and sturdy, larger and stronger than other men. It became quite clear they had come from far away. Abraham eyed them uneasily as they approached his tent, but another emerged from behind them, this one dressed in shining robes of white, but he hid his face beneath a hood. The two men approached Abraham and his tent, leaving third to wait behind at a distance. Abraham right away recognized the man in white, feeling the presence of his Lord. He threw himself before their feet and bowed to worship the King of Kings.

"My Lord!" he exclaimed. "What has brought you to my tent?"

"Your lord brings you good tidings Abraham," he said. "In one year we will return you, and you will have a son."

Sarah shook her head, trying to contain her laughter. What sort of sage or soothsayer did this man believe himself to be? Her husband was roughly a century old and she wasn't far behind. Both of them had seen many years. She had given up on Abraham's delusion of a promised son many years ago, how could she not. Both of them were manes of white and garments of worn and wrinkled skins. She herself could barely be bothered to pull herself from bed in the morning. For almost a century now she and Abraham had hoped and prayed for a son, and this stranger comes along and predicts it now? How absurd!

"Why does your wife within herself? Does she doubt the promise of the lord because both of you are old? Do you not believe the same God who created all things can also fulfill his promise to provide you with a son?" He asked.

Sarah's eyes widened. She pressed her hand against her chest to feel her heart skip a beat as her stomach turned. Who was this man that he knew her inner thoughts? How could he have heard her? Was Abraham right all this time? Had the Most High God, promised them a son? In either case, He seemed a man she didn't want to anger.

"I didn't laugh good sir, and I'm sorry you must have misunderstood."

"I know you laughed." the man said with a smile. "In any case, we must leave you now."

The two robed men before them beat their chests and offered a polite bow before they turned away, but their master in robes of light lingered for a moment while they marched ahead.

"Where are you going?" Abraham asked them.

"I am sending them to judge the city of Sodom," he said. "There is evil thereof every kind. The streets teem with sin and indecency. The men prey on the women and the young, and the people act out in violence without remorse or punishment. They worship every kind of false god as they indulge in every intoxicating substance, their own detriment. The city cannot be allowed to remain on the earth, lest its rot and pestilence begin to spread. So we will burn the city to the ground."

Abraham gasped, reaching out a hand as he approached the man in white. His hands trembled as he thought of Lot and his family who'd made a life there.

"My lord!" he cried, throwing himself at his feet. "You are a good and just God. Surely you will not kill righteous men with the sinners." he reasoned. "If your angels visit Sodom and find even fifty righteous men who serve you and obey your commandments will you spare the city?"

"I will spare the city for the sake of fifty righteous souls." the Lord agreed.

"My Lord, you are just, and I am but dust before you almighty God. May it be far from me my lord to believe myself wiser or more just a judge than you. But my lord..." Abraham humbly asked. "Surely only lacking five men you would not destroy the city, would spare the city for forty-five righteous souls?"

The Lord nodded again. "For forty-five righteous souls, I would let the city stand."

"What about for forty good and honorable men who please you, Lord? Would you let them die for the sins of their city?"

"I would spare the city for forty righteous souls."

"Forgive me once again, my Lord, but I am but your humble servant. What about for thirty my merciful Lord?

"For thirty men surely I would spare Sodom."

"I have been too bold, my lord, forgive me. But if I may humbly ask, will you spare Sodom for only twenty souls to serve your name?"

"For twenty righteous people, I would spare Sodom from my wrath."

"Do not be angry with me, lord, please?" Abraham cried out one final time, trembling before the Lord. "I implore you! For the sake of only ten righteous people will spare the city of Sodom, lest they are taken with the city?"

"For the sake of only ten, I would spare the city and let my servants live." the Lord nodded solemnly once more, but his stone expression never changed. Abraham could hear it in his voice, but even so, he prayed for the lord to spare his Nephew Lot. "I must go now." said the Lord and turned away.

* * * *

The gate opened before the angels and they entered the city to be greeted by many unpleasant sights, and sounds, and even smells. The air was thick with the smell of spirits and burning opiates. The streets ran with mostly naked men and women dressed in extravagant costumes. Fights erupted on every corner, many of them turning fatal. The angels had barely just entered the city and already it revealed its deep corruption.

"Excuse me, gentlemen," Lot called to them from afar. "Are you new here?"

"You could say that." the slightly taller of the two spoke first, his voice deep and commanding.

"Have you traveled far?"

"We have." the second one spoke.

"I'm afraid this city isn't very hospitable to strangers at first. But they get used to you after a while once you learn the way of thing."

"We're not staying long." the first said flatly.

"I see, well the inns are bound to be full this time of year. Please, stay with me. I'll provide you a hot meal, a cold drink, and a warm bed."

"That's quite alright," said the second. "We'll be staying in the square tonight."

"You don't want to be out here at night." Lot shook his head hardily. "Come on, I won't take no for an answer!" he insisted. "Believe me, I'm one of the few here you can trust."

The two looked at each other silently for a moment in mutual pondering. After a few seconds of consideration, they exchanged a stern nod and looked back to Lot.

"Very well." said the first angel. "Lead the way."

"You won't regret it!" Lot assured them with a hard pat on the back. "My wife cooks a good a lamb. Do you eat lamb?" he asked, leading them through the crowded streets. Along the way, they received several inquiring looks and even unending stares. Men whistled, and a few even reached to try to touch the angels as Lot led them away.

"Don't pay them too much mind. The less attention you give them, the better."

"Where are you going, sweetheart?" One of the men, painted in cosmetics and clad from head to toe in sparkling jewels. "Come back!"

"Hey Lot!" cried one of his neighbors, a drunken tavern server. "Who are your new friends?" she asked with a wink, licking her lips.

"Hey, Lot!" cried another neighbor, leading a host of lusting souls their way.

"Hey, Lot! Who are these fine specimens?" another cried.
Many more hooted and whistled their way as Lot beckoned to hasten their pace and after what felt like years, he finally came to his home. "We should be safe soon," he reassured them. "Just hurry in now!" he urged them through the door."

"Hey Lot!" a crowd followed after him. Lot closed the door behind him, staying outside to keep his troublesome neighbors at bay.

"These men have come under my protection. Please leave!" he

cried, pointing to the way behind them.

The crowd persisted and Lot had no choice but to flee inside, barring the door behind them.

"Lot what's going on out there?" His wife demanded. "And who are these me you've brought to our home."

"They are guests." Lot said. "Those men out there want to have their way with them. You know how they are, like hounds, especially during their fertility festivals."

"Just give them what they want. They're going to break down our door and kill us all!"

"Let us in Lot!" the door pounded, almost as if to fulfill her premonition.

"We just want to say hello!" laughed another member of the crowd.

"We need to leave now!" the first of the angels said.

"Leave? What is he talking about Lot?" His wife asked.

"What are you talking about?" Lot turned to them in question.

"God has sent us place judgment on Sodom. Our decision is made." the second angel said. "Sodom will burn tonight.

"What you can't..." Lot's wife began to gasp. "Our whole lives are..."

her thoughts were cut short when the crowd began to pound at their windows and kick at the door to force their way in, shouting, laughing louder as they did,

"They're right!" Lot gasped. "We have to go now!"

The door fell from its hinges, crashing loudly as the crowd burst. A single, soft thrust from the first angel and he pushed a group of them away by merely extending his right palm. The second angel rose his hands into the air and spread them, closing his eyes. The crowd began to panic, some of them staring at the hands, other looking around in frantic terror. Their eyes opened as wide as they could manage, but nothing...

"I'm blind!" the first man said.

"I can't see!" said another. In their panic, they began to run and flail about, and many of them even begin to swing on one another. Blood flew in spurts as fists clashed in the air and the panicking blind began engaged in an endless, drunken brawl.

"We have to go now!" The angels commanded in unison, grabbing the women and Lot by hand to lead them through the streets and alleys of the city. The sky began to stir with clouds and flashed with scarlet hues that seemed to forebode the disaster to come.

"Whatever you do!" one the angels warned them sternly. "Do not look back, no matter what you must keep your eyes on the path ahead!"

"Do you understand?" the other angel asked. Lot and his family nodded and turned to follow the angels, hastening their pace as they drew closer to the gates. The gates lied open before them, and they made their way through and as far as they could manage into time that they had left.

"Don't look back! Don't look back!" Lot frantically reminded his wife and daughters.

A deafening crashed followed a loud boom that reverberated for miles and startled those who heard it even from a distance. The stone of the city walls along with all its impressive architecture crumbled, then shattered, collapsing to the ground. A blinding glow of red and orange swallowed, screaming city whole to silence its cries at last forever.

Lot's wife stopped, freezing in her tracks as they distanced themselves further from Sodom. Her thoughts turned to all her friends and all their prized possessions. Their home, their sustenance, their closest friends and neighbors, all gone. Where would they go now? Would they flee to the mountains, or hide in the lands of the kings who once had captured them? Would they crawl back groveling to Abraham? Everything she ever knew had faded in an instance.

"My love!" Lot screamed after her, but never daring to turn his head. "My love, come quickly, please!"

"Lot..." she gasped, whimpering. "Lot where will we go? Everything we ever knew is gone!"

"We don't have time, come my love!" he called to her again, but his cries fell on deaf ears.

She turned her head, her eyes watering, mourning for the life they were leaving behind. Her eyes caught but a glimpse of burning, smoking city before they could see no more. Her form went stiff, and her breathing heavy before it stopped completely. Her feet turned first, and then it spreads up her legs and through her torso. With a final gasped she breathed her last, her lips, then her eyes, and up to her crown were a white as ivory and as hard as a stone.

"No!" Lot shrieked, but the angels bid him forward when he tried to turn to see her. "I must see her!"

He demanded, tears flooding and snot pouring as wept in agony. "Please! I must see her!"

"We have to go!" the first angel insisted.

"Now!" agreed to the second, as he urged his sobbing daughters forward with them.

The city glowed with burning embers for a time, but eventually, it faded. In its place rose clouds of smoke, spraying the area with its mists of black, then gray, then white, until it cleared completely. In the city's place lied only dirt and ash. For years it lands stayed barren, and its air was strangely silent.

"What happened to Lot and his daughters?" the woman asked the girl.

"They survived," the girl told her. "And would flee to the mountains, never to see Abraham again."

"That's so sad!" the woman said. "And his poor wife!"

"Death and tragedy are the prices of sin." the girl explained. "God fulfilled his promise to Abraham. A year later he bore a son and made of him a great nation."

"If only Lot had stayed with Abraham. They could have been part of it too." the woman remarked.

"Some people want an easy life. In Sodom, there was work, food, shelter, all of life's conveniences." the girl explained. "Lot and his family had that in Sodom, but what God had given them would have been made to last..."

Chapter 4-Egypt's Prince
God's Prophet

The woman watched with wonder as the story of God's interactions with man unfolded before her eyes. As she listened to the girl speak and watched the scenes unfold before her eyes, she somehow seemed to forget the terror that once overwhelmed her. Once trembling hands and knees grew still, and her heart had long returned to a normal pace. She breathed easily now, even as the little, feeling her grow more at ease, slowly released her hand. She walked across the void that stood between them and the screen. Her eyes lit up and her body took on an eerie yellow glow.

"I have seen all these things," she explained, but to no clearer an understanding for the confused woman who stood before her, but she continued. "God had a plan for humanity, beginning to end, and He so loved them that he made carried that plan through to the point of giving everything. But first..." she explained. "He sent his messengers."

"His angels?" the woman asked.

"The angels visited the prophets and the apostles, God's anointed." The girl smiled as the screen crackled and flashed behind her. "But

God so loved His creation that He understood their need for one another, and out of love, He chose to use people to save other people. He sent messengers and prophets into the world to spread His message, and most of all, to prepare the way for His ultimate to gift to mankind. To deliver that gift, He would use His chosen people, the Israelites."

"The children of Abraham?" the woman's eyes perked up, her curiosity sparked.

"Yes. Abraham had a son."

The woman watched with a smile as images came to life before her. Abraham and Sarah wept with joy as the babe emerged at life and Sarah held him close. After a few moments of hugs and kisses accompanied by joyful laughter, she handed him off to the proud new father.

Abraham laughed with tears in his weary eyes as he took the boy with a pair of trembling and wrinkled hands, weak with age. The woman's smile widened as she watched him take the boy through his first steps, and as his mother's smile brightened as she spoke His very first words. As the boy grew in stature, Abraham grew in joy and pride with his miracle son. The woman could see it all over his face. Yet soon his smile would turn to a grimace of despair.

"No, lord!" he begged softly, alone by his bedside as his wife slept peacefully, unaware of what God had told him. "Please, not my only son!" he wept. "The boy you promised me, the one who you would make a nation of? Please, lord, I'll give you all my cattle, all my wealth. I will trade the great nation that was promised to me if I can but keep my son."

Soon the woman cried with him, shedding a tear of her own as she watched the old wrinkled man nodding with a frown.

"Very well," he said, fists clenched. "You shall have your sacrifice if my Lord demands." Not a wink of sleep would visit Abraham as he sobbed the night away. God had asked too much, yet Abraham was a man of faith.

The scene faded into black, blinking for but a moment before a mountain faded into view. The screen zoomed to Isaac, and his father Abraham as they marched up the mountain path. Each of them carried a walking stick and some minimal supplies for the journey. Isaac from sipped his waterskin, looking up at his father with a smile. This would be the first time Abraham would take him with to offer a sacrifice, at least that he would be old enough to remember.

The boy looked around, confused, yet his tongue at first, should he question in his own father. Surely he knew what he was doing. Even so, he was worried. Something seemed amiss. His father had never forgotten something so important before, even in his old age.

"Father," he looked up to Abraham in question. Abraham turned his head to a sharp left to meet his face with his sons. Isaac had startled him, breaking the uneasy silence between them. He could hardly look the boy in the eye. "I'm sure it's not my place to ask, you've done this before but..." he hesitated a moment. "Aren't we supposed to bring a sacrifice? Like a lamb or something?"

Abraham nodded, pursing his lips as his stomach churned at the question. He couldn't tell the boy what he had planned. He might try to run away and what would it accomplish anyway. It would need to be a quick, clean kill to shorten the boy's suffering. No reason to prolong the inevitable. Abraham knew better than to toy with God; He would have what was His. Even so, he was sure that something was amiss.

"My son," he managed with a forced smile. "Don't worry. God will provide us a sacrifice. I am sure of it. This is a test of our faith."

"How can you know?" he asked.

"Because God," Abraham answered, taking his son by the shoulder to lead the rest of the way up the path. "Is a God who keeps his promises. I know this to be so, and I would live by it. You too must believe my son."

"Father?" The boy's eyes grew wide as Abraham set his supplies on the ground and bid him do the same. Abraham urged him along, and the boy obediently placed his pack on the ground. His breathing became uneasy as the wrinkled hand tightened around his shoulder, and led him to the altar.

"Do not be afraid of my son." Said Abraham, his voice cracking and his right eye releasing a single tear. "Now, lie down."

"Father!" the boy cried, his breathing growing even heavier, and his limbs twitching. "Please!" he cried even louder as he bound him by the hands to the altar. He kicked and squirmed but to no avail as Abraham tightened the bindings around his legs. He tightened the ropes around his wrists and legs to ensure they'd hold him in place. The boy squirmed and screamed, but even above his terrified shrieks, he could hear the pounding of his heart. It grew in volume to deafening levels. As he struggled to breathe through an expanding chest he wondered if it would be the last sound he'd ever hear. He'd have his answer soon, he thought, as Abraham cleaned the blade. Tears flooding now he asked his God once more for mercy.

"Please God," he sobbed. "Please, not my sweet boy!"

"Father, please!" the boy cried, joining the old man in his weeping, and soon the woman joined them both. The girl nodded at her, she understood. Though she had seen the story a thousand times in a thousand lives, it was one of many that tugged the hearts, even of the higher beings.

"What kind of God would ask a man to kill his own son, much less His chosen prophet?" she lashed in tearful cries.

"Watch..." the girl said calmly.

The scene continued. Abraham with tears streaming now raised his knife into the air and brought it down to kill his son.

"Abraham." called a booming voice from above. "Abraham!" it called again, louder to still his blade.

"Is that you, Lord?" Abraham asked, with gaping mouth and eyes, knife hand trembling.

"Did you believe that I would break my promise to you? Did I not promise to give you a son and make of you a great nation?" He asked. "Still your blade, for I your God will provide a sacrifice. My most precious lamb in place of yours."

A lamb bleated from nearby and emerged from a collection of bushes. Abraham put him his arm and head down, sighing sweet relief as he watched little creature prance his way.

"Thank you my God!" he cried, now with tears of joy. "Thank you!" he cried again. "Forgive me for ever doubting you."

"Know that this is my promise to you Abraham, that through your people I will provide a sacrifice, so that all men may be saved, so that you may be restored to fellow with me," God said. "For I have longed for you to return to my arms, to hear the sound of your voice calling to me. Long have I shed tears waiting for humanity's return to me, and with them the restoration of all life in Heaven and on Earth."

Abraham ran to his son to cut his bindings and release him from the altar. With tears and cries of joy, he wrapped his arms tightly around him. He swore he'd never come so close to losing his precious son again.

"Oh thank you God!" he exclaimed again, this time softer and choked by tears as Isaac returned his tight embrace.

"Thank you, God!" the boy repeated. "Thank you!" he cried with tears of his own, trembling in his father's shaking arms. A beam of golden light poured down through parting clouds upon them both, sending warm buzzes through them both.

"I have provided a sacrifice for you Abraham, and so will I provide for my people, through your people. This is my covenant with you, Abraham, the covenant of the sacred lamb, the Lamb of God." said the booming voice.

"My majestic lord, I and my people follow after you all of our days, forever and ever!" Abraham gasped.

The scene faded and once more, the screen went black.

"So God spared him, he spared Isaac." the woman observed.

"Yes," the girl answered. "He made of him a great nation, just as He promised. Not only that but through Abraham and Isaac's people, He gave humanity a Messiah. But the path ahead would be difficult for God's people."

"Why?" the woman asked.

"Because people of God's nation would suffer trial and tribulation." the girl explained. "Just as anyone must before they become great. As time passed, God's people would experience a great famine. Crops began to dry and rot, and eventually, life wilted away and the ground stopped producing completely."

"What did they do?"

"Through God's chosen servant, they won the favor of a great empire, Egypt, who would accept the family of Joseph into their midst as refugees. For a time, the Egyptians and the Hebrews lived in peace. Eventually, though, God's people began to grow in number, and they grew rapidly just as God had promised."

"This sounds like a blessing."

"It was." the girl said. "But the Egyptians didn't see it that way. They were content to use the Hebrews for labor and to exploit them for wealth, but as their numbers increased, they feared the increasing refugees might turn on their hosts after resenting their lesser treatment."

"Did they?"

"The Egyptians wanted to make sure they didn't have a chance..." the girl continued.

The screen fizzled again and rumbled lowly as the scenes returned to view, and once the story came to life as the girl continued its telling.

"Conditions for Hebrews only got worse as hatred for them by the Egyptians grew, and suspicions began to arise that the Hebrews may overthrow the Egyptians, and even make them slaves themselves."

"What did they do?" the woman asked. "Did they try to kill the Hebrew people?"

"Not all of them, at least not at first, but they took extreme measures to keep them in their place, even attacking the very heart and future of the Hebrew family," she said. "The move that Pharaoh, Egypt's ruler, would make next would threaten the very future of their existence."

"What was that?" the woman asked.

"They went after the sons of God's people." the girl explained.

Pharaoh tapped his fingers angrily on the arm of his throne where he rested his hand of many rings. The rings clanged against the metal of the throne's frame. His face rested on a single stone expression. The women, most of the old and feeble, who stood before him could clearly see it in his eyes. The king was angry.

"The Hebrew people continue to multiply..." he sighed, tapping his foot. "Including their boys. Why is it that I see young Jewish men prancing about the streets of my empire when I have ordered all of the kingdom's midwives to put the little runts to death?" Pharaoh roared in rage. The women flinched, stepping back as their ruler stood to his feet. The oldest of the women spoke first, retaining her calm composure despite her panicking companions who cowered behind her.

"My lord and my god, supreme Pharaoh, ruler of the Nile and master of all things. You must understand these Hebrews breed like rats. These women aren't like the Egyptians, they're another breed completely these Hebrews." she explained, waving a tough and wrinkled hand for emphasis. "They pop their little ones out before we can even get there, and wouldn't you know it, the little ones gone. Just like your sorcerers and their tricks, they somehow make them disappear. Then somehow they turn up again when they're grown. What can we do?"

Pharaoh growled at the woman and clenched his fists. It seemed today their supreme overlord would choose the path of restraint.

"They do breed fast. Their numbers grow like flies in our waste piles." he agreed. "All send orders out to all the soldiers and garrison guards. In fact, I will make it a law. Anyone who sees one of those Hebrew boys and they must kill them. We'll still let the girls live." he sighed. "But that still includes you. If you *do* see any boys born, you kill them. I will not be mocked in my own palace."

"Of course my Pharaoh." the woman said with a curtsy and turned with Pharaoh's men to be escorted from his presence.

"Will we really be killing the boys now, as Pharaoh commanded?" one of the younger midwives asked when they arrived far enough from the palace and Pharaoh's many ears.

"Of course not," the older woman scoffed. "The things about brutes like him, they're dumb. No need to acquiesce to the demands of this monster the gods have cursed us with a king, he'll continue to believe the tale we've spun for now."

"But what about his new law?" another midwife asked.

"We can't protect them forever." the woman sighed her agreement. "But we don't have to kill them either. We won't be the monsters we've seen in our ruling class. As far as it concerns the midwives, the boys continue to live in accordance with our sacred duties."

"They seem like kind-hearted women," the woman said. "It's good to see there were some good people in the old world, even outside of God's chosen."

"God does not judge as we judge, nor does He see as we see." the girl explained. "God's chosen were ordained to bring God's

116

message and life to *all* people. God blessed those who were righteous and those who were not he tore down. In the same way, God blessed the midwives, who were good to God's people."

"How so?" the woman asked.

"Eventually, they would marry and experience the joy of motherhood, blessed by God with families of their own."

"Even the older women, it seemed they had no desire to marry."

"They did." the girl said. "And God knew their hearts. They were lovers of life, especially God's most vulnerable life, the smallest of Adam's children," she explained. "So he blessed them with children of their own."

"What about the Hebrews, did Pharaoh succeed?"

"God protected His people, and eventually, he would free them through one of His greatest prophets. Through him, God would introduce His laws to God's people, and eventually, lead them to the land that God had promised the nation of Abraham."

"What was his name?" The woman jumped, turning her head in a start back to the screen that rolled out before her. The images faded and flashed once more, and she was greeted by the soft calls of a cooing babe. The woman held him close, tears of joy streaming still even days after he had entered into the world.

"Moses!" she spoke his name with love. "My sweet little Moses!" she exclaimed in a soft whisper, rocking him in her arms. The man forced a smile. If he had born in any other time, nothing would have brought him greater joy than having a son, but this was not one of those times. This was not a time of joy or life, not for a Hebrew boy.

"How much longer do you think we can hide him?" he asked a sense of frantic urgency in his whispers. "If they find him, they won't just kill him they might put us to death too for our deceit. Are you willing to risk that, are you willing to risk bringing the wrath of Egypt on both of our families?" he asked.

"Just a little longer." the woman whispered sadly, staring into the tiny eyes. There she saw love, pure love, but there was something else too. Hope lied in his eyes. This boy had a purpose. She just knew it. "Please my love, just a little longer with our baby boy."

The man nodded, taking the boy by his tiny hand. He wanted that too. "Just a little longer." he agreed. The doors to the tent opened.

"Come on you scum, another day of honest work!" a man exclaimed, bursting in with a comrade.

"Quick, hide him!" the man gasped. "Under the blankets keep him quiet."

The woman nodded, gasping as well, and her eyes darting to and fro in terror as she hid the little one, holding him close in her attempts to soothe him. "Shhh! Shhh! Shh!" she gently shushed as he stirred within her arms, whining softly. "Just stay quiet my lovely boy, just for a little bit."

"Come on you!" said one of the armored men scorning at the woman's husband. "Back to work with you, this useless pile will join you when she's recovered!" he added, gesturing to his wife.

"I will see you soon, my love."

"Soon." she agreed, staring ahead, hoping and praying the child would remain quiet. Miraculous! God answered her prayers and the men left just moments before he began to cry. Once more, she shushed him and held him close, rocking the boy in her arms. She knew her husband was right. They couldn't hide the boy forever, and trying to would doom them. She sniffled and wiped a tear from her as she stared at the little face. "I won't let them kill my son!" she said.

She waited until her husband left for a long day of labor, out of sight and out of mind. After that, she waited for the babe to fall asleep. She flinched, watching him stir in his slumber as she retrieved him from his resting place. Still wrapped up and sound asleep, she breathed relief. She turned her head left and right, then behind her; no one was looking. She places the child into the basket and shut the lid to hide her precious treasure. With a low grunt, she lifted the basket, feeling the strain on her knees. He was a heavy, healthy boy; she smiled. Only three months old and she could barely bear to see him go already.

The journey seemed like an eternity, maybe because most of it was spent looking over her shoulder or swallowing her grief to choke back tears. The waters of the Nile rushed before her in all their glory. She swallowed hard with her approach. The river was hardly known for its hospitality. She could pray her boy would survive the trip. Yet her trust was not in nature but almighty God.

"I know you will spare my son," she whispered. "You have a plan for his life!"

She waited by rolling waters for the moment. She watched as the river's unforgiving current carried reeds and blades of grass along with fallen branches and other debris. Already she could see the ride would hardly be a smooth one, but her trust was not in the river or in the unforgiving gods of Egypt.

"Go now, my son. I love you!" she gasped, releasing the basket into the Nile. She tried to breathe but her lungs denied, perhaps crushed beneath the weight of her heart. It stilled, skipping beats as she watched her little one float away. She reached out a hand as if to take the basket back. Too late to change her mind now. The currents of the river froze for no one, not in the scorching deserts of Egypt, and much less the baby Moses. Who was a little Hebrew boy condemned to die anyway? Who indeed?

The woman fell to kneeling and hid her face, weeping, wailing to be heard even over the rushing Nile currents and through the unending sands of the Sahara.

"Moses!" her deafening wails rose to clear blue skies, but not even a cloud was there to hear them. "Moses!" she screamed louder than before. She wailed for but another moment before falling to quiet sobs. Her son was gone forever. She wondered if she'd ever heard from him again. Would anyone?

Only time would tell for sure and it would so soon enough. The basket bounced with the rushing of the river's currents. It floated, swaying with the rushing waters as it went. A sharp rock nearby rose to meet it in its course. The basket rushed forward towards the stone but swerved in time to avoid crashing into it. The baby began to whimper then to whine, especially as it looked around for its mother, but instead found itself in its crudely woven vessel traversing the Nile rapids. The basket flew into the air again, sending the basket soaring, the baby crying, screaming with it. It landed with a heavy splash and miraculously remained afloat with the cargo inside and intact.

The current slowed at last as the river's path widened and came to a crowded clearing. There the women tended the clothing ready to be washing in the cooling waters of the river. Along with them, children ran playing games on land while others splashed, laughing in the water. Though the older children waded far and deep, even the bravest among them dared not go out too far lest they are washed with the forever moving waters that rushed on by. Even so, they stopped for a moment to admire an odd sight that greeted them in their splashing games. The babe's cries at last rose above the running water and chatter that accompanied the children's playful laughter. The children gasped, some screaming and other giggling with glee at the sound.

"There's a baby in there! There's a baby in there!" a little exclaimed, jumping up and down.

The woman walked with richly sown gowns that suited her title and status. One look at her, and her servants fanning her to cool her smooth and silky skin, and it wasn't hard to tell. This young woman, in all her beauty and prestige, was the daughter of a king. With each step, she took as she approached most went silent, except for the children who continued in their banter and childish games. Each step carried grace and elegance as she walked, planned and timed at every perfect moment. Her straight posture and her shining jewels said it too; this was a princess.

She cracked a smirk as she walked by the small children, the only ones who didn't fawn over her all the time. She supposed that could be the reason she enjoyed their company more than most.

"Do you see that?" she asked one of her servants, a younger woman, but not much younger than her.

"They're all gathering around that basket," she observed. "You don't suppose there's a snake in there do you?"

"I certainly hope not, and if so, not a venomous one."

"Perhaps we should get one of the guards to..."

"Nonsense." the princess held up a hand to silence her. "Let's have a closer look, shall we?"

The children continued their giggling and their murmuring, though some of them turned to gasps of wonder when they saw the princess approach with her cohort. All of them cleared the way with her passing. She pressed her lips to another smile as she confidently approached the small gathering that cleared before her.

"What is this?" she asked.

"He was just floating there." one the little girls told her. "And then he started coming towards us, so we rescued him."

"You rescued him, did you?" the princess laughed. Now she was *sure* it was a snake. "Let me see." she pressed her fingers against her lips to cover her gaping mouth. The babe cried louder with her approach, looking up at her desperate, but now hopeful eyes. Her hands moved to her chest as if to hold her heart in place lest the little one takes it out while tugging its string. "You poor thing!" she exclaimed. "How could someone let this happen to you? Where are your parents?" she demanded, sounding indignant.

"He's probably one of those Hebrew boys my lady." her servant clarified.

"Savage people! Leaving their kids to drown like that. Father is right to fear them!"

"Your father recently ordered that all of their baby boys be put to death." the servant pointed out. "The mother was probably trying to save him."

The princess paused momentarily, nodding with a frown. "My father is a bit of a savage himself, I suppose. But..." the baby cooed in her arms, laughing for the first time since his voyage on the river. The princess couldn't help but return the smile with a grin of her own, even a laugh. She stared at the small face for what could've been hours. She'd always wanted a child of her own, and could she really let this little one die so cruelly because of her father's overzealous ambitions?

"Get this boy some milk, and a collection of our finest silks." the princess ordered her servant.

"My lady?" she looked at her question.

"He will be my son," she declared. "Now do what I've told you! He is a prince of Egypt now."

The servant did as her lady commanded and gathered the finest swaddling clothes for the boy and fed him the finest milk, reserved for the sons of Pharaohs, princes of Egypt. Moses was raised accordingly as an Egyptian in an Egyptian household. He learned the language and the ways of the Egyptians and all his life he lived as an Egyptian.

In full prince's attire, hair and all, the boy stood proudly with his Egyptian brothers in their father's throne room. There they received a proper Egyptian education from Egypt's most brilliant tutors and had access to the ancient empires' deepest wellsprings of timeless knowledge. The boys, though, preferred to be outside playing or watching the builders at the site of the pyramid.

"Do you think I'll be buried in something like that someday?" he asked the princess once.

She pursed her lips into a familiar smile, one that Moses had grown to love and always returned with one of his own. "Maybe so," she said. "You are, after all, in the family of the Pharaoh Egypt's greatest ruler. You may hold a high position in his court one day."

"But why does he keep some people as slaves?" he asked, looking to a group of Hebrew men, sweating in the fields nearby, many of them faint under the heat of the Egyptian sun at high noon.

"Sometimes..." she said sadly, hesitating. She seemed unsure of whether or not she even believed the words that passed from her own lips sometimes. It had always been that way, especially when discussing the affairs of the state, and especially when his grandfather was around. "A ruler must make difficult decisions. Somebody has to gather the crops for harvest, and somebody has to break stones in the quarries, while some people need to build these beautiful monuments to Egypt's greatness and the greatness of her kings. So how does a king decide who has to do what?" she asked. "If we didn't have men like these to gather crops, we wouldn't eat. Does that make sense?"

"I suppose so..." Moses said, scratching his head. She didn't seem convinced either.

The woman watched as the little girl explained Moses' life and upbringing. He grew up in an Egyptian family and went to school with Egyptian boys. He worked with the Egyptian royal family and often oversaw many of the Hebrew slaves, yet he never seemed happy as he did. He never seemed happy at all, much less in the image of him standing on the palace balcony. From there, he could see the prosperity of Egypt. He was born into power and prestige that most Egyptians lusted after. Any Hebrew boy would have gladly traded lives with him, and yet he was never happy.

"He doesn't even know who he..." the woman remarked.

"And yet deep down he does..."

"How so?" the woman turned her gaze to the girl in question.

"All spiritual beings have that gift. We know when we are out of harmony with God when we wander outside the plan, He has for us. We can feel it in everything we do, every breath we take. Even the fallen angels feel it. It is the source of their eternal torment."

"So God punishes us for straying from His plan." the woman guessed.

"No," the girl said flatly. "We just know, we feel it when we are not connected to our Source."

"And what happened to Moses?" the woman asked. "Did he die a great prince of Egypt, never knowing his true place as one of God's people?"

"Actually," the girl said. "He became the greatest among God's chosen, the messenger of God who would deliver his laws commandments from the mountain where he alone would meet the Creator in person."

"How could he do that when God's people were in chains under the heel of Egypt?"

"Moses knew in his heart where he belonged..." the girl continued.

The screen changed again, and Moses could be seen walking through a field of barley in the bright afternoon. The sun bore down, more ruthless than usual today, and the slaves could feel the heart.

"Some water for you my friend," Moses whispered, handing a water-skin to the oldest and the weakest of the men who looked like he'd be the first to fall to the summer's heat.

"Th-thank you great master." the trembling man stammered, barely standing straight as he poured the water down his throat.

"Come on! Come on!" one of the foremen shouted, walking up and down the lines of working men who tended to the crops. "Faster! Faster! You little runt!" he scorned at the youngest and smallest of the group, their newest recruit for the fields. "Unless you'd rather be in the quarries!" he smacked the whip out and it slithered like a snake, striking with the same wrath and precision. The young man screamed in agony, tumbling to his knees.

"I'm sorry master! I'm sorry!" he shrieked, trembling as the foreman cracked the whip again, then a third time.

"Don't apologize to me, Hebrew filth!" he scorned, spitting on the young man, kicking sand in his face for extra effect. "You are filth, do you understand me?" he demanded. The man grunted, then whimpered when the man kicked him in the chest. "Do you understand?"

"Yes, great master?"

Moses trembled as he stood before the scene, watching the foreman's cruelty. He had come to inspect the pharaoh's fields for the coming harvest many times before. He had expected to see the Hebrew men subjected to cruel conditions, but this time seemed different. Was it something about the young man in question, or just that he had seen it so many times before? He watched the foreman kick him a second time, this time in the gut with a scowl. His own stomach turned on impact. His eyes lit up with like rising fires. He had seen enough.

"What is the meaning of this?" he demanded, storming over. "Do you intended to kill all of our working men before the harvest even arrives?"

"Just having a bit fun..." the foreman smiled, proudly sporting his whip over his shoulder. "And sending a message. It encourages others to be more productive. Works every time."

"Well, it ends today!" Moses declared, clenching his fists and straightening his posture for emphasis. "We are Egyptians. Not animals."

"Are *WE* though?" the man growled, adding a low snicker. "Everyone may look at your nice clothes and your nice hair and your nice jewels and see a prince of Egypt, but most of us who aren't groveling at your grandfather's feet know what you really are."

"What are you talking about?"

"You can't tell me you haven't heard the stories." the man said tauntingly. "Your mother found you in a basket in the river. She felt sorry for you and shed a few tears for the poor little abandoned orphan boy, except you're not an orphan at all?"

"That's enough!" Moses warned him.

"You're a poor little Hebrew boy who was supposed to die!" he continued the taunt. "I always knew you were one of those vermin, but since I can't touch the royal princess's pet, I think I'll just play with this once instead!" the man laughed, lifting his foot to kick the younger slave again.

"That's enough!" Moses said again, this time screaming. "Leave him alone!" Without another warning, he charged the foreman's way and tackled him to the ground. The foreman fought back, pinning Moses on his back, but for long as the more limber man would wiggle out and retaliate with an elbow to the chest.

"Dirty Hebrew!" the man cursed. In a rage, Moses stood and drew his blade. Before the man could take his whip, Moses charged again, this time with his sword outstretched and cut the foreman down. The sword cut through the man's chest and clean to the other side. The man gasped, eyes wide with horror and shock before he gagged and coughed up falls of blood. Moses watched in horror as the man wriggled and writhed at the end of his blade, blood spurting, and the life leaving his eyes before he finally breathed his life. The slaves stood stunned in total, some trembling, others murmuring among themselves. Though slowly, they returned to their work with no desire to involve themselves in a quarrel among their Egyptian masters, much less the conflict of an Egyptian prince.

Moses watched in horror as the lifeless body tumbled to the ground, the weight of landing with a thud and leaving a cloud of sand with its impact. His hands trembled and his mouth gaped even wider while he glanced at the stream of blood that stained his blade, and now his hands.

"What have I done?" he exclaimed in horror, his stiff form drenched in a nervous sweat. "What will I do?" he added the more pertinent question.

He turned his head and then his body with it as if it to look around for witnesses. The slaves minded their work, some of them shaking their heads. Moses frantically dug a hole in the sand nearby. Breathing, panting heavily he dragged the body to fill the rushed grave. Like a storm, he rushed to move the sand back in place to hide the body and when the deed was done, he ran away as fast as his legs would carry him from the scene of the crime. All that he could do was pray for mercy from whatever gods may be. Would the gods of Egypt show him mercy, did they even possess such a thing, or could he be forgiven for the sins of his Egyptian brothers by the God of Abraham? A murderer and a fugitive, he would need a miracle, and it seemed he was running out of gods to provide him one.

A few days and night passed, dragging on like years for Moses who had hardly slept a wink. Most of his days, especially at the Pharaoh's court, were spent looking over his shoulder. At any moment, he wondered if his next breath would be his last outside the dungeons of the pharaoh's wrath.

The sun bore down once more, hot as always, but Moses hardly notice. His focus remained on his pounding heart and sweating palms as he wondered when they'd find him out.

"Moses!" a voice called out from the silence behind. Moses turned, jumping and gasping to meet its familiar tones. "Are you quite alright?" the man asked, standing tall and towering above Moses.

"Yes, Pharaoh, of course," Moses said.

"Well, you might want to deal with that." he pointed over two a pair of slaves shaking fists and waving fingers at one another. "I understand the petty squabbles of lowly slaves should not be our concern, but alas it is part of your duties Moses, to make sure everything is running smooth, just as it is mine to make sure the kingdom is running smoothly. Understand.

"Y-Yes Pharaoh. I-I'm sorry." Moses stuttered.

"No matter, just be more attentive, and Moses?" Pharaoh inquired, eyebrow raised. "You're not yourself lately."

"Yes, great Pharaoh I've just been having trouble with sleep lately. I'm sure it will pass."

"Very well see that it does." The Pharaoh admonished. "But don't hesitate to see me if there is anything you need. We are family, after all," he added more softly and with a forced, stern smile.

"Thank you, Pharaoh. I'll be sure to..."

"Moses, the slaves."

Moses nodded and without another word turned to deal with the petty dispute. It seemed the conflict had escalated to the two turning to games of tug-of-war over farming tools.

"You're going to get us all in trouble!" One of the slaves admonished the other, tearing the plow from his hand. "You'll ruin all the crops and they'll put us to death. Better you than us all."

"What is the meaning of all of this?" Moses asked, drawing starts and whimpers from the group.

"This idiot was about to break all of your tools, great master, I was just trying to show him the right way, but he refuses to listen to reason."

"Why do you fight among yourselves?" Moses asked. "Are you not all slaves to the Egyptians? Are you not all Hebrews?"

"And what of you?" the man spat back indignantly. "Who made you the leader of the Hebrew people? Are you now our judge? Either crack your whip on who you deem deserving, as all great Egyptians do, or we have nothing more to speak about!"

"Do you believe me to be cruel like all Egyptians, have I not been kind to all of you slaves?"

"Oh, how kind of you throwing us the crumbs from your table!" the man mocked, his face changed, first to a startled frown but quickly to a mocking smile. "Are you angry now?" he asked. "I suppose you're going to kill me like you killed that Egyptian foreman?"

Pharaoh turned his solemn gaze in their direction. Moses could have sworn he spotted daggers in Pharaoh's eyes as he watched him briskly walk their way.

"Moses?" he called out as he approached. "Is there something you want to tell me?"

Before he could receive an answer, Pharaoh would arrive only to see that Moses was already sprinting away.

"After him!" the pharaoh ordered the guards that escorted him.

They swiftly obeyed their king's orders, rushing after Moses, spears ready for the kill. Moses had gone too far though, and they were sure the deserts would deal him swifter justice than they could hope to in such a chase.

"He's gone my Pharaoh!" the leader of his cohort cried, panting and leaning on his knees. "I'm sorry."

"The deserts will surely claim him. Where will he go?" he waved his hand at the guard. "Tell the men to come home. If he is seen, let it be known he is fugitive of Egypt. Kill him!"

"I will help spread the word my lord!" the guard beat his spear into the ground to emphasize his commitment to the pharaoh. "If I see him, I'll bring you his head myself."

"Did they ever find Moses?" the woman asked. "Where did he go after that?"

"God protected His servant and messenger Moses. He allowed Moses to slip away to another land where, for many years, he would escape to a life of simple pleasures. He married, and even bore a child and lived an easy life as a humble shepherd." the girl answered. "But it was never meant to last. God's calling for Moses could neither be revoked nor escaped. He was God's messenger and the leader of God's people. He would be the prophet who would lead Abraham's children out of Egypt and teach them the laws of their heavenly father."

"So what happened?" the woman asked.

"God found Moses in a field. He was tending to a flock of sheep that belonged to his father in law Jethro, was a respected priest in the lands of Midian when God called him to a new life, or one could say an old one."

When Moses faded into view, the woman could clearly see that he had grown. A full beard complimented an aging face, but his many years had been good to him. He was a husband now and a father who enjoyed the simple things in life. He enjoyed his work the most, tending to the sheep. They were simple beasts, loving and submissive. They were easy to manage, and they rewarded their caretakers for the task with kindness and affection. The fields were always quiet too. Moses loved that. Here he could feel close to God's creation, far from the oppression of Egypt and their taskmasters. He pressed his lips together in a bittersweet smile. Sometimes he did worry for his family, his people by birth. While he tended these sheep in peaceful solitude, they labored at the end of pharaoh's whip. He wiped a beam of sweat from his face, which perhaps hid a tear or two as he wondered...what did his mother look like?

His train of thought would prove to be short-lived, interrupted by an unfamiliar sight. His heart jumped when his eye caught burning glow in the distance. It flashed before him, though far away the light was blinding. A solitary bush sat tucked between the sandy hills, set ablaze and engulfed in flame. Despite the roaring flames he barely saw a speck of smoke, and the bush itself remained in tack. Neither the leaves nor the bushes burned, and the trunk stood solidly, holding the rest of the plant in place. The flames danced and sparkled, growing hotter as he drew closer. Drawn by the unusual sight, he continued his approach despite the sweltering heat. He hid his eyes behind his hands from blinding flames but drew closer still.

Despite the blind light, he tried to steal a peak between his fingers. What could be? He wondered. What kind of bush was this that engulfed in flame, it was neither burned nor even singed. Not even a hint of damage could be left behind, but the flames continued burning never fizzling out. What fed them and kept them blazing, if not the burning bush? Even more to his amazement low roars erupted from the flames as the ascended into the air. A mighty wind seemed to stir them and with it came a shouting voice, deep and loud like roaring thunder.

"Moses!" it called to him, seeming to shake the ground beneath his feet, or maybe it was shaking him. "Moses!" it called again commanding his attention. "Remove your sandals. This is holy ground."

Moses gasped aloud, eyes gaping, and head turned to heaven. Who could this be? Was this one of the gods of Egypt? Not Osiris this far from the Nile, could it Ra, the lord of the sun himself? Surely it would be in his character to speak from a mighty blaze. But somehow Moses knew even before the voice corrected him.

"I am the God of your father Abraham, of Isaac and of Jacob!"

Moses gasped again, this time trembling and throwing himself face-first to the ground. He hid his face in the sand, not daring to catch a glimpse of the almighty, his Creator. He knew himself unworthy of even a glance.

"I have seen my people's suffering in Egypt, Moses. You have seen it too."

Moses considered turning his head upward, his curiosity aroused, but he dared not in the presence of his God.

"Like you, my heart weeps for the children of Abraham. I have seen their forced labor, their ill-treatment, and the deaths of the sons and the tears of their mothers. Your people's prayers have reached me and I have chosen this as my time to act and I have chosen you as my messenger." he said. "Now go to Pharaoh and you will demand that he release our people. Then we will avenge the blood of Abraham and set my people free."

"Me, Lord?" Moses shook his head. "Who am I? Who am I to go to Egypt and demand from Pharaoh himself? I'm a wanted criminal there, and when I speak I get nervous and...Especially in front of important people..."

"I will be with you, Moses, and I will protect you and provide you with the words you need. Go and trust me, and you will deliver my people. I know you want to see them free, and you are the one that I have chosen. As I sign to you, you and your people will worship me on this mountain. Now go and free my people from Egypt."

"Me, Lord?" Moses asked, almost trying not to laugh. "To them, I am just an Egyptian one of their former slave masters. Most of them probably don't even remember me. What do I say when they ask who I am to presume to tell them they should follow me? I'll be a laughing stock. Who will I say sent me?"

"You will tell them you were sent by the God of Abraham, of Isaac and of Jacob, the God of the fathers of Israel. The elders of Israel will listen to you; I have already seen this. Together with them, you will go to Pharaoh and demand he releases the people of Israel so they may worship me and be free. Pharaoh will not give up his slaves without a fight but fear not for I will strike them with my wrath in the form of many plagues. When he has seen what my wrath can do then and only then will he listen to reason." God explained. "After that, the Egyptians will be begging you to leave and will shower with gifts of gold and silver and articles of fine clothing, and all manner of gifts to bestow upon you and your children. You will plunder the Egyptians, and I will bring them to ruin for what they have done to my people."

"Lord, why me?" Moses insisted. "The Egyptians will not listen to me. Why should they care what a simple old shepherd has to say, much less one who is claiming to speak on behalf of their slaves? What will I do then when the great king of Egypt refuses to listen to me?" he asked.

"That staff in your hand, do you see it?"

"Yes, of course," Moses answered. "Throw it on the ground."

Moses obeyed, casting the staff to the sandy ground beneath his feet. A loud hiss sent him lurching back and staff transformed before his eyes. Plain wood turned into scales, and the long and limber body of a snake appeared it should have landed. The snake turned its gaze, hissing at Moses, taunting him. Moses stepped back further from it, panting, gasping for terrified breaths. The snake straightened its form as if in obedience and the scales turned back to wood and the serpent's body folded back into the carving of a plain and wooden staff.

"Pharaoh will see what the Lord your God is capable."

"S-surely lord there is someone else you can send. Someone who won't s-stutter every time he speaks." Moses still objected. "Just send someone else please."

A wind picked up brushing the flames, which soared into the air. They roared and crackled as they picked up a thunder rumbled lowly nearby. The ground shook beneath Moses, who continued to lay face down before the burning bush, groveling and crying out for mercy.

"I have chosen *you* as my messenger Moses, *you* as the one who will deliver my people from Egypt and who will teach my people the laws of my kingdom. Do you fathom so little your calling and the gifts I have given you that you would refuse my commands out of fear, that you would deny my plans for your life because you think yourself unworthy?"

"I *am* unworthy lord! Send someone else!" Moses begged, beating his fist in the sand close by for emphasis.

"Your brother Aaron will meet you soon. He will go with you and will speak on your behalf, but *you* will go to Pharaoh and *you* will lead my people to the Promised Land, to a land that is flowing with milk and honey and to the land I promised your fathers."

Moses nodded from his position on the ground. He would obey. There he rested for a time, lying on his face as the flames continued to dance before him. Over time they fizzled out, dimming as the day went on before they finally faded altogether. God had left that place, but Moses lingered nonetheless for just an hour more. Still, he could feel his Creator's presence, and though he felt at peace, he also felt a sense of shame. How could he refuse the demands of God Himself? Who was he to disobey? Why had God ever chosen him anyway?

With doubts still lingering in his mind and weighing on his heart, he turned away and forced himself on. He needed to find this "Aaron" God had mentioned, but where would he even look. What did the man look like? He supposed he would soon find out as God would arrange for them to meet in the wilderness. Who was he to question God yet again? The images on the screen faded to black for but a moment before they faded once more into view. This time they revealed the majestic Pharaoh palace upheld by mighty pillars of stone and guarded by massive statue warriors. The Pharaoh sat on his throne enjoying a moment's peace, the first he'd had all day and perhaps the last he'd have for some time. His heart began to feel uneasy, and it did seem too calm. A creaking of the door would soon confirm his deep suspicions. This peace was never meant to last.

"Great Pharaoh!" His servant called to him. "There are men here to see you. They are the elders of Israel, the representatives of your Hebrew subjects and have requested an audience. Among them is a man who claims to know you personally. He calls himself Moses."

"Moses?" the Pharaoh's eyebrows flared in his surprise. "There's a name I haven't heard in ages. Send them in."

"Should we arrest him?" one of the guards asked.

"If he is with the elders he has found refuge among his people the Hebrews. Let's not risk a slave revolt just yet." The Pharaoh waved his hand to coax the guard from his blade. "Let's hear what they have to say first."

Moses entered with the elders of the Hebrew people, and Aaron stood by his side with a staff in hand. The elders spread out before the Pharaoh in two lines with Moses and Aaron forming a third in the front. The Pharaoh and his Egyptian cohort eyed the set of Hebrew leaders with suspicion and contempt.

"Why have you come to the palace of the pharaoh?" he asked.

"You have enslaved our people," Aaron said. "You have beaten us, forced us to work long hours, and you put our sons to death the day they are born so that we are forced to hide them from you and your midwives. You are trying to exterminate us. It is clear we are not welcome, though our labor still is, we can see we've overstayed. For that reason, we are taking our leave, and we are asking you Pharaoh, let our people go."

"Why should I do that?" Pharaoh asked.

"Because you..." Aaron began to pace confidently while Moses watched nodded, supporting him silently. "Are holding God's people hostile. We are the children of Abraham, the anointed and the chosen of the highest God. You do not..." Aaron stopped and stared into Pharaoh's eyes for emphasis. "Want to invite His wrath."

143

"We have gods too, and rituals and prayers, and great spells. My wise men are feared by kings and high priests alike. Our gods outnumber your God, and our magic and our secrets are ancient. Are you sure you want to toy with Egypt, or do you believe it has only been our earthly armies that have made us the most powerful kingdom on Earth?"

"A demonstration then..." Aaron said with a smirk, and caste his staff to the shining marble floor. The staff transformed, startling the Pharaoh, but only momentarily. He eyed the slithering beast with disgust in his eyes, stepping back from its approach. The hiss startled him once more but only before he clapped his hands to call in his wise men. As he had told the Hebrews, the Egyptians had tricks of their own.

The robed and bearded men entered, their eyes pale like blind men, but most of them could see more than most. Pharaoh nodded to them and responded by lowering their heads in a respectful bow. They threw their staffs to the ground. A chorus of hisses erupted as the room filled with snakes, crawling on the floor. The Egyptian snakes circled Aaron's and threw daggers at it from their eyes. Aaron's snake eyed them each calmly as if sizing them up one by one. The wriggled back as it hissed aloud and cocked its head their way. The first snake fell fast as Aaron wrapped its maw about it and sank its fangs into its neck. The venom quickly rendered the snake cold and limp, allowing it to swallow its victim old. The magi of the Pharaoh stepped back in horror, murmuring among themselves. They gasped aloud crowding against the wall away carnage. One-by-one they watched their snakes fall to Aaron's, its body growing larger, fatter with every snake it swallowed. They shook their heads with trembling hands in disbelief as they scattered about the room until the wisest and oldest among them called the room to order.

"These men..." he exclaimed in wondrous whispers. "These men serve the one true God."

"This is not a failure of the gods!" Pharaoh cursed aloud. A loud crash startled the room as the Pharaoh stood in rage, kicked his throne onto the floor. "This is the incompetence of my magi! *My* Hebrew workers are going nowhere!"

Moses turned to Aaron, smacking him on the shoulder to steal His gaze. Aaron turned his ear and leaned to listen, nodding as he spoke.

"The Lord has spoken," Moses explained, his aging voice trembling. "Pharaoh will not hear reason. We must move on to the first plague."

"As the Lord commands." Aaron nodded solemnly.

The woman watched in horror as Aaron and Moses stood with elders late in the evening, nearly dusk. Aaron moved his staff over the water, and together they bowed their heads in prayer. The water sparkled in the light of the sun, clear shining quartz, but as the elders stood in silence, they began to bubble. In minutes a cloud formed in the now murky waters and they begin to darken and change in color. People nearby began to gag from the stench that arose from the rose as it turned before their very eyes to blood. Men, women and children screamed in horror as they rushed from the slimy waters and onto dry, clean land. Animals that had been drinking from Niles waters began to gag and collapse. Thereby its banks they died, along with the crops that drank from its banks and their canals that borrowed its sustenance.

Pharaoh stood over his balcony watching in horror as the river, the very life-stream of his Empire, died before his eyes.

"Osiris!" he exclaimed. "Where are you now!" he gasped. "Surely we must submit to this Hebrew God."

"I would not be so sure my lord." said a robed man behind him.

"What do you mean?" the Pharaoh asked. "You should see this."

The Pharaoh followed, nodding His head obediently, and entered the throne room where his magi were waiting for him.

"Do you see this fresh basin of water?" the wise man asked.

"Not many of those left now the Nile has been cursed. What manner of God is this that he can overcome the very power of the

Egyptian gods who protect the river?"

"Black magic, my lord, see?" the man waved his hand gently over the basin. To Pharaoh's astonishment, the water transformed before his very eyes, just as the Nile had. He dipped his finger in the sludge-like substance just to see if his eyes had betrayed him, but it was very real.

"Those Hebrews are a wicked lot, and I'll give them that, it's an impressive trick. I think their problem is they have too much time on their hands to practice the dark arts. Let's make them work harder."

"A fitting punishment for these trouble-makers in your kingdom" the magi agreed, bowing politely to his king.

"After all that..." the woman turned to the girl. "Pharaoh still refused to let them go? The Nile was the life stream of his Empire, and it provided water to his people and their crops. Was he not afraid?"

"He was a proud man who did not want to appear weak." the girl explained. "And his Empire enjoyed the benefits of Hebrew labor. He had been born a believer not just in the gods of Egypt, but as Pharaoh in his own godhood. He saw himself above all people, not only his subjects and the people of Earth but above even the Creator Himself. That would be his downfall as it would be the downfall of many men. It would cost him dearly."

"And his people," the woman observed. "Did they deserve to suffer for his disobedience to God?"

"No, not necessarily," the girl offered a reassuring smile. "But they followed a cruel and unjust ruler, and they choose to worship false gods, even after more signs followed, and they treated God's people no better than cattle. In fact, cattle were less disposable. Would say that Egypt was a just empire?"

"No, but they didn't all deserve to suffer." the woman said sadly.

"That's why we must consider how our actions affect others. The plagues continued..." the girl continued her story.

The screen flashed with many images. First came the frogs, erupting from pond, stream, canal, oasis, and every fresh body of water that remained. Women screamed and children fled to their homes to get away from them, but the frogs were in there too. For days the frogs plagued the Egyptian people shutting down streets and festivals to their pagan gods. They disrupted trade and even drills for the Pharaoh's army, leaving his kingdom vulnerable to attack. Cities and villages sent emissaries and representatives begging for relief as the frogs made life impossible to bear. Everywhere they went, they left filth in their wake and kept residents up for hours into the night with their constant croaking. Even the halls of the palace wouldn't remain safe forever.

Pharaoh sat on his throne, dismay all over his face as the incessant

148

things hopped around his throne room. He kicked one away from his throne and smacked away another off of his head. The doors to his throne room swung open. His servant kicked away some things, almost tripping more than once.

"Our Hebrew friends again, my lord." He said. Moses and Aaron entered behind them.

"You've made your point!" Pharaoh cried. "Just take these things away from me. I can longer bear their constant croaking tunes that play into the night, nor can I hear the weeping of my people. Life is impossible in my kingdom because of you and your God. Please have mercy, just take these things away from us and you can leave, just never return!"

Moses and Aaron nodded to another with a smile, and the frogs croaking came to an instant halt. One by one with rapid plats, they fell dead in their tracks. The air stank of their corpses within the hour and the people of Egypt scooped them up shovel after shovel and piled them in endless hills.

"Word from Pharaoh!" a young man came rushing to Moses and Aaron who received the note of papyrus with a grimace.

"Let me guess..." Aaron sighed.

"He's changed his mind. He says he needs the extra help. He wants the Hebrews in his words to 'clean up the fields they ruined with that black magic stunt they pulled with my river'"

Moses joined Aaron is yet another solemn nod. "Then, God will continue to reach out to our Pharaoh friend. The plagues will continue."

A swarm of gnats began to circle the frogs rotting corpses, which seemed to pile up faster than Pharaoh's workers could stack them, let alone bury or dispose of them. Out of the rot, the tiny winged things began to infest the kingdom and once more the pharaoh's palace wasn't safe. The palace reeked of perfume and burning incense day and night. Day and night his sages and his herbalists spread herbal oils and burned leaves of every exotic plant that they could import. Nothing would rid him of the things, yet still, he refused the Hebrew people their awaited release.

The Pharaoh entered the magi's chamber to see what they had accomplished in the days since he had set them to the task of matching this dirty Hebrew trick. Together they scrambled through every book, covered in dust from dusting off endless ancient tomes. The elder among greeted the mighty pharaoh only with a shrug of his shoulders and shake of his head. Even they could not match the evils of the Hebrew magic. Perhaps there was more to this God than there had seemed, but Pharaoh pushed the thought from his mind. He'd not be bested by these savages.

Pharaoh would soon live to regret his decision, however, as would many of his shepherds and keepers of livestock. One by one through the kingdom they fell to some kind of unknown pestilence. More likely, a dark curse the Pharaoh reasoned. Riots ensued throughout the kingdom as thousands of his subjects starved and his wealthiest merchants and farmers faced destitution from their loss of livestock. Even worse, the pestilence began to spread to men and women. Boils began to form on their skin, some that became so big and so intense they used sharpened rocks to scratch them, even to the point of bleeding in exchange for brief relief. The pharaoh, even effected himself bathed in oils, perfumes, and soothing creams, but nothing helped. None of his magic, none of his physicians, and none of his herbalists could help, yet as Pharaoh refused to relent and bow to his Hebrew subjects' demands for freedom, the plagues continued.

Hail fell for days, killing and injuring those who found themselves caught in the onslaught. Homes and shops were torn apart by its endless rains, and wares began to rot as merchants found themselves unable to transport them on perilous, icy roads. The ice beat down outside the Pharaoh's palace and his people screamed outside for refuge, Pharaoh sat with a scowl, clenching his fists in bitter defiance.

"The Hebrew people..." The Pharaoh managed to force the words out even though weary and bloodshot eyes. "Are going nowhere. Let them continue their black magic, their secret arts, and let them continue to pour the wrath of their God upon us. They will forever be slaves, until the day the last of their kind at last dies by my hand. They're not leaving!" he scorned.

"That's what you want me to tell them?" His servant asked.

"That's what I want you to tell them!" Pharaoh turned his gaze away and back to the wall ahead, where it always stayed these days. 'As you wish mighty Pharaoh!" the servant departed with a bow.

The woman gasped as she watched swarms of locusts fly over the lands of Egypt. Like a cloud, they enveloped the land tormenting whatever poor souls couldn't make it inside in time. They devoured every living thing in their path, including precious crops and what sickly cattle still remind. For days they confined Egyptians to their homes until at last, they cleared, only to be followed by utter darkness.

A shadow swallowed the light of the sun by die and covered over the stars and moon by night. When the Egyptians closed their eyes at night, they did so in utter darkness and when they opened them, they were greeted by the same. Some of them longed for slumber so in their dreams they could remember what it was like to see. The memory of light became dim by the third day, and it had felt like they were dwelling in darkness for months.

A loud crash sounded as dishes fell and broken and the chair turned over. Pharaoh cursed aloud, stumbling in the dark and dreading the day he'd been reduced to this.

"Pharaoh!" Moses called to him in the dark.

"Moses, is that you?" Pharaoh recognized his voice. Slowly the sky cleared, and the Pharaoh's sight returned to him. Moses came through the doorway to reveal his voice. "How did you get past my guards?"

"I suppose I had a talent for not being seen today," Moses said with a sly smile. "Will you now let my people go?" he asked. "After watching your river, the very heart of your empire dying? After watching your people tormented by frogs and stench followed by gnats and swarms of flies? After watching your cattle and your people fall ill to pestilence and disease, will you let my people go? After stumbling for three days in darkness, will you let us leave in peace?"

"I am a reasonable man." Pharaoh sighed. "You may leave." he agreed bitterly.

Moses and Aaron nodded and bowed politely, turning away to gather their people.

"But you leave your cattle behind!" he scorned after them. "They belong to Egypt!"

Aaron and Moses stopped abruptly, pausing for a moment before they turned in unison.

"The cattle belong to God's people. We need our cattle to present sacrifices to our God," he explained. "As I'm sure you can understand first-hand He is not one whose wrath we have a desire to provoke. The cattle are ours. We bought them, raised them, tended to them, fed them in our fields, and we are taking them with us. Not a single lamb or any other beast, not even a single hoof is to be left behind!"

The two waited for a response and when none was given, they took his silence as acquiescence.

"Your people aren't going anywhere. Ungrateful savages. You belong in my fields, and someday in Egypt's forgotten graves!"

Moses remained silent for a few uneasy moments. Pharaoh waited, though not patiently, for him to finally speak.

"It doesn't have to come to do this. We were family once. Please be reasonable. Please don't make do what my God is going to ask me to do if you refuse."

"Your black magic surely has its limits. Soon the gods of Egypt will avenge us. What will you do then against Egypt's wrath? Your people deserve to be forever slaves for what they've done to my people, and they shall be forever slaves. I offered you the freedom, and you spit on it. For that, I will ensure your people stay here forever until one by one, your sons are finally dead and your people's existence no longer will be a bane to my kingdom."

"My people came to your people as our neighbors, for help, and for refuge. For years we lived in your lands together with your people in peace. We trusted you and your hospitality, and we respected your laws, and you made us slaves. Then you began to kill our sons in your river. From the very day, our boys opened their eyes you ordered your midwives to close them. For that, you will know the pain of losing a son."

Pharaoh stood from his throne and gestured his guards to draw their blades. "Do you dare come into my throne room to threaten my family?" he demanded.

"We make no threats," Moses said plainly. "We simply tell you that you have provoked the wrath of the God of Israel and it will cost you dearly. Every firstborn son in Egypt will be taken at nightfall. The angel of death will claim them. You will not see him nor will you hear him, but in the morning you shall see the bodies of your eldest sons left behind by their touch.

"Leave my palace now!" Pharaoh demanded, pointing to the door. "Before I take your head to hang on my wall behind my throne!"

Moses and Aaron obeyed and waited for nightfall after they sent out instructions to the people. He joined Aaron and his family as they carried out the ritual themselves. Aaron dipped the cloth in the blood from the freshly slain best and began the task of painting his door frame in its tones.

"Care to give me a hand?" he asked Moses.

"I suppose," Moses stood with a smile. "You've helped me enough through these trying times. I do appreciate it."

"You've become a better speaker," Aaron said, patting him on the back. Moses scraped the cloth up and down the door. He watched solemnly as the wood took on its scarlet hues. "His son was my cousin...I knew him..." he said sadly.

"They are our oppressors. They killed plenty of cousins and brothers and sons." Aaron reminded them.

Moses nodded. "Maybe so, but there is always a tragedy in death. Sadly it is the price we pay for sin since Adam. Even by this blood, we cannot escape; all of us will find it someday."

"But we will find our place paradise, surely as we follow the one true God into the Promised Land. We are His chosen people."

"Indeed. We should get inside." Moses said, sounding more urgent. "The sun is setting. It's almost time."

Moses and Aaron sat together with their families in a silent and simple feast of unleavened bread. Their candles burned dimly that night, especially as the shadow passed over them outside, but they focused on their time of prayer and feasting. Moses broke the bread passed it out to each person, leaving a prayer of thanks to God for His mercies, and for Israel's deliverance. This was the first Passover feast.

Darkness fell over the streets of Egypt and everyone slept soundly. For the first time since the plagues began, in what felt like years, the empire was finally quiet. Everywhere was quiet. Though men and women slept peacefully in their beds, for the first obtaining much-needed rest, all would not remain well. The woman watched with gasps as a black wisp, flowed dark sails tossing in the wind, and hovered along the streets of Egypt's cities. One by one it visited sleeping boys and men, all of them the eldest son, the firstborn of their households. One by one, the figure stroked their cheeks with its long and slender claws. Each as it did boys short and tall, men, young and old, breathed their last. Wails and weeping would be heard from mothers above all else, but a single street or a single corner in Egypt would be free from their cries that day.

Pharaoh wept over the bed, profusely sobbing as his hands trembled tightly grasping the lifeless young man's cheeks. Though ready to inherit the most powerful kingdom on earth, the Pharaoh still could see him only as his little boys. There he wept as he remembered the day when first he held him, squirming in his arms. He had always been a fighter, a stubborn boy, just like his foolish father.

"Great Pharaoh?" His servant asked, after standing there for some time. "I'm truly sorry to interrupt..."

"Just tell them to go. I won't change my mind this time. They have my word."

"My lord?" the servant raised his tone in question.

"Just tell the Hebrews they can leave, and take everything with them. We'll even shower them with gifts if they take their leave. I've seen enough death already."

"As you wish Pharaoh!" the servant bowed.

The people of Israel gathered with Moses as they headed for the Promised Land that Moses had told them about. He could hardly believe that this day had finally come, the day that God had promised. He had been sure that the Israelites would never follow a simple fool like him. What was he but a spoiled prince who lost his temper and killed a man? What was he but a fugitive shepherd who fled the calling of God and hid in a mountain? What was he but an infant abandoned to die before he could even speak? Yet God chose him to lead these people, and there were more of them than the eye could see.

"What do we do now?" he asked Aaron. "How will we provide for so many? Where will we go with them all?"

"Didn't you say God was showing you?" Aaron elbowed him with a wink and a laugh. "You're not going to get us lost for a few decades, are you?"

Moses sighed.

"You'll be fine, God has brought us this far he'll bring us through the rest of the..."

"Moses! Aaron! Moses Aaron!" a young a man cried. Sweat drenched the lad from head to toe, and his widened looked like they had seen a ghost, but alas they'd seen something far worse for them.

"What is it, boy? Speak!" Aaron commanded him.

"The Egyptian's have sent a massive army our way. They're going to kill us!" he cried. "We never should have come out here!"

"Moses is this true, Pharaoh is pursuing us?"

"His armies are so wide, there is no escape for us!" the boy continued. "The only way to flee him would be to drown ourselves in the nearby sea. We are doomed."

"We should have stayed in Egypt as slaves," another man cried in the background. "At least we'd be alive!"

"At least my daughters would live!" another woman joined.

"Calm yourselves people of Israel!" Moses called to stir them from their distressful murmurings, even as he heard the thunder of Egypt's horses, and the rumbling of her mighty chariots coming their way. Others began to panic as they watched the massive army closing in on the horizon. There was no escape.

"We must surrender!" said another woman

"We'll be punished!" objected another man in the crowd.

"What choice do we have?" the woman demanded.

"We choose to have faith, my brothers and sisters, in Abraham!" Moses called to him, beating his staff into the ground to gain their attention. "He has punished our captors and our oppressors. He has starved them and plagued them with darkness and pestilence. He has harassed with his smallest, but most vile of creatures, and he has taken their firstborns, their very future. Do you think their

160

armies terrify the almighty God, the Creator of heaven and earth who will make of our father Abraham a great nation? Have faith!" he cried. "He will deliver us!" he raised his staff in the air before the waters, and they began to stir. At first little happened, but they began to stir some more, and this time they bubbled.

The whole ground around them began to tremble. A low rumble startled the gathered cloud and called their mutterings to silent order. They watched in wonder as the waters splashed sporadically into the air and then began to rise and split in two. Miraculously the water stood like towers, like mighty waters looming before them. They gasped in awe, watching the fish and the other creatures of the sea continue their daily routines in obedience to their Creator. Together the Israelite moved, cheering and hailing Moses as their great prophets and fearless leader. Even more, they sang praises and ancient songs of glory to their God. Some of the learned among them joined in reciting scriptures of triumph and praise. Others joined and pranced across the gap, but not for long as Egypt's horses and chariots began to roll in. The Israelites picked up their pace, screaming, clamoring for the end of their watery tunnel.

The last one, a small boy ran through, Egypt's armies just behind. He tripped and looked back in horror as Pharaoh's soldiers came after him, screaming for blood. His mother ran with all her might and speed after him and grabbed him by the hand. The waters began to stir and bubble again. The woman yanked her son with all her might and dragged him, screaming just in time from harm's way. The towering walls of water folded and collapsed. With mighty splashes and gurgling screams, they closed in on Egypt's armies. Their horses wined, and their mine cried on in terror only to have their cries muffled by heavy water. The chariots fell apart on impact with the thick clusters of water that crashed into them, and the sea refilled the debris of them floated to the top along with some of the army's supplies. Within an hour hundreds of corpses floated to the top, Egyptian men and their horses both who met their fates at the bottom of the Red Sea, a sea of blood that day.

The Israelites watched safely from afar, many in stunned amazement at what they'd seen. Their God had performed a miracle, and through the outcast Moses, the chosen prophet of God. Together they cheered to celebrate their triumph, dancing, clapping, and singing they worshiped thanked their most high God. At least for now...

Chapter 5-The Wicked Hearts of Men

Then Moses and the Israelites sang this song to the Lord:

"I will sing to the Lord, for he is highly exalted.

Both horse and driver he has, hurled into the sea.

The Lord is my strength, and my defense; he has become my salvation.
He is my God, and I will praise him, my father's God, and I will exalt him.

The Lord is a warrior; the Lord is His name.

Pharaoh's chariots and his army he has hurled into the sea.
The best of Pharaoh's officers are drowned in the Red Sea.

The deep waters have covered them; they sank to the depths like a stone.

Your right hand, Lord, was majestic in power. Your right hand, Lord, shattered the enemy.

In the greatness of your majesty, you threw down those who opposed you.

163

You unleashed your burning anger; it consumed them like stubble.

By the blast of your nostrils, the waters piled up.

The surging waters stood up like a wall; the deep waters congealed in the heart of the sea.

The enemy boasted I will pursue, I will overtake them.

I will divide the spoils; I will gorge myself on them.

I will draw my sword, and my hand will destroy them.

But you blew with your breath, and the sea covered them.

They sank like lead in the mighty waters.

Who among the gods is like you, Lord?

Who is like you—majestic in holiness, awesome in glory, working wonders?

"You stretch out your right hand, and the earth swallows your enemies.

In your unfailing love, you will lead the people you have redeemed.

In your strength, you will guide them to your holy dwelling.

The nations will hear and tremble; anguish will grip the people of Philistia.

The chiefs of Edom will be terrified, the leaders of Moab will be seized with trembling,

The people of Canaan will melt away; terror and dread will fall on them.

By the power of your arm, they will be as still as a stone, until your people pass by, Lord, until the people you bought pass by.

You will bring them in and plant them on the mountain of your inheritance, the place, Lord, and you made for your dwelling, the sanctuary, Lord, your hands established.

The Lord reigns forever and ever."

Exodus 5:1-18

The woman watched with a fond smile on her face as the Israelite leaped for joy and danced in the hills of the desert, some of them playfully tumbling down. Some of them laugh while all of them joined Moses in songs of praise and thanks to their Creator, their deliverer, and their provider. After years of captivity and slavery in Egypt, they were free, and for the first time, they could set out to form their own country of their own people. The little girl smirked as she watched the woman enjoying their moment of victory. Laughter and wild roars of applause joined with songs of worship as the Israelites rushed with Moses to claim their freedom.

"They seem so happy." the woman said, breaking the silence as they watched the scenes continue together. The Israelites continued to wander the deserts frequently stopping to make their homes in tents, and of course to search for freshwater. Their searches seemed in vain, always turning up dry, but for a time at least they continued to cling to faith. God had delivered them from Egypt, and he would surely not let them die in the desert, would he?

"Would you be happy?" the girl asked. "If for years, you watched your people suffer and die and were forced to perform hard labor while languishing in poverty? If you were forced to hide your sons or watch them be murdered by a king who once provided you with a refuge? Would be happy if by some miracle you were delivered from all of this. Would you rejoice if first-hand you saw the one true God, whose existence you had questioned as a slave in Egypt to pagan masters, part the very seas to free you?"

"Of course," the woman agreed. "They should be happy should they not be?"

"Indeed." the girl agreed. "But the hearts of men are fickle things. They only live in the moment, and faith does not come easy to them. They live in a world where they are forced to rely on what is seen, which has given them despair and emptiness at every turn. How then can we expect them to trust in the unseen, unless shown the way by people of faith?"

"Is that what Moses and Aaron were?" the woman asked. "Men of faith?"

"They were chosen by God to deliver His people, and to bring His laws and His message to mankind, but they were one of many, a small part of the story, but a significant one. They were the beginning the foundations of God's holy nation, which would be ruled by God's holy laws, at least that was the intention." the girl sighed. "But alas the fickle hearts of men."

"Did they turn from God again?" she asked. "Did they betray him? Did they try to overthrow him as they did in Babel?"

"Not so much," the girl explained. "As they forgot about him completely. Sometimes when God is not what humanity wants Him to be, they try to create one in their own image, but often it starts with creeping doubts. We lose sight of what we see on the mountain at our highest point, but in the valley, God is forgotten. In many ways, the Israelites would experience such a thing, while the messenger of God dwelt alone on the mountain. He would return to lead his people through the valley, only to find a people who had lost their faith." the girl continued. "But it all began creeping doubts that formed when God presented his people with tests of faith."

Moses held himself up with his staff, barely able to take another staff. He felt more lightheaded than before, and the faint feeling only grew worse. The merciless continued its scorching of the earth and with it, Moses and his people. Drenched in sweat, they continued their course through what seemed like the endless desert. They and their cattle seemed the only living things left for miles, but that surely wouldn't last long. Food supplies were running scarce, but even worse, they were running out of water. Their tongues cleaving to the roofs of their dry mouths, they panted desperately for more water, but the rationing continued. Supplies had to last or they wouldn't.

"Is there no water anywhere," Aaron cried, throwing himself to his knees theatrically. "Anywhere in this blazing, endless, forsaken desert?"

"I think I see more sand over there..." Moses remarked, pointing his staff with a chuckle.

"Good to see you still have your sense of humor, even in all of this," Aaron remarked. "Not like this sour lot we've been stuck," he said, looking around.

"At our age, you have to have a sense of humor even in the worst of times, but more importantly, we must have faith. God did not lead us out here to die." Moses reassured.

"Tell them that." Aaron sighed, paying another glance to silent, but murmuring crowd around them. "I don't know if I can handle one more mother's pitiful look or another death-stare from that old man over there."

"We'll find water soon. Trust in God." Moses insisted, unshaken at least on the outside.

Moses began to lose faith himself as endless wasteland continued to greet them. The cries of babes joined the whimpering of their mothers to stir his heart, and he could barely take a moment more. There had to be water somewhere! The sun continued to beat down on them, and more than once, Moses was sure he heard the sound a trickling stream or a bubbling spring. More than once he swore he saw an oasis surrounded green stalks and a few small trees, only to blink and find his eyes were deceiving. A moment more of this wandering, and it would drive him to madness if his people's increasing complaints didn't do so first.

Moses' vision began to blur, as he felt fainter. A few times, he tumbled to his knees, helped to his feet by passersby, but he forced himself onward. His breaths became longer, more forced. His chest felt heavier, and his stomach tighter as nausea set in, but he shook his head and freed himself of the feeling and when all seemed lost...

"Water! Water! I see water!" cried a little girl, skipping Moses' way. "It's right over here."

Moses stumbled again; this time, he was sure he would collapse. Aaron caught him by the arm with a wide smile and hearty laugh. "Come on, you're not leaving us yet my brother," he said. "The girl's right, it seems there's a body of water here in the lands Marah."

"Could it be the miracle we've been waiting for?" Moses stuttered, struggling to pass the words through his dry lips.

"I've already sent scouts ahead, so we should know soon enough. Come on then, let's get you a waterskin either way. You need it."

"My people need to drink..." Moses insisted. "Take me to the water first."

Aaron nodded, forcing a smile. Moses had always been a meek and soft-spoken man, but it could never be said he wasn't a stubborn one. He obeyed, helping Moses to the waters, but even as Moses descended to his knees, the scouts arrived to report to Aaron.

"Aaron," one of the scouts called to him. The grimace on his face and the dread in his voice seemed to indicate the news was anything but good. "We've tested the waters and examined them closely," he explained, hesitating, shaking his head. He pursed his lips together in a frown. "We can't risk it. These waters are bitter in taste and murky in appearance. They're infested with all kinds of things. If we drink these waters, we'll be no better than the Egyptians when our God turned their Nile into the blood. I'm sorry, but we must strongly advise you don't drink these waters. We need to move on and find water somewhere else."

"We won't make it anywhere else!" Aaron growled. He paced back and forth behind Moses, who simply sat on his knees paralyzed, speechless. What could he even say? He saw the water himself, staring into its murky depths. His dry mouth wanted to drink it as did his parched throat and his spinning head, but he knew better. This water would kill his people, likely in a matter of days, yet he also knew that Aaron was right.

"What do you mean we can't drink the water?" cried a woman who overheard nearby. "My little girl is dying. If she doesn't drink soon..." she paused, gasping at the very thought. "You have led us here to die!" she scorned, waving her finger at Moses. "Is this the deliverance we were promised, by the God you claim speaks to you?" she demanded.

"We've been duped. We're all going to die under this sun!" another man cried out, adding his voice to her dissent.

"We need water now, Moses, what are we going to do?" an elderly woman cried to him for help.

"Please, can't we just drink it and try? I'm so thirsty" said the little girl, the excitement gone from her voice and replaced by anguish.

A crowd slowly formed and began to circle Moses and Aaron in. A deafening chorus rose with their arrival of dissenting voices demanding answers. The people were thirsty, and they wanted answers from their leader. Where was God's providence? Wasn't he his messenger? Perhaps he was a false prophet, some went so far as to suggest. Moses began to tremble, hands and knees both as he tried to back away from the growing crowd, only to find they had closed them in. Aaron clenched his fists, shaking a little himself, but standing firm ready for a fight if need be.

"Lord God!" Moses muttered as the crowd closed in, hands and voice trembling. "Have you led your people to die, and your servant to be killed by their hands? Please God, what will my people drink, show me how I may save your people!"

Moses a soft voice called from somewhere in his head. *Moses,* it called again, drowning the angry cries that rose around him.

"My God is that you?" Moses asked, not even able to hear his prayers above their deafening roars at Aaron tried to hold them at bay. Suddenly noticed turned his head, his eyes catching a small scrap of wood that lied nearby the water's shores.

Throw it in said the voice. Moses managed to squeeze by the angry crowd, even as Aaron began to lose his grip on them and they drew closer still. A loud splash brought them to a sudden halt. Stark silence fell as the ripples spread from the floating scrap of wood as Moses tossed it in. The waters sparkled under the light of the sun, but with a new glow. Their murky depths cleared and the water transformed miraculously before their house. The cold spring now flowed clearer than the purest quartz and the people jumped up and down cheering.

"Moses! Moses! Moses!" they began to chant, but Moses quickly turned their praises to where they belonged and they continued to sing to the highest God who cleaned the bitter waters of Marah before their eyes.

The woman watched with great anticipation and then a wide smile as they came to the beautiful springs of Elim. There, no less than twelve springs bubbled with fresh, clear waters that provided the Israelites with a small paradise in the desert. Palm trees sprouted up around them, providing much-needed shade, and long-awaited relief from the merciless desert suns. For a time, they enjoyed the Lord's provision and set up camp there, but it was not the Promised Land, and indeed it paled in comparison. Day and night, Moses dreamed of it. God had described as a fertile land of prosperity and health. It was a land, He had said, that flowed with milk and honey. What could such land be like, and when could his people call it home? Some of the Israelites looked back as the ventured on from Elim, but Moses kept his eyes fixed ahead, ready for the home that God had promised him. With that hope in mind, he packed the last of his belongings and with a friendly nod and smile to Aaron, prepared to leave.

Days turned into weeks and weeks must have turned into months as once again supplies began to dwindle. Yet day by day, the Israelites moved forward, living on what God provided, though not without complaint.

"More complaints," Moses guessed, shaking his head at Aaron. "Am I right?" he asked, sweating as his legs continued to carry him forward under the heat of the desert sun.

"Lately I can feel them before anyone even speaks to me," Aaron said, looking around at the many faces. Some of them scowled at him and Moses in bitter anger. Others looked away with the pitiful faces of sad and hungry children and the mothers who struggled to feed them. "And they're piling up. These people are never short on hunger and thirst."

"We'd be better off if we stayed in Egypt." an older man interjected in their conversation. "At least there we were fed. Everyone else thinks so too," he added to nods and silent murmurs of agreements.

"And yet there were we, not slaves, and when we tried to leave, did they not try to murder us?" Moses asked. "Yet God drowned our enemies before our eyes on the very path He used to free us. I know that times are hard, but we cannot be discouraged now...the Lord will..."

"Will what?" a woman interjected. "Give us more flatbread or a few more drops of water? In Egypt, we could eat all we want, and they took care of the Egyptians did."

"The Lord will provide then," Moses reassured and paused in a moment's prayer. God answered their prayers. Baskets of sweetened loaves of bread began to fall to from heaven. Later that night as Moses blessed the meal and gave thanks for God's provision, he sent sparrows. The Hebrews rejoiced as they used their slings to shoot the birds from the sky and proceeded to roast them over their campfires in a triumphant feast. As they traveled, their Creator continued to send His blessings to His people. By night he provided fowl of the air for meat and by day sweetened loaves of bread for His people to eat. Frequently he led them to springs of fresh and running water. Even as they traveled in the harshest deserts, they wanted for nothing.

"They deserts were harsh to any travelers, especially in those times," the girl explained. "Much more to outcasts and escaped slaves without a nation like the Hebrew people."

"Yet God provided," the woman observed. "They didn't just survive; they ate meat, fresh bread, and fresh cold water. With God taking care of them, they lived like kings compared to other tribes."

"Indeed. God took care of His chosen people. And yet..."

"They turned away again..." the woman guessed flatly, almost sounding disappointed, but somehow she was beginning to see the patterns. "What happened this time?"

"They came to the mountain to receive God's laws," the girl explained. "But only Moses was allowed to climb to the top to meet face to face with God..." she continued.

175

Moses fell forward on his hands and knees as he came before the peak of the mountain. He was sure he'd never make, that his old legs would give out before he reached the top. By some miracle, he came to the mountain's peak and stood above the surface of the world he knew. His thoughts turned only briefly to his people and to his brother Aaron as he struggled to manage things below. Aaron was a bolder man than he, Moses reasoned, he'd be fine. In many ways, Moses was little more than a sit-in and a go-between for God. Aaron did all the heavy lifting. Still, Moses wondered, what did God want with him up here?

The silence almost seemed deafening, though it was disturbed by harsh and eerie winds that could be heard for miles. The whistling of them proved perhaps more unsettling than the silence itself. Moses looked down with gasps of wonder at God's creation. He smiled just barely able to make the crowds of tiny people who waited for him below. He could see them, only barely, but he knew they could not see him, not from so far below. So it was with God, he reasoned, yet what did the Almighty want with him? Why did he call him back to Mount Sinai? Only time would tell.

Moses continued to pray and to wait in silence as he meditated on God's greatness, His knowledge, and His truth. The anticipation built as he continued to wait for his Creator to pay a visit as he had promised. His heart slowed, and his stomach tightened with the anticipation as he wondered what could be taking Him so long.

After a moment's distraction, Moses brought his mind back to silence and returned his thoughts to God as he waited patiently.

A low roar resounded, and the ground trembled slightly. Moses whimpered as he stirred on the ground, struggling to remain upright, but on his knees. Another rumble came, this one ringing in the skies like thunder. A thick cluster of gray parted into two sets of clouds, the very heavens opening as a crack of lightning followed by roars of thunder split the very heavens. Beams of light poured through as deafening cracks of thunder continued to announce their arrival like beating dreams.

"Moses!" said a loud and booming voice. Its tones were deep and its volume commanding, but it spoke softly and soothed Moses as it gently called his name. "Moses!" it called again.

"Yes, my Lord!" Moses exclaimed, his voice cracking as he could barely speak.

"I have brought you here to teach you my people's laws. You will teach them to my people, and teachers of the law and judges will be appointed among you. They will carry out my laws, and your people will prosper and they will thrive if they but follow the instructions I give you today." the voice explained. "Listen carefully and be eager to learn Moses, for this very important task, has fallen to you. You are my messenger and the first of my great teachers. You are the prophet of the highest God. Are you ready to show my people the way?"

"I am ready Lord, to learn your ways." Moses gasped in awe. "Teach me, and I will learn. Command me, and I will obey."

"I will start with the first of my commandments, the greatest of my laws: First and foremost know that I am the Lord your God. You and your people must worship no other God but me. I am greater than the gods of Egypt and the gods of all nations. I am greater than the gods of this world. I will not share my place of glory with gods that have been created in the imaginations of men. Do you understand?"

"I understand Lord," Moses affirmed, bowing forward, his face on the ground, for emphasis. "We shall worship you and only you, our one true God."

"You shall make no idols, statues, or graven images, or false gods to be worshiped. I am the Lord your God, and I will not tolerate idolatry."

"We shall not be an idolatrous people, my Lord." Moses agreed, nodding firmly.

* * * *

"Why can't we see him?" one of the men demanded. "Why can't we see God or Moses for that matter? He's been gone for ages, and we've just been sitting here!"

"God has commanded the people to keep their distance. Only I may enter, or high priests if they consecrate themselves and are approved to go up. Anyone else who tries to take a glimpse is going to drop dead. Understand? Aaron bit his lip, frustration was evident. "Now please just go, nobody's going up the mountain."

"Just listen to it from our perspective Aaron. Moses, our brave and fearless leader who brought us into a desert to die..."

"Out of slavery from Egypt..." Aaron interjected.

"Yeah to *die* in a *desert!*" The man insisted, sounding even more frustrated. "And he's now sitting on a nice cool mountain time while we sweat down here and wait for him to finish talking to a God we are not allowed to see or hear. Is that right?"

"Essentially yes," Aaron sighed. "Now can you please go back to your tents?" murmurings rose to voice their objections,

"We need a god we can see!" another man demanded. "No more invisible man in the sky."

"The Egyptians had gods, and they knew what they looked like why can't we?" a woman demanded from the crowd.

More voices rose to make their objections known, and they demanded something tangible for Aaron. Aaron clenched his fists scowling. Why *did* Moses get to enjoy the quiet of the mountain with almighty God while he had to stand down here and deal with the riff-raff? He shook his head, wearing resignation all over his face. He finally released a heavy sigh. He gave up.

"You know what?" Aaron cried, raising his hands to hush the crowd. "Fine. You all say you want a god you can see. You all long for your days of luxury in Egypt. You all want something to pray, something complains to, something to cry to? You all want something to blame all your problems on?" he cried out. "You can pay the price, and we'll all make something together. So everyone give me your gold. Give me all your Egyptian gold."

The crowds continued to mutter, but this time in question as they reluctantly obeyed. They removed their chains, rings and passed around their golden ornaments.

"Everything now, gather it all up!" Aaron beckoned them. "Necklaces, bangles, rings, good luck charms every bit of gold you have from the good old days of Egypt!" Piles of gold began to form at Aaron's feet. "And you lot!" he pointed to a group of men standing idly by. "You build a fire. We're going to make ourselves a forge! Did anyone here learn to sculpt while they were in Egypt?" he asked. "Any sculptors among us? He asked again. A few men and women stepped forward, bringing their tools with them and watched as Aaron melted the gold down over the fire.

"Is this a good idea?" one of the younger priests asked Aaron.

"Why not?" Aaron asked. "Look how happy they are. I've never seen them so excited about anything," he said, admiring the crowds of clamoring and chattering people, many of whom gathered to watch as the craftsmen and laborers teamed up to build their new god. "This should at least keep them busy while Moses is taking his time on the mountain, should it not? And they're happy, why not? They have their god!"

The woman watched, shaking her head with soft disgust. Like God often did she found herself disappointed, but not surprised.

"After all that," she said, still shaking her head. "After they were freed from slavery, and watched God wipe out their enemies and perform miracles before their very eyes, and after he provided for their every need as they traveled in the desert, and even with the hope of a new a home, the Promised Land, they still turned to other gods?"

"Yes," the girl answered flatly. "That is what they did and would continue to do for thousands of years," she explained.

"And what did God do?"

"What God continues to do," the girl explained. "He honored His promises with Moses." she continued.

Moses watched in astonished wondered as the beams of light that poured down on him began to glow even bright. They buzzed loudly, but God's voice boomed over them, dominating the air.

"I present to you my laws written so they may never be forgotten, on a stone so they may never be broken."

The pair of large stone tablet descended on the beams of light, landing one on each side of Moses. With trembling hands and twitching fingers gently brushed their smooth and shining surface with gasps of wonder. The stone was soft and warm at the touch, but solid maybe even unbreakable by the feel of them. Their very touch made his hands tingle, and the feeling shot through his arms and overwhelmed his trembling body. They seemed to energize him at the touch, and yet he scarcely wanted to meet their surface with his skin ever cautious in their handling.

"I promise you, my lord, we honor your laws forever and ever. As long as there is breath in our bodies, my people and I will keep your commandments and steadfastly follow your teachings and your word."

"Is that so?" asked the booming voice.

"Surely lord it is so!" Moses exclaimed softly. "For we are your people and your humble servants."

"Yet even now your brother and our messenger Aaron is defiling his answer by leading a project to build a golden calf and your people submit their prayers and their songs of praise to it even now as it has just been finished. Have they forgotten the God that created the world they live in, who breathed the breath of life into their bodies, and who reigned for thousands of years long before even the gold existed from which they made their new God?"

"It is not so, Lord!" Moses gasped. "Surely this is some sort of mistake, some sort of misunderstanding!"

"They have turned from me to worship a god they have created. There is no mistake. They have grumbled against you, my humble servant since the day they set forth from Egypt. They witnessed my miracles. They were brought from slavery and death. They were fed and provided for in my world's harshest deserts, mercy not afforded to most. Yet already even as you speak to me on the mountain above their very heads have defiled themselves with false gods. I am nothing to them, and what are they to me?"

"I will correct them, my Lord, they are in need of guidance. I will tear down their idol, and I will instruct them in your ways, and Aaron will be the first to hear from me. Please lord forgive me, I will fix this immediately!"

"There is no need, Moses," God said softly. "You are the only faithful one among them. I will destroy them. I will send fire to consume them, sand to bury them, or perhaps I will drown them with the Egyptians. You, my faithful servant, will live, and I will give you a new nation."

"Surely Lord, you don't mean that. These are your chosen people, and they are my people. They are my friends and my family!"
"They are wicked and worship false gods at every turn. They are ungrateful and full of sin. They will corrupt this world and will soil my name. I disown them as my chosen. You and I will start new."

"You promised to deliver us, to deliver *these* people, my Lord!" Moses objected. "You promised this to your people and to your servant Abraham. You made a holy covenant with your people. Lord, surely you are an honorable God and surely you can be a merciful one too." Moses called, his voice choking in tears. "Please my God. Do not wipe out my people. Keep your promise and your covenant to us, and be the God I believe you to be, faithful and just, merciful and full of grace! I beg you, my Lord, if not for them then for the sake of your servant and your messenger whose heart will break to see you wipe them all out and turn your back on this sacred covenant!" he said.

"They have become corrupt, they thank their false God for bringing them out of Egypt, and how can they be saved?"

"You, my God who brought them out of Egypt may also bring them out of sin, for sure you did not bring us out into this desert only to betray us to death. Have you not made a promise to Abraham, to Isaac, and to Jacob? Will you turn your back on that oath now or will you spare my people and fulfill your promise?" Moses cried in tears. "Spare my people. Please!"

A moment of silence fell between them. Moses felt uneasy. He knew the silence too well, as did he know the familiar sound of the whistling winds as he waited. For a moment, he wondered if God was even still there, and yet still he felt his presence.

"They will be spared," God said softly. "But make sure they are dealt with."

Moses stormed down the mountain angrily to a chorus of brass instruments and ungodly chants as a group of men and women joined hands and danced around the calf. There they presented burnt offerings and songs of praise as they bowed down to the calf. Wild cheers erupted as Moses brushed past them all, and rushed to Aaron.

"What is this madness, and what this, this..." Moses began to stutter again, overcome by rage. "This monstrosity, this abomination!" he waved his hands to the calf.

"They wanted a god," Aaron shrugged his shoulders. "So I gave them one..."

"Tear it down, now!"

"Don't give me that look!" Aaron objected. "What did you want me to do? A riot was forming while playing games of hide and seek with God in the mountain; meanwhile, the crowd was going to tear me apart. I had to do something!"

"Take it down!" Moses cried ferociously, pushing the calf into flame, the last burning sacrifice this festival would see.

"Are you so quick to forget your God?" Moses demanded. "The God who saved you from the wrath of the Egyptians, who performed miracles before your very eyes, who brings food to you day and night constantly complying with your selfish demands for things like meat! You should all be grateful to be alive, and not slaving away in Pharaoh's fields forced to drown your sons to appease Egyptian paranoia! Yet here you are living like they day, dancing like they do, worshiping false God's like they do!" he scolded them, eyeing Aaron most of all. "Since you all enjoyed your lovely festival so much I invite you to partake in the spoils. Burning that abomination and grind it into dust and ash! When it's done, add it to some of our water supplies. Everyone take a drink, starting with you, Aaron!" Moses commanded. "Then the high priests, and every person here who bowed down to that thing. With every sip remember the bitter taste of Pharaoh's luxury and the promise of sweeter things in the land that God has promised us!"

"When did they arrive in the Promised Land?" the woman asked.

The girl hesitated as the scenes paused before them. She seemed sad. "Moses never saw the Promised Land, nor did anyone there," she said.

"Why not?" the woman asked, sounding disappointed. "Because Moses, in his anger disobeyed God, and because his generation continually grumbled against God and His provision. His Promised Land would be given to a worthy generation, a generation of faith."

"Yet if God's people were so rebellious where could such a generation be found?" the woman asked. "And was it even worth being found. Humanity seems so hopeless."

"They are," the girl responded plainly. "But that is why God had a plan. Moses was only laying the foundation for that plan. The greater plan would come from the seed of Abraham and would find His foundation in the laws of Moses. But God does not perceive time as people do. His plan would take place over thousands of years."

"That's an elaborate plan. Why does He go so far for creations that are only going to betray him again anyway, as they have so many times before?"

"Because he so loved them, because he loves *us*..." the girl answered. "It was that love that gave birth to the universe, and it was that love that would restore life to it once more. Only that love could conquer sin and death."

Chapter 6–The River of Jordan

Then Jesus came from Galilee to the Jordan to be baptized by John. But John tried to deter him, saying, "I need to be baptized by you, and do you come to me?"

Jesus replied, let it be so now; it is proper for us to do this to fulfill all righteousness. Then John consented.

As soon as Jesus was baptized, he went up out of the water. At that moment, heaven was opened, and he saw the Spirit of God descending like a dove and alighting on him. And a voice from heaven said, this is my Son, whom I love; with him, I am well pleased.

Matthew 3:17

Joshua knelt by the pile of blankets where Moses lied down. Cold sweat drenched his wrinkled form, yet he shivered from some icy breeze that only he could feel. His hands trembled, and the rest of his body soon joined as he only grew weaker. After some effort and a bit of light grunting, he managed to force himself up to at least meet the younger, healthier man's gaze. Joshua choked back his tears, refusing to bear his weakness to his friend and mentor, especially in his final days. Moses needed him to be strong. Everyone needed him to be strong.

Moses shuddered weakly as Joshua gently laid him back.

"You need to rest my old friend," he whispered softly. "You need to regain your strength."

"I have no strength left to regain," Moses managed to say, trembling and stumbling between his words. "The days have come to pass, and the Lord has declared that I am soon to see the grave."

"Don't say that!" Joshua urged him, forcing hope into his voice even though inside he knew the truth. "You will lead your people into the Promised Land, as the Lord promised."

"I have betrayed the Lord's covenant by being an unfaithful servant to him. I have disobeyed the Lord and I have grumbled against him. I'm no better than all these other drying out old ingrates." he laughed, managing to wave his hands for emphasis. "He has declared I will not see the Promised Land, at least not in person. Perhaps He will allow me to watch you lead our people home from beyond."

"Don't say that!" Joshua insisted again, his eyes welling with tears. You've brought us this far. We need you. *I* need you."

"You need only our mighty God, the king of kings and Lord of lords, the God of Abraham and Isaac." Moses corrected him. "It is too late for me now, and for this generation of grumblers. We don't *deserve* to see the Promised Land. We behaved like savage, unbelieving wanderers of the desert and so shall we die. But *you* there is still hope for you and your generation. Yours will not be the generation of grumblers, but a people of fearlessness and faith."

"Moses!" Joshua sobbed as he watched the weariness set in on Moses. It clearly showed in his drooping eyes. The life slowly faded from them as his breathing grew slower, but steadier.

"You will do so many great things, Joshua!" he called softly. "Make your people proud and remember to always serve the Lord. Serve Him, and you and your household, and *our* people will prosper." His eyes fluttered only for a moment before they closed forever and his head fell back into his bed. One last sigh and he breathed his last. Joshua could see it in his eyes. Moses' soul had gone. He was gone forever. Joshua collapsed, burying his face in Moses' blankets. He wept profusely. His tears gushed like roaring river currents, merciless and unrelenting.

* * * *

The waters rushed before the crowds as they approached the banks of the Jordan River. Somewhere they found a clearing large enough in the tree and the shadowy canopy they provide, large enough to pass through with all they had. Flocks of cattle joined with men and women along with their children and their belongings. The crowds murmured and the animals frayed, falling more silent but not completely as they approached the shimmering waters. A deafening roar joined the river's current along with the songs of various birds to overshadow their quiet conversation. Almost at once, the marching crowd came to a grinding halt before the river's shores. This, it seemed, was the end of the road for the traveling Israelites.

"We'll have to go further down the river, see if it cuts off at any point. Maybe there's a bridge, or a shallow end we can cross" someone suggested.

"This is the way the Lord has shown us." Joshua insisted. "We must move forward!"

"We'll drown!" a woman cried out from the crowd.

"The Lord will deliver us just as he did out of Egypt. If he split the waters of the Red Sea are you so quick to believe he will allow drowning in the Jordan? Where is the ark?" Joshua cried out, his voice carrying some distance among the crowd. "Show me the ark!" he demanded again.

The light was almost blinding in its radiance. The sun seemed even brighter when its rays reflected from the golden surface of the massive, heavy box. On either the side the sparkling cherubims knelt, praying and declaring the lordship of the Most High God. The priests winced under its weight, holding the ark in place by the polls they had attached. Even as they struggled with the load, and with beams of sweat running down their faces, they dared not release the ark. To them had been entrusted the sacred responsibility of carrying it all this way. The ark meant that God was with his people. It had kept them alive all this time and without, they were sure, they never would have made it all this way. To drop the ark was to surrender the very presence of God Himself. To disrespect it, they had learned in times past, meant certain death.

Joshua forced a smile, though his tone was solemn when he saw the ark. He bowed his head in sacred reverence, watching its approach. Upon his order, the people gathered fell completely silent, first those closest to the ark. Each man and woman gathered along with children they admonished to silence, bowed their heads and closed their eyes to show their respect.

"Send the ark forth!" Joshua ordered, not a hint of hesitation.

The priests seemed less than enthusiastic. Suddenly the strain of the arks unrelenting weight seemed light in comparison to what they were asked to do. Each man's heart skipped a beat, and each man swallowed hard. Would they simply throw themselves into the merciless waters of the Jordan? Would they be swept away, or sink to drown on the river's floor with the heavy ark? Yet how could they disobey their leader, the man who spoke for God Himself? With a few deep breaths and just a few more moments of hesitation, they prepared to breathe their last. Their knees trembled and their hands with them as they fought to keep their grip on the poles that held the ark. Despite the stiffness in their knees, they forced themselves forward, closer to The Jordan's banks. The currents never ceased, crashing against the sandy and rocky shores. The waters bubbled before them, lightly at first. The bubbling grew to mighty torrents. The ground seemed to shake beneath them, though they wondered if it if they should dismiss it as their own trembling knees. The shaking rocks and rumbling earth seemed to disagree, as did the other gasping Israelites watched as the waters began to stir. White like rushing rapids, the waters began to split before them. Parting like a rolling scroll the waters piled up and a mass of dry and rocky ground formed before their eyes.

With every careful step, the priests released a gasp each foot they moved forward. With every step they expect to breathe their last, only to cry out in wonder as yet again the waters parted with their approach. The crowds followed cautiously behind at first, but they piled their hesitation turned to cries of joy. Before the day concluded, every man and woman danced and cheered with joy, crossing the Jordan River into the land that God had promised them. They, the chosen generation went forth with Joshua to claim what God had promised. Joshua laughed aloud, wrapping an arm around his wife as he joined his family to cross the Jordan into the new lives that God had promised them. This miracle alone was proof enough. God was with them, and he would continue to provide.

The jubilee would continue even further when they marched to Jericho, though the Israelites had their doubts.

"What are your reports?" Joshua had asked his spies.

"Their men are giants!" one exclaimed. "We can't go in there!"

"There's too many of them!" said another.

"They have weapons. Lots of weapons! They're not like our cheap blades either. They have master smiths in the city. I suggest we go somewhere else."

"I agree." another spy put in. "That's the best option if we want to live. Really it's best these people don't even know we exist lest they come after us. My advice: steer clear of Jericho."

Joshua nodded solemnly, his lips stiff and his jaw clenched as he considered their reports. He turned his attention to two of his men in the corner of the tent. They had been oddly silent.

"And what of you?" Joshua asked. "What say you?"

"We should go in!" said Pinehas, the quietest among them until now. "We'd be fools not too, and we already have a pretty good layout of the city. We had help from a local whose family we ask to be spared, but beyond that the city is ours. Every inhabitant must know it by force if need be."

"We don't have the numbers!" another spy objected.

"There are riches beyond measures, the lands around are fertile. Jerichos a good city. We should take it!"

"It would be a suicide mission. Do you not value our lives?"

"Have you no faith?" Caleb put in, also silent until now. "Do you not believe that the God who delivered from Egypt, and who split the very waters of the Jordan River to bring us here can deliver the city into our hands?" he asked. "We don't need the might, the numbers, or the weapons. We serve the God of Abraham and Isaac. These are the lands He led us to, are they not?"

"They are." Joshua agreed.

"Then we should go!"

The spies murmured amongst themselves for but a moment before Joshua motioned them to silence, nodding to the other two spies. Silent gasps of disbelief soon fell to silence, but before a few soft objections. The tone soon changed; however, as Joshua walked up and down the line of spies, looking at each of them squarely in the eyes. "Go, we shall," he affirmed. "We will take Jericho."

Though many bore anticipation the Israelites marched fearlessly to Jericho, their hearts still filled with joy and their mouths with praise after crossing the Jordan with their courageous leader, Joshua. The trumpets sounded first announcing their descent upon the city in the night. The soldiers of Jericho stirred from their posts, weapons ready but unprepared for what they saw next.

Armies of Israelites swarmed down on them, blazing torches igniting their way. Roaring trumpets joined with beating drums and shouts of victory along with songs of praise. Some of them danced while others clapped with glee. The soldiers of Jericho stood stunned at what they saw the frenzied Israelites swirled about the city seven times and what happened next would shake streets of the city themselves.

It began with a low rumble, then loud cracks and falling stones crashing to the ground below them. The trembling ground threw them from their feet, and most were buried in the debris. The walls of Jericho crumbled, leaving massive clouds of dust and piles of scattered rocks. With their walls torn down and their armies decimated and in panic, the Israelites claimed the city before the next day ended and once again shouted cries of praise to the King of Kings. Joshua stood, the loudest among them as he claimed the broken walls of Jericho in the name of the Most High God.

"Many miracles came from the Jordan" the little girl explained. The scenes before them blurred and faded to black, but only for the moment. In seconds the light returned and the river came back in view, though this time the scenes were quieter. Only a few men could be seen by the riverside, the most notable among them a weak and sickly man accompanied by a younger servant.

The older man towered over his servant, his stature tall and his build were sturdy. He was clearly a strong man, but not stronger than the forces of nature and the ailment that befell. Spots of rotting flesh and peeling scabs covered him from head to toe. He winced noticeably from the agony that befell him, yet he preferred the pain to the parts he couldn't feel at all.

"I still don't see why we had to come all the way out here." he spat between fits of coughing and heavy wheezing. "The waters in Damascus are just a soothing are they not? Probably cleaner too," he said scowling at the rushing waters of the Jordan. "Seven times in this cesspit?"

"You came all the way out here to see this prophet did you not?" the servant asked. "And with a letter from the king himself. Yet now you would spur his instructions? Even if he's a mad man, you've heard the miracles this man can perform. If his God can do what everyone in these lands is saying He can do, then I would say it's worth the journey is it not?"

"I suppose" the man sighed, grunting as brought himself to his feet. Even before this pestilence had overtaken him, his body bore many scars, yet they were scars of pride that made him a hero, not like these spots of rotting flesh. He scowled again, unwrapping himself to reveal of his living, yet decaying carcass. The smell of it alone would have been maddening, had he not grown used to it. "This prophet better be telling the truth." he sighed.

His toes curled as they made contact. The water felt like ice to the touch, yet when he found the courage to wade in deeper, he found it soothing. He drew a deep breath, stealing the air from the cool breeze that fell over him. He shook his head one more time and closed his eyes. Water splashed and ripped as he emerged his head in its cooling depths. He emerged with another splash and shook his head and hair as dry as he considers. He looked down at still rotting flesh with a heavy sigh. Nothing. He descended a second time below the Jordan and emerged again. The rotting spots burned and itched now, irritated by the river's current. Still nothing. A third time he went down again and reemerged, but still nothing. His servant could see the disappointment in his eyes.

"Four more times, Naaman!" he cried out to encourage. "Seven times as the prophet told you!"

Naaman nodded, throw what a doubtful frown and went down a fourth time, then a fifth and twice more. He rose a seventh time. Nothing seemed very different. He sighed and shook his head, rubbing his eyes free of the irritation the water and its filth had brought him.

"A journey wasted..." he grumbled, but then something changed. The burning and the itching faded quickly like they were never there at all. His shoulder, his chest, his knees, all spots once number suddenly reeled from icy waters, but the cold was more than reassuring. He could feel again.

Naaman shook His head again, free the excess water from his dripping locks of hair. The servant gasped, watching as he came ashore. His skin shimmered, soaking wet and shining in the sun. All the rotting spots had vanished, his skin was as clear as a newborn baby's.

"You're healed, my lord!" he exclaimed. "The prophet's words were true."

"So they were!" Naaman exclaimed, but softly, hardly able to believe what he had seen. "Healed by the God of the Hebrews..." he remarked aloud.

"How are the waters of this river split apart for God's people, just like they did for Moses in the Red Sea? How is it they can heal the sick and afflicted?" she asked. "The river doesn't seem so special to me."

"And yet many miracles have happened here, and God chose to

place it in the Holy Land, the nation of His chosen people. Sometimes God uses unlike things to reveal His glory both among His people and in His divine creation." the girl explained. "So it was with many things. The Jordan River, the Hebrew people, the Town of Bethlehem, and the little vessel that would be the King of Kings."

"I don't know what you mean." the woman said, confused. "What are all of these things?"

"You will understand soon." the girl reassured her. "But first you must understand what happened next. After the Israelites took Jericho, God would overtime fulfill His promise to Abraham. Through Abraham's descendants, he made a great nation. The Israelites became a great people. They enjoyed wealth and power, peace and prosperity. Yet they were not great because of these things."

"Then what made them great?"

"Neither wealth nor power made Israel a great nation. Their greatness came neither from the vastness of their treasures nor from the mighty of their fearless armies. Everything they had was given to them by God, the Most High. They were great because they served the God of Israel, the source of their victory, their wealth, and everything they were. They were great because they followed the one true God, and because their nation would one day host the Messiah."

"The Messiah?" the woman raised her voice in question.

"The Israelites forgot what made them great." the girl went on, seeming to dodge the question for now. "They turned from God and indulged in the wickedness of the world around them, and each time they did, they fell to captivity, slavery, and even slaughter. They never learned. They never stopped choosing their own wickedness over Him. That's when He saw it...humanity had no hope. They would never change."

The scenes before them faded once more on the screen that flickered before them. Instead of black this time, they faded to white then to scenes of crystal cities with golden streets. Blinding rays of white and gold bore down on the heavenly cities that covered God's kingdom in heaven. Choirs of angels permeated the air with serenity and lasting joy. The golden gates of the city stood high, adorned in sparkling jewels. White steps shimmered in the radiance that bore down on the city from God's throne at the highest point of them rose to the holy place where the Creator sat. His eyes glowed with burning glory, yet sadness swirled deep within them as he gazed at His creation from His kingdom in the heavens. A cohort of His most trusted angels gathered closely around the throne as God addressed them in solemn town. Front and center among them stood Gabriel and Michael, and in between them a young and fresh-faced man dressed in robes of blinding white to match the Creator's. He bowed his head softly with a radiant smile before the throne and took the Creator by the hand, planting a gentle kiss. His love bore the warmth of eternal and perfect love, and his smile the joy of heavenly peace.

"Father." he greeted the Creator with a warm smile that matched his.

"My son," a booming voice responded one that could be heard by every angel in heaven, and even the fallen ones below though they could hardly understand Him. "My only begotten Son."

"I know why we're here." the young softly spoke, his tone somber but unafraid.

"Then you know that you are the only one who can save them," God spoke softly now, almost moaning in his grief. "And I am sure you know that if were any other way..."

"I am not afraid to do whatever I must to save our lost creation, nor do I hesitate to obey the will of my father. I am your son but also your humble servant. My love for you is deep, as is my love for your kingdom and your angels, and all of your purest creations. But my heart also weeps for the precious souls of the earth who have been led astray."

"Only a pure and perfect sacrifice will cleanse and purify their sins." God explained, speaking to His son but turning and raising

His volume as if to also address His gathered angels. "They are hopeless in other ways, and they will never change their ways on their own. They have become too corrupted."

"Then what must we do?" asked Gabriel. "What will we present as a sacrifice?"

"Not what but who..." Jesus explained.

Michael's face fell ill as he realized first what they intended. "He would have to live among them?"

"What are they talking about?" one of the angels in the back demanded.

"I must be born, grow, and die, just as they do."

"And suffer..." Michael pointed out, not hiding his grim tone. "And the death will not be a peaceful one. Not if you are to be...a sacrifice."

"Jesus?" Gabriel exclaimed, understand now as were the muttering angels. "He will be the sacrifice, to die by the hands of your own creation? Is there no other way."

"There is no other way," God said grimly. "He will live among them, he will become them, and he will be the sacrifice to atone for their sins and restore their connection with their Creator. Our children can finally come home." His tone seemed bittersweet. His love for His creation bubbled with the anticipation of restoring once more the relationship He'd had with them in the beginning, and yet the price. The only thing He loved more than them, was His only son, and yet His love was so deep.

"I want to do this," Jesus reassured him, feeling His heartache without a word between them. "I'm ready..."

"They don't deserve you," Michael said plainly. "Either of you."

"Yet still we choose to love because love is what we are. Without love, none of the creation would have ever come to be, and without love, it will cease to exist in Harmony with us." God told him.

"Love, life, and the Creator then are one." the girl explained. "No one can claim to know true love apart from God, and no one can claim to know God if they have not known true love."

"What is true love?" the woman asked.

"It is agape. Love for all of creation, limitless love that neither nor fails. It is love without conditions and completely free from any selfish motivation. Neither man nor angel has ever known such a love. But I've seen it. I searched for it and followed it until I found it."

"What did you find?" the woman asked.

"Perfect love. It's not that kind of love that can be explained. You have to feel it for yourself. You have to see it." the girl answer. She nudged closer still and took the woman by the hand, squeezing tighter. "You can know that love, but you have to see it for yourself. I can only tell you, show you what I've seen, but you'll never know it until you confront it on your own."

"How do you find it?" the woman asked.

"You seek it," the girl answered. "But the more you seek, the more you realize you're never going to find it all. Eventually, it finds you. I can't make you experience that yourself, but let me make you see what I have seen. Close your eyes."

"Close my eyes?" the woman asked, uncertain.

"Have faith." the girl reassured her, squeezing her hand again. "Close your eyes."

Her eyes sealed shut. She refused to open them despite her nagging urges to. She turned her head down as if staring at her feet through her eyelids. The world around them slowly seemed to fade away. She couldn't feel the little girl's hand or the cold and lifeless air around them anymore. The stark silence of space soon faded, and a radiant light came into view. A beautiful chorus of birds teemed in the air. The song seemed throughout the river's banks and shores. A bright blue sky faded into view. The rays of a scorching passed gently through the canopy of the trees that sat on either side of the river. The roar of its mighty currents soon faded in to join the birds in their lovely choir, as did the cracking of sticks and the rustling of reeds as the little arrived to approach the river's clear, inviting waters. She knelt by the rushing currents and gazed for a time on its shimmering waters. Clear as crystal, she could see her reflection on its shining surface. Schools of squirming catfish soon crowded to the spot, overshadowing the image of her face. The water scattered in ripples to river a floor of rocks and sand, not so different from the gravel beneath her knees. She cracked a smile as she took a moment to admire the trees, the reeds, the fish, and even some of the insects that fluttered around her. The plains of the Jordan seemed a miracle in the merciless desert that surrounded them. It was the very miracle of life itself. In bringing life to where there was only suffering and death, in many ways, the river represented the one who had treaded its water so long ago.

"Two-thousand years." the little girl whispered as she extended her finger to the bubbling waters of the restless The Jordan. "So long ago, yet not long ago at all. A timeless a sacrifice, an eternal love." Her hand stretched forth, drawing slowly closer to the cooling waters. Ripples spread seemingly even before she touched the river's surface. The water cooled her finger's tip. Her finger tingled, and her ears rang. A certain buzzing spread through her finger and up her arm. Her heart pounded, and her breathing was heavy as the tingling spread through her shoulders and up her head to her very round. The feeling rolled down her spine and enveloped her like a newborn baby in a brand new blanket. The ringing in her ears grew louder almost too deafening levels. Her body went lighter than air and she felt as if she might leap from if she lost focus.

Her heart rate slowed and her breathing grew lighter. Over time the feeling faded and a soothing warmth replaced the chilling shock that overwhelmed her. On the water's face, she saw the vision of the men who gathered more than two millennia before. The man who stood in the heart of the gathered crowd spoke boisterously, "Repent! Repent for the kingdom is near!" one by one men and women who gathered to hear the prophet speak lined up to be baptized. There is holy waters of the Jordan he submerged each man, woman, and child to be baptized to repentance. Each one emerged from the waters restored, a new creation, cleansed and free from the bonds of sin. Each day more and more gathered, even to the point of the prophet catching the eye of a king.

Yet one man approached who brought the prophet to his knees. Dressed in rags, he came out from the crowd to many murmurings. Who was this man? They wondered. Who was this man who wore locks of greasy hair and shaggy beard? Who was this man covered in dirt and sweat, who was this homely man dressed in torn and dirty rags? Yet the prophet knew full well who stood before him.

"My lord! My lord!" he exclaimed. "This is the one of whom I have spoken, the man of whom I have prophesied. This is the one who will save God's people, remove the sins of the world."

"John." the man greeted him by name, though the two had seldom met before he looked at him with eyes of tender love that surpassed a father's or a brother's. "Rise, John. I must be baptized."

"Who am I? John exclaimed. "That I should baptize you?" he asked. "You are the one who takes away the sins of the world, the Messiah, the savior of all mankind. You are the son of the living God, yet you ask *me* to baptize you?" he gasped. "My mighty lord, it is I who must be baptized by you, for it I who must repent and be saved. I am nothing."

"You are the one whom I have chosen to prepare the way. You have baptized with water to symbolize repentance and purity from sin. You have also been chosen to baptize me on this day and in this holy river." Jesus answered. "I am to be baptized to fulfill what is to come. You have been chosen for that purpose, and so I ask it of you as my child and as my servant. Baptize me so I can begin my father's work."

John nodded solemnly. He breathed deeply, his hesitation obvious. "I am unworthy to even untie your sandals, my lord, to even be in your presence or to kneel at your feet. Yet I will not refuse what my lord has asked." With only a moment of silence falling between them, John took Jesus into His arm and prepared to baptize. A splash announced His descent. Jesus went under, sinking below the rushing waters of the Jordan. After a moment that must have felt like days for John, his breathing uneasy as he held the Messiah under, he brought him up. A splash came again but was hardly noticed.

An angel choir flooded the area and filled the air with warmth. A cool breeze soothed the gathered crowd but quickly picked up to a mighty gust of wind. Fluffy clouds parted in the sky with a low rumble like thunder, but no sign of a storm. A beam of light flashed through the air, blinding all who saw it for at least a moment. The beam washed over Jesus and expanded growing brighter still. A booming voice descended from the crowds, echoing and all but deafening those who heard.

"This is my son whom I love," said the voice, carrying with it a gentle warmth and unyielding love. "This is my servant and my beloved son, with whom I am well pleased."

The little girl watched with eyes of wonder as the crowds gasped and fell to silence before the stunning scene. Not a man or woman could believe their eyes or ears, yet there it was before them. They had witnessed the baptism of the Son of Man and the birth of the messiah's ministry. But why, she wondered, was *she* seeing it? Why was she being shown these things, this vision from more than two-thousand years ago? She looked up, startled, her heart-stopping for but a moment. She swore she heard something. A whisper. She gasped aloud, and she was sure it spoke her name. She turned her eyes to the right then to the left then glanced behind her. It carried like a whisper in the wind, just barely heard over running water and singing birds.

She breathed deeply, her heart racing. She found herself in the dark, water still running, and trees still on every side. They cast a shadow over her, drowning out the light of the moon and every star in the sky, except for three. She could almost see faces in each one. The kicking of sticks and gravel startled her from behind. Three robed men past by her, heading to the east where the stars loomed over them in the distance. Each man seemed to follow his own star, but all of their eyes were fixed one. One star towered over the other three, shining brighter than any other in the heavens.

"The star will lead us to Bethlehem!" she heard one of the men exclaim on their journey. His voice echoed, faded somewhere in the distance as he the three vanished somewhere into the trees. "It will lead us to *him*. The child of promise, the King of Kings!"

Morning Star she gasped aloud she would be sure she heard it speak this time. It startled her, but oddly she couldn't feel a bit afraid, just perplexed. Where was this voice coming from? Did it have something to do with the vision in the water *Radiant?* It spoke again.

"Who are you?" the girl asked in a soft mutter, knowing it could hear her even in a whisper that it matched its volume.

You will show them the way. It spoke again, ignoring the question. *Venus,* it emphasized the name in echo carried for several drawn-out moments, repeating itself in a gentle breeze that picked up once in awhile. She looked back at the water, running her finger through cool and soothing depths. The face appeared, the man who was baptized in the river. *Venus* the whisper spoke again, this time louder, but softer. It seemed to be coming from the water; the face of Jesus. In the eyes, she saw perfect love and peace. She got lost in the eyes as most beings do, heavenly, earthly, the Lord of Hosts seemed to have the same effect on all of His creations. She became enamored with the face, the face that looked at her with a joyful smile, almost laughing. His eyes might have even been welling with tears of joy only at the very sight of her, but who was she?

"Venus," His voice was clear now. Soft and reassuring, it called her name softly. Her eyes welled with tears. Her tiny hands trembled, overwhelmed by the sight of her Creator, shaken by the sound of His sweet and soothing voice. In them, she found the essence of perfect love. She looked around, gasping, startled. Night had fallen, and darkness covered the wooded area by the river. Where had the day gone? She stood quickly to her feet, gazing around trying to find some source of light for her eyes to fixate on. Clouds swirled about the sky blocking out the moon and most of the stars.

Morning star the whisper came again and then she saw it. A single star twinkled in the sky, shining brighter than any star she'd seen before from earth or in all the heavens. The star and its light

213

expanded to illuminate the night. Its rays bore down to reveal a fruit tree in the distance. Her stomach growled. It looked so sweet, so succulent. Twigs snapped and reeds rustled with every inch she forced her way forward. Yet she swore some of the noises weren't her own, and even when she stood still she could hear the rustling of the leaves, the crunching of gravel under sandals. She paused to look around. Was something following her? Through the dim light that made it her way from the distant star, she seemed to see a shadow cast by her with every step. Was it hers? No, she saw the shadows. She swore she counted two, and the second was taller than her own and stronger too in build. The shadow was of a man. Just as quickly as it had followed her with every step, it vanished.

A cool gust of wind picked up, setting her off balance. The reeds swayed along the branches of nearby trees. The winds stopped, and the branches with them on every tree, except for one. Leaves rustled and the branches continued to sway. Her heart jumped as she edged closer to the fruit tree. A thump sent her stepping back, but her gaze caught the spot on the ground before her. Another thump, her heart jumped again. She chuckled, startled by what she knew was just another piece of fruit. Then she saw the shadow's source. A man had cast it over her, but not just any man. He was just the man she had been looking for. She'd felt so lost before he arrived, so empty, and so alone. Yet in all searching she would discover, it was *she* that was found by Him. But who was she to be so worthy of such unyielding love?

Dressed in tattered rags with long and ruffled hair, he leaned against the fruit tree with a smile. The light bore down on him from the moon and stars that arrived, the sky clearing. Even so, without them, he seemed to radiate with light His own. It must have been from His radiant smile, His radiant eyes of love.

"Venus," he said with a smile, His voice soft and bubbling with affection. The very sound of it left her breathless, so soft, and so loving. He spoke her name with tenderness, and love she'd never known in all of her existence. Her eyes welled with tears at the very sound of it.

"Master!" she cried, running to him with open arms spread out, falling to her knees when she reached His feet. Her eyes flowed more freely now, gushing and dripping by His sandals.

"Morning Star," he whispered tenderly, another loving smile. He bent to meet her gaze and caressed her gently on the cheek. With a smile, He lifted her face, moving her gaze to meet His own.

"How do you know my name?" the girl asked, eyes wide and moist, sparkling with tears.

"Because I have called you by name out of the void, from nothing. I have chosen your name, your face, your very soul for this divine purpose. You will show them the way."

"I am no one!" the girl exclaimed, sobbing. She threw herself on him, hiding her face in His chest, overwhelmed by the warmth of His embrace. *So unworthy,* she thought, lying in His arms as he wrapped them around her tightly. "I am nothing" she managed a sobbing whisper.

"You are *everything!*" said the Messiah, embracing her more tightly. "You are my chosen, my treasured creation, my precious child. You are loved, you are worthy, you are *all* to me," he said. "Now show them the way..."

The waters of the Jordan began to bubble. Warmth permeated its lightly steaming currents, vapors floating. A bright glow overtook the river, illuminating the clouds that floated over them. The vapors were soothing to the touch. They carried a sweet aroma that soothed her to sweet and restful slumber. It must have been for hours that she lied in His arms, fully at peace, basking in His love.

"I have never known a deeper love, a love more true, than what I found at the River of Jordan." the girl explained, the sun fading back in view. The woman trembled slightly, tearing up a little as she listened. She could almost feel the loving tenderness the girl had felt. She could hear it in her speech and feel with every word she spoke. What is it like, she wondered, to be so loved?

"It was at this river where God performed many of His greatest miracles. The waters split to make way for God's chosen people to take the city of Jericho, men were healed here, and lives were changed here." the girl continued. "But most importantly, He was baptized here. God revealed Him here as His son and most beloved servant. It is here that it all began."

"Who was this man?" the woman asked. "That he performs such miracles that He loves so tenderly?" she asked.

"I've told you before, He is the Messiah and savior, Lord and King of all that is, was, or ever will be. He is the Creator, the Word, and the light of existence itself. But He is so much more..."

"How can he be more than what you've said?"

"You'll never understand that until you see Him for yourself like I did." the girl explained.

"Then how can we find Him?"

"You must seek Him. Look for him in every corner of the world, look for him in every step you take and every breath of air you take from His creation. Look for Him in the heavens and on the earth, but most importantly, look for him in depth. Seek Him in the quiet place and search for Him in the depths of your heart and soul." she said. "Pray, read, meditate, seek, ponder, but you'll never find Him."

"What is the purpose then, if he cannot be found?" the woman asked, sounding almost heartbroken, her own eyes moist with hidden tears. The little girl looked up at her with solemn eyes and face. Fiercely, she locked the woman's gaze to her own. Her eyes like unending pits stared intently in her own. Her voice trembled, the tone matching the intensity the woman spotted on her face.

"He finds *you!*" the girl replied in whispering gasps.

Chapter 7-The Son and the Lamb

"These are they who have come out of the great tribulation; they have washed their robes and made them white in the blood of the Lamb. Therefore,

"they are before the throne of God and serve him day and night in His temple;

and he who sits on the throne will shelter them with His presence.' Never again will they hunger; never again will they thirst. The sun will not beat down on them, nor any scorching heat. For the Lamb at the center of the throne will be their shepherd; 'he will lead them to springs of living water. And God will wipe away every tear from their eyes.

Revelation 7:15-17

"The love I saw that night," the girl explained, staring into the woman's eyes. "Is the same love He has for you and your world. It's a love so deep He was willing to give the thing he loved the most."

"What was that?" the woman asked.

"I was there when He explained it to all His angels and when He spoke to His beloved, His only begotten in heaven."

"His son?" the woman asked.

"His only Son. The only one who was with Him in the beginning when there was nothing else. He is the only one who truly knows His thoughts and deepest feelings. Yet He so loved the world..."

"You were there when it all happened?"

"A lot of us were there. Some of them don't remember, but they were there."

* * *

A white radiance fell and bathed the streets of gold adorned with precious stones of every color. The crystal cities shimmered in the light that fell from the great white throne that watched over heaven. Shining rays fell like pearls, gifts upon the city to the saints and the angels who gathered to worship. There in the light, gave thanks to God for all eternity. Angel choruses rang through the streets and all the way to the pearly gates. Misty clouds fell upon the city to cool the air with their soothing dew. God and His Son and walked to gather on the platform where the great white throne presided over the kingdom. The cities seemed so small from here, even the pearly gates in all their glory. From here, they saw every person scrambling far below and every cloud floating in the sky beneath. Like ants, the people scurried through streets and flowered meadows and grassy hills. People laughed and played, danced and sing. The music rose with songs of joy gleeful chatter. Even the angels appeared as ants from hearing as the Creator walked with Earth's Messiah.

The little girl watched from several feet away from where she had been tending to the platform that held the great white throne. She watched and listened, cracking a smile as she could feel the warmth and love between them. Just as much, she could feel the love they had for their creation. So much that they were both willing to pay the ultimate price to fight for it. Silence fell between them for a moment, but as they stared into the distance, their face said it all. She watched as the Father addressed His Son. He breathed deeply, a heavy sigh to announce His reluctance. He placed a firm hand on His Son's shoulder, clasping tightly and forcing a smile. He tried to speak, but at first, all he could manage was an uneasy silence.

He stared into Jesus's eyes with a sour grimace. He tried to hide His emotions, the agony that tore His heart in two. He tried to conceal the tears that welled up in His eyes and to slow His heavy breathing lest His Son should notice. Jesus cracked a smile, and God returned it. They both knew better. God's Son was the only one who could truly feel what he felt at every moment and vice versa. Though distinguished persons to the mortal eye, they were one. Even through tears of joy, he managed to find laughter, gazing on His only Son. Somehow even knowing the sacrifice he'd have to make, He found the strength to enjoy the moment and retain bright and youthful look in His eyes. God forced another smile as He embraced His Son, laughing but also sobbing. He could hardly tell which one He wanted to do at any moment since he lived in every moment at every moment. It was a strange thing living in all of the time at once, and His only begotten, His beloved, was the only one who understood that. Soon though...

"It will be a strange feeling, I imagine," Jesus said. "Living in only one moment at once, trapped in a single moment of time. What will it be like not going back or forward at any given moment? It must be a strange thing to experience in a straight line." God chuckled in spite of Himself, Jesus joined in unison, seconds later. "You'll be weak, especially at first."

"A helpless babe. Not looking forward to that." he laughed.

God smiled. "You'll hardly remember it once you become a certain age."

"Age." Jesus shook His head. "But, I won't get old at least..." God grimaced noticeably. "That part will not be easy."

"I know." Jesus nodded, closing His eyes tightly as he almost felt it. "Does it have to be so...agonizing?"

"It is the consequence of sin, and I'm afraid that's what they've sown." Jesus nodded, "I understand completely." he said. "I just wish it didn't have to be this way. For their sake, I mean. There's so much suffering, and not a single soul is spared from it, and some worse than others. So much sin, so much corruption, and so much injustice it makes me want to weep even now. The worst part of all this is that the ones who deserve it least among them are the ones who suffer most."

"The children." God agreed. "They always suffer for the sins of their fathers and mothers just as all creation must suffer for the sins of Adam and Eve. For that reason, the Son must suffer in place of the Father. The blood will be your part of the sacrifice, and this will be mine. If it could be any other way, you know as well as I do that I would go myself."

"I know," Jesus said. "For we are of one mind and one heart, Father and Son. I will be your representative to your creation. I will show them the way back to you. I won't fail you, I promise."

"I know you won't." God smiled, so proud of His only Son. "I am well pleased with you, and I love you. I want you to know that."

"Our creation may be imperfect, but it is also very remarkable you have to admit that." Jesus smiled, looking over the stars and the planets in every system, along with the world's endless wonders. Comets joined with shooting stars to provide spectacles all across space only to be devoured by black holes that scoured its depths. All the while, the people on Earth remained so focused on their own affairs in their own small world. Someday, they both, they would grow. Eventually, they would see that there was so much more. In some ways, that was what would make it all worth the sacrifice. Even in all their sins and with all their flaws, both could see what humanity would someday become. They saw what they would be when at last, they reconciled with their Creator.

"Are you sure we can't send one of the angels?" Jesus laughed.

"I wish it were so simple," God responded, chuckling. "It has to be a pure and holy sacrifice, completely flawless and set apart from all of creation, and it has to be the ultimate sacrifice. I must give up what I treasure most to win back my creation."

"Then, I will do what I must," Jesus said. "Should we gather the angels? Tell them our plan?"

"Yes. It's time."

The angels gathered by the great white throne, as many as could fit on the platform. The others hovered around them carried by thick clouds, gentle breezes that held them by their wings. All of the heavens fell to silence as God, and His only begotten called for the assembly. Only silent murmurings fell between them, wondering what all of this could be about. Even their murmurings faded over time, and their noises yielded to utter silence, except for the whistling of passing winds.

"We have come to a decision," God informed them. "He's going."

Their murmurings soon picked up again as the angels joined at once to express their concerns. Disagreements fell between them, and their murmurings slowly rose to loud chatter, then to boisterous debates. Shouts of dissent joined with calls for loyalty and then with demands for silence. Shrieks arose as well as even the cherubim began to chime in, and all of the heavens nearly descended into chaos when roaring thunder shook them to their knees. With a boom, it struck and called them all to silence.

"He will show humanity the home."
"Why do you care so much about these people, anyway?" An angel asked, "Wouldn't it be so much easier to destroy them all and start all over again?"

"They are my children, made by hand and endowed with my very breath my very divinity. They are my image, my chosen. We will save them." God said plainly. "And my son has also agreed to this."

"You know that our enemy Lucifer is master on Earth. You'll be sending your Son out to be slaughtered. He'll manipulate your creation, your 'children' to murder Him, and they'll make a spectacle of it too. You know this?" Michael informed them.

"We'll be counting on it." Jesus stepped in. "In fact, I already know which of my trusted disciples he'll use to betray me."

"He's going to use one of your disciples?" An angel shrugged His shoulders. "Wonderful. But why would he bother going to so much trouble."

"To try to hurt me, poison me against the mission by making me bitter through betrayal."

"Lucifer was always one for theatrics," God added, chuckling in spite of situations seriousness. "In any case in doing all of this, Lucifer will actually be playing right into our plan. He'll be providing my Son here as the ultimate public sacrifice, a pure and perfect lamb. He will be the atonement for all of humanity's sins. As soon as Lucifer thinks he has my Son trapped in the grave, He'll take the keys to life and death set our faithful free."

"Lucifer will think he's won by slaying our Messiah, but in reality, he'll be doing what we needed to be done along. That's actually brilliant enough to work." Michael remarked.

"Thank you," Jesus said with a cheesy grin.

"I can see where dying publicly will present a sacrifice, and I can see where it will expand the message on earth through martyrdom, but if Jesus dies won't humanity interpret that as a sign that He is not who He actually is since it would make Him, you know, mortal?" an angel asked. Other angels agreed, adding mutterings to voice their uneasy agreement.

"As I said, Jesus will take the keys to life and death, and then he will be raised from death and return here to heaven."

"Yes, but they won't see that."

"It will be a bodily resurrection," God explained.

"We're going to bring the body here?" Michael asked, raising an eyebrow. "A mortal body?" Other angels seemed to equally voice His doubts, some even expressing disgust at the thought.

"That thing are going to be quite a mess when those humans are done with it." Gabriel put in, almost chuckling. The little girl couldn't help but laugh herself as she listened in, and thought of it herself. Mortal flesh? Here in heaven? It seemed unconventional, but who were any of them to question God and His only Son? The discussion continued for some time, but the plan seemed pretty clear and straight forward.

First, Jesus would be born into a humble household, but of noble lineage to fulfill the prophecy that He would come from the line of a human king named David. For 30 years, he would grow and learn and live as any mortal man, and he would eventually become a teacher among God's chosen people, the Jews. As a teacher, He would show the people the way to the one true God, and fulfill the incomplete scriptures that circulated among them.

He would show all men and women what they must do to be saved from sin and death. He would be baptized and begin a three-year ministry. Twelve men would follow Him, His closest friends, and His chosen teachers to act as His apostles.

After three years, he was to be publicly executed, though free from sin and all wrongdoing, a pure and innocent lamb, but not just any lamb, the Lamb of God. He would be the ultimate sacrifice for sin. Lucifer, of course, not knowing this, would conspire to have Him executed to stop Him from fulfilling His role as Messiah. In doing so, His own hand would do the deed in presenting him as the sacrifice to redeem mankind and reunite them with their Creator. Jesus would then conquer sin and death and be raised from the dead, so he can present himself to His disciples to carry out the rest of His plan on Earth. Jesus would then return to heaven in His pierced and scarred mortal body to heaven until he returns for those among humanity the plan was able to save.

"We're not allowed to know when?" Gabriel asked, crossing His arms.

"Only myself and my son are allowed to know, I'm afraid," God said softly, nodding. "But when it is time, we will be ready, and everyone will know. The second coming will be announced with a trumpet. For now, we will have to prepare the way. We will use my chosen among humanity to go and convey my message first.

There will be teachers and prophets who will bring the secrets of heaven to man as they were once hidden by Lucifer and by man's obstinacy.

Meanwhile, you, my faithful angels, know your role. You must keep the demons at bay and act as my messengers in spiritual places to humanity. I must now speak alone with my Son." God told them all. The angels and the cherubim and all of the gathered heavenly creatures slowly dispersed, quickly obeying their Creator. God waited with His Son in silence and watched them depart. Silence remained dominant in the air, even with the quiet chatter as the souls dispersed. Still, only that same familiar warm breeze filled the air now after Michael, the last angel left. God nodded, and Jesus returned it with a firm nod of His own and a severe frown. God returned it with a forced smile.

"We've done so much together," God said. "I can hardly make myself send you away."

"We have some time before that."

"No amount of time is enough for us, you know that." he sighed.

"In a moment passes a thousand years and in a thousand years only a moment."

"Yet we have all time..." Jesus said. "We are all time."

"Do you remember our faithful servant Abraham?" he asked.

231

"Of course," Jesus cracked a smile. "And His Son Isaac. I remember how loud he wept how he begged you to spare His Isaac's life. And now here we are, making the same sacrifice."

"But no lamb will take your place..." God said grimly.

"But, you still won't lose your son."
"I'm not sure you understand..."

"I remember the look on Abraham's face when we asked him for that sacrifice..." Jesus trailed off. "You've had that same look since the day we made Adam. I know the agony you feel for I feel what you feel, but like Abraham, we will be faithful until the end, and like Abraham, we will know abundant joy when it's over."

God and Jesus stared over the streets of heaven in silence for a few more moments. Golden streets and crystal cities teemed with life below. Angels sang, and souls rejoiced, but with heavy hearts, all the two could think about was the sacrifice of Abraham.

* * * *

Abraham rubbed His chest firmly. It felt as sore as did His stomach from the tightness all day. He tried to hold the pain. Sarah didn't need to see him fall apart. Still, Abraham was only a man. He wondered if God even understands that now. He choked back the tears crawling out from the tent. He glanced behind flinching as Sarah seemed to stir from her slumber. He sighed

232

relief when she returned to her back and to steady breathing. She was still asleep.

The boy slept too, like a rock not even stirring from His rest. His watered slightly, but he held it back for fear of losing control. If he started crying now, he'd wake them both. He had to be strong for the family, for God. He had to carry this out to the end, though he was sure he could never do the deed.

He left the tent and stumbled into the night. His knees nearly buckled more than once as he wandered off. He was getting too old to wander off on His own like this anymore. It was a miracle he even produced the seed that made Isaac, let alone for Sarah, to give birth. Neither of them could go through it again. God knew that. So why would he ask him to do that? He swallowed hard against the lump in His throat. His eyes swelled up, and the tears began to force their way through. He stumbled into the woods.

At last, he could endure no more, so he tumbled to His knees. He wept, whimpered, and sobbed what felt like all night long. He struggled to breathe through all the tears and snot he cried so endlessly.

"Why, God? Why?" he moaned, sniffling between His words.

"Why even promise me a son, why tell me what a great nation you'll make of me only to ask me to do this? Why are you asking to kill my baby boy?"

The little girl watched from a distance, but even from where she stood, she could see the pain on the Creator's face. He watched Abraham weep and listened to sobbing prayers with a heavy heart. He couldn't tell Abraham what would happen next. Not yet. In time Abraham would see that He had a plan and that He would reveal Himself as a God who always keeps His promises. The pain of Abraham was necessary, though, so humanity could understand. The pain of Abraham would soon enough be God's pain, though the world would mourn for Abraham. Some would even scorn him for the choice he made. Yet God knew Abraham would never do it. He'd never have to with what He had planned.

The girl watched, anticipation in her eyes as she watched her Creator see His plan unfold. The night quickly yielded today, and Abraham gathered His belongings and His most precious treasure.

"Come, Isaac," he called to the boy. "Are you ready?"

"I'm ready, but where's the sacrifice?" the boy asked.

"God will provide." Abraham nodded firmly, His voice choking, but he hid His tears well. He'd had plenty of practice and plenty of preparation the night before.

They reached the top of the mountain where Isaac was bound placed on the altar, squirming, weeping, terrified. Abraham trembled as he lifted the knife into the air. God's servant moved

His wrists to bring it down, but His arms wouldn't budge. He froze. Why couldn't he do it? Of course, he couldn't do it, he thought. How could he? He tried so long to have a son. Sarah had already forced him to send Ishmael away, how could he murder Isaac too? His eyes welled with tears, and His entire body trembled. He collapsed to His knees, losing hold of the knife. The blade clattered to the rocky ground beneath His knees. He buried His face in His hands. Again he asked, "God, why are you making me this? I just want to know why?" After a moment of silence, he nodded with a frown. He wiped His eyes and nose and regained His composure.

"It's OK, father," Isaac said. "Please, just don't make it hurt."

Abraham nodded again, standing, staggering to His feet. He lifted the knife again, hardly able to see straight through His tears and sore eyes.

Then he heard His answer. The bleating of a lamb startled him from behind, a pure and spotless creature, an innocent lonely lamb. Its footsteps pattered gently as he ran to Abraham. It rubbed His head against the old man's shins, looking up with anticipation, almost as if it knew. Abraham caught the look in the eyes, and His heart raced, staring into them. There was something different about this lamb...

A voice from shook the rocky ground beneath him. Its booming thunder startled Abraham and roused him from His sobbing.

"Abraham," the voice called to him. Abraham turned His head to the beam of light that fell from heaven, somehow making its way through the gloom of the day. "Abraham!" it called again.

"Yes, Lord!" Abraham cried back.

"Take that knife..."

"Yes, lord?" Abraham's became wide.

"Turn to your son..."

"Lord?" Abraham asked but obeyed, turning to the altar.

"Now cut him free, for I have provided you with a perfect and spotless lamb. I have provided the perfect sacrifice, so you don't have to. Do you understand?"

"Yes, Lord!" Abraham cried with joy. His hands and voice still trembled, but His tears were gone in but an instant. "Thank you, Lord!"

God smiled but shook His head. He knew he didn't understand how could he, how could he understand the sacrifice the King of Kings would have to make? He was only a man, and though they were capable of love, they could never understand His love, not yet. They could never understand its vastness, its depths, or its endlessness. Yet it was that love that forced His hand. He knew He had no choice but to do the thing that pained Him most. How could He? How could he enjoy a life of splendor and glory, a life of perfection and infinite power with His only Son and then ask Him to suffer and die? How could he ask him to be humiliated at the hands of His fallen creation? How could He ask him to do this? Yet the Son shared the father's love or else he could say no. He tried to get Him to say no if he really wanted to, but Jesus's love was just as deep as the fathers. It was a reckless but an eternal one. It was that love that would undo all the evil of Lucifer and His plans on Earth. He'd never see it coming. Still, God was unsure about what would happen next, would His Son be ready?

"Son," he said with a deep breath, hesitating. "We need to talk."

"I am ready for everything I need to do." He answered, knowing what His Father would say before He even spoke. "And yes, I know what will happen on the cross. I know that it's more than just an execution, just a physical sacrifice."

"Then you know you are to take all of the sins of the world on yourself. I won't even be able to look upon you. You will be cast from my presence, and as soon as you breathe your last, you will awake in the kingdom of hell, surrounded by Lucifer and all His fallen angels, and surrounded by every torment that belongs to them."

"And I will claim the keys to life and death and rescue the saints who are held captive, and then I will be resurrected and reunited with you, just as your creation will be."

"Are you ready to take on the consequences, the separation from me and all that it is holy? Are you ready to be stripped of access to the holy kingdom, and drenched in all the sins of the world? Are you really ready for that? Are you ready to take on the pain and the darkness of every unholy act? Every violent attack and every kind of abuse will be yours to bear. Every rape will be your burden, every unholy act will be within you. Every wicked thought and every wicked scheme devised by man will be borne by you, and every vile action and word will be on you. You will be separated from me, and I will have nothing to do with you. I will revile you, and curse you, though I don't wish to, but I must punish all that is unholy, and you will become the essence of sin. You pay the ultimate price so humanity may be spared." God explained. "Are you ready for that?"

"I am ready," Christ assured him.

"I know you are," God said, His voice nearly cracking. Another moment of silence fell between them, but they told each other more in those moments than any creation could have said in a thousand years. It was that way with them. They chose to speak slowly, sometimes to live in the moment and to enjoy it, but they never have to. Soon that would change for the Son, as he would inhabit a mortal body.

"I will miss you."

"And I you, but you will always be with me and I with you, for even as I inhabit mortal flesh, we are separate but one, forever and ever."

The two stepped forward in unison. Silence fell one last time between them before they joined in a tight and warm and embrace. It was hard to tell how long it lasts. I might have been a thousand years, and it might have been a few short moments. It couldn't have been long enough, God thought, not with what He was asking His only Son to do. He admired His love and courage. He wasn't even going to Earth, but he could barely stomach the thought of His own Son going. If only he could go in His place.

The scenes of heaven faded before them, and the woman and the little girl found themselves standing once more in darkness. The void of space surrounded them, but the warmth of heaven seemed to linger. A light each did as well, of some angelic tune that came from heaven, and with it an orchestra of soothing harps.

"He loved His Son so much. You can see it all over His face. Why would He give Him up for a sinful creation?"

"None of us can understand that love, but we can experience it. We can feel it, and by doing so, we can't help but share it and pass it on to others. That's the way with God's love, it never seems to stay in just one heart for long. Yet that love carried a

239

higher price than any of us could ever understand, for none of us can know the loneliness of God."

"It seems like most of us should envy the supreme master and Creator of the universe."

"Because we are not Him, we cannot understand the loneliness that comes with such a title, to be above all else, to know everything before it happens. What must it be like to have no one to interact with who understands what it's like to carry the weight of the universe? God had no one except for His Son, who was the Word and was with Him in the beginning. Yet for love, He was forced to give up that precious gift, His only beloved."

"Would the world even be ready for such a sacrifice? Could they even appreciate such a love?" the woman asked.

"That is why," the little girl explained. "They needed to prepare the way. That is where the prophets came in."

"Who were the prophets?" The woman asked.

"Jesus inhabited mortal flesh because mortal flesh follows mortal flesh. Sadly, humanity relies on their physical senses more than spiritual discernment, so people need people to follow. Along those lines, God chose people from among humanity to be His prophets and prepare the way for the coming of Jesus. They would reveal the truth of the one true God to all of humanity and would establish a chosen nation to host the Messiah."

"And Jesus would be king of that nation?" the woman asked.

"Not exactly," the girl cracked a smile. "He would be called the King of The Jews, for He would be their Messiah, but they would never acknowledge Him. He would be born in a city that has no room for Him and turns Him away. He will be born in a dwelling place of animals, and yet He will be hailed and worshiped as the king. The king of that nation will try to murder him, and he'll grow up as a refugee in a foreign land. He'll spend the majority of His life preparing for ministry. Eventually, he would become a great teacher with loyal disciples and crowds of adoring followers. Yet, at the end of His life, he was to be alone and rejected by even His own father. There, on Golgotha, He was to die in shame only to conquer death and wash away the sins of humanity."

"So greater than any king could ever be." the woman gasped. "Yet no one would ever know it or acknowledged."

"Many would and many would not, Jesus came for every lost soul on Earth, but He and God that some people would reject their gift. Even so, they made the sacrifice..."

"For love..." the woman whispered in wonder. "All for love."

"All for love." the girl agreed. "You'll know that love soon enough, I promise you."

Chapter 8–The Star of the

Only Begotten

*After Jesus was born in Bethlehem in Judea, during the time of
King Herod, Magi from the east came to Jerusalem and asked,
"Where is the one who has been born king of the Jews? We saw
His star when it rose and have come to worship him."*

*When King Herod heard this, he was disturbed, and all Jerusalem
with him. When he had called together all the people chief priests
and teachers of the law, he asked them where the Messiah was to
be born.*

"Bethlehem in Judea," they replied, "For this is what the prophet

has written: 'But you, Bethlehem, in the land of Judah, are by no means least among the rulers of Judah; for out of you will come a ruler who will shepherd my people Israel.' "Then Herod called the Magi secretly and found out from them the exact time the star had appeared. He sent them to Bethlehem and said, "Go and search carefully for the child. As soon as you find him, report to me, so that I too may go and worship him."

After they had heard the king, they went on their way, and the star they had seen when it rose went ahead of them until it stopped over the place where the child was. When they saw the star, they were overjoyed. On coming to the house, they saw the child with His mother Mary, and they bowed down and worshiped him. Then they opened their treasures and presented him with gifts of gold, frankincense and myrrh. And having been warned in a dream not to go back to Herod, they returned to their country by another route.

Matthew 2: 1-12

God looked into the distance. First, he looked to the north and to the south. Then to the east and to the west. He could see into all that, and all that would ever be. He could see the wonders he would create and how they would fall from glory. He could see their downfall, but also their restoration. He smiled at the thought. It will have been worth the sorrow and the grief. The love He had for them was so deep, even before they ever came to be. But right

243

now he could only see the nothingness. The sight was less than easy on His eyes. The Son stood by nodding, knowing what the Father felt before He even spoke. The Spirit stood by as well, floating by in silence, but in agreement with them both. He was the divine Creator and so it was in His nature to create. What else could he do?

Nothing existed. Black nothingness, meaningless void, they were all that He could see, but what did it matter anyway? No eyes could see but theirs, so who would appreciate their creation anyway? The silence deafened them to the point of streaming tears and muffled cries of grief. The loneliness almost seemed unbearable. How could such a divine being, one who was all-knowing and omnipotent, be so weak? How could He feel such pain and loneliness? The silence said it all and the void that lay before him painted a vivid picture of the sad the truth that surrounded Him. What was the point of existence at all, this painful awareness, and this endless knowledge? What was the point if no one existed share it with?

He knew then what He wanted to do. All three of them knew even as they hovered over the still and lifeless waters. The waves tossed and the ripples went out into the endless void.

"Shall we make something?" The Son said with a smile, placing a firm hand on His father's shoulder. He chuckled, turning to the glowing whisper floated with them in the mists of stirring seas that surrounded them. "Or maybe *someone*, he added with a wink and a nudge."

"Not yet." I want him to awake to the world we created for him and His children.

"Wait until he sees Eve." the Son chuckled with glee.

"I can already see His face as he stirs from His slumber."

"Looks terrified, doesn't he?"

"As all men after him will be when they first meet their partners. God laughed. But, for now, let us focus on our first creation."

"They will be impressive. Jesus grinned now. The stars, the moons and planets will truly be glorious."

"It will be nice to have something to look at in the void."

"Don't forget mine..."

"The Morning Star." God smiled, love twinkling in His eyes as he spoke more warmly now. "Precious little Venus."

So she's going to show our glory to all over the world, is she? Jesus asked. I can't wait to see her shine.

The wisp that was the Holy Ghost whistled and swirled before them, cutting off the conversation. The waters tossed with the heavy waves that crashed around them. Splashes then full-scale eruptions of the sea's excess flew into the ear as the waters began to move with the force of the Holy Spirits power. A low rumble sounded first like a mighty horn than a little higher to ring like singing trumpets. Then a mighty, booming voice as Father, Son, and Holy Spirit spoke in a roaring voice that crashed like thunder and echoed throughout the voice.

"Let there be light!" and overtime as the Godhead spoke the world into came into being. The heavenly bodies formed across the vast expanse of space, once a hollow vacuum. Cracks and splitting rocks would have roared throughout the darkness, but only silence traveled in the endless sea of black. Fires sprang up as spheres as ignited with a sweeping blaze. The planets formed from the wreckage and along with them the sun and the systems many moons. Stars sprang up forming solar systems then galaxies and universe expanded.

A light whimper and she stirred from what must have been eternal slumber. Her vision blurred, but she could just make out the other lights as they floated in the distance. Where was she? What was she?

"Venus," a soothing, though muffled voice called to her. Venus. It spoke her name with reassuring warmth.

"Are you..." the little girl asked, shuddering where she lay, "my maker?" she asked.

"Yes." said the Master, resting a reassuring hand on her. Her forehead tingled at its touch and it set her mind at ease and stilled her pounding heart. "And I have given you the gift of life," He explained. "But I have also given you my light. I have given you these gifts that may share them with your sister in creation."

"Earth?" she asked. How did she know the name?

"You will show her my light when her world needs it most." He explained.

Her eyebrows raised in question. "I don't understand," she said.

You will, he reassured her. "When the time is right. Until then enjoy the gift I've given you and marvel at your sacred place in my creation. I love you, my child, and so I have brought you into being."

"Why?" she asked. "Why did you do all this; why create all this?"

The Master smile. "I have created what I have loved. All that has existed has existed in my love. Know that you have been created because you have been loved."

"Darkness and silence." the girl said plainly. "Nothing else existed in all the face of the deep and the void. The universe was empty, formless, and lonely. It was before I ever came to be. I can't imagine what a sad sight it must have been, all that space and nothing in it. No stars, no planets, no beauty or light, to please these eyes. Just nothingness. How deafening the silence must have been, how sad it must have been to have no one to speak to or listen to." she said, almost whimpering at the thought. "Except..." she trailed off.

"There was one." the woman guessed.

"The Father had the Son. The two of them were one even in the beginning. The Son was with the Creator just as He was the Creator."

"How can the two of them be separate people, able to talk to each other and love one another, but also be the same, one distinct person but also separate three?"

The girl cracked a smile. "How can you understand that when you can't even understand how God experiences time or how He lives in all things and all places just as He occupies all time?" she asked. "How can you hope to understand the many and vast mysteries of God until you first understand the essence of what He is?" she asked. "Until you can understand God's love, there's a point even asking about the other things," she said. "And when you understand this, you begin to see how true love starts with caring for others and for the self because true love does not discriminate, love only loves. Love is not satisfied unless it is extending itself to others, growing, forever multiplying. That is how a God who loves His son more than anything else can give up His son for His creation, even though he Loves Him as just as much. That is why the love of God is a perfect love. It is not a love that is 'because' it's a just a love that 'is,' it is agape love." she said. "God's love was that way, unsatisfied to remain in itself. So he created."

"He made the heavens and the earth. Humanity."

"First, he made so many beautiful wonders both the universe you know and live in, and the kingdom of heaven in all of their natural beauty. I wish you could see what the old Heaven was like compared to the Earth." the girl told her. "It was so much brighter, so much more beautiful. Just like the new Heaven and the new Earth, it was free of disease, sorrow, or corruption. No imperfection existed there. Except for the rebellion that required Him to cast out Lucifer out with His rebellious angels after man's creation, everyone lived in peace and harmony. Everyone and everything lived and moved in obedience to God. Heaven was an orderly place where everything always made sense. Everything always went according to plan and in accordance with God's laws and commandments."

"The old heaven didn't sound so bad."

"It wasn't," the girl admitted.

"But God wanted more. Earth, even in all its sin and corruption is much more interesting with man."

"Why are they so special?" the woman asked.

"Because they can do what God can do, no other creation can." The girl said plainly. "They can do what neither the angels nor any existing being can do."

"What's that?" the woman asked.

"They can choose." the girl answered. "And through their choices, they can change God's universe."

"The demon's and angels can't?" the woman asked.

"They can only do what God allows them to do, but God gave the ability to choose other to Adam and Eve, and they passed it down to their descendants. Spiritual creatures like angels and demons can do some things in God's realm, but producing any real change or alteration relies on influencing God's most gifted creation: man."

"Why would He create something so dangerous?" the woman asked.

"Love." the girl explained. "For love to be true, it has to be given freely by someone who can otherwise choose to withhold it. God longed for that love, so He created it in man, knowing the risks."

Darkness fell, covering the face of a universe that once was but had yet to be. A frightening silence drowned out all noise and threatened to also swallow thought and even feeling from the poor souls devoured by its depths and doomed to drift forever. Some would consider it a blissful fate, one to be envied. Floating in the void and lost to all thought and feeling meant no desire and therefore, no loss, no pleasure, and thus no pain. The vacuum of space may have been less than glamorous, but it represented order, consistency, and the absence of change. Life was chaos and change, loss and agony were bound to be the result, especially for restless souls. They would be anxious like they always were but could handle it if they'd just wait. They wouldn't. They didn't have the patience. He knew that because He knew all about them. He knew what they would do and what they would become. Everything He knew told Him that it was wrong, but He wanted to create them anyway. With chaos came calamity, but also exhilaration. The tragedy was the price to pay for life. There was no other way.

"Are you sure about this?" The Son asked him.

"Are we ever unsure of anything?" the Father asked, smirking.

"Of course not, I like how it's turning out so far..." he said, grinning as he watched the stars form along with planets and the moons that surrounded some of their orbits. Comets shot across the sky along with blazing stars who had seen their final days. Many of them expanded the endless abyss that man would call "black hole," but for now, their creation would be blissfully unaware of these pits of vast destruction.

"We can already witness their faces when they see one for the first time."

"It's a sight to see, for sure," Jesus laughed.

"Their faces, or the black holes."

"Both." they chuckled together.

The heavens formed over time and then the planets, and of course, the Earth in all its glory. Together the father and the son called life from water, land, and sea and watched with joy as each one came forth just as they envisioned before they spoke it into existence. Frequently, they glanced at one another, smirking as they the anticipation on the other's face. They couldn't wait until the last creation, the greatest of them all.

"What should we make them look like?" the Creator asked His son.

"Let's make them in our image, inside and out. They'll love, feel, create, and everything else we do. It'll be just like having another son." Jesus laughed.

"They will accomplish amazing things," God said, trailing off as he considered the wonder of what even His smallest creations would someday become, and what they could have become if only they had remained under His guidance from the beginning until the end when at last they could join Him in eternity.

God stood over the shining city, bathing in the light that draped down from His majestic throne where presided over Heaven with His Son. Jesus looked sadly into the distance, feeling the heaviness His father felt. They could hardly keep secrets from each other, let alone hide heavy burdens.

"Remember, when I formed Adam with my hands?" He asked. "When I took Eve from by removing His rib and forming him a companion?"

"Remember when Eve bore children for the first time?"

God smiled, but it was hard to keep it from turning to a grimace. "Poor woman. It wasn't easy watching her experience that pain for the first time..." he trailed off for a moment. "It won't be any easier watching you." He said. "I want you to know that, even after I forsake you. It brings me no pleasure."

"We are holy. We cannot be around sin. I knew what had to be done when opened Adam's eyes for the first time, and even before that, when we made the first star."

"And what of our star?" God asked, referring to a different star they were to meet along with the angels.

"She is ready to play her role just as I am ready to play mine," Jesus answered.

"Then, we should gather our circle one last time," God said. "Heaven must prepare itself for a war that will last for thousands of years. This plan is the only hope to save humanity."

"I love them as much as you do."

"Sometimes, I think you love them more."

"Some of them will think that," Jesus laughed, grinning even after he came to silence for a peaceful moment. "I am inclined to disagree. We are holy and cannot tolerate sin. What is love without righteousness but abuse and injustice, and what is righteousness without love but oppression and punishment? But even more, what is the Son without His Father, and what is the creation without their Creator? I am in you, and you are in me. Grace and truth, humanity needs the fullness of God.

A small group of God's most trusted angels and heavenly servants gathered as God called them from their places in Heaven and their stations on earth. This gathering appeared much smaller, as God let only a few of His most trusted in Heaven in on the details of His plan for humanity. God and His Son were at war with the devil, a cunning adversary, and a relentless one at that. He'd be making plans to counter their every move, and in many ways, their plan counted on him doing just that. Yet every detail, every word, every prophecy, every step on Jesus's path and every moment of His life would have to be just right. God knew, of course, it would be, but that was because He also knew who He could and couldn't trust.

The small cohort of loyal angels included Michael, Gabriel, and Raphael, to name just a few of God's closest angels. Gabriel would be God's highest messenger, bestowed with the honor of visiting the soul who would serve as the holiest vessel for humanity's Messiah. The angels were not the only ones who would play a role, however.

"Do you really think we can trust them to save themselves?" one of the angels scoffed at the idea, still unsure even after they came this far.

"They follow one another. They need teachers they can see and touch, teachers like them." Jesus explained.

"Just as they'll need a Messiah like them, but not like them..." God explained. "Sanctified vessels of the truth to carry my light into the world that Lucifer has darkened."

"And the girl..." one of the angels asked. "Is she ready?"

"She's here now," Raphael informed them, cracking a soft smile as he gently coaxed her forth. A soft hand reached to grab the little girl's, though she shied away at first. "Come now, little one, your role is a crucial one. You will carry God's light in the world, and you will show them their Messiah. How will you show humanity your light in their darkness, if you cannot even reveal yourself in

Heaven's day to the Creator and His angels? Your calling is the divine little one, and so you are. Step forward into the divine company."

Her light certainly seemed dim in comparison to bright and shining stood that sat on the glorious throne before her. His light all but blinded her in its pure, undying radiance, how could she even hope to compare to His glory? She found some relief in the gentle smile and loving eyes she saw there on His face. The eyes met hers. His eyes swirled like endless worlds before her. She lost herself in them when His gaze met her own. His smile brightened her day even more than the light itself. He seemed so happy just to see her, so proud of who and what she was. She was a shining star, a candle to illuminate a dark universe, or so she was told. Yet, her world was lifeless, a void and empty rock.

"Your light is so beautiful." the Creator gasped, His smile growing. "I can't wait to see you let it shine for my children on Earth."

"Is that my mission?" the girl asked. "To send your light to Earth?"

"To show them the way to my Son," He said, presenting the Messiah. His face was gentle too, and His presence reassuring. A soothing aura exuded from him, bringing peace and reassurance. More calming even than the presence of the Creator, He set her at entirely at ease. She smiled wide, but her hands of feet were still as she stood silent, overcome by His peace.

"It will be my honor to present your people with their salvation."

"You're an important part of our plan." Jesus shot her another loving smile, catching her even further off guard as His eyes met hers. In a single blink, she felt her entire life borne before him without a moment's time to also try and conceal her thoughts and memories, her dreams, and deepest fears.

The angels gasped and murmured among themselves, impressed as they watched her light grow. A light hum rang in the air, its tune as beautiful as the songs of the seraphim. The star expanded in sparkling rays that joined in rivaling the light of Heaven as it prepared for its journey into the Creator's universe. Her heart fluttered at the thought of being assigned such a critical mission. She was bringing light into utter darkness, hope into hopelessness. Was she really worth it? Would she even be ready when it was time? Only the day would tell her for sure and only when it came in all its glory. She could hardly wait, especially to see the Messiah in His delicate state. Pure and perfect innocence in the most precious of earth's holy vessels. No one even see Him coming, even the one who planned His demise. It was undoubtedly a brilliant plan, she thought, and an inspired one. She didn't know whether to feel humbled or honored in being part of it.

She could see the love in His eyes when He talked about His creation. She could hear the tenderness in His voice every time he reminisced about Adam and Eve, and His precious billions of children, each of whom he could list by face and treasured name. To know that she would play such a significant role in saving something He so loved was the ultimate honor, the highest service to her Creator. She only hoped she could live up to the esteem He placed in her.

"And what of the prophets?" Michael asked. "Are they ready?"

"I have seen each one from the day they are born to the day they die to the day they enter our kingdom to ascend to my throne and receive their just reward for service to the kingdom. The prophets are ready." God answered firmly. "I have chosen them myself, and I know they will prepare the way for my son to bring our light into my lost world. The prophets will teach, and my faithful will listen, and they will prepare the souls of Earth for the day of the Lord."

"Their path will not be easy." Gabriel pointed out."

"My messengers will sometimes need to be sent to set them on the right path, and I will appear to them when I need to. But we will be watching over them every moment, and setting everything into place." God answered. "I cannot take them from the trials they endure, but I will watch over them. My word will guide them, my hand will protect them, and my heart will receive them when their last days on Earth have arrived. The prophets are ready!" he said again, more firmly.

"And what of my angels, my warriors, and messengers?" he asked each of them.

Michael nodded first, a solemn gaze but one with a definite hint of loyalty in the eyes.

"Ready, willing, and able!" Raphael answered with a hearty nod.

"Ready!" Gabriel nodded, pounding a nearby table with His fists for emphasis.

"And you, my light?" he asked the little girl. "Are you ready to shine, my precious light?" he offered a reassuring smile.

She returned it with a smirk of her own. "I'm ready," she said, her brightening.

"Then let us prepare," Jesus said, breaking His long silence

"I will send out the souls of the prophets," Michael said with a bow. "We'll make sure they make it Earth safely, and everything goes according to plan. Lucifer's sure to throw us some surprises along the way."

"No surprises for us," Jesus smirked. "Venus," he startled the girl, calling her by name. She wasn't sure why it frightened her. She knew that he knew all things, but maybe it wasn't that he knew the name that caught her off guard. Perhaps that it was that He bothered to use it at all. He was a king and a prince, but he called her by name. Who was she to deserve such an honor, but that's how

Jesus was, and the Father wasn't so different. Up close, it was often hard to tell who was really who.

"Yes, master?" she asked.

"Please," He said. "Just call me Yeshua."

"Yes..." the girl stuttered, uncertain of herself, but slowly coming closer to a state of peace as he seemed to draw her into a sense of calm with His soothing tone and gentle eyes. "Yeshua?"

You should go with Michael." He told her. "He'll be sending the most important souls of my creation into the world, the prophets to mankind. They are my messengers in human flesh, my voice in a world that refuses to hear my name."

"It'll be a sight to see." Michael chuckled, turning His head to motion her His way.

The girl hesitated, completely silent. After a moment to consider, she affirmed her agreement with a subtle nod and followed Michael. Jesus and the Father followed closely behind as they drove off of the platform that held the heavenly throne. A blue sky dotted with fluffy clouds carried them safely off of its edge. They floated safely on its face, walking on air as they flew down to the cities of Heaven. They passed through golden streets and crystal palaces along with villas of granite and mansions of shining marble. Bathed in the white and golden rays of God's glorious light, the kingdom of Heaven was a sight to see. Everywhere they turned, harmonious music rose to greet their ears with pleasant tunes. Laughter joined with chatter, and sometimes shouted of joy. The scent of sweet treats and fragrant perfumes permeated in the brisk and soothing air that carried the very essence of peace. Everywhere they looked, contentment and joy dominated the streets and faces of those who ran through them, except for one.

The girl clasped father's hand, looking up at Him with a compassionate smile and pity in her eyes. He forced a grim smile of His own nodding as He took the small and tender hand in His hand. The hand was massive by comparison, and tough like leather but not less gentle, no less healing in its touch because of it. It was the hand that forged the face of the universe, and that gave her the precious gift of life. She wanted to ask what was wrong, but she knew. Looking at His face, she could see the pain and feel it too. She had never seen a more profound sadness, and she never would again, except once. She saw it once on one of His prophets' faces. It was the face of a father about to lose His son.

"Is there no other way?" the words just slipped from her mouth. She wasn't sure why she asked. Who was she to question the plan of the Creator, the King of Kings? Who was she to ask such a question when He was in such pain. She half-expected an angry scolding, at least a harsh look, even a deep sigh as he'd brush her question away. Instead, He showed her a loving smile and gave her hand a reassuring squeeze.

"If there were, I would do it. I am holy God and cannot be around sin, but only a perfect and untainted sacrifice can remove my wrath from them."

"You love them that much?"

"We both do?" Jesus answered for Him, a gentle smile of His own. "Come, we're almost here."

They came to a celestial island tucked away in hovering clouds, also floating high above the city. On its heart lay pools of steaming water, sparkling as they bubbled before them. On the other hand of the stirring spring, she saw a small structure of ancient stone adorned with stained glass windows. It resembled a mausoleum. Wildflowers sprang up in the fields of grass the surrounded the spring and building. The wings of butterflies fluttered along with those of gentle songbirds gliding overhead. Reeds sprouted up, gently tossing in the peaceful breeze that followed them as they approached.

"What is this place?" the girl gasped, looking up at the Creator with wide and inquiring eyes.

"The souls of humanity are here, in particular, my most important souls."

"Why are they so important?"

"These are the souls of my most faithful and trusted servants. The people I have chosen to spread my truth and carry my name into my creation. They will share the truth of their God and Creator with their brothers and sisters in humanity."

"So these people already exist?" the girl asked. "Even though you have sent them to be born yet?"

"Their souls are in the palm my hand," he said, raising His right hand in the air. The doors of the ancient building swung open with a loud creak and a hard crash. A blinding light lashed out from the doorway, with what appeared to be hundreds, thousands, maybe millions of smaller lights that went worth. "Even before I send them into the world, I know them by name. Their stories are already written by hand. I know their hearts, their fears, and their dreams. I even know how many hairs are on each of their heads, their exact genetic code."

"There's so many of them!" the girl exclaimed.

"And I made each one different and special." he gasped with a proud smile. Michael nodded from nearby as he approached to interrupt their conversation.

"Are we ready to send out the prophets?" he asked.

"Bring them to us first," Jesus told him.

"Of course," Michael said with a bow.

"The prophets..." the girl repeated what the angel said.

"Yes..." the Creator answered. "They will bring my Word into the world, and they will prepare the people to receive my Son."

"And I will show them the way back to the father," Jesus spoke with joyful anticipation, almost like He couldn't wait to go. God didn't seem so sure, the girl noticed. Best not bring it up, she thought as the angel returned. He carried with him an extensive collection of white orbs, glimmering before them as they hummed with life. "We know each of them by name." He said glee in His voice as He took each orb into His hand and called it by name.

"Abraham," He said. "He will leave behind His life of wealth and luxury in the Godless lands of Ur to create a new nation. He will be the father of many, not just nations, but people of differing faiths will call themselves children of Abraham. His nation will give Birth to the Messiah..." he grinned in spite of himself. "Me!" he added with glee.

"And Isaiah," the Creator chimed in, taking one of the orbs into His own hands, looking down at the soul with wonder and love in His eyes. "His prophecies will predict the coming of my Son. He will rebuke kings, and His prophecies will bring great men and great nations to their knees. His prophecies and His warning will be vast, but widely ignored just like my Son." he turned sadly to Jesus. He nodded firmly with a solemn frown. "Isaiah's a vital role. He is ready to be a great prophet."

"Don't forget my favorite," Jesus said, chuckling.

"Of course," the Creator joined him in a laugh. "Good old stubborn John the Baptist. I can't wait for us to see the look on His face when he lies eyes on you for the first time."

"When the bold and boisterous locust eater falls to His knees." Jesus laughed. "I look forward to my first meeting with him."

"I'm sure His mother will appreciate the rise you get out of him in the womb." the Father laughed. "Are you sure you want to do this?" He asked one more time, though. He already knew the answer.

"You know I am," Jesus answered.

"We will be sending them out like lambs among wolves," God said. "The same will be true of the apostles you send after you, and the same will be true for you when you are on Earth. You know that I will be with you, and I will perform miracles through you. I will watch over you every moment, but it won't be the same as it is here. I won't be next to you at all times I cannot walk among them, you know that their sin is too great."

"I will be fine."

"And when the time comes, and you separate from me

completely..."

"I'll be ready..." Jesus answered. "And when I've conquered death, I will be ready to rise again to your side until it's time to return for our lost creation."

"You will be at my right hand, and your name will be above all others. Call forth the prophets. Send them into the fallen world to live and to teach among the lost. Send them out to call the sinners to repentance and to bring our lost lambs home. "

The orbs of light floated into the air, growing brighter and humming louder in their ascent. Together they formed a growing light that must have resembled the burning sun from far enough away. The light reflected from the waters of the spring as they stirred before. A misty dew rose up, and the water began to sparkle, then to glow. The lights grew brighter against its surface until they appeared as fluid light itself.

Michael watched, sword raised, and ever vigilant as they prepared to send them out. A small cohort of his most reliable angels joined him, ready for the unexpected in their flight. Each of them stood up straight, still as statues except to gaze back and forth, always on the lookout. Splashes rose from the spring as the stirring waters crashed now, and a heavy wind picked up. Jesus called the first name forth.

"Abraham." A roaring thunder carried in the air to accompany His voice, and the winds picked up again. The light grew, its luminescence expanding as its ring increased in volume. Jesus pointed, and the orb flew forth down into the heavens, plummeting to the earth. Michael nodded solemnly to His angels and leaped from His position to follow the spheres. The other angels glided into place and dived to join him in planned formations. The girl tried to hear over all the chaos of the storm, but couldn't make out certain names here and there.

"Elijah!" Jesus cried, and another orb flew forth, thunder picking up with this one. "Moses!" he cried again, and another sphere shot out at His command. "Daniel!" he called, louder this time and another orb went out. On and on it went for what felt like hours as the girl got lost in the spectacle. Each ball rang with eerie tunes, leaving trails of sparks and linger streams of light as they went forth. It was a beautiful sight to see, God's prophets going in to rescue His world from darkness. Still, she wondered what might wait for them below.

"And what of you, my child? The father asked, startling her from the side. "Are you also ready to shine for your Creator?"

"What must I do?" the girl asked.

"You must find Earth and show her the light. She is lost. Can you do that for me?" God asked her gently. She nodded, eyes and mouth open, unsure of what He was really asking her to do. "You will show my lost creation the way to their Messiah when He goes into the world. I think He's almost ready."

A moment of silence followed as Jesus watched the last orb hovering before them. The light fizzled a few times, but a stubborn light, it remained. It edged slowly towards its destination to join the others, eager. Still, it patiently awaited its master's command, always faithful and obedient until the end. Jesus nodded with a smile, just as he expected. He couldn't help but laugh as he watched it restless flutter back and forth, waiting with anticipation for His command.

"John the Baptist!" he spoke the name plainly and watched the orb fly forth. Quicker than all the rest, it raced to catch up with the other hands in their migration to Earth. Jesus turned with a smile, but also sad eyes to His father, who waited for Him a short distance away. The father stood with a straight posture and clenched fists. His stiff form could hardly move, but he found the strength to edge a few steps forward, and then ram front-first into His son. His son moved first, but two joined in a tight and warm embrace, one that could have lasted all eternity. The little girl could almost feel the lump in the Creator's throat as their hug ended, and they backed away. The savior nodded firmly to Michael. The two exchanged a solemn gaze, and Michael returned to the nod.

"Into the water, my Lord," Michael said, frowning.

Jesus bowed and nodded firmly one last time to His father. The father took Him by the hand, silently insisting He guides Him to the waters. Their hands remained entangled, even as Jesus waded into the waters. Deeper he went and they covered His ankles, and then His knees. The Father watched with His sad eyes as His son's hand slowly slipped away. His heart skipped a beat. Only their fingers were touching now and began to move away. His heart sank when the last finger slid from reach, and He could feel His son's touch no more. Even more, it dropped when He watched Jesus sink beneath the waters, His head emerged at last. He arose, transformed into a ball of light, not so different than the others except pure and free from blemish. Unlike the other spheres, His light neither flickered, dimmed, nor fizzled. It was a perfect light and brighter than all the rest.

"Yeshua," God spoke His holy name, with welling tears watched His soul fly forth to join the others. Silence fell and lingered for a time between them, except for sobbing and sniffling as God stood otherwise still as stone. The little girl stood silent, staring, watching the Creator cry. After some time of tears and sobbing, then utter silence, He turned to greet her.

"Now, it is your time to shine. Are you ready to show the way?" He asked.

The girl nodded, though she wasn't sure. It didn't seem so hard, what He was asking, yet she was sure she'd mess it up.

"You're going to perform beautifully. You're going to light up heaven's skies, and people are going to be talking about you for thousands of years," he said, reassuring her. A certain eerie calm overtook her as she hears the gentleness in His voice, saw the love in His eyes. Even His mere presence, the feeling of His touch as he gently held her shoulder seemed to carry with it a heavenly reassurance.

"All that I'll have to do is just...shine."

"Just shine the light that I have given you." the Creator smiled. "That is all you have to do."

"Will it hurt?" she asked. "When I'm sent into the world."

"All things hurt that are worth the effort and the time. It might hurt a little, but I will be with you in all the pain, and what follows will be everlasting joy."

"I'll do it," the girl said. "If you really want me to, but I'm sure you could use someone else. They'll do so much better than I ever could."

"I want you to do." He answered love and laughter in His voice. "And I chose you for this extraordinary task, but it requires you an exceptional soul. Are you ready?" He asked, extending His hand.

The girl cracked a smile, for the first time, a very real one. Anticipation overtook her. The fear that she once felt seemed to pale in comparison to the excitement. She couldn't wait to allow her light to shine, to show people the way to the love that she had found. She couldn't wait for them to see it too. She reached out her tiny hand, and He took it into His own. He gently guided her into the steaming waters. Her feet touched the surface, sending ripples throughout the spring. She flinched. She didn't think it'd be so cold. The pool had looked so inviting before, so warm.

"It's ok" He reassured her. "You'll get used to it. Just take it nice and easy."

She carefully waded deeper, weighing, and measuring her every step. The water touched her knees and rose to meet her thighs as she waded ever deeper. She felt her hand slip from the Creators as she began to drift gently out of reach. She gasped at first, struggling to still her pounding heart and heavy breathing.

"I'm still here." He reassured her, His voice setting her at ease. The waters stirred and flowed around her, humming, ringing. They seemed warmer now. The steam was also calming, purifying. She basked in its soothing essence for just a moment before she waded deeper. The waters splashed, tossing to and fro around her. Up to her neck now, she waded deeper, taking one last breath. Her chest felt tight, her frightened heart pounding with anticipation. She breathed deep and swallowed her fear. Silence fell and joined with darkness to overtake her. Closing her eyes, she held her nose in preparation. One last splash and she dove below the swirling waters. Their peaceful, soothing essence overtook her.

The Creator watched with a somber smile as an orb light rose from below the spring's misty surface. He watched the rise and over above the fog and listened to it hum. It seemed to sing the sweetest tune of all the other souls, and except for Jesus's, its light was brighter too. The Creator cracked a smile as he prepared to send her forth. He knew she'd make Him proud, despite her doubts and fears.

"Venus," he called out and gracefully extended His hand to point and send her into the universe. The orb hovered away from the spring and sprang out to join the other souls, but this one didn't make it quite to Earth. God watched with a loving twinkle in His eye to see it stop somewhere in its course. There it spun around the Earth, hovering in the endless void. Yet its light shined, brighter and brighter to overtake the Earth at night. Only the moon could match its luminescence, and only the sun could outshine its beauty.

It was the brightest of the lights that could be seen from Earth, especially on that one holy night. Only one light shined brighter than hers that night, and it was a light that could not be seen with the eye. It was the light of the hope and salvation that came with the promise of new life in Him. It was the light of a Messiah born in a humble manger to be forsaken by the people He came to save. How could should ever to hope to match that light? Yet it was her light He chose to show them the way to His.

The light flickered but only grew in the endless night of the void. The field of infinite space and planets along with stars and the countless heavenly bodies faded away. She watched as the scenes before her faded to white and then to nothing. The humming screen before them flickered and fizzled out to match the endless void that threatened to engulf. The woman flinched as darkness fell, and they found themselves once more in the unending void after the destruction of a universe that was no more. The little girl felt her fear and squeezed her hand tightly, looking up with a reassuring smile.

"The light will return soon enough." the girl said.

"You were the light," the woman said. "The light of the world, the star that showed them the way. The light that guided the other lights."

The girl nodded.

The woman could barely see her in the dark, but she could feel the affirmation somehow. "But why are you here now?" she asked. "Earth is gone."

"I was sent to find my lost sister."

Silence fell for a moment as the woman pondered her words for a moment. What did she mean? Somehow she could already feel the answer. There had been something about the little girl from the moment they met that seemed different. Her voice, her presence, they seemed so reassuring. Even though they'd only met, she felt like they had known each other for than a few millennia. "Are you..." she started to ask her lips were quivering. Why did she fear the answer? The woman's eyes welled up with tears. Her hands trembled, and her breathing turned to rapid shudders. The girl nodded, her eyes wide.   Without a moment more of stillness, they squeezed each other in a hug that could have lasted a thousand years, but would still be over all too soon. They released each other from their arm and, with some pause, returned to their places at each other's sides. The girl looked up her, eyes still watering.

"When I heard that you were left behind, my heart broke. I begged Him to send me, but that was already His intention. He knew the Earth needed her Morning Star one last time to show her the way home."

"Is that why you're here, to bring me home?"

"The home you knew is no more." the girl said sadly. "But I'm here to show you our new home, but first you have to understand..."

"Understand what..."

"What He did to save us. How it all happened."

"Then tell me. Show me." the woman said. Everything seemed to unravel now as if the scales were falling from her eyes. Things seemed clearer, and yet so many things remained so unclear like a long-forgotten dream. Why did so many questions remain unanswered?

"Before my light could show them the way the other lights had to go ahead of me."

"The prophets." the woman said.

"One of the prophets would foretell the coming of Messiah, Jesus. No one would even know the truth of His prophecies until thousands of years after he died. Then when everything fell into place, I was ready to shine my light. I revealed the path of the magi, spread the truth to all the nations of the world."

"The magi?" the woman asked.

"Watch." said the girl as she grabbed the woman's hand and pointed to the screen. The screen crackled and flickered before it came once more to life, first with scenes of blinding white. Then they shifted into blue skies and desert hills. The lands were dry and barren, sand as far as the eye could see. The sun bore down on them, but the Wise men did not relent. They would find the Child of Promise. They would find Him if they had to search the four corners of the world.

The campfire burned and flickered, crackling as it gave warmth and light to the weary travelers who found themselves in the desert late at night. Nothing but sand lay before them as far as the eye could see, but it wasn't ground or the terrain that lay before them that concerned the three companions.

"You truly believe he is here, someone in these lands." the first man asked, the fairest of three with eyes the sea at midday and hair like fire in the night.

"I am sure of it." said the second man. The darkest among them, skin resembled more ebony, and His eyes were more like night. "This is where it has led us. These texts are not wrong, my friend, I assure you. We are talking about thousands of years of writing, research, and observations of the heavens by men who would make our wisest scholars today look like fools."

"I just hope your right." said the third man, breaking His silence as he sat by the fire, staring at the sky. "I hope *it's* right. We've come all this way."

Silence returned the company of the three robed men who sat by their campfire in silence as they soon prepare to retire to their tents for the night. They had come far, but what they saw was correct. It would be well worth the journey. History would remember this trip. They were sure of that.

"It is beautiful." said the third man, breaking the silence one last time before they retired. The other two agreed in silence, looking up the star that loomed above. Its light dominated the night's skies, from which the moon seemed absent tonight. Yet Star of Bethlehem shined brighter than all the other lights compensate tonight. It had been for many nights now, and the three robed scholars were sure that they knew why. They just had to see Him for themselves.

"The Child of Promise." the second man remarked as he doused the fire. It hardly made a difference with the light of Venus bearing down on them. "Won't that be a sight to see?"

"That it will," said the first. "You have your gifts ready?"

"Of course."

"Guard them with your lives. All kind of bandits, criminals, and the like roam these lands."

"They wouldn't dare steal from the King of Kings." said the wise man. "Good night, my brothers."

"Good night." said the third man, happy to at last yield to the silence that fell between them in the night. He was the last to enter His tent, giving him another chance to steal a peek. He looked up at the star in wonder. A deep sigh, and he went to retire for the night. He hoped they would find the child, and soon, lest their efforts were all for naught.

A cold wind picked up. It whistled in the desert to sing an eerie tune that would nonetheless fail to disturb their slumber. Their journey had been long, and it would be longer still. The sands shifted with the wind, tossing against their tents and setting their animals ill at ease. They made it safely through, however, as night yielded to day. The stars faded, and the sun began to rise over the distant hills to conquer the night. Even with it gone from sight, however, the star was still there in the heaven's ready to show them the way when darkness fell again. The scenes faded to a blur, then to white. The woman and the little girl returned to their former place, the screen flashing and flickering before them as they returned to present-day.

"You were the star," the woman said. "The one that announced the coming of Jesus the Messiah?"

"I was a light that was sent to provide a guiding light to Earth when she was lost." the girl answered. "That was more than once, but back then, it was to announce the coming of a great Messiah. Ultimately, I was sent to find my lost sister."

"Me?" the woman asked her. "Were you sent to find me?" she asked.

"Before God could send His son to save us. He sent His prophets to prepare the way. One of the greatest among went by the name of Isaiah." she explained. "He would prophecy the coming of the Messiah, Jesus of Nazareth."

The woman took her hand, her eyes fixed back on the screen. "Is that him?" she asked, as the image on the screen focused in on His face. The girl nodded.

"I expected a handsome man, or someone better groomed. Wasn't He to be a king?"

The little girl giggled in spite of herself, it was true He wasn't a handsome man, as the word had said He wouldn't be. He was so much more though than what He had appeared. "He was, and He was the greatest king there ever was." the girl answered. "But He was also to be forsaken, just as the prophet had foretold."

"The prophet Isaiah..." the woman said. "Who was this man?"

"He was a prophet from a line of prophets, but he was more. He was God's anointed, His instrument and lips into the world to prophecy of one greater than himself. He was one of the greatest prophets Israel ever had, but they forsook him too. If only they knew the truth of the prophecies. If only they knew how right he was."

"What else did he say?"

"Many things." the girl answered. "And many things were said by him." the girl continued to her story as the screen flashed and flickered before them. The screen seems to grow now humming lightly as if to draw them in. The woman's head rang along with the little girl's as the humming seemed to work. The story was all around them now. I almost felt as if they stood among the servants. From there, they watched their nearby king. The proud king nodded firmly as he inspected the impressive structure. He almost cracked a smile, though he dare not let it show.

"An impressive wall to say the least." he kicked the stone and nodded one last time, His affirmation and the sign of His approval. "Well done," he said to the nearby masons.

Chapter 9-The Prophet

Isaiah

Who has believed our message and to whom has the arm of the Lord been revealed?

He grew up before him like a tender shoot, and like a root out of the dry ground.

He had no beauty or majesty to attract us to him, nothing in His appearance that we should desire him.

He was despised and rejected by mankind, a man of suffering, and familiar with pain.

Like one from whom people hide their faces, he was despised, and we held him in low esteem.

Surely he took up our pain and bore our suffering, yet we considered him punished by God, stricken by him, and afflicted.

But he was pierced for our transgressions, and he was crushed for our iniquities;

The punishment that brought us peace was on him, and by His wounds, we are healed.

We all, like sheep, have gone astray. Each of us has turned to our own way, and the Lord has laid on him the iniquity of us all.

He was oppressed and afflicted, yet he did not open His mouth; he was led like a lamb to the slaughter and as a sheep, before its shearers are silent, so he did not open His mouth. By oppression and judgment, he was taken away. Yet who of His generation protested?
For he was cut off from the land of the living, or the transgression of my people, he was punished.

He was assigned a grave with the wicked and with the rich in His death, though he had done no violence, nor was any deceit in His mouth.

Yet it was the Lord's will to crush him and cause him to suffer, and though the Lord makes His life an offering for sin, he will see His offspring and prolong His days, and the will of the Lord will prosper in His hand.

After he has suffered, he will see the light of life and be satisfied; by His knowledge, my righteous servant will justify many, and he will bear their iniquities.

Therefore I will give him a portion among the great, and he will divide the spoils with the strong, because he poured out His life unto death, and was numbered with the transgressors.

For he bore the sin of many and made intercession for the transgressors.

-Isaiah 53

King Uzziah found it more difficult to conceal His pleasure with every stone he inspected and even more so as he stared into the abyss to the bottom the wall where he stood on top. He tossed a small rock down, chuckling as he watched it descend into the abyss below them. The walls were impressive, to say the least, but not nearly as impressive as the towers. From their peaks, His men would see threats for miles, and when they arrived, they'd never stand a chance.

From the top of the tower, he could also see the beauty of His kingdom, and the landed that God had blessed His people with. In a land of desert and desolation, they found fertile plains and valleys. From so high up, he could even see the swarms of livestock that grazed in lush and fertile grasslands. He could almost make out distant cities, bastions of Israel's might and wealth. They'd come so far since; first, he claimed the throne. He was young back then, so naive. It seemed insane that all of this could have been built by a 16-year-old king. Yet even in all its glory, it paled in comparison to God's blessings and His creation. Even in all of His accomplishments, the king did not forget the one he served.

"Long way down," he said to His servant nearby.

"It is," the servant agreed. "And it is an impressive wall, but wait until you see what else your men have come up with."

"Is this the special project we've been working on?" The king asked, trying to somber His tone and hide the anticipation from His voice.

"It is, my king." a soldier said nearby. "Our engineers are quite proud of it, and so am I if I may so. But please. Let me demonstrate and let the device speak for itself."

"It is a mighty weapon, my king!" the servant giggled, rubbing His hands together with glee.

"I can't wait to see it." The king said, following the soldier to where the heavy blank concealed their proud achievement. The soldier motioned to a few of His cohorts nearby, and they rushed to join His side. He directed them each to their post, and they removed the blanket together. It required some effort, but the blanket came untangled and freed itself from the siege machine they mounted in its place on the wall. The king grinned, unable to contain himself now. He clapped His hands together, laughing aloud as he watched them load an over-sized spear on what appeared to be an oversized bow.

A few men struggled to hold the heavy ammunition in place and pull back the massive string. New recruits, no doubt, the king thought as he watched them with a smirk. Another man joined to help and cranked the machine as the spear fell in place. The gadget creaked rocked around but held itself in place the same. A loud whip and the string snapped from its place and the arrow as far as the eye could. The long and heavy spear flew straight and true, crashing into a distance tree. The spear shot straight through the bark and brought down its mighty limbs and branches. The king laughed aloud and clapped His hands in His exhilaration, watching as it tumbled from its place once rooted in the earth.

"Most impressive!" he exclaimed. "Let's see the enemies of God's people approach our walls now!" he dared them.

"As if they could even scale them now." one of the nearby soldiers chimed in.

"They won't get close enough now," said Uzziah with a sly smile.

"I don't think Israel's been safer under any king." said the servant.

"Come," the king commanded the gathered men. "Let us give thanks to almighty God for good fortune and victory over our enemies."

"To the temple?" asked the servant asked.

"To the temple," the king agreed. "Whatever I accomplish asking, we must never forget the goodness of God who watches over our nation in a land of wolves."

"Couldn't agree more." said the soldier as they departed.

The safety of the wall continued to reassure them for sometimes as they ventured through the streets of one of many of the country's prospering communities. King Uzziah had proven himself to be a fine king of Israel, having fortified many of the nation's cities and providing for the protection and security of God's people. More than that, the kingdom prospered under His reign and wise counsel. There had hardly been a king since Solomon so great, but what made Uzziah great was more than that he made a fine king and skilled administrator. Even as a mighty and respected king, Uzziah never forgot who the real king was. A spiritual revival had taken place during the time of His righteous and holy reign. Uzziah would be forever remembered as one of the righteous and holy kings of Israel. His dedication to God and His reverence for the Lord of Lords was all but unmatched among the nation's rulers, and indeed the many rulers of the earth. How could such a king ever fail the people of Israel? How could such a king ever fall from the favor of the Lord of Hosts?

The temple loomed before them in all its glory, God's holy tabernacle on Earth, where the men and women of Israel came to pay homage to the God that made them great. The king bowed His head in holy reverence, His servants and soldiers following His lead.

"It's not much further now," he told them. "Prepare your hearts to pray and to enter the presence of Jehovah, Israel true and mighty king."

The entryway of God's holy place came to the king and His small and trusted circle, who followed close behind. Some flames flickered around the holy place, but it seemed a little darker than usual. Their footsteps could be heard but little else. It seemed quieter than usual too.

"Where are the prophets? Where are God's holy priests?" the king asked allowed.

"It seems they're away. I'm sure whatever they're doing is more important. We can wait." said the servants. "Perhaps we should stay outside until the men of God return."

The king looked around for a moment. His eyes darted back and forth, admiring the impressive structure of the sacred temple. A soft breeze picked up, startling the small group, but little other sounds would echo through the temple. The pattering of steps would prove a sole exception with every step they took.

"Is anyone here?" Uzziah called out the temples halls and empty chambers. No one answered except for echoes of the king's voice.

"Ah!" he exclaimed, pointing to the crudely carved altar that stood before them. Candles surrounded the small but holy structure, and incense of precious fragrances rested on its face. The king pointed up, nodding as he took the censer in hand. He stopped to admire the simple but elegant design for a few moments. It was a said relic, he thought, His knees shook at the very thought of holding it, an instrument usually handled only by the priests. "The altar of incense. Here we may offer our prayers to God."

"We should wait for Azariah and the other priests should we not?" the servant asked. "For the priests must light the incense and usher in God's holy presence."

"I am the king," Uzziah said casually, as there could hardly be a difference. "Am I not God's anointed, Israel's holy and righteous leader? Was I not blessed and christened by the prophet? Did our God not choose me to be His representative, His righteous administrator, and judge, here on Earth and in God's holy kingdom?" the king asked, smirking, raising His eyebrows. "I'm sure the priests have more important affairs to attend to, so where a priest cannot be, perhaps a king may serve," he said, retrieving the incense.

The soldiers and the servants gasped as they watched him grab the incense without a moment's hesitation. How could be so sure of himself? Their hearts raced, but they dare not call their king into account. Who were they to question the ruler of God's chosen? Even if it were their place, they preferred to keep their heads attached. They swallowed hard against the thought of being the first to speak, and the first to see the sword as punishment for insolence.

"Let us give thanks to our Lord." said the king. His hand moved slowly, still shaking, and he dipped the incense in the flickering flame. A cold breeze picked up, this one whistling eerily as it passed. It sent a cold chill down every spine, drawing gasps as they watched the flickering flames fizzle. The incense smoked a lot, but the spark soon died, and the incense failed to light.

Azariah stood stunned, His beard hanging down along with His extended jaw. His eyes went wide with shock, and His hands were set to trembling with rage. Who was this king to assume the place of God's anointed? He motioned to the men behind him, and the crowd of priests poured into the temple. The servants and soldiers gathered with the king stepped aside and bowed their heads, dare not looking them in the eyes. The men stood as still and silent as the mountains as they watched Azariah approach the king.

"What is the meaning of this?" he asked. "Do you assume the authority that God has granted to His holy priests? Do you believe yourself both king and prophet of Israel that you assume the place of God's sacred and anointed?" he demanded.

"I am God's anointed, am I not? Did the prophet not christen me with oil, was I not anointed as ruler of God's people on Earth?" he asked, speaking softly at first.

"You are a ruler and administrator and defender of God's people. You are not His priest, and you are not His voice to the people of Israel. You are dishonoring God by even being here right now. Leave now before you provoke His wrath!"

"Don't presume that you can give me orders, priest!" Uzziah cried to echoes across the temple. He threw censer to the floor in a rage, and its bronze clattered and joined the echoes in the tune of rage they sang. "I am your king, and you obey me, not the other way around! Do you understand me?"

"Be careful, King Uzziah, God, will not be mocked!" Azariah warned him. "Leave now!"

Uzziah kicked the altar, crying out in rage. "I will not leave the temple! I will not be ordered around by..." he trailed off as gasps of horror and shock called him to silence. The priests and the servants

290

and soldiers joined in utter silence, their mouths gaping, and their eyes widened as they watched. Whispers broke the silence as they murmured among themselves, looking back and forth between Uzziah and their peers.

"What?" the king demanded. "What's wrong with all of you is there something on my..." His arm went stiff, His fingers curled, gently stroking the rotting flesh. He gasped and trembled, stammering as he struggled to speak. What was this? He looked down at His other hand in wide-eyed horror. He couldn't even bend His finger, and His arm went number and lifeless as the scarring overtook it.

"H-How?" He tried to speak, but could barely manage more than a word or two. His knees gave way at last, and he fell to kneel in tears. Utter silence fell, broken only by the weeping of a once-proud king. "Why?" he managed another word, the question that haunted him the most. Azariah stared in silence, scowling at the sight of the infected king. The high priest knew the answer, and Uzziah knew it too, he could see it in His eyes. Hours must have passed in silence as Uzziah knelt still and cold like stone, staring at the altar. He must have begged all day for God to change His mind and show him mercy. Just like all the rest, though, God watched on in silence.

One by one, the priests departed until the high priest stood alone, watching the once proud king as he begged in vain for mercy. An eerie breeze passed again, whistling the same familiar tune. One by one, the soldiers and the servants followed as the final priest departed, and only two remained.

"God has made His decision." the prophet told him. "You have disobeyed God's commandments, and you have shown arrogance before His rebuke. You will die, and you will be succeeded by your son Jotham," he explained. The priest frowned for another moment before he turned away to leave the king to come to terms with the fate the God decreed for Him. "It really is a shame," he turned His head and called once more before departing. "You were a good and righteous king, but God is a holy God who cannot allow sin to be free of consequence. Your pride cost Israel a good king today, Uzziah."

Over the next few months, the prophet's words would prove to be the truth. The king resigned himself to fate and watched His son succeed him before His final moments. The passing had not been an easy one, but peace had found him in the end. Jotham could see it in His eyes, just before he breathed His last. For months, or what felt like years they'd watched as the king grew worse. Leprosy had spread and claimed him limb by limb.

"Have we determined what is to be done with the body?" a servant asked the new king.

"He is to be buried with His ancestors to join them in holy rest. He'll be buried near the cemetery of a great king. An honorable burial for an honorable king." Jotham said, His tone somber as he stole one last glance at His father's lifeless body.

"A fitting tribute for sure. May he rest in paradise with the fathers of Israel and with God's righteous kings."

"May he indeed." Jotham nodded in agreement. He watched with sadness, but a certain sense of peace as they took His father's body. There was little time to mourn. He was the king of Judah now and had a job to do. The time had come to His father and His people proud."

The images before them faded once again and yielded to endless white horizons. The blinding had become familiar now, but no easier on the eyes as it overtook their vision. The little girl squeezed the woman's hand again. A whistle rang like that of swirling winds, and cool gusts of its force washed over them. The endless white began to vanish once again, and the world around them faded back into their line of sight. The darkness seemed to dominate, but flickering flames offered some illumination. A white beard dangled, tangled, and poorly groomed, as the prophet turned His head to the nearby ink well and dipped His pen.

He pressed the tip of the pen gently against the papyrus scroll and scribbled the ink on its crumpled surface. He spoke aloud as if there were someone there to hear His tale. Was he speaking to himself or someone else? Was he speaking to God perhaps, or one of His angels? Maybe, the girl and the woman reasoned within themselves, was he speaking to the children of Israel and all God's people who might someday read His prophecies. Maybe God was showing him something they couldn't see.

"It was that same year, the year of the death of King Uzziah that I saw it..." he paused for a moment and succumbed to heavy breathing, just recalling it. He tried still His racing heart and relax His trembling hands, but to no avail as he recalled the vision. "It was that year that I saw Him. No words in any human tongue could describe what I had seen. Who was I that I was to be shown the God of Israel, who was I that He chose me to be His prophet?" he asked aloud to no one in particular.

Something must have doused the flames of the candles nearby because a shadow fell over the room, rendered the girl and the woman blind. A stark silence fell, broken only, but what seemed a muffled, constant gust of wind. A dull gray came into view first, a heavy fog descending. The winds continued to whimper and roar, clearing a path in the imposing fog. A looming staircase stood before the gasping prophet. He cried out in fear, but only muffled groans came out. He edged forward, His footsteps silent, and with caution climbed the staircase. He looked first right then left, and back and forth with every step. Every scratch and every tap against the stone, every little breeze stopped His breathing and set His heart to pounding.

The steps seemed endless, but the light grew brighter to provide a glimmer of hope and soothing warmth along the way. The mist glowed as the light expanded in luminescence with every step that he climbed closer. His ears picked up a certain ringing that resembled angelic tunes and choirs. Harps and gentle flutes joined in to complement the ambiance. The patter of bells would also add to the heavenly orchestra as he drew closer to the height of the looming staircase. Beams of gold and white passed through the fog's translucence now as Isaiah nearly approached the top. A warm gust of wind picked up, and the dew evaporated while remained began to clear away like the parting of the scroll before it dissipated. The clearing of the fog revealed an impending platform that held a great white throne that glimmered in the light. It must have been carved from pearls in diamonds from its beauty and its glow, Isaiah reasoned. A mountain of a man sat upon it clothed in glorious robes of pure light. His glowing garments draped down over the throne and down the platform like waterfalls that formed a lake of light before him. Its glow oozed out, stopping only at the prophet's feet.

Isaiah's mouth gaped, and His knees buckled, as stiff as trees. He collapsed to the knee, overwhelmed by what he saw and by whom he stood before. Could it really be Him? He wondered. His eyes were like burning suns and His hair like beams of moonlight. When he spoke, it shook the heavens, beginning with the steps beneath the prophets already trembling knees. From above, he felt the wind of angel's wing. The cherubim circled overhead armed with golden spears and silver bows at their sides but also playing peaceful harps as they sang praises to their king. Six wings protruded from their backsides. Two covered their feet and the other two their faces in shame before the Lord of Glory. The remaining two spanned like wings of eagles. The feather shined like crystals in the King's light as they circled over Him continuing to proclaim His glory at every moment of every day. They sang and sang without ceasing as if it were their only purpose in existence.

"Holy, holy, holy is the Lord God Almighty! The Earth is forever filled with His endless glory!" over and over, they sang.

Isaiah swallowed hard against the sinking feeling that overtook him as the eyes like fire, turned to him. The heavens shook when he opened up His mouth to speak. The roar overtook the heavens and the angels and the cherubim. The prophet reeled most of it from the deafening boom that shook him from His knees. His palms smacked the steps before him hard to break His fall before His face had met the stone. The roar was deafening, but the prophet couldn't hear what God had said. He turned to one of His cherubim, who bowed before His king to acknowledge the command.

Smoke arose from the bowl of burning embers that glowed beside the throne. The King reached His mighty hand took the brightest piece of burning coal. The cherubim took it from His hand obediently and fluttered away to Isaiah. The cherubim reached out its tiny hand, not seeming to mind the burning coal. Isaiah saw it, though, and that gasped aloud as it drew closer. Surely God had sent the angel, he thought, to punish him.

He had seen the Lord of Lord, the Creator of all things, what other man had lived to see the sacred Father and lived to tell the tale? What man was worthy of such a sight, such a memory? He bowed His head with cherubim approach to preparing for His demise, for surely God was punishing Him for stealing this unworthy glance. Who was he to behold the face that even the cherubim were not allowed to see? He flinched and shied away from the cherubim's approach.

"Please!" he cried, stuttering and struggling for breath. "Please forgive, I'm sorry! I am unworthy! I am unworthy! I am unworthy!" he shrieked louder and louder, tears drenching His sweltering cheeks.

The angel held the prophet's head in place with its top wings and pinned His legs with the other two as it used the force of its body to knock him on His back. Isaiah landed with a thudded, squirming, struggling, but it was all for not. His arms legs went stiff like dying trees as the angel forced the coal against His lips. Isaiah tried to scream in agony, but the cherubim held His mouth in place. A muffled cry instead was trapped inside His throat and chest. He reeled in pain and squirmed with terror until, at last, the pain was gone, and he went limp. Lying down, he breathed deeply for a moment before the cherubim peaked over His all but lifeless body. The cherubim reached out His other hand and helped him to His knees. With a smirk, he said, "Don't be afraid. Now, you are cleansed for the master has made you clean."

"I am unworthy, a sinner!" Isaiah insisted.

"Your sins have been atoned for, and your guilt has been wiped clean." the cherubim reassured him. "The master has made it Himself for you are His chosen prophet."

"How can I be His..." Isaiah began to speak, but the voice like thunder rolled out again, commanding the attention of the heavens. This time the prophet could hear more clearly.

"Whom shall I send?" the voice boomed and reverberated throughout His godly kingdom so everyone there could hear.

Isaiah could feel it in His chest, like a fire burning. He could feel it in His breathing and in His very heartbeat, along with His shaking hands and knees. How could he deny the calling of the God he claimed to serve? How could he neglect to share His word with His people who have so long turned away?

"Here am I, Lord!" he cried out, standing to His feet in triumph.

"Send me!"

"You must go to the people of Israel and give them my message. They will turn deaf ears to it, of course, and they will refuse to hear it. Tell them this: 'You will be ever hearing, but never understanding; you will be ever seeing but never perceiving.' I will make their hearts calloused; make their ears dull and will close their eyes. Otherwise, they might see with their eyes, hear with their ears, understand with their hearts, and turn and be healed."

"For how long must this be, Lord?" Isaiah asked the Creator.

"Until their cities lie in ruin and are abandoned and havoc has been wreaked across their lands. Until their fields are barren of crop or cattle and their houses are empty and desolate. Until they are taken away as exile and slaves in foreign lands, and until I have sent every last one of them away from home they have taken for granted. The land will lie completely in waste and ruin, and only a portion will remain. Even that portion will be taken away as I allow it to be laid to waste once again, for my people have forsaken me. I will cut them like trees, but as trees leave stumps when they're cut down, so will I leave a holy seed among God's people, the holy stump that will serve as the last hope for Israel and all mankind."

Lightning flashed before them, and the cracking of thunder nearly split their ears from its deafening boom. The stones of each step collapsed, one-by-one before them, and the world around them seemed to shatter like breaking glass. The broken pieces were soon reduced to dust piles and what sights remained before them faded from view forever. The vision ended, and Isaiah returned to His place of quiet prayer and contemplation. The prophet's eyes shot open. He shuddered and gasped as he stirred from His trance and found himself once more in the dark and quiet of the night. Cold sweat drenched His forehead and dripped down His face and neck. Was it a dream? No, it was much more he knew, a vision from God. The light of the lamp flickered once more as the prophet returned to His scrolls and His writing. He pressed the pen once more to His papers and continued.

"I still don't understand it," he said. "Who am I to be called a prophet of God? I'm no one remarkable for sure, and certainly no one worthy of high prestige. Yet, I go, for my God has called and His leads I shall follow, no matter the cost."

The prophet scribbled for just a few more moments before the lamp began to dim. No more oil. He was nearly finished anyway, and the prophet thought as he eyed the dying flame and wrote the last few words.

"Tomorrow, I must go out to the people." he said. "To whoever will listen, and even to the great kings of Israel and Judah, though their ears will be deaf and their hearts will be hard to God's message."

The prophet found rest, at last. His slumber remained undisturbed by dreams and vision at least tonight, yet when he awoke, the fire burned again. As the sun rose, so did the prophet and the calling of

300

His King. Would they listen though, he wondered. The Hebrews were a stubborn people, even more, so their rulers and their kings. The false prophets were also sure to challenge him, yet how could he be afraid when he spoke on behalf of the God of Abraham and of Israel's people? He was ready to speak His prophecies according to the instructions of His Lord, but would they be ready to hear the prophet's words and warnings? He had His doubts.

When he approached the place that God had sent him to, he began to speak. With every word, a crowd picked up and slowly began to gather. The prophet hardly noticed. He could barely even hear himself as he spoke the words that God had told him to. Often the words flowed freely, and he never quite felt in control. He was a more a mouthpiece than a man at all for His words were not His own.

"The kings of God's nation turned their backs on Him. They have worshiped false gods and turned their backs on our traditions. They have consorted with foreign and wicked kings, thinking their alliances will save them, but just when they're safe, God's wrath will come. Like an assassin in the night, your allies will betray you. Israel, you will be conquered, you will be captured, you will be exiled, and you will be enslaved. You will be banished from your own homes because you have forsaken the one who delivered the Lands of Promise into your hands. They will be stripped from you, and you will live as captives. You will be destroyed by the very gods you worship and the nations whose wicked ways you have chosen to embrace. You will be destroyed, oh Israel, because you have forgotten the one who saved you!" stark silence fell as the prophet spoke. The crowds gathered still, but all were quiet, and all were still, their attention glued to the prophet's every word. "The nations of the world will overcome God's people. They will be rooted like trees rooted out by their stumps," said the prophet. "Yet one stump shall remain, a holy seed who will save the wreckage of Jerusalem. He will be the messiah and just king to the people of Israel and to all the nations of Earth." The prophet paused, waiting for silence to return as the people mumbled among themselves. As the soft chatter faded and the people returned their attention to the prophet, he continued to speak. "It will be a story of two cities. There will first be the corrupt and wicked Jerusalem. They will be a wicked people, and they will turn from their heavenly king to the gods of this world. Their kings will build idols, and their priests will burn offerings to them. The people shall worship them, and in turn, the wrath of Jehovah will burn their cities, tear down their homes, and ruin their fields and their livestock. There will be no mercy. They will cower in fear, and they will die as exiles and slaves because they have rejected godly counsel and turned to the wickedness of the kingdoms of Earth." he shouted aloud, waving His hands and pacing up and down to crowd to drive His points home. His voice carried with remarkable strength for some weary from age and rough living. "But there also shall be a new generation, and so God will build a New Jerusalem. Out of the

Stump of Israel, the holy seed of the Messiah, God will build a new city and a new nation of God's chosen." he continued. "He will establish justice and righteousness with truth and peace throughout the nations of Earth. Every man, every tongue, and every nation will visit the holy temple to pay tribute to God, and Israel will once more be restored to her former glory. The Israel of today has turned their back on God!" he cried and paused to rest after raising His voice for emphasis, His head down. "We have violated the old covenant, and we are worthy of nothing but wrath and destruction. Yet God has turned a loving eye on Israel, and in His heart, He has found merry where we have deserved the only wrath. He has found patience where we have shown only obstinacy, and He has found love when we are worthy only of being reviled. Hear, people of Israel and Judah, hear people of God's city, Jerusalem. God has extended two hands to you. In one, He holds healing, redemption, and infinite mercies. In other, He holds the wrath of the ages and the fury of Heaven. What hand, Israel, do you think He will extend to you if you continue to turn your back on Him in all of your ways? For though will destroy our holy city. He will build it up again." he said. "The New Jerusalem will be a land of peace and mercy. Enduring prosperity and eternal justice established by the very reign of our God. The New Jerusalem will come through the holy seed, but we will reject Him. We will reject Him as we have rejected the ways of our fathers and turned to false idols. We persecuted Him as we have persecuted the prophets of God. We will turn from Him and His teaching just as we have turned from

303

the teachings of the Holy Scriptures and the divine law. Yet though He is bent, he will not break, He will be an eternal kingdom. No one will be able to break, and nothing will be able to tear it down. No nation will rise against Him and stand. He will be the light the way, and the truth for all mankind, a beacon of light in a world that knows only darkness."

A wind picked up, but aside from that, only silence could be heard along with the occasional song of birds flying overhead. Not a single soul stood before the prophet in anything but utter silence, not sure what to make of the prophet's message. Their eyes stuck to him like glue, and their ears remained ever open. The prophet looked at them with only zeal in His eyes as the message He spoke burned him from the inside out. Even if he wanted to control it, he couldn't help but speak. The message wasn't really even His at this point, it was as if God was speaking for him, through him. Isaiah was only along for the ride at this point. Yet the human in him trembled, frozen in paralyzing fear. What if they didn't receive His message? What if they decided to put him to death like the prophets before him? Who was he to speak against the kings of Israel?

He continued speaking for what felt like hours. He wasn't sure what he actually said sometimes, His memory always fuzzy, and His mind and body weary from trance's rush. It was often hard to keep up with all the words that fell so freely from His mouth and often beyond His control. Night fell by the time he returned home to rest and silent prayer and contemplation. He slept well that night, His eyes heavy, and His wind was fleeing him more with every day. His sleep was not without its troubles; however, for soon, he would have to approach the very king of Judah. It wouldn't be much longer now, and he so despised the court of kings. The politics came with the calling, the prophet knew, but he so despised them. Even more, did he despise the wickedness of kings in all their arrogance? His fear of losing life had long faded, and it often paled in His comparison to the wrath he felt for kings who lead God's people into wickedness. Yet despite His passion, and despite the times he'd faced it, the fear of death never went away completely, except when he remembered that fateful day. The vision had felt so real. When the cherubim touched His lips with coal, he felt so clean, so humble, yet so overjoyed before the presence of His God. He wouldn't trade that feeling for anything and looked forward to the day he could join His king.

Why him? So often, he wondered. Why couldn't he have had a simple, peaceful life like other Hebrew men he'd seen? Yet the faithful prophet rarely wasted time on trying to understand the ways of God. He was but a humble servant, placed on Earth with a holy message. His job was to deliver it, and so he would speak to whomever God instructed. His eyes closed at long last, and the prophet finally found His too-elusive slumbers. Like other nights, though, he was sure His sleep would be disturbed by godly visions and cryptic dreams.

* * * *

King Ahaz sat on His throne, weary from a day of tugging at His hair and biting at His nails, a habit he had trouble ceasing these days. The troubled days that stood before the kingdom of Judah seemed to be working His nerves as of late. Little sleep came to him in times like these, and when it did, nightmares plagued it of war and ruin. He all too often envied the lives of shepherds, so free of trouble and such heavy burdens, he'd prefer the peaceful pastures over the courts of kings. Yet, now he fought with all he had to keep His throne and His kingdom in its place. He refused to be remembered as the king who lost Jerusalem.

Yet two kings conspired against him to force him into an alliance against Assyria. How could he be asked to go to war against such a mighty nation? The snake, King Pekah, had rallied Northern Israel to His borders and soon enough to the holy city's gates. No doubt that two-faced Rezin, king of Syria, would send His armies to assist His dogs. They had made their feelings clear; it was "join or die!" Yet in their unholy alliance, they failed to realize, the king of Judah had allies too.

"Your greatness, King Ahaz!" a servant called from across the throne room, two steps from the guards who watched over His throne room.

"Go ahead," King Ahaz ordered His servant. "Speak!"

"May I present to you His majesty King Tiglath-Pileser III of the kingdom of Assyria."

"May he enter," the king commanded. The guards stepped aside and allowed a cohort of servants, males, and females, both young and easy on the eyes. Their king entered shortly after they lined up to form His entryway, each bowing before their king as he passed. King Ahaz couldn't help but smirk. The man had always loved to make an entrance. He found some comic relief in all of the theatrics, and yet he couldn't help but admire His style, just as he admired the king himself. His armies were unmatched, and the wealth of Syria was unsurpassed. He could learn from such a king, and together they could be the fiercest force the world had ever seen.

The silver and gold gleamed along with precious gemstones as they rattled from the foreign king's silken garments. His narrow eyes stared intently at the king of Judah, and he pursed His lips with His contempt. He clenched His fists, trying to hide His disdain for the smaller nation that would soon be on its knees before its rightful lord. Yet these were trying times. Of course, that weasel Rezin would join with Northern Israel. These were trying times indeed, and Judah had much to offer in this fight. Like it or not, King Pul needed Ahaz just as much as the king of Judah needed him. A deep breath and stiff upper lip and the king of

Assyria approached the foreign king's throne.

"King Pul," Ahaz gave him a warm greeting with His approach.

"It's always an honor to host such an esteemed guest. You are always welcome in my courts."

He rolled His eyes and sighed heavily. Skip the flattery, he wished to say but couldn't. He glanced at a nearby adviser who pushed out His hands to urge him forward, adding an encouraging smile. The king gritted His death and grunted lowly so Ahaz couldn't hear.

"Just as we discussed now, be civil with the little king," he whispered. "He is going to make us very rich today."

King Pul nodded and drew a deep breath. He drew closer to the king and accepted a servant's offer for a seat. The king seemed all too eager to welcome him to His table and had His servants serve him up a feast. But there was more.

"May I present to the tribute that you have requested, and then some my lord." King Ahaz announced to ordered silence. "We have brought you silver and gold from the royal treasury of Judah and precious stones as well. We have also added to our gifts, precious treasures from our sacred temple's treasury."

Isaiah pursed His lips in rage, joining in the court's contempt. The people of Judah whispered their doubts but dared not voice them too loud in the presence of one king, let alone two. Isaiah watched in baffled horror as the servants entered carrying chests of gold and silver, accompanied by the priests of the temple. Could His eyes be deceiving him? Could His ears by lying, Isaiah wonder? He had to believe it so, for the king of Judah would never steal from God's anointed, to buy the sword of a foreign king.

"We have discussed our terms and our desires for this alliance. If you want our help against the northern alliance, then you must agree."

"What terms must I agree too?" Ahaz asked, raising an eyebrow, but hardly flinching as he waited.

"You must agree to bow to your rightful king and submit to those who preside over you in the high place. You will submit to the authority of Assyria. You will be our allies and warriors, and we will be your protectors in your time of need. You pay tribute to us, and you, as king, will swear fealty to me."

The court of Ahaz rang with whispers and murmurs of distress. The servants and councilors of Ahaz seemed uneasy with the terms. Isaiah listened from just outside, but only for a moment before he strode into the throne room. He watched and listened, standing at a fair distance to the king and His court. Far be it from the prophet to intrude on matters of the state, he thought with a scowl and a stiff upper lip. Even more, would he be troubled by what he heard next?

Ahaz stood and held His hands in the air to gesture His court to silence and began to shout. "Silence!" he cried. "Silence!" he cried again until their mumbling died down. "I remind you all that without Assyria's armies, Jerusalem will fall. We are outnumbered, and we need allies. This king has been kind enough to offer us help, and I say we should hear him out."

"Your people will be my subjects, and your kingdom will be a state of our empire. You will obey our laws and will follow our traditions so that our people may be stronger as one."

Objections began to rise again, but King Ahaz quickly raised His hands to silence them. "And what does Judah receive in return?" "You will have the protection of Assyria's armies, an ally in this war, and all future wars, and everything that Assyria has will be yours. You'll have access to our trade routes, our resources, our infrastructure, and all of the wealth of my empire will also be yours. Meanwhile, you will remain a free state, free to have your kings and your laws along with all of your favorite Hebrew traditions. You will also forever live in peace and prosperity under my glorious reign."

More soft chatter began to rise, some of the conversations among Judah's counsel sounded more optimistic now. "We will gladly give you time to think it over. Seek counsel and consult your advisors, your prophets, and your soothsayers. You're free to have your process. Just know that the sands of time cease for no one, not even a king. Judah's gates cannot and will not withstand the armies of Pekah and Rezin, but neither can their armies withstand mine. Consider my proposal carefully and send word as soon as you are able. A great lion has prey to devour; I will not wait long." Without another word, even as Ahaz raised His voice to speak, the King of Assyria turned away in silence, and His cohort soon turned to follow. A dramatic exit too, Ahaz shook His head with a heavy sigh. Those, he found far less endearing.

The court began to clear after a time of discussion, uneasy feasting, and a few formalities. Isaiah waited patiently for an audience with Ahaz, though not so patient with what he'd seen. The noise died down, and the crowds began to clear until only a few servants remained behind to clean up along with a few guards to watch over their king. They hid somewhere in the background, fading into the scenery and the shadows cast by the late-night torches as the feasting hall began to clear. An awkward quiet fell, the king staring sadly at His half-eaten plate.

"Not hungry?" Isaiah asked him, tearing him from His thoughts.

"The prophet himself honors me with His presence. Word has spread of your message, a tale of two Jerusalems, some have called it," he said. "Tell me, good prophet, which is my Jerusalem?"

"I suppose that is for its king to decide, for the king is the guide to the people. Sadly, their eyes blind to godly authorities, except for in times of need, and so God acts accordingly. The people look to the king, and when given a choice, they choose a king that reflects their own virtues. The kind of king you are will be the kind of kingdom Judah becomes. God's kingdom is an eternal kingdom. Is yours?"

The king smirked, smacking His hands together and bowing His head, humbly, or perhaps in resignation. "The prophet always speaks the truth, or so they say," the king remarked. "Will my kingdom fall to foreign nations, to wicked kings, and will my people be exiles and slaves?" he asked. "I've heard that you have seen God in a vision. I look around, and I see frightened people threatened with war, looking to their king for protection. Shall I give them a book, a scroll of prophecies to comfort them? What would those scrolls say of the invasion I am threatened with from King Pekah and His friends in Damascus?"

"You seem to know a lot about my prophecies and my message," Isaiah observed.

"I have familiarized myself with the prophets, dead and alive, as any king should I receive a proper Hebrew education, and kings tend to make it their business to what prophets are saying of them. I suppose I could use some words of comfort from the God we pray to here in Judah."

"Do you pray to Him?" Isaiah asked. "Or do you trust in the mercies of ungodly kings and the treasures of their vile courts and treasuries?"

"I suppose you are referring to our friends in Syria." King Ahaz surmised. "Politics is a dirty game. Unfortunately, we cannot be pure and sanctified if we want to survive in this world of wolves. I suppose that is why the sanctity and purity of God's presence is reserved for prophets and priests, who, but they by surrendering their full lives to Him, can keep their hands clean?"

"Perhaps you should trust in the power of Jehovah and not in foreign kings and dirty politics." Isaiah countered. "It doesn't suit the king who holds the holy city."

"Tiglath will provide the holy city with protection and prosperity."

"And what does he ask in return?"

"Only that we make ourselves His protectorates."

"He seeks to subjugate you, and he will introduce His false gods to your people who will bow down to false idols at the end of His sword. I suppose you will enjoy the wealth he shows you with, but it will come at a cost. Assyria will betray Israel, and they will be conquered. Yet if you, my king, will trust in the strength of the Lord and remain faithful to Him, you will have the victory of Pekah and all of the northern kingdom. You will win by the sword of the lord, but if you trust in the sword of a foreign king, it will betray you." Isaiah said. "And am I to understand you're bribing

Assyria with a tribute from the coffers of the holy temple?" he demanded.

"I am a king," Ahaz sighed. "It's a heavy burden to bear and one I wouldn't expect you to understand, Isaiah. I trust in the promises of God, but my kingdom doesn't need promises. We need armies, and we need supplies to get through this war," He drew a deep breath.

"And we need someone to give our enemies what they deserve for once," he added with a scowl.

"Then the king has made His decision to trust in the rulers of this world." Isaiah sighed and turned away. "I fear, the great king of Judah, your decision will cost the people dearly."

"They will thank me," said King Ahaz. "When they're bellies are full, and their heads are still attached to their necks and not at the end of northern spikes." the cried out in His defiance. "We and our allies will prevail over the northern alliance! Tell Pekah that's my prophecy to him!"

* * * *

King Ahaz watched, His eyes gleaming as the armies of Assyria gathered, blocking out very sunlight with their march across the lands of Judah. He watched with hope restored to His eyes and once racing heart, as a shadow fell over the kingdom of Judah. Horses joined with armored infantry and archers as far as the eye

314

could see. King Tiglath-pileser watched with glee but also determination in His narrowing eyes as His arms swept over the plains and the valleys and down the hills at His command. The horses racing stomped their hooves like thunder across the lands of Judah and Israel trampling whatever crossed their paths and crushing it like dust. The sound of it was deafening, but the song it sang that day would ring forever. The mark left on the lands of Israel would be felt for years to come.

The king smirked as he watched His armies pour into the Promised Land. Soon they would all be within His grasp. How convenient it seemed, that every today just fell in place. Northern Israel would soon belong to him, and His enemies in Damascus would be on their knees to join them. Judah belonged to them, a subjugated protectorate with a weak, subservient king, and all the gold and silver of Judah's temple too. How could these days be any better?

The armies of the merciless king swarmed across the lands like locusts, devouring everything that they could see. Men, women, and children all were murdered where they stood. Villages were wiped from existence, farms were burned to the ground and, the crops soon joined them in blinding bogs of endless smoke. Assyria showed no mercy and, in time, all of Israel was on its knees before this foreign king, and their allies followed soon. All of Israel could be heard wailing, and the only kingdom in the Lands of Promise was not heard weeping. Judah found no mourning in these days, least of all their king in all His splendor, at least not yet. If only he knew how the people of Israel would suffer because of him, if only he knew as he watched King Tiglath-Pileser III swallow the lands of Israel, and soon even Judah, before His eyes. Yet Israel would someday take note, and King Ahaz didn't seem to mind.

Often Isaiah could see visions of the king and the lavish life he enjoyed, but even more, he saw the cost it would bear Jerusalem and the cost it bore all of Israel and all God's people. It seemed unfair, the prophet often thought, that the people should suffer for the mistakes of their kings, yet it was their mistake to trust in the kings of men. Even since before the days of Saul, the prophets and the master had warned against them. Even now, he could see Ahaz consuming the feasts of Pagans. He grew fatter with the spoils of the wealth afforded to him by His friendship with the Assyrians, but Israel paid the price even now.

King Tiglath sat with advisors, frowning with determination as he watched from His high place in Damascus to inspect His new holdings. A smirk returned, at last, to His face, ever-widening as he watched His little pet in Judah eagerly approach. It was a special day when kings swore fealty to their true masters, he thought. He couldn't wait to see the little Hebrew where he well belonged, on His knees.

"King Ahaz," Tiglath greeted him, warms wide open, and the hands at the end of each one adorned shining rings. "It is good that you have arrived at long last. The time has nearly come for the remaining kings to swear their fealty to me and the empire of Assyria. You have been an example to the other kings here, and so I would like you to present yourself first."

"It would be my honor, of course, my lord," Ahaz said with a bow. Tiglath smirked again and shook His head, so humble, the loyal dog.

Music played, and women tossed their bodies to and fro, spinning them in perfect circles as they move to seduce men drowned in wine and lost in feasting. Men juggled torches while others swallowed knives to please the drunken crowds. Chatter joined with laughter and endless songs of cheer; a man could hardly hear His thoughts. A call to silence wiped the noise away, and eerie it fell among the hushing crowds. The Assyrian king held His hands high to shush His gathered court and soldiers who gathered to celebrate His recent conquests, but now the time had for the conquered to honor the king themselves.

"Step forward, Ahaz, King of Judah," he commanded, and the king moved swiftly to obey His lord.

"Thank you my king, and from my humble stores may I present to you a tribute, gathered from the people of Jerusalem, and the remnants of the treasures of our holy temple, a gift of thanks to our savior, our king, and our mighty lord from the lands of Syria. The

317

people of Judah thank you," he said kneeling, and bid His servants forward. They carried a heavy cart filled with chests of gold, silver, and precious treasures to present them to the new emperor. They, too, fell before their knees in a humble sign of Judah's surrender to the rule of law and the king who would uphold it.

"I, King Ahaz of Judah," the king spoke loud enough for all to hear, though His head stayed bowed. "Do swear fealty to you on behalf of all of Judah and all her people, and her people's children, and their children who will be forever your humble subjects. I do swear to uphold your laws and sacred edicts. I swear to be your sword in times of war need, and in times of peace and plenty. For all our days will Judah follow into wealth and poverty, into sick and into health, and into life and death, the word and law, the strength and power of King Niglath-Pileser III?" The king lifted His hands to gesture Ahaz to His feet. The king obeyed His silent gesture with a silent nod and stood to roaring applause throughout the court.

"Our first king has sworn fealty to His proper lord," King Niglath announced to the patrons of His festivities. "His people will fight for Assyria, will serve Assyria, and will obey Assyrias laws. In turn, they also will serve the gods of Assyria and embrace the ways of our people."

Ahaz swallowed hard, hearing it aloud, and even harder with what was to come. "And even more so he has another surprise for us all tonight. As a gesture of His good faith, he and His family shall join

318

us along with His own son tonight in the ceremony of flame. It is my wish that you all will attend to see it."

Ahaz's wife shot him daggers of a deadly breed. He'd rarely seen the look in her eyes, but he knew that it meant trouble. Even so, he feared her less than their new king.

"This had better not be what I think it is," she warned him sternly in harsh whispers.

He squeezed her hand to reassure her, leaning close. "All for the best, my wife." he whispered back. "We do what we must for the survival of Judah, of our family." he stared her in the eye. Her expression softened. She tried to hide the frightful gaze in her eyes, but closed them instead, nodding. She understood. What else could they do? If only he had known, she thought, how much he'd make their family suffer by allying himself with these foreign kings. Was any of this worth the soul of their own son? She had her answer with the loud crash that clattered nearby. The golden chalice fell on the floor, still half full of wine. Some of it had spilled on the drunken Niglath's lap, and some of it on the rug beside His sandals. She shook her head and hid her eyes in shame. She recognized the chalice from the temple where she had gone before to sacrifice to Jehovah, their one and only God. Until now, it seemed...

"How many more wonders will these compromises accomplish for our family, I wonder." the woman scorned under her breath. "I hope the treasures we reap from this are worth the souls of our children Ahaz, as much as they were worth the soul of Judah and Jerusalem."

"I simply know our place," said Ahaz in a final whisper before he turned away. "You should know yours. You are the wife of a king, but not an invincible king. You are no queen of Assyria."

The night would fall, surely a symbol of the new dark days to come for Judah. The fires lit the night, though, so they could see the sin they plainly tried to hide in darkness. Ahaz's wife tried to hide her eyes from it, but she couldn't help but watch. So she did. She watched in terror as her son, her precious baby, their firstborn and eldest son, passed through the flame. She listened, her heart wrung with rage overcome only by fear, so she could not express. With contempt in her eyes and seen in the tight pressing of her lips as her husband repeated the prayers and joined them in the vows to present the little boy as a living sacrifice to Moloch.

A grim look befell him as their eyes met, but he quickly forced His gaze away. He could hardly bear to them as he watched them give their son away to the gods of foreign kings who would now force the people of Judah beneath His thumb. It would be only one of many offerings he would give to false gods and idols. He gave sacrifices, burn incense at their altars, and join their priests in blasphemous prayers.

After a while, the king seemed to enjoy it. The people of Israel saw it, and she would see it too as he lost His soul to their idols and their wealth. He lavished himself with their treasures and filled His stomach with their wines and rich foods. His throne was often surrounded by Assyria's many luxuries and pleasures, and the king would lose himself in them at the expense of Judah's people, and God's holy city in Jerusalem. That is why it would be decreed that he was to be buried apart from all of Israel's kings. He was a traitor to God's people. If he only knew how they'd suffered for it while he lived His life in luxury, at the feet of their enemies' wicked kings.

Judah and Israel must have lost thousands of her children in those years to exile and to the swords of predators and tyrants as well as enemies of Assyria's wondrous king. Judah too would see many depart to exile and servitude. Others would be plagued by destitution and oppression, forced in slavery, and to live as crushed and conquered people. The iron fists of King Niglath-Pileser III would soon seem soft, however, when a new master would come in the form of Babylon, who God allowed to conquer the holy city.

The old man eyed the door frame intensely, moving the brush in even strokes to spread the fresh blood over its splintered surface. The young boy sat nearby, watching His grandfather move with care, but also the urgency. He never saw His grandfather move so quickly before, yet His voice retained a soothing calm as he continued to tell the story.

321

"So God commanded Moses and the Israelites to spread the lamb's blood over their door frames," he explained, His voice quivering, but as it always did with age.

"Do you really think God will protect us?" the boy asked over the sounding alarm bells ringing and people rushing around and shouting outside. The old man forced a smile, but the boy, though young, was hardly deaf and blind. He could see the fear in His eyes and could hear the terror in His voice, though he tried to hide it.

"I know that one day we will dwell forever with our ancestors in paradise where we will find peace on Abraham's bosom. My precious grandson, we will be among the angels and, at last, find eternal rest," he answered. "Whether that day is today, well, that is for Jehovah to decide."

The boy drew back in terror, further into the tiny home, hardly a stronghold of protection, but where else could he go? The songs of war began to rise outside and among sang screams of fear and agony, clashing swords and cracking flames. Fraying and whining horses soon joined the choir, along with cries of war from the crazed warriors they carried on their backs. The boy all but shrieked aloud before His grandfather cuffed His mouth.

"Hush boy," he commanded. "They'll hear you," he said as the door swung open. Together they dove and hid behind the bed, praying the men of Babylon wouldn't find them.

"Anything valuable here?" one of the men cried gruffly.

"Wait!" shouted a snarling soldier nearby. "Over here!"

The boy's heart stopped as he watched the warrior tear a shelf away. All noise went muffled, the items of the shelf were crashing on the ground. His breathing heavy, he drew a deep gasp when the second man of Babylon ripped the bedding from its place and overturned its sturdy frame.

"Over here," he called to His cohorts, who quickly moved with grins to examine them. The boy screamed in terror as two men grabbed hold of him, His eyes welling with tears as he watched two moves retrieve His groaning grandfather.

"Please! Leave him alone!" he shrieked and squirmed.

"This one's got spirit!" a soldier laughed, struggling to subdue him.

"What should we do with them?" asked another

"The boy is young, but he's strong and healthy. He'll make a good house slave if he behaves; if not, he'll be an asset to the quarries when he's older." the tallest among them spoke boldly and with authority. "The old man is useless. Kill him."

"Grandfather!" the boy shrieked, snot and saliva flying from His weeping face. His body flailed about as the men dragged him away, and he watched the others draw the sword approach the weak, old man. "Leave him alone!" he cried before they shut the door to spare him the gruesome scene, the Babylonian's only mercy.

The sounds of war and terror went quiet, and the flames grew dark as smoke swallowed the city, and many breathed their last. The black dominated once again, and the noise died away to yield to quiet emptiness. The nothingness of the void returned for only a moment before a flash brought in fresh scenes again. A river roared with the rushing current while tree provided shade by its lush and fertile banks. The prophet sat alone in the cool it provided from the heat of the day. So many years had passed since. First, he had that vision, and God had called him to prophesy to the Hebrew people and to their kings. So white, he went with age from years of hardship, and to what end? If only the prophet had known the day, His prophecies would be fulfilled. If only they knew the one of whom he prophesied if only he could have seen His face just one time before he died. Yet the prophet would cling to faith and remain loyal, steadfast to the end in following the calling of God. Just he predicted death he predicts a new life.

The prophet continued with trembling hands and now worn and bony fingers to scribble His words and His prophecies onto the scrolls.

"God will allow Israel to be oppressed and enslaved because of the wickedness of her people and her kings. Babylon will subdue her and crush her under His heel. They will be oppressed and will be forced to practice their traditions in dark and quiet places. Certainly, there will be those to their own detriment who will join the men of Babylon in their idolatry under threat of sword and offer of mercy. Yet some will remain faithful, and prophets will arise among them too. And one day God will even show mercy to His people in their time of trouble." he said.

* * * *

The walls of Babylon stood strong, but not nearly strong enough for the might of Cyrus the Great, a name feared throughout the lands of the east. He would unite many of the Asian kingdoms, and he would restore the ancient traditions of God's people. Jehovah Himself, some said, had anointed the King of Persia for this very task.

The proud king smirked as he stood before the walls of Jerusalem, His armies at His back. Horses lined up with chariots, and catapults, and a man ready with a ladder. The archers raised their bows first, however, preparing to fire the first shot, but not until their king commanded.

"Hold!" the king cried, urging His horse forward and up until the wall of shields and spears that stood before him. He grinned now, watching the eyes of His young soldiers light up with fury and thirst for war. "Men of Persia!" he shouted as loud and with as much vigor as he could. "Are you ready to show the world what you're made of?"

"We are ready!" they cried.

"Are you ready to make your families proud, to please your kings, and to be rich from glorious plunder!" he cried, raising His sword in the air and charging down their ranks on His furious stead. The men shouted and cheered in return, beating their shields to start the orchestra of war. The engineers rushed to their siege machines and loaded their ballistics in pace. At king's command, the archer shot first, however. Their arrows flew into the air forming a death cloud that drowned out the sun and flew over the wars of Jerusalem. The trumpets rang, and the drums pounded, the men cried out in terror and rage, and the battle began.

A loud crash and the first stone landed, forming a cloud of dust in its wake. Another followed shortly after, and the archers tumbled from their place on the high tower. The siege machines continued to assault the holy city along with onslaughts of arrows, and it was only a matter of time before the gates would give way. King Cyrus watched with pride in His eyes from a high hill as the battle ensued. His horse frayed, restless, and ready.

"Shhhh!" he brushed its mane gently to calm it. "Not until the gates are breached, then we enter Jerusalem and take what is ours!"

Soon enough, the trumpets will sound and battle cries would arise, and the king knew it was time. The gates cracked and shattered before their very eyes, splitting to pieces. The Persians poured in, shields, swords, and spears in hand as they entered. In days the city was his.

* * * *

Some time had passed since they cleaned up the bodies and rubble that piled in the city of Jerusalem. Crowds of Hebrews gathered alongside Persian soldiers and servants of the Persian king. Cyrus the great dressed in shining robes of silk. He adorned himself with chains of silver and gold and rings equipped with precious stones. A neatly groomed beard complimented the elegance of His crown.

A moment of silence followed the festivities and ceremonies, along with many commemorations. The king retrieved a clay tablet from His servant and addressed the people of Jerusalem. He glanced behind him a few times before he spoke, admiring the old wreckage of what once was a sacred temple to these conquered and exiled people. Those were the ways of the old kings. He pursed His lips with determination. He would unite these lands, and he would bring peace. These, he thought, looking to the old wreckage of the holy temple, were the ways of old kings. They were long dead and gone, and none of them had built an empire as large as his. His ways were better. He was proving it.

"People of Israel," he announced. "I am now your king, and your country is part of my kingdom. As such, you are under my protection and my laws," he explained. "As your king, I am pleased to announce that the cruelty of Babylon is over. You have been enslaved, exiled, and oppressed. Many of you were forced to abandon the ways of your people. It is the way of weak kings to wipe out the identity of the people he conquers, but I am more than a conqueror. I am a uniter and a leader. As with all the peoples under my rule, you shall be treated with dignity and kindness. I will respect your customs just as I would ask any of you to respect mine. No more men will be slayed and imprisoned for worshiping the gods of His household and of His people. No longer will you be persecuted for worshiping your God. You are Jews, and under the reign of Cyrus the Great, you shall be free to be Jews. I honor your God, oh people of Israel!" he said to cheering and roaring applause, but it wasn't over yet. "Furthermore, furthermore!" he cried, raising His hands to try and calm them. "It is not right that under your old rulers, your people were forced from their homes under exile. As your king, I will right the wrongs of old kings. It is time for your people to come home. All of those who were exiled in Judah and Israel may return home, and furthermore..." he said, trying still to calm the joyful, roaring crowd "Furthermore, I am calling on your lost people to help rebuild your sacred temple, that you may properly honor your God, and celebrate a new beginning. Death to the ways of the wicked kings of old, I, Cyrus the Great promise you times of peace, prosperity, and, most importantly, of change!"

* * * *

The old and aging prophet trembled as he tried to scribble the words onto the scroll. It took some struggle at first, but with determination, he pressed the pen against the page.

"There will be hope, and there will be despair, there will be peace, and there will be war, but in all times, men will be in rebellion to God. There is no hope for mankind, not even for God's people." sighed the prophet. "Yet there is one. He will come long after I'm gone. He will be called Immanuel, "God is with us," and he will be the hope and salvation of all mankind." the prophet breathed deeply, staring off in silence. His eyes watered a little but soon became dry, weary from so many years of searching and waiting. He stared off sadly, another moment. If only the people of Israel had listened. If only her kings had heeded His words in His life. But the prophet knew better. "We will reject him, condemn to die as a criminal. Yet He will save us all. He will restore us to the Creator..."

Chapter 10-Prepare Ye the Way

The new king of Judah rose to the throne with His head hanging low, the new responsibilities of a king weighing heavily on him. There had been much work to do, and undoing the evils of the previous king would be no easy task. Isaiah took him by the hand for a moment, a silent gesture of His blessing and perhaps His empathy.

"It is no light burden you bear," Isaiah said. "Restoring Jerusalem to its former glory after the evils of your father's reign."

The young king cringed noticeably. Isaiah offered a smile of pity, but there was little more than he could offer in the way of comfort. It was no easy thing for a young king to bury His father, let alone to disavow him in His death. Isaiah knew, however, the new king would have to learn from the mistakes of the old or else be doomed to repeat them. So many sons had done so before, forever doomed to repeat their fathers' mistakes. What had to be done next would be a heavy burden for any son to bear, but it had to be done.

"He will not be buried with Israel's other kings then," Hezekiah agreed, reluctance in His voice, but determination in His eyes.

Israel would follow God, its true and rightful king.

"He was obstinate, disobedient, and all of God's people were enslaved because of Him. To do otherwise would be displeasing to God Himself." Isaiah said, trying to hide the pity from His voice. "I know it is no easy thing to be king, but it involves making difficult decisions."

"All idols will be torn down," said Hezekiah. "Even the kings of old who betrayed the laws of God. No king is above that!"

Isaiah nodded His approval. Hezekiah was a righteous king and one who served God, but sadly such kings were never meant to last. The hearts of kings were wicked and fickle things, and it was rare to find one that didn't spurn the favor of God at some point. Power and corruption, Isaiah learned over many years, often went hand in hand. When Hezekiah passed the throne to Manasseh, sadly, the apple fell far from the tree. The old idols soon returned, and Israel, in its time of peace and prosperity, turned its back once more on the very God who freed them. When Isaiah spoke against the king, he did not respond in kind.

"I grow tired of your condemnations, your tales of doom and gloom," said the king as he dragged the prophet before him in chains.

"I speak, but what God commands me, you have brought the wickedness of your corrupt grandfather Ahaz, and you will drag

Israel into the condemnation, and they were once more be conquered because of you."

"Your words are words of rebellion. It seems to me," said Manasseh. "That you seek to dive my kingdom, to tear it down the very middle that I may be deposed as king. Your treason and your insolence will no longer go unpunished prophet. Since you would divide us all, we shall divide you. Take this man away for His treasonous words and His venomous false prophecies and saw him in half!"

The guards dragged the prophet away, but he did not resist, nor did he cry aloud. Instead, he lied limp, resigned to His coming faith. The prophet knew His time had come. He had known for a while now, but before, it was only a matter of waiting. He closed His eyes and whispered a final prayer in His final breath. A peaceful sigh, he prepared himself to meet His king. He was ready.

* * * *

"He died, killed by a king like so many prophets..." the woman said. "How many times must the people suffer for the wickedness of kings?" she asked.

"It is the hearts of men that are wicked," said the girl. "That is why they need a savior. They looked for a king, but He was a king like no other."

"Then they silenced the one voice that would have shown them the way to Him when Isaiah died, did they not?" asked the woman.

"He wasn't the only voice that spoke of the messiah," the girl corrected her. "At least three other prophets predict that a great Messiah would be born in Bethlehem and from the line of a great king of Israel named David."

"Who were these men?" the woman asked.

"There was a great prophet by the name of Micah," the girl explained. "He too preached the message of Isaiah..."

The screen lit up and expanded before them. A low hum and a high ring joined together to sing a lively tune as the sights and sounds faded in. The humble prophet sat silently at His desk, scribbling with His pen in the latest hours of the night. Only the candlelight provided a dim source of illumination as the prophet continued His writings, but he was too far behind to stop now. He was determined to record every action, every word, and every accurate detail of the histories of His king. A loud voice roused from His writings, setting His heart to racing and cutting His next breath short.

"Nathan!" called the guard. "The king wishes to speak to you."

"Of course," Nathan sighed, pressing His hands against His chest to slow His heart. "One moment." he took a few minutes to catch His breath, fetched His robes and followed after the guard.

An elegant throne room housed the king, His head hanging low as he sat in deep pondering. He rubbed His chin and looked back and forth, tapping His foot uncontrollably as he waited, anxious on His throne. Only a few torches provided light in the dark and cloudy evening, which allowed little to pass through the open velvet drapes. He turned His head up, looking to the door, wondering where the prophet was. He wasn't sure why he was so on edge when at last times of peace had fallen, but there was always work to be done. The guards, too, stood intently, he noticed. Armored men stood with sturdy spears staring straight ahead, their gazes solemn and their forms as still as statues. Vigilantly they stood ready for a fight at any moment and ready always to protect their king. David smiled in spite of himself. He certainly appreciated the loyalty he seemed to inspire in His men. His eyes widened, and the room echoed with the sounds of clattering armor and raising wooden spears as the heavy doors squeaked open, and a visitor came unannounced.

The guards stood ready to block the way to the king when a familiar face came through the doors with an armored escort. David waved His hands, a silent command to drop their spears and step aside. The guards obeyed, clearing the path for the prophet to allow him through.

"Nathan!" David greeted him with a smile and outstretched arms. "I am glad the man of God could come to me at this hour. I fear sleep will be eluding me all night if I don't discuss this with you."

"What is the matter, my king?" Nathan asked.

"Look around you, Nathan," David told him. "What do you see?"

"I see a great throne room in a king's palace, King David."

"Indeed. I have made for myself a house of cedar, but the Holy Ark, where does she stay? Who am I to house myself so lavishly, while the very symbol of God's presence in Israel wanders about aimlessly with no place to rest?" he asked. "I don't want to overstep my bounds as king, but..."

"Whatever you have planned, my lord," the prophet cut him off. "Then do it. Because I assure you, my King that you are in God's favor. He had given you victory over your enemies, and He will make you a great king. He will stand with you wherever you go and whatever you do so long as you continued to serve Him, follow Him, and honor His name."

David nodded, leaning back on His throne. He rubbed His chin once more in thought and smacked the arm of His throne. "Excellent. I shall take what you've said into consideration. Thank you, Nathan."

"Of course, my king, may the Lord be with you," he said.

"And also with you, Nathan. Good night."

The night dragged for what felt like hours as Nathan stirred in His slumber, restless for some reason unknown. His chest constricted, and His breathing became heavy as he tossed and turned all night. His legs twitched, His toes curling, and His fingers fidgeted relentlessly.

Nathan said a voice out loud, a rude awakening that nearly sent him tumbling from His bed. The prophet caught the other end just in time to stop His fall and pull himself back in, but only just before the voice called to him again. *Nathan* said the voice again.

The prophet struggled for a time to slow His breathing and still His trembling hands, but in time he found the courage to sit up and look around the room. No one could be seen, but a third time he heard the voice again. *Nathan.*

"Is that you, Lord?" he at last found the courage to speak.

Tell the king these words, said the voice as it slowly trailed into a whisper. Nathan nodded, staring intently at the ceiling, blinking only when he needed to. He stared and nodded, and occasionally waved His hands and even spoke aloud in conversation, as if receiving detailed instructions.

"Yes, yes," said the prophet frantically, "Yes, Lord! Certainly, Lord!" he continued.

Darkness soon yielded to dawn as the prophet found slumber at last, and it was dreamless too. The gentle song of birds gently whisked him from His sweet and peaceful dreams, and Nathan was ready to address the king. The cool breeze carried the morning dew to cool softly cool His kin. Nathan said a silent prayer before he began His day and then prepared for His conversation with the king. He could hear the festivities already as he approached the feasting hall to enjoy a breakfast with the king. The smell of fried eggs and toasting barley greeted His nostrils, enticing him more with His approach, but the prophet was not merely here to eat.

"Nathan," David greeted him warmly. "I can see it in your face already. Have you a word for me from our almighty Lord?" he asked. "I haven't displeased Him, I hope. Can I be at is ease, my prophet, and friend? Am I still in God's favor? Tell me its good news."

"It's good news, actually," Nathan offered a light chuckle. "The Lord is pleased with you, but he does have a message."

"Hmmm! Very good!" David clapped His hands to call the hall to silence. The lively strings died down along with winded instruments and merry tunes. Chatter ceased, and the people, over time, came to silence and turned their attention to the end of the table where the king and prophet conversed.

"Ladies and gentleman," David raised His glass. "To our honored guest, Nathan, the man of God Himself, my trusted court prophet."

Everyone raised their glasses and came to silence to offer the prophet their attention and sincere respect. The prophet smiled to the king in silent thanks for the courtesy.

"The Lord has said 'I have not had a dwelling place since the days I brought my people from Egypt, though I have made you dwell in a house of cedar I have not established for myself a dwelling place but have moved all about. Yet the day is coming when I will establish your house and the house of Israel. Your kingdom and your lineage, King David, will live forever as God's people continue to carry His truth and His laws, and one will come that will make your name and your lineage greater than all other kings. Long after you have passed from this world, one will succeed you who will inherit my kingdom in my glorious name. His kingdom will endure forever and ever, and so will House of David through Israel's true and eternal king."

The hall remained in utter silence for a time, even as the prophet turned away without another word. He staggered to the door to exit the hall, seemingly drained from delivering the message of His master in Heaven. David may have smiled, but he pondered the meaning of the prophecy. What could it mean? If only he knew it meant that His descendant would be king, not of Israel but all kings and of a new nation of justice and righteousness.

"Who is this king that he will live forever to reign over all men?" he wondered aloud. Their silence seemed to echo His questions along with the uncertainty that would dominate the room. The feasting hall went still and silent. Time itself began to stand still, or so it appeared. The torches dimmed, the flames dying slowly. The room grew darker before it faded completely, and the screen returned its formless void.

"There was one more, wasn't there?"

"There were a few prophets that referred to the Messiah, born in Bethlehem and descending from the lineage of the great King David." the girl agreed. "Then, there was the prophet Jeremiah."

"What can you tell me about him?" the woman asked.

"He was a great prophet of the Lord, but the people of Israel were unworthy of him. Some people called him the 'weeping prophet' because of His great lament. He was called to be a prophet at such a young age. Such a heavy burden to bear for someone who had experienced so little of life, but it was a time when God was once again using the young to pave the way for a great revival. After Jeremiah, Israel would see a spiritual awakening under Josiah, the righteous child king."

"Perhaps symbolic of the child born in Bethlehem, the little king who would bring light to the world." the woman mused. The girl giggled in spite of herself. She so enjoyed watching her sister learning and seeing her eyes slowly open for the first time.

"God has always chosen to use unlikely messengers," the girl added. "But Jeremiah would confront the false prophets of Baal, and he too would predict the demise of Jerusalem before the might of Babylon."

"They never listened to His prophets," the woman sighed.

"Many of the prophets conspired to take His life." said the girl. "But they failed, and time and time again, Jeremiah proved that God was greater than idols of Israel's wicked minds and hearts."

"The wrath of God is coming for those who have led the people of Israel astray. God's sheep are lost because they have been misleading by false shepherds that have come as wolves in the clothing of lambs. Woe to them and woe to those who are destroying Israel and her people with their wickedness their falsehoods, and their idolatry. Woe to those who have offered their own children as burnt offerings to false Gods, and those who trust in the words of Baal's priest. Woe to Israel, destruction is coming if she does not change her ways!" the prophet announced, as the light of a shining sun eased him into view. "But the days are coming, my brothers and sisters in Israel," he added, more hope in His voice, and more optimism in His tones. "For one day, God shall send a king who is righteous, who is perfect and holy and follows God's way. God will raise up a righteous branch from the tree of King David. He will reign forever and ever, and no one will ever succeed Him." he cried. "And so will God raise up Israel's rightful king to reign for eternity in Israel and over all creation. This is what the Lord has decreed that there will be hope for future generations through a just king and a holy messiah!"

"A man from Bethlehem, a man from the people of David," the woman remarked. "All of these prophets were saying the same thing as Isaiah."

"They prepared the way. They built the road to salvation by pointing the way to the Messiah, but the people didn't listen. Isaiah knew they never would. They would forsake Him, and he would be pierced for their sins. Their hands would slay Him for blasphemy, while His death would be their very salvation, the great reconciliation with God."

"So many prophets spoke of Him, but when He came, the people weren't ready for Him. They still wouldn't listen?" the woman asked.

"They were sent only to pave the way," the girl said. "So that future generations could be saved. A great empire rose up to that would devour all of the empires before it."

"Rome," the woman said. The name just came to her. She sighed, wondering if she'd ever get used to this.

The girl shot a grin, but the woman didn't notice. "They would conquer Jerusalem, and they would build roads through their glorious empire. Little did they knew they were paving the way for His apostles to spread the message that brought mighty Rome to its very knees."

"Did the Roman persecute the Jews as well?"

Under Rome, they would be allowed to maintain their traditions and their identities as Jews, but they were subject to Roman taxes and unfair laws. They were expected to fight for Rome, but beyond protection from greater evils, Rome did little to fight for her in return. Rome treated God's people as they treated all their captive nations, as lesser things." she explained. "Nonetheless, God used Rome to pave the way as well, and it would be Rome who carried out His martyrdom, His redemption for all mankind."

"Wasn't that His own people?" the woman asked.

"They often accused each other throughout the years, but it was both," the girl explained. "Rome executed Jesus at the behest of the Jewish priests. Jesus died for all mankind, slain by them to save them all."

"There was one more prophet, wasn't there?" the woman asked, hesitating.

"There was," the girl said. "His name was John the Baptist. His entire life, he'd wait to meet the Messiah before he baptized Him, but little did he knew they met very young." the girl giggled,

342

recalling the story.

"Oh?" the woman asked. She seemed intrigued, breaking character to disarm herself for a wider smile. Her eyes perked up as the girl gestured her back to the screen that rolled out again before them. It brightly flashed with images of Heaven. The angels and the cherubim swirled about the Father and His heavenly throne from where it rested at the highest point in Heaven. Their hearts and wooded instruments joined with their majestic vocals for a joyous tune, but one that did little to lighten the mood. God looked one last time on His Son before His final departure. His heart sank as he watched him fly away, but he could still feel His presence.

Michael looked over with a frown. It would hit His king the most, but the angels would miss Him too, Michael knew it. Jesus brought a certain vibe to Heaven, His wide smile only adding to its majestic light and joyous choirs. God watched as he floated down to Earth to be born among His creation. He watched with a heavy heart and sad eyes.

"I love you, my son," he whispered to Him one last time before he left the kingdom for His trip. "I want you to know..."

"I know..." the father could hear Him whisper back with equal love and tenderness.

"But I still want you to know," God insisted. "Even after what we have to do. It won't seem like it. But I'll still love you. I'll be far from you, but my heart will still be with you, and my thoughts will still be on you, my precious Son. My precious and holy Son..." His eyes began to well with tears as he felt the presence of His only begotten fade away into the world of sin. He was there as He was in all things, but not a part and not among His creation like it once was. His Son lived among them now, hidden by their sin, His light clouded by their darkness. He seemed so far away now. He could feel Him, but only faintly, and soon enough, He knew not at all. Yet though He knew all things, he tried not to think on those things, for even the King of Kings, the master, and Creator could feel the hurt and pain setting in already. He had felt it only once before when Adam and Eve first ate the apple and made themselves unworthy of Him through their sin. The separation and the loneliness formed a pain He had never known before. This time it was even worse, or at least He knew it would be when the appointed time would come at last.

"Good luck, my son." He whispered. A tear of joy came now, as He smiled down on His precious mother, Mary. The pure virgin with a tender heart and blameless soul, she was the perfect vessel of untainted innocence, the Holy One, the Christ Himself. If only she knew how precious it was, the gift she carried.

He watched her with a smile of pity as she wept. He watched from Heaven with a tender heart, melting as he beheld her tear and listened to her soft whispers.

"I don't understand how this is possible." she cried. "I've never been with anyone, but who will believe me now?" she asked, crying alone just outside her town of Nazareth. Only the rocks and sands were there to hear her, or so she thought.

"I am with you, my child," God said, weeping with her. He addressed both Mary and Jesus in a single breath and, with no less love for either, through Christ was His only begotten. "Gabriel," he turned to His mightiest messenger.

"I am here, my Lord!" he acknowledged.

"Are you ready?"

"I will go tonight, my lord!" he affirmed, adding a salute and a bow to further assert His loyalty and His determination to carry out His mission for His king. "The precious virgin will see me in her dreams."

"Remember," said the Lord. "You must also go to Joseph, so he will know He has a virtuous wife and that she carries the messiah, the savior of all," he added.

"I will visit him as well, my lord," Gabriel said. "And I know he will receive my message and show kindness to Mary. As you know, my Lord, He is a godly and honorable man."

"That is why I have chosen him for this humble calling," God agreed. "Now go and serve me well, my faithful messenger, and report back when you've delivered my messages and my songs of good tidings."

"As you wish!" said the angel before he flew away.

The angel bowed one last time and turned to join the other angels as they followed Michael to Earth. He fluttered away, beams of light stretching out and following the gliding of His brand new wings, drawing streams like white rainbows across the heavens as he flew to Earth. His majestic glow illuminated the night's sky for a moment in what appeared to be a flash of lightning. He was not alone, however, in casting the light. The angels of Heaven descended in armies upon Earth, swords in hand, and battle cries rising. Humanity and the rest of the world's creation remained blissfully unaware their movement, unaware of the Great War that was to be fought around them in the unseen spiritual realms. It was battle for Earth and humanity, for creation itself. It was a war between life and death, sin and righteousness, and between the armies of Heaven and Hell. All that was or would ever be was at stake unless, of course, God simply destroyed it all in the blink of an eye, but He loved them too much for that, so that war continued. The horns sounded, and the demons of Hell were roused from their stations on Earth and in the lower places, and they rose to join the fight. The Son, the Only Begotten, was headed to Earth to become a man. God had a plan to save His creation? Whatever it was, the demons knew they had to stop it at every cost. If only they had known they were far too late. God was always ahead by a thousand years or more. Still, the devil persisted, but the angels made it through with Michael leading the way, His fiery sword in hand, cutting through the legions with His angel warriors at His back.

The devil charged in from nowhere, the mightiest of all His warrior demons. His fang bore out like spears as he snarled at the angel Michael and lunged with His twisted blade in hand. The blades clashed in the air, and the devil struck, nearly knocking Michael from His footing. Michael quickly rose to meet the second strike with a hard block and a kick that sent the devil tumbling. The angel grinned as he watched the devil turn His gaze to Gabriel and the other angels escorting him, who soared from the fight and into creation. Satan glared their way, growling, roaring in rage, and called His demons back to Hell to regroup.

"This isn't over!" he cried to Michael, hissing. The angel called His angels back to Heaven to report the battle's end to His King in Heaven.

The angel arrived at the temple and watched for a moment where the priest was praying. Both of them admired the beauty of the singing outside as the others worshiped. Zechariah sat in silence alone, however, as he began to light the holy incense. He paused for a moment before dripping them in the flame to prepare His heart to enter in. The incense lit and burned, setting ablaze. The priest watching for just a few seconds as the flames ascended from their surface and blew them out. The smoke poured into the sanctuary, leaving a sweet fragrance, an aroma that always brought him peace. Why shouldn't it? He often wondered since it represents the presence of His Creator. A soft breeze picked up, igniting the embers and the tips of the incense sticks. Footsteps startled the priest, but when he looked around, there was no one to be found.

"Hello?" he called into the silence, but no answer.

"Hello!"

The priest jumped, flailing and crying out, trying not to scream. The angel caught him only moments before he slipped and fell on His back.

"Be careful," the angel laughed. "Almost fell there."

"Who are you?" the priest demanded, stuttering. "What do you want?" he pushed out His hands as if to keep the angel at bay, backing away from the tall and glowing being.

"Be at peace! Be at peace!" the angel raised and opened His hands to reassure him. "I am not here to harm you, in fact, I think you'll find what I have to tell you does what the opposite."
"What do you mean?" Zechariah demanded. "What is the meaning of this? You barge into the quarters of a priest during the lighting of the incense, and then you come to me speaking in riddles?" he demanded.

"My intentions are noble. I assure you," said the angel. "I am a messenger of the most high, an angel of the Lord," he reassured him. "I am here to deliver good tidings, which I am quite certain you'll be happy to hear."

"And what news is that?"

"Your wife is with your child,"

"Impossible!" Zechariah exclaimed. "My wife cannot conceive, and even if she could, both of us are too old to bear children."

"And yet there your wife Elizabeth is, pregnant and ready to bear you a son at any moment," he said. "The Lord has answered your prayers, Zechariah, rejoice! You are going to be a father, and Elizabeth is going to be a mother. He will be a delight to you and your household, but even more importantly, he will be a joy to many people. Just make sure he is never allowed to consume wine or any strong drink, for he is to be sanctified." the angel explained.

"Are you some kind of mad man? I already explained to you, my wife and I cannot conceive. How can I be sure this is, isn't some twisted joke? How do I know what you're telling me is the truth?" Zechariah demanded. "

"Because the Lord Himself has declared it," the angel answered. "And He has sent me, Gabriel, His esteemed messenger to tell His holy priest in person."

"I have a son?" the old priest asked, His hands trembling with the excitement. He could hardly believe His ears. The angel smiled widely, beholding the mortal's joy.

"You will have a son," the angel affirmed. "You will name Him John, and His name will be great among all nations. He will bring many of the lost sheep of Israel home to their rightful king. He will be a great prophet, going out in the spirit of Elijah to declare the word of the Lord. He will prepare their hearts for the coming..."

"The coming? Zechariah asked.

"The coming of the Lord," the angel explained. "Your Son will prepare Israel's people to receive the Lord, and by His words and His message, their hearts will be made pure. He will prepare the way for the coming of the Messiah!"

"How can this?" Zechariah asked in bewildered whispers. His eyes well with tears of joy and His entire body shook as he ran to find Elizabeth. They were having a son, a baby boy! "I have to tell Elizabeth!"

"Go, and give thanks for the blessings the Lord has bestowed on you, for God has given you a son and Israel a prophet to prepare the way for the Lord."

A few months had passed since Gabriel's visit. The marketplace teemed with excitement that day, crowds gathering to buy and sell, and to enjoy the activity of another busy day in the markets near Nazareth. Endless chatter could be heard and joined with arguments erupting from merchant stalls, the sounds of children laughing playing as their parents searched for good provisions. Mary found relief from the heat of a scorching sun beneath the tent of a nearby merchant when a familiar face greed her from a short distance.

"Mary!" the woman exclaimed, outstretching her arms as she ran to greet her fellow mother-in-waiting.

"Elizabeth!" the younger lady called, a grin lighting up her face with the sight of a familiar friend. "How have you been?" she asked as she approached.

"As expected," she said, pressing her hands gently on her stomach. "This little one is taking His tolls as always..."

The woman chuckled for but a moment, but her laughter quickly to turn gasps and groaning. The woman stumbled forward, clutching her stomach in agony. She winced aloud even as Mary caught her in her arms to stop her face from meeting the dry and rocky ground beneath them.

"Are you ok?" she exclaimed, helping the panting woman to her feet. Elizabeth took a moment to regain her composure, her face still flustered, and her forehead sweating as she struggled to regain her balance.

"I think I'm fine now..." she said, her eyes dazed and her face confused. She glanced around in disbelief and shook her head, her eyes still wide with her amazement. "Mary," she began to say between heavy breaths.

"Yes?" asked the younger virgin.

"Have you noticed anything different about your Son since you've been carrying Him? Has there been anything strange going on with your pregnancy?" she asked.

"Well," Mary hesitated, stopping to ponder for a moment. "I mean nothing I hadn't heard other women talking about when they were with child. I don't think anything strange has happened, no. Why?"

"My son was not just kicking me," she said. "He was pushing, no leaping," she paused a moment to regain her breath. "Like he badly wanted to see yours, he pushing my very womb towards yours," she said, almost laughing when she took the time to think about it.

"I suppose they're going to be close friends someday," Mary offered with a smirk.

They paused a moment, an uneasy silence falling between them. Mary broke it first, lightly giggling. Then together, they burst out laughing, not seeming to care who in the market place stopped to stare at them, many of the women rolling their eyes as they happened by.

The remainder of the day came and went without event or trouble, yet in the back of Mary's mind, she wondered. Could it really be true, could her baby boy really be the King of Kings, the child of prophecy? Who was she to receive such a wondrous gift? Surely others existed who were far worthier than she, and yet God chose her. Why? When the sunset and supper passed in silence between her and Joseph, she allowed the thoughts to come to bed with her. Throughout the night, they ran within her mind and whisked her off to sleep. She stared at swelling belly with a smile on her face, her chest warm and toasty with the love she bore the little one before He even left her womb. She couldn't wait to see precious king open His eyes for the very first time. All in time, she thought as she closed her and laid her head by Joseph's.

The much older couple slept soundly that night, yet before she drifted off to join her husband in His slumber, Elizabeth, to place her hand flat upon her womb. Her frail and bony fingers gently stroked the stomach as she hummed a soft tone to soothe her little prophet off to sleep. She glanced and offered a second smile to her gray and wrinkled husband, who lay next to her. Neither of them ever dreamed they'd have a child, yet here they were a little man of God on His way into the world. She wrapped her arms around the sleeping priest and closed her eyes to claim her blissful slumber.

What kind of men would these young babes become? Both their

parents often wondered and pondered their futures throughout the night, as many parents did. Yet years would pass before they'd ever know how great they would become. Years would pass, but they would know, the world would know even though they would reject their message. The sun would rise soon enough as dusk gave way to dawn and a new day began. The cycle would repeat itself many times for many years before the prophet became of age to prepare the way for Israel's king. Yet when it happened at long last, a new day began for not just Israel, but all of Earth and God's divine creation. If only their mothers knew just how bright that day would be when their sons would change the nation and the world.

The locusts sang throughout the night, even in the chilling air that picked up as darkness engulfed the desert lands around them. Stars sparkled in the crystal clear skies that soared above the distant hills. With them, the moon rose to light the world in place of setting sun, and the locusts' song announced the coming night. A locust all alone on His own pranced about, rubbing its tiny limbs together. It sang its subtle tune, such a quiet song without its brethren, but loud enough to reveal it in the night. The massive arc hovered over it, an impending blur and shadow, but the locust failed to notice. The finger and the thumb swooped in like a charging hawk and snatched it by its wings, which failed to flap.

The little creature squirmed and wriggled, suspended by its wings but to no avail. It swung its tiny limbs in a final vain attempt to escape its fate. A light crunch and a tiny wooden stake cracked its shell, cutting through its chest. Impaled, it hung over the crackling flames, which devoured at once. It's burned, crisp body dangled in the air and roasted for a moment more before the stick swung over and drenched it in a sticky pool of honey.

The bearded face smiled widely at the little treat, a grin of yellow teeth. His eyes light, and he groaned with pleasure, crunching the sweetened, roasted locust.

"The sweetness of God's bounty and provision," he chuckled to himself. He often mumbled to himself these days, for he was better company than most. He had so few folks to talk to these days, except when he was preaching and baptizing in the name of the coming savior. Until the day they met, he waited. He crunched a few more, savoring its gamy flavor and swallowed hard with another smile as he left His damp and earthy dwelling place to view the stars one last time. Would he come in the night? He wondered. He crossed His arms to hold himself in a warm embrace and shivered in the path of the whistling desert winds. His rags of camel hair strayed in the wind like threads, nearly unwinding as they blew, but somehow holding in place. A leather belt dangled over His waist, torn and tattered from years of use, but somehow held His garments in place. With eyes wide and filled with hope, he stared into the starry sky in silent prayer and anticipation.

"Someday he will come," he reminded himself in hopeful whispers.

"Someday..."

He took a moment more to draw in the beauty of the heavens as they presided over the wilderness around him. The moon and stars were a sight to see, not a cloud or storm insight to impede their wonder. He wondered if he'd ever lived to see that star he'd heard about as a child, the one that shone brighter than all the others around the time he came into the world. It must have been so beautiful. He bowed His head a moment in humble prayer. After that, he sat in silence, waiting, soon to return to His humble abode as he felt the chill in the air picked up. He should get some rest, he reasoned, tomorrow would be another long day at the River of Jordan.

The moon and the stars began to clear away, yielding to the rising sun and her ruling light. The songs of birds soon replaced the songs of locust to announce the dawn's arrival. A warm breeze replaced the chill in the air, and the holy lands came to life again. John followed the sounding roaring currents until he found the path to the Jordan. Crowds had already gathered in anticipation of His arrival. His following seemed to be growing these days. He wondered if that meant it was almost time. His heartbeat faster at the thought, and His chest tight with excitement. He couldn't wait to His king. The chattering and laughing crowd hushed with His arrival and prepared their hearts to hear him speak.

John the Baptist approach the center of the crowd's attention, dressed as always in camel hairs and tattered sandals. With His belt loose and flopping, he walked and up and down the masses and looked them over. The river current continued in its course, the river's waters bubbling as they passed nearby while the birds in their soothing tunes. John the Baptist's tattered sandals sifted sand and crunched the gravel as he paced, but other than all of that, there was utter silence. He grabbed the crowd's attention with a mighty shout, like one from Heaven that boomed throughout the gathering and roused the snoozing crowd to the prophet's message.

"You have learned the old laws, you have studied the prophet, and you have all been instructed in the ways of the lord," said John the Baptist. "So you know that the prophets have spoken and that they have warned us of the coming wrath of God on high. Yet you have also heard of His abundant mercies and of the rightful king," he told them. "Some of you have called me a prophet, but I am here to tell you the one coming after me is one of whom I am unworthy to even untie His sandals! He will establish a new covenant with Israel and a new kingdom to rule over all kingdom administer God's justice on Earth. He is greater than I could ever hope to be. I have baptized you with water, but I tell you, he will baptize with fire, and with the very spirit of God!"

Men, women, and even children waded into the waters to be baptized by John. Lines waited for him as far as the eye could see, and one-by-one he received. Splash after splash could be heard as

357

he baptized each man and women who came to receive repentance, dunking them under the raging water and lifted them up into new being. He was the way, the voice in the desert, preparing the way for the king, and the king's lost sheep came to him for life. Yet even as he received each one who hung on His every word and received His baptism with joy and gratitude in their eyes, he looked to Heaven waiting for the great king who he hoped would one day baptize him. His lost eyes always turned to Heaven, yet they never lost the vigor and the passion for His mission here on Earth.

"Repent and be baptized!" he cried, repeating His message for all who would hear it. "For I tell you," said the prophet. "The Kingdom of God is near. Prepare your hearts and make room for the savior, the rightful king of Israel!" he continued to preach. "He will not be like the wicked kings of old like Ahaz who threw in His lot with wicked and godless kings, or the kings of today like Herod who has shamed Israel by taking His brother's wife! Repent Israel, repent, for the kingdom of God is near!"

The river's water bubble once more, shimmering in the light of a high sun in a clear and perfect sky. The woman watched in wonder as time itself seemed to pause, and John the Baptist and His crowds stood as still as the mountains. Silence fell and hung in the air, with not even the birds making a sound, but river The Jordan still roared, its current flowing forward with force, and the woman could hear its depths cry out to her. She could feel the fish of the sea, swimming in its cold and murky depths, she could feel the birds watching overhead, and she feels the trees basking in the warmth of the sun as it bore down their branches and leaves. Her heartbeat faster as she felt the anticipation of the gathered crowds who waited to hear the prophet speak. Then she began to sob, overwhelmed by a sudden sadness. Venus put her arm around her.

"It's ok, she said." You're just remembering." "Remembering what?" she asked.

"Your connection to Earth, her creation, her life, her people, all fell away from their Creator. You're feeling the life and the destruction at the same time, the sin and the salvation of Jesus," she explained. "But don't cry," the girl insisted sadly, her pitch rising to reassure. "The prophet was sent to prepare the hearts of the people to receive the king who had a plan to save His people."

The woman wept and wrapped her arms around the girl. They sat for what felt like forever until a kind of whiteness enveloped them both; a warmth ran their bodies, bringing them to peace. A sweet and gentle face approached them, wrapped in golden rays of light. The sparkle in His eyes reassured them as he cast a loving smile their way. "What has been broken can be restored." he placed His hands upon their heads, and they rang with soft and otherworldly tunes. The screen fizzled out, and its scroll-like surface rolled into itself, closing around them. In a moment, it was gone, and so were they.

The blackness of the void was blinding as the silence that dominated its spheres was deafening, but it never lasted long. The Creator never seemed to care for it. There was more. He wanted them to see, with their own two eyes as it happened. The blurry lights faded in with birds singing and waters rushing.

Chapter 11-The Promise of New Life

For God so loved the world that he gave His one and only Son, that whoever believes in him shall not perish but have eternal life. For God did not send His Son into the world to condemn the world but to save the world through him. Whoever believes in him is not condemned, but whoever does not believe stands condemned already because they have not believed in the name of God's one and only Son. This is the verdict: Light has come into the world, but people loved darkness instead of light because their deeds were evil.

Haunting melodies soothed them from afar, but from where they could not be sure. Blurry images tossed and waved before them along with shades of gray and white, but beyond that, their eyes grasped very little. In time their vision would return to them, and the sights they'd see would stun the woman, but the giggling girl not so much. She looked up at her eyes, burning brightly with joy and life.

"Do you know where we are?" she asked, standing on streets of gold and sparkling gemstones. The crystal towers, temples, and elegant estates shimmered before them along the way. Angels soared over them through fluffy clouds. Peaceful harps strummed around along with joyful flutes and choruses of angels who joined together to praise their king.

"Isn't it beautiful?" the girl asked, grinning up at her.

The woman looked over at her with a flinch. She had nearly forgotten about Venus as she admired the beauty of Heaven. Laughter and joyful chatter greeted them wherever they went as they traversed the shining golden streets. A great white staircase loomed before them ascending into the clouds.

"Is that...?" she began to ask, stuttering. "Is He at the top?" she asked.

"The Father," the girl answered. "The Creator of everything that ever was is or will be. Just as we met the Son, now we will meet the Father." the girl explained.

"I don't know if I'm ready," she hesitated.

"Come on," the little girl reassured, extending her hand. The woman took it and smiled when the girl wrapped her petite fingers around her own. "He's not as bad as people think. He cannot be around sin for He is a holy God, but when His Son paid the price for all sin, He made us holy too," she explained.

Each step seemed so long and tedious, but perhaps that was

because of her racing heart and heavy breathing. Maybe it was because of all the questions raging through her mind, which she knew she'd never find the courage to ask. A heavy fog set in now to remind her that they were getting closer now with the higher climb. An eerie wind whistled in the air, but a calming one. A gentle warmth carried in its passing. Her breathing became easier when the fog began to clear, and to her surprise, her heartbeat began to slow when she saw His face. Just like when she saw the Son. She could see the sparkle in His eyes and could feel His love, ever stronger as she drew closer.

Her knees shook with every step. Even with the little girl to urge her on, she found it harder to move forward. With a wide smile, he gently drew her forward and waved her to His throne. A pair of cherubim landed at each side of them to escort them to the seat of the heavenly king. The warmth grew in intensity, and the light expanded in its vibrant glory as she drew closer to the king. Her knees failed at last, as she arrived at the base of His towering throne.

"Do not be afraid, my child," he spoke with a booming, but a calming voice. "You have been made pure long ago and in times yet to come."

"What do you mean?" the woman looked up Him, confused.

"You do not see time as I do, not yet," He answered. "But you will," he reassured her. "And you will feel it too." He said. "Yet even now though I am in Him and He is in me, I feel the loss of my only begotten Son." His voice trailed off, a single tear pushing out from His eye.

"You miss Him?" the woman asked.

"Just as I missed you, my special creations, my beloved children," A measure of joy come to His reassuring echoes as He spoke with a voice like soft thunder. "I can feel His loss, though, for where He is I cannot be. He is among sin in corrupted flesh in a world I can no longer dwell in as I once did in the beginning when it was only Adam and Eve."

"Before the fall," the girl interjected.

"Before the fall..." He sighed deeply. "Yet He went to them in helpless form. He almost didn't make it..."

The Creator watched from afar with sad and worried eyes; His voice was trailing off one last time before he yielded to the silence. His Son looked so helpless now, the smallest and weakest of their king and His dwelling place. He shook His head, but He knew it had to be. Even so, the stables were hardly fit for a king, let alone the Son of God and His people's king. They were so unworthy of Him. So why did He go to all these lengths, and why was Jesus so quick to agree? None of this made sense, but He couldn't help it. He loved them so...

* * * *

Mary came home to Joseph, who rushed frantically around the home to gather various supplies and stuff into sacks. Mary stopped in her tracks, but he hardly seemed to notice her. He rushed outside, brushing past her with an arm full and rushed it to the beast who waited for their journey.

"Oh!" he cried, startled as her elbow collided with His own. "Sorry, my love," he said. "You've come back from the market?"

"I have," Mary said, struggling to regain her composure and sighing relief as none of her own supplies reached the ground. "What's going on? Are you going somewhere?" she asked.

"*We* are going to Bethlehem," he corrected her. "And it's a long way from Nazareth, so we may need some of that supplies you've brought home with you."

"Why do we need to go to Bethlehem?" she asked.

Joseph shook His head, sighing and rolling His eye. "Good old Caesar and His decrees. We must appear for a census in the city or town of our origin, that means you and I are going to go to Bethlehem."

"Almost half of Israel must be from the town of King David's birth. Imagine how crowded it will be," she said.

"That's why we need to hurry," Joseph insisted. "We'll need to be one of the first travelers there if we want to find an inn, and need I remind you that you're pregnant?" he asked.

"And not exactly early on," she said, looking down at her bloated belly, drawing a chuckle from them both. "I may be ready to give birth any day now."

"Which is why," Joseph insisted, urgently packing what he could. "We need to go. We don't want you giving birth to our Son in the streets of Bethlehem for all to watch now, do we?"

"We'd give them so good entertainment." Mary laughed.

"Who needs the coliseums of Rome when we could watch you give birth in Bethlehem," Joseph shook His head with a sly smile. "Come on, we'll need to leave soon!"

Joseph's words proved to be far too true. Many travelers joined them on the roads, but the journey was far and anything but hospitable to them on their way. How long had it been, she wondered. She panted and stumbled weakly along, clinging hard to Joseph and His sturdy shoulder as he held her close to His side.

"We should stop somewhere to rest," he said. "You're growing weaker."

"I don't want to have this baby in a tent in the middle of a desert, no midwives to watch after him and no bed to him in as I give birth." she sighed.

"We have to take care of you, though," Joseph insisted. "And the baby!" he added more firmly to remind her.

"But the census," she gasped. "You know how the Romans want their taxes. They'll have you on a cross if they think you're disobeying the emperor and His edicts."

"A plague upon the emperor of Rome, my wife, and child, are more important."

"Come, Joseph," she insisted, wrapping her arm more tightly around him. "We can do this. Just a little further."

She must have blacked out once or twice on the road, unsure of what she went as she stumbled weakly forward. She wasn't sure how much time had passed before Joseph finally put His foot down and called them to rest. The dipped below the horizon. Night had nearly fallen anyway, so Mary agreed it was time to rest.

"Will you wake me up if the baby starts coming," Joseph laughed aloud in jest.

"If he does, you'd better *not* wake me up," she warned him sternly. "I don't want to feel any of it, even now. In fact," she added before laying her head on her husband's chest. "Do me a favor, and don't wake me up at all. Even when the sun comes up, don't wake me until we're in Bethlehem in a nice room, with our baby squirming in my arms." she grinned and giggled, planting a quick kiss on His lips.

"You are a sneaky one!" he snickered, kissing her back before they closed their eyes. Sweet rest came at last, and the sun would rise before they woke.

The wise men could see it too, the sun rising in the east as dawn triumphed over the night. The magi sat alone by the campfire as His companions slept, eyeing the distant sun as it cleared away the other heavenly bodies. He couldn't seem to keep His eyes off the point where he saw the star. Even though the day had long erased it, he stared intently. His narrowed fixed hard at the place where it rose to show the way to the man who would be the King of The Jews and the man who would topple sitting tyrants.

He looked away from the flames for a moment to examine His sleeping friends. He cracked a smirk at one of them snoring and shook His head. He stole another glance of His wooden box, sealed tight to conceal His gift for the newborn king. He turned His head to the other and sighed deeply, wondering. They were precious treasures, that much was sure, worthy of a king, but were they worthy of the King of Glory? The face of Herod flashed through His mind once more as he reflected on it. Shivers ran down His spine at the ghastly image. Something about that king had rubbed him wrong, but he couldn't put His finger on it. The other men seemed keen on returning to him once they were finished so he would provide for their journey home, but he had advised against. He always seemed to have a sense for these things.

"Make sure," the king had called, with a certain uneasy look in His eyes before they left. "That if you find him, you return to me so that I may also pay my...proper respects," he remembered the sinister smile all too well, and all too well from history, he knew the ways of kings. The others stirred from their slumber, cutting His thoughts short.

"Already awake, my friend?" one of them called over to him between fits of groaning and rolling in His tent.

"Awake and ready to go," he said. "I even made us breakfast." he offered with a grin.

"A man after my own heart," said the third magi as he departed from His tent with weary, but eager eyes. "I'm hungry enough I could eat a flock of sheep."

"Eat then," said the first magi, staring into the flame. "But eat quickly and remember why we are here. I am ready to see this promised king."

"I'll drink to that," said the second magi, raising a wineskin in the air. "To the Child of Promise, and the signs in Heaven are showing us the way."

"Hear! Hear!" said the magi, forcing a smile.

* * * *

Mary cringed one more time, watching the sun fail once more as night rose to take its place. The skies remained clear and beautiful tonight. The stars and the moon lit up the heavens, especially the one star, the brightest of them all. It almost seemed to follow them everywhere they went, watching over them. Despite the serenity of the lovely display of lights and glory, she dreaded the coming of the night. She needed rest, but she didn't want it. She just wanted the journey to be over, the agony of the tiresome walk, and pregnancy to be done at last. She just wanted to sleep in a bed with a roof above her and solid walls around her child as he's born safely. She didn't want to stop for rest one more time; no matter how tired she may have felt, she just wanted to get to Bethlehem.

"Just a little further, my love," Joseph reassured her. "Can you make it?" he asked.

"I can make it," she grinned widely, silently giving thanks to God as the lights of the crowded town came into view.

The crowds poured into the city. The couple, with all their things, struggled to squeeze in and navigates the streets of the city, teeming with noise and life. Everywhere they stepped, someone brushed their elbow or bumped their shoulder. People rushed from every side and scrambled to find a room and much-needed provisions. Roman soldiers scowled, many of them young men who tried to conceal their fear before the crowds of Rome subjugated people of Israel, all of whom poured into the city for a common cause. They, like the soldiers themselves, were here on the business of Rome. Joseph and Mary avoided looking in their eyes through brass helms and solid armor that hid frowns of contempt behind their bravado masks.

"I just need a room for two!" Joseph shouted over the counter at the innkeeper who stood stunned before the crowds who pummeled him with coins and demands for rooms. His hands trembled as the crowd began to shout in anger and clamored for the counter of the inn.

"You must have at least one room!" a patron demanded, but to no avail for the innkeeper would hardly hear him over other rising cries of rage. Roman soldiers stepped in, extending their impending spears in a show of force and shouted orders for the people to step back. Joseph and Mary stumbled back, the unarmed guards pushing the crowds back to support their comrades in the gaps between their spears.

"Order! Order!" shouted one of the Roman guards. "We will have order!"

Mary paled noticeably and whined aloud, but neither Joseph nor anyone else could hear her whimpers over the demands for space, nor would they have heard her collapsing to the ground if not for what happened next. Joseph caught her in time to prevent her from hitting the floor, but a puddle rushed out in her place and splashed on the wooden floors. The patrons backed away, crying out in their surprise, along with the soldiers of Rome who even found themselves set off balance and stepping away from the scene.

"I'm in labor!" Mary screamed aloud. "Please, someone help! I'm about to have my baby!"

"Joseph's hands trembled, and His breathing turned to rapid gasps and wheezing. He tried to shout out in anger, but it came out stuttering, though he persisted nonetheless.

"What are you waiting for?" he demanded. "Help her! Can no one spare a room for a woman in labor?"

The innkeeper stuttered and struggled as well, "I simply have no rooms, I don't know what to..." Mary screamed in agony, cutting the man off shortly before he could finish.

"Come on! Come on!" the innkeeper's wife stepped in, huffing and puffing as she rolled her eyes. "We're not letting this woman give birth in the crowded streets of Bethlehem to be tramped along with her little one! Are you so heartless, my husband? The least we can do is bring her to the stables where they'll be safe and a roof over their head for the night."

"Yes, of course, the stables!" the innkeeper exclaimed. "Bring them immediately!"

The labor seemed to last all night, most of all for Mary, who screamed throughout its painful journey. Joseph shook His hand when it was over, barely able to feel it as His newly wedded wife nearly squeezed it off. His entire body shook with Mary, who shuddered weakly where she lay back on beds of straw and dirt. Animals frayed and whined nearby as their stench joined with the warm Bethlehem air to create a less-than-pleasant ambiance.

Even so, the couple smiled wide as the baby stirred and whimpered in His mother's arms, and His Father cooed at him to draw a smile from him. The crowd had quieted and cleared by now, but in the distance, three more visitors waited to see their king. Mary's heart jumped along with Joseph's as they turned to greet the men dressed in shining jewels and robes of silk and fine linen. Their impressive steeds frayed nearby as they dismounted, stepping forward with eyes fixed upon the newborn king. Their faces solemn, turned to greet them, and turned to humble and friendly smiles.

"So you are the mother," said one of the magi, stepping forward to introduce them. "We have come from very far away to see your son."

Mary flinched, squirming and positioning herself closer to her husband for protection as he stepped forward.

"Please," the man stopped in His tracks, extending an open hand as a sign of His pure intent. "We mean no harm." he fell upon His knees and locked behind him to signal the others to follow suit. The other magi stepped forward to join him and knelt as well, holding out their boxes. The wood was smooth, elegantly carved with an ornate design, and carried in it precious gifts for the precious king. "Your Son is the Child of Promise. We have followed the great sign in the sky to get here to find him."

"Did you speak to the angel too?" Mary asked them, hesitating, but feeling a little bit at ease as they conversed.

"No," he answered. "We are wise and learned men who have spent years studying tomes and ancient prophecies along with the ancient arts and sciences. We have learned to read the signs in the sky and followed him here to find the Child of Promise."

"What do you mean by the Child of Promise?" Joseph asked.

One of the other magi looked at Joseph. "This child will be called the King of The Jews." the man explained. "He will take away the sins of the world and administer a just rule and establish a righteous kingdom."

"His reign will last for all of eternity." added the third magi.

"And what is this promise?" Joseph asked. "What is this promise that our child will bring, why do you call him the 'Child of Promise'?"

"Because His rule promises humanity a return righteousness and unity with the divine. His reign will bring the promise of truth, justice, and peace. His birth represents the promise of a new life for all people on Earth. It is our belief that this king must survive at all costs because His existence will change the course of history, and will alter the world in ways that humans will likely not understand for many millennia."

"He is the king of hope, of restoration, and new life for all of mankind." said the first magi, still kneeling. "Please allow us to present the royal family with gifts worthy of a king."

"First," said another of the magic as he rose to step forward and present His box to the king. "A king should have a proper tribute. May we present to you precious treasures from our land. Gold, for the newborn king, may it help you on the journey ahead."

"What journey do you mean?" Mary asked him, but the man fell to His knees, completely silent. He bowed His head and closed His eyes as he paid homage to the infant monarch who playfully cooed and reached out His hands as if to bestow His royal blessings. The next man stepped forward to present His gifts, kneeling before the manger, ignoring the piles of straw beneath His knees. He opened His box of precious herbs and incense, a holy tribute to a holy king.

"To the holy king and honored priest. He will establish godliness throughout the Earth and pass down righteous edicts and decrees. He will cleanse the land of evil and unrighteousness. By Him, wickedness shall be cleansed from Earth. He will smite evil and reunite man with the divine, as it was foretold in the beginning..." he said. "And so I present this frankincense to our noble lord and holy priest."

Joseph and Mary tried to speak, but they could hardly manage a word or even a question, though many raged, before the third and final magi presented himself to them. He lowered himself to one knee and bowed His head humbly to their Son, who squirmed playfully and closed His eyes. Even in His rest, he stirred, and pointed to the magi in front of Him, granting the man an audience.

"My king," the oldest of three smiled through His white and well-groomed beard. "My precious little king," he said, lifting His head. He opened the box to reveal a bottle of sparkling crystal. Precious perfume lingered inside, resting its shining, bubbled surface.

"A king will need a proper burial," he frowned, sadness in His eyes as if he could see it happening then. "When the day comes, of course, but believe me, there is time before that happens," he reassured the woman, looking in her eyes to offer peaceful reassurance. "But that is why we must move quickly. Your little king is an important man, but please..." he paused, looking to Mary and Joseph, then back to the slumbering babe as lay still in the hay. "Please accept our humble gifts. May they be a blessing to you on your journey, and may the king remember His friends from The East when he reigns and glory. Our humble thanks." he said.

After a moment of reverent silence, they rose without another one, only silent nods, and turned away to return to their countries. Mary Joseph waved back as each man offered His "goodbye" bow and salute, and they watched them ride away.

"Who were those men?" Mary wondered as the night went on, but to no one in particular. She knew that Joseph wouldn't have answers, even if he were awake, so she released the matter and soon joined her him and their little man in their peaceful slumber. But it didn't last long. It never seemed too...

The oldest of the magi stirred in His slumber as they rested at their camp. Darkness covered them as did the cold, but it wasn't the desert chill that deprived the learned man of rest. First, it was screaming. Women, men, and little babes cried in agony and terror as armed men began to raid the city. The images flashed before the old man's eyes and horrified him, images of blood and gruesome death. Little lads and even baby boys shrieking as they were dashed before their parents' eyes, even as they begged and cried for mercy.

"There's only one 'King of the Jews!'" he heard Herod's distorted voice say as His twisted face flashed into His view as if standing right in front of him. "Allow me," he said with a grin of bleeding fangs and glowing eyes like fire. "To pay him proper worship too," he snickered as he licked a silver blade, dripping with royal blood.

The old man gasped, shooting up from His place in His tent, and wheezing for air, rudely awakened from His disturbing nightmare. Cold sweat drenched His forehead and His quivering hands, even as he crawled to wake the other two. His pale face and wide eyes told them everything before he even spoke, so he only needed five simple words to make them understand.

"We can't return to Herod!" They nodded both at once as they bore the same expressions, and their faces said it all. The two of them had seen the dream as well.

* * * *

Mary and Joseph, too, we're tossing and turning in their slumber, sleep had not come easy, but when it came it wasn't silent. A familiar face arrived again, His familiar voice, urgent, though

379

reassuring.

"You must go to Egypt now!" the angel urged them, His voice echoing as they awoke. The echoes rang along with the cries of screaming babes and crying mothers, and over and over again, it warned until, at last, it faded, and they woke fully. "The mad tyrant is coming, Israel's unholy king. You must go to Egypt. Save your Son, save the newborn king!"

"Joseph!" Mary pushed him hard to wake him. "Joseph, we need to leave!"

The cruel hand of Herod would soon be far from them now. The journey had been long, but by some miracle, they survived. The people looked different, and so did the buildings, and the people here worshipped false gods and followed strange customs and beliefs. Still, they reasoned, it wasn't uncommon for Jewish refugees to find their place in the lands of Egypt. It far enough outside of Herod's reach and from beneath the thumb of Rome that they'd survive for now.

The waters of the Nile River rushed before them, a refreshing sight after a long and hard journey across what seemed an endless desert. The endless river's sparkling surface shimmered as it faded into view, more glorious with every step. People gathered 'round their cooling waters for a swim and for refuge from the scorching of the summer's sun. Some waded in its cool waters and watched from afar as the river teemed with life.

Fertile plains and meadows sprung up around it, along with farms of tall stalks of grain and barley, a bountiful harvest, also fit for a king. Children laughed as they swam in the Nile's waters, splashing and dunking each other while they engaged in child's games. Joseph and Mary found their place in a gathering of parents who watched from afar, praying to the gods they worshipped for safety as they watched their children from afar to make sure they remained in the safe places. Some men armed with spears watched for foes and wild beasts, but gathered people for a time, at least, seemed to welcome the Hebrew refugees into their midst. The baby squirmed and giggled, looking up with smiles and eyes of wondered at each person that they passed, blowing a few a kiss it looked, a gesture of His love.

"You're new here," one of the mothers smiled at Mary, admiring the little one in her arms. "Don't worry," she reassured the couple, noticing their worried and out-of-place expressions. "You'll find your place. This little community is welcoming to strangers, at least in time," she said. "And you may find other refugees are on their way, so you'll not be the only ones for long. Even so, I welcome you."

"Thank you," Mary said, stammering timidly.

"Don't worry," she said. "In time, you'll find you belong. Many have come here like you, to find the promise of new life in the lands of the Nile, and I promise you they are generous and they are bountiful. You'll be fine here."

In time the woman's words would prove true, though the couple wouldn't stay forever. The boy grew and learned for a few years in Egypt. He played with other boys and girls as he learned to walk and talk, and to interact with others. He learned the ways of the world, but at an early age, He learned more quickly than the others, especially in the ways of God and in demonstrating the difference between right and wrong. Not once in all His years did he misbehave or lash out in anger at Mary or Joseph, but He wasn't a normal child. He was often seen staring at the stars for hours at night and looking into the sun while he rested with many thoughts. He was gentle with living, like little birds that often came to him without Him even calling At times he'd say the strangest and most profound of things that went beyond even their comprehension. What kind of child was this, that he was more learned than them, especially in the ways of the Jewish faith?

For many years they watched Him grow and learn and change in Egypt. He played with other children, but it wasn't home, and it wasn't meant to last. The time would come word would be sent from Heaven that it was safe to return to their homeland, when the dangers of the king, at least for now, had passed. Yet the times of wicked kings would never be over completely, especially tyrants who thirsted for blood to keep them in power. Yet for now, the little king could return to His rightful place in Jerusalem, the City of David, and the people of Judah. There the little lord would find His rightful place as King of The Jews, but though the people there would never notice Him, much less the priest he would to shame with His wisdom and knowledge of God and Holy Scripture. There he'd visit until he returned to His home in Nazareth to continue to the rest of His life before He'd fulfill His divine and holy purpose. Nazareth was far from Egypt, but there He found His home and His new life. From there he'd offer new life to all His people, the little growing king in Nazareth.

Joseph and Mary watched with pride over the next few years as their little boy grew, yet deep inside, they knew He wasn't really theirs. They could often see it in His eyes when he looked into the heavens or stared up at a nearby tree. They could also hear it in His voice when He spoke of heavenly things and engaged local rabbis in dialogue on spiritual things. It was an odd thing, to say the least, to watch the little savior grow, knowing that one day he'd be their king. It was hard to believe that such a bright and simple smile could hold the promise of new life.

* * * *

The lights and gentle melodies of Heaven died away before they found themselves once again before the ruins of the old and burning Earth. The woman looked away, but only for a moment, startled by the sight that haunted the path of her vision. The world continued to burn, the flames still raging somehow as it spun in its place in the void. Aimlessly it spun, alone and in the dark, and void of life, it would continue forever until the flames at last consumed and died away for lack of fuel. Then what would remain but the void that had existed with God in the beginning before anything else that ever was.

"Man took my gifts for granted," the Father said. "It really was a shame. I gave them such a lovely world, so vast and so full of life and wonder."

"And look what they did with it," the woman crossed her arms with a frown. "They burned it, poisoned, and exploited its treasures until nothing was left. They used the precious gifts you gave them to destroy each other, and to ruin your creation, this beautiful world."

"They were poor stewards," He said. "But they accomplished so much with what I gave them. Imagine how much more they could have done if they obeyed, and if you could see what I can see right now," he smiled widely. "You'd see how much they'll grow and what they'll become someday when at last, we're reunited as it was meant to be in the beginning."

"It's too late now," the woman said, sobbing. "They've destroyed everything. It's gone now."

"The old creation can never be restored," God agreed sadly. "But I will create a new heaven and a new Earth, but first I had to save those who would be saved, those who would be restored to their proper place near my heart and in my arms. How I miss them so!"

"That's why you sent your only begotten..."

"He will bring them home, he will bring them back to us into the eternity that was meant to be..." he said. "A new life, the Creator and the creation in a holy union, as it was always meant to be..."

The woman turned and looked over at the little girl, who stared sadly at the old Earth at different times. They soon joined her in looking down at little Jesus of Nazareth as he would begin His new life to prepare for His ministry on Earth, and mission to save God's missing souls and lost creation...

* * * *

The little boy Jesus smiled widely as they approached the gates of the Holy City. He could almost feel His Father's presence, though it wasn't the same as when they walked together in Heaven. He could hear the temple, deep within His heart, calling His name and drawing him near. He, with anticipation as priests and rabbis, happened by along with the common people on their way to the temple for pilgrimage and sacrifice. How he longed to see it, what would it hurt to steal a glance? Just one little peek, he reasoned, they'd hardly notice he was gone.

"Jesus?" Mary looked over, and her heart skipped a beat, then two, then three, and she was sure it would stop completely. Her chest closed, and her breaths grew short in her panic. "Joseph? Joseph!" she tugged as His robes.

"Mary, what's wrong?" he turned His head sharply from he tried to barter with the merchant, clearly agitated, but not showing it.

"It's Jesus!" she exclaimed. "He's wondered off; I can't find him anywhere!"

"Oh, wonder!" Joseph moaned, turning away abruptly from the merchant and storming off to find the missing boy. "Jesus!" He cried into an endless crowd, thumping a few bodies he and His wife stormed off on their journey to find their missing son,

"Jesus," Mary shouted too, looking in every direction as they wandered away from the square. "Jesus?"

Jesus meanwhile sat in a circle with rabbis and Pharisees and other high teachers, cracking a smirk as he opened the dusty tomes to show them some of the old texts...

Authors note:

There was a void in my life where I felt trapped within my own imagination and was not being able to portray it. I have always been a strong-willed person, a true testimony to God. What I have learned throughout my life is to not let the imagination float inside your mind. It must be released into the universe, after all, your own imagination will unlock who you really are as a person, and by faith, and you become your character that God meant for you to be.

I have always enjoyed writing in silence. Some know that I write and most do not. I want these books to come to life and myself to inspire a spark of imagination within every human. When you truly focus on yourself, you ultimately learn a lot. We do not realize how much we are capable of doing until we do it. If you do not have belief, borrow it from someone that does, it can be the only thing that saves you. The glow of a human is further brightened when the kingdom of heaven is found within them on a specific frequency. A man defeated is no more than dust in the wind. But if a man is not, he will be willing to stand against the fiery gates of hell with a smile.

You need to live and breathe the part in order to become a part. Humanity is bleeding... why did you bite that fruit Eve? The forbidden tree has spoken and the plagues cast across planet earth.

The hate, the destruction, the pain, the suffering... Death smiles at us all. But for what?! Why must we create earth just to destroy it? Humanity is bleeding and raging hatred towards us all but shows no love. Love is stronger than hate. Bleed yourself to purity and drain all the hate. The Second Coming of Christ can only restore the abyss that humanity has fallen into.

My imagination ignited this, but my faith wrote it. Detach yourself from the generational and traditional societal norms, and you become cleansed with purity, specifically when you build that connection and only connection with God.

A world of chaos. A world at war. Be careful when the devil yawns, but be glad when the angel dawns. Armageddon? Heaven or Hell? Which one will it be? Lord! Heaven is the one for me! When will this hate and corruption end? Whatever happened to a simple handshake? Respect! Honor! Words they say, but no actions follow. We went from centuries of honorable men leading entire armies to brother's cheating one another. Pity! From the temptation to discipline. This corrupted disease, temptation. An overpowering effect on one's kind. Resistance is proof of strength. But pleasure is a tingling weakness that makes you lose all cares for everything. But the actions you are a part of is an irresistible act of rebellion and can be calming to a furious soul. Every step towards temptation leads you into darkness. Is there such power as endless love? Battling for that irregular heartbeat. That one of a kind. The search for endless love. Will never cease for it is a repetitive dream that one will never awake from. A fantasy that we forever crave. To be a part of it. If this is the reality that we all live in. Then there is no right from wrong. The forbidden fruit has long been eaten, and temptation is now everlasting. With no escape. The mind is trapped. Forced to choose between the worlds of values and the fearless world of passion. There is no judge beside you. Life is a game, and the winners are the ones who end their days Feeling satisfied...

Made in the USA
Middletown, DE
03 October 2020

21069338R00225